tip in

book 1 of the lakeside green coyotes

josie mae

Book Cover by Caravelle Creates

Chapter Headers by Samantha and Deb at Ink & Velvet Designs

First Edition

This is for all of the people who make fan edits of athletes. We see you and we salute you. Thank you for your service.

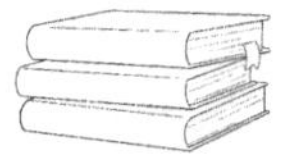

Chapter 1

MAYA

I stared at the bitch cup sitting on the table—an unfortunate consequence of playing beer pong at The 151—and shook my head. I was *not* drinking that.

"Come *on*, Maya," my best friend, Iris, said from nearby. Despite the chilly mid-October air outside, her face was flushed from the heat trapped in the house. I pulled my hair off my neck, already drunk enough that I wasn't worried about whether I looked good or not. There was never anyone worth impressing at these parties, anyway.

"I don't want to," I admitted, shaking my head. "I can't. I can't do it."

It wasn't exactly party girl cool of me, but I'd seen the combination of drinks poured into that thing. If I had any concern for my well-being, I wouldn't bring it anywhere near my body, let alone drink it.

"Come on!" someone groaned from nearby. He smacked his hands playfully onto the table, and everyone else joined in.

"Ma-ya! Ma-ya! Ma-ya!" Iris chanted, clapping her hands gleefully. The only reason she was allowed to be a bad influence was because she was really good at taking care of me when I was hungover. There was no one else in the world I'd rather have as a roommate when shit hit the fan.

I took a deep breath. I'd done so much in my life—including kicking that 250-pound football player in the nuts last year when he tried to make a move on me. I could handle a bitch cup. The bitch cup was going to be *my* bitch.

I picked up the cup, the eyes of everyone else around the table on me, and chugged as hard and fast as I could. I chugged like my life depended on it, because it kind of did. If I stopped, the taste would catch up and I'd gag (best case scenario) or throw up on everyone's shoes (worst case scenario).

I threw the empty cup down moments later to cheers from the table around me. I laughed, playfully bowing. I—as someone who embodied the multiple Leo placements in my chart—loved the attention. And the people who hosted the parties at 151 Marshman Ave—affectionately referred to as just The 151—loved me, so I could get away with causing a scene.

The table cleared as people shuffled in and out to start a new game. Iris walked over to me, throwing an arm around my neck like I was a quarterback who just threw the game-winning pass. Our limbs stuck together with sweat, and the sensation of my hair pressed against my neck was making me nauseous. Saliva pooled in my mouth, a glowing neon sign that I was going to throw up if I didn't get moving.

"You good?"

"I feel so sick."

She snorted. "Okay, let's get you outside."

Iris took me out near the bushes, and I put my hands to my knees, taking deep, intentional breaths. Every type of alcohol was swirling around inside of me all at once, and I was worried it was going to push me over the edge.

"Oh, vodka is coming through so strongly," I said, nearly gagging.

"You are the most powerful woman alive. You are so strong and capable. Everyone loves you," Iris said.

The cool air was helping. It was a particularly crisp night and really felt like fall, dropping to the lowest it had so far in the school year.

I loved it. I grew up in the heat of the Arizona desert, where 'cold' was any day below seventy-five and any night below forty-five. I adjusted quickly to the weather here, mostly to spite the people back home who said I was stupid for moving further up north, but if all went well, I'd probably stay here even after graduation. In my mind, I bought my heavy winter coat freshman year with the intention of never looking back.

Admittedly, there wasn't much to go back to even if I wanted to. My hometown of Engleston housed an old high school boyfriend from before I came out, a bunch of former classmates in real estate and construction, and my mom, who'd been waiting since the day of my birth to be an empty nester. I was willing to adjust to any climate to get out of there; Lakeside Green University just happened to be the school that offered me the most money.

Iris, however, was responding to the cold like any normal person would. She hugged her arms tight to her body and subtly hopped side to side, doing her best to make me not feel like a pain in the ass for keeping her out here. Her booze blanket wasn't doing much to protect her, and neither of us was stupid enough to risk bringing a coat to a house party of this size. The one thing no one had warned me about before moving was how expensive dressing against the cold could be; I was *not* letting someone snatch what was practically an inheritance away from me.

"We should go back inside," I offered, watching as Iris practically started doing jumping jacks to stay warm.

Her teeth chattered. "Take your time."

I took another deep breath, fighting off the swirling, sickly feeling consuming my body. I had a pretty good sense of when I was going to vomit—this was definitely not my first rodeo—and

I wasn't getting that feeling now. But that didn't mean I felt good; I still felt like I'd been tossed into a washing machine and put through a spin cycle.

"I'm going to be so hungover tomorrow," I moaned, squatting to the ground. "I already feel like shit. It's only going to get worse from here. Why did I do that?"

"And that's okay. It's Thursday. You have one class tomorrow, and it's not until the afternoon. We just got through midterms, so it's smooth sailing until finals." Iris's tone was supportive and warm. She had the best gentle parenting voice—never patronizing, always kind. "I can pick us up In-N-Out after my shift tomorrow."

Iris was so impossibly sweet it was hard to believe she was a real person. She worked as an in-home caregiver for the elderly on most weekends and on the days she didn't have class, being the perfect saint that she was. She was in school for nursing and was so spectacularly good with people. We balanced each other well; she was the Pisces to my Leo, the *I bought us Pedialyte* to my *I'm viciously hungover*, the girl who would practically kiss me on the forehead and tuck me in after I'd spent all night drinking too much and flirting with the hot lesbian DJ on campus.

"An angel on earth," I said. I would definitely be hungover tomorrow and probably have the spins tonight in bed, but I considered not throwing up to be a victory. "Can you get me a milkshake?"

"Of course."

"Oh, that sounds so good right now."

"I know." Iris nodded with a deep understanding. I could hear in her tone that she was holding back a laugh, and I realized the alcohol was hitting me. My speech was slurring. "Do you want to go home? We have food at the apartment."

"But you wanted to find that basketball player," I protested.

"He'll probably be at another party, like, next weekend. It's not a big deal. I'll just find him later."

"No, I *need* you to find him," I said. I put my hands on her shoulders. "Iris, you need to bag the hot basketball player from your sociology class last semester. It has to happen. I want this for you. He's tall, he's beautiful. I'm sure he's talented."

"Our men's program isn't actually that good—"

"He's an *athlete* either way. Playing at a college level at a D1 school. I know his arms are crazy."

Iris sighed with acceptance. "His arms are crazy."

"He could probably bench you."

"I think I want him to."

"That's the spirit!"

I nodded, mentally getting myself together enough to go back inside. I wasn't at the point of needing to wave my white flag yet; I could still keep it going for at least another hour or two, especially knowing Iris's love life was on the line.

I shook out my hair, flipping my head over to give my neck a chance to breathe. The cold was finally starting to seep into my bones, and it felt so good. It was times like these that I understood the concept of an ice bath.

"How do I look?" I asked when I came back up.

"Never better."

I doubted that. Even though the haze of alcohol—the kind of drunk where I was probably going to flirt with myself in the bathroom mirror later—I knew I looked like a mess. I didn't particularly care; the smudged makeup, messy hair thing was cool, and I was hot enough for it to seem intentional.

Or, at least, drunk enough to convince myself of that.

"Let's go find your man," I said, reaching for Iris's ice-cold hand to bring her back inside.

The warmth of the house hugged us like a blanket immediately upon stepping through the sliding back door. It was only rounding on one a.m., so it was still packed.

"Water?" Iris offered, raising her voice over the music blasting from speakers placed around the house and the cacophony of voices and laughter. When I crinkled my nose, she gave me a thumbs down and pushed me toward the kitchen. On the way, I waved at familiar faces. We were in our senior year, so I'd been seeing most of the same people at the same parties for years now.

I didn't know how many of them could really be considered friends.

Other than a handful of people in my life, I'd never been particularly good at permanency. Friends rotated in and out, crushes never lasted long, and relationships lasted even shorter. I'd gotten just enough therapy to know it was rooted in how my mom raised me, but I wasn't therapized enough to particularly care. Life was more fun on the move, existing as the manic pixie dream girl rather than best to bring home to mom and dad.

It wasn't to say I didn't deeply love everyone and everything, though. When I thought about the more permanent fixtures in my life, my heart tugged with a kind of affection that could make me cry at the drop of a hat. I was just hard to pin down, and I'd always preferred it that way.

Iris got me a cup of sink water—temperature tested using her wrist—and handed it over to me.

"Do you see him?" I asked.

"Not too loud!" Iris laughed, smacking my shoulder. "And no, I haven't really looked."

"That's a total lie because I can literally see you scanning the room for him," I said. "Not even an *attempt* at being subtle."

Iris groaned. "This is so stupid. Do you think he's even going to be here?"

"Amelia said he was supposed to be," I said. Amelia was one of three who lived in The 151. She lived on the same floor as Iris and me our freshman year and had the very important role as our party host from the very beginning. Amelia's sister was a senior at Lakeside Green at the time, so Amelia always had the best alcohol and the best party invitations.

Things only got better when she moved in with one of the girls from the women's basketball team and another from the women's hockey team. The 151 had accidentally become a hub for athletes and a lesbian haven basically overnight. It wasn't often that the male athletes on campus came anywhere near our parties, but one of Iris's crush's green flags was that he was a semi-regular here. Amelia had only ever had good things to say about him—not that Iris or I really knew, because Iris was too shy to say anything to him and she refused to let me see what he looked like. I'd tried stalking the men's basketball website for any indication as to who he could be, but Iris had been a locked box.

"Maybe he's sick. Or at another party. Or somewhere on a date." The words came out in one long stream, riddled with uncharacteristic anxiety. She pushed her blonde hair behind her ears. "Not my night tonight." She looked at me. "Where's your crush? I think we should focus on you instead of me tonight."

I scoffed out a laugh. There was no genuine crush in my life; I hadn't had one, a *real* one, since probably high school. It felt pointless and, frankly, stupid to spend so much time caught up in what someone else was doing and to care so deeply about them. I hated waiting by the phone and obsessively wondering if they were ever thinking about me. I'd gone through the developmentally necessary and excruciating humiliation ritual of high school love, and that was good enough for me. It wasn't at all that serious in retrospect, but it'd felt like everything at the time. The thought of being older now and having experienced more and knowing more—it felt real. It felt *serious*.

And I didn't have time for things like that.

That wasn't to say I was completely shut off from the idea of dating. But I wasn't going to open myself up to something if there was even the tiniest bit of a chance I'd get my heart stomped on in the process. I had to be sure.

Unlike me, Iris was a believer. She was raised by two happily married parents and really put her hope in happily ever afters and serendipity and the possibility of forever. I loved her optimism and sometimes ached to have even an ounce of it.

But because of that, I was always worried that Iris would end up disappointed and hurt. I wanted to keep her cheerful bubble going and never burst it. I didn't believe in true love for myself, but I definitely believed in it for her.

I had to turn her night around. I wasn't going to let the nicest person I knew continue to go on without some kind of bite from her crush.

I looked around the room, skimming over the faces. I'd been to enough parties here to be able to guess which social group everyone belonged to—the theater kids, sorority gays, unaffiliated partiers. And then, across the way, I saw them: the athletes.

"Come on," I said, dragging Iris behind me.

Chapter 2
THEO

I did not want to be here.

"Another beer, T?" GJ asked, waving her can in front of me.

"I'm good." I brushed her off, pushing the can out of my face.

She threw herself down onto the couch next to me—way too close. She was the only person I ever let in my personal space like that off a basketball court. GJ tended to be my exception to a lot of things, though.

"Come on, *Theodora*," GJ teased. "It's just a beer."

"Leave my great-grandmother out of it, *Georgia Jane*," I shot back.

GJ was unfazed. She'd always been better at teasing me than I was at teasing her. We chalked it up to how she'd grown up with siblings and I hadn't; she had more practice. "Drink up."

"It slows me down."

"It also gives life meaning." She wiggled her eyebrows at me. "Come on. Just one more."

"We have practice tomorrow."

She clicked her tongue. "Your excuses are getting thin. We always have practice. And our first game of the season isn't for, like, two weeks. Alcohol will be completely dispelled from your body within the next twenty-four hours."

I looked at her half-pleadingly to leave me alone, and she threw her arm over my shoulders. Our long limbs fell into each other, her arms not as strong as mine, but her legs a little bit longer.

GJ Mitchell—Georgia Jane Mitchell, *Georgia Jane* reserved for her mother and myself when I wanted to piss her off—was my right-hand man. She was a junior and the point guard on the team who would inevitably follow after me as captain next year after I graduated. I loved her game and loved playing with her. I'd never had a friend who'd understood me in the way that she had, down to us being lesbians whose types were not each other.

GJ threw herself back into the couch, playfully crossing her arms and pouting. "I hate that I can't peer pressure you into anything. Makes this a lot less fun."

I shoved my shoulder into hers. "It's called standing firm, you should try it sometime."

She snorted. "You need to take a very long, deep breath. That's all I'm saying."

"I'm *relaxed,*" I protested, immediately disproving my point.

She cackled, throwing her head back. "No one who is actually relaxed would say it that way."

"I'm..." I tried to find a way to defend myself, but came up short. "You always act like basketball is my entire life. You make me sound so boring."

"Basketball *is* your entire life," GJ said. This wasn't the first time we'd had this exact conversation. We'd known each other for years, playing against each other at a middle school and high school during travel AAU. Both of us were on the fast track to D1 recruitment, so we heard each other's names and saw each other's faces a lot despite growing up in different states. It wasn't until we ended up at the same university that she finally said to me, *You don't have much fun, do you?*

I didn't need another go-around of the same conversation. Maybe basketball was my entire life, and people thought I was boring and stiff and whatever other uncreative adjectives they could think of, but that had always been who I was. I knew what I was about. I didn't hold myself on a tight leash because I'd been told to or someone asked me to. I held my own leash—always had, always would.

"Mags—how would you describe GJ?" GJ said, yelling over the music. We were all huddled together in the way we always tended to be at parties. We had friends off the team, but there was a strong sense of community between a good number of us. We had friends in similar circles and ended up at similar parties.

There wasn't a group of people I beefed with more and loved more than them.

"Our motherfuckin' *captain*!" Mags shouted, clearly drunk. Mags was a shooting guard and also a junior, like GJ. Off the court, things were mostly cool between us but we butted heads on the court pretty relentlessly. Mags was a hothead with a big mouth—and was also, frankly, a ball-hog, even though none of us were allowed to say it. She was an acquired taste, and I didn't think I'd ever fully get there, but her talent was undeniable.

"Right," GJ said and turned to me.

"That's a good thing!" I insisted.

"That's a *basketball* thing," GJ said.

I nearly rolled my eyes. "Right. And I need to find other things to do and life is bigger than basketball and..." I said, reciting off all of the things that GJ had said to me over the years.

"Or just people to do."

I couldn't help it—I immediately started blushing. I turned my face away from her, shaking my head. "GJ."

"I'm being so serious. You're a senior in college. This is it for you, and then you're leaving me forever. I can't let you go off into the world having kept yourself in a locked box. *This* is your time to have fun. Get stupid. Go fuck some girls—"

I winced. "Jesus, dude."

"Fine, go *make love* to some girls or whatever. I don't care. Get drunk. Get laid. I know you're about to have women falling all over you when you make it into the big leagues, but it's different right now. It's college. Flings that happen now really mean nothing."

"It's not guaranteed."

"That women are going to flock to you when you're playing in the W?" GJ scoffed, like that was the dumbest thing anyone could ever say to her.

"No, that I even make it to the W," I said, punching her in the shoulder.

She laughed. "Man, if you *don't* make it to the W, there's no hope for the rest of us. It's over at that point. I might as well give up now and actually start paying attention in class."

My stats were the one area of my life I didn't come by modestly. I'd learned over the years that I preferred to let my numbers speak for themselves. I was on track to beat the all-time scoring record in men's and women's college history before graduation, make first team All-American for a second time, and conference player of the year for the fourth time. And possibly most importantly of all, I was prepared to bring my school its first-ever women's basketball championship ring before I graduated. After three seasons of feeling like we were close but not quite there, I had a really good feeling about our team this year. I was ready to go out with a bang.

I was, with no ounce of modesty, one of the most decorated female college athletes of all time and by far the top basketball player my university had ever seen—men's or women's.

Logically, I knew that. I knew I was good—better than good. But I also didn't expect anything. Despite pretty much universal predictions that I was going to be a first-round draft pick for the WNBA, I never assumed that things would line up. The odds were in my favor, but never one hundred percent.

As much as I appreciated GJ's attempt at cooling me off and giving me the chance to slow down, I didn't see a good reason to. There was always a way to be better, even if my only competition was myself. There was never a time to take it easy or prioritize things like getting drunk and getting laid. I had to focus.

"The season's too soon for me to start taking a break now," I said. I was a little more easily distracted in the official offseason, but that wasn't saying much. My flings were confined exclusively to the summer and were few and far between. They tended to be weird more than anything else, just some random person I met at a party who I kind of knew, or a friend of a friend. I preferred to take care of whatever needs I had by myself; it was less messy that way.

I refused to admit it to GJ, but that was more of the reason that I avoided fooling around more than anything else. I could handle the casual aspect and didn't feel particular about who I was having sex with. But I did feel particular when it came to navigating life afterwards. There was part of me that wanted the girls to basically vanish from the face of the earth after. No mess, no potential for feelings, no hooking up more than once.

It'd also gotten increasingly more difficult to maintain any sense of normalcy in dating as I'd become somewhat of a celebrity on campus. Everyone here knew me or knew of me. Even if the girls didn't actually care that much, it took away some of the fun. I wanted to be able to be a college student who got stupid sometimes, but there was a lot of risk that came with it now that I was public-facing. I knew people I'd hooked up with texted their friends about it, mostly because they'd *tell* me that they were going to tell everyone they knew, like I'd find it funny or appreciate getting bragged about.

It was hard for me to imagine any world where I actually ended up with someone because it felt impossible. Teammates and people close to my teammates were all hard nos, but they also felt like the people who'd understand me best. It didn't exactly leave me with much.

"What about her?" GJ asked, clearly ignoring everything I'd just said to her.

Without thinking, I looked up and locked eyes with a girl who was looking in our direction. Her hazel eyes stayed on mine. I expected at least one of us to give in, but we didn't. Her lips turned up in a small smile, effortlessly continuing her conversation with her friend next to her through it all.

"She's been looking over here for, like, five minutes. I don't know what she and her friend are talking about, but I feel like it has to be us," GJ said, and with good reason. It wasn't anything the girls were doing in particular; it was that GJ tended to have that effect on women, and I also, admittedly, did too. We were tall, muscular, celebrated college athletes and publicly queer. We had our pick; it was usually our choice to engage with it or not.

And unlike me, GJ always wanted to engage.

But as GJ eyed the girls from across the room, I felt weirdly possessive over the brunette I'd made eye contact with. She was mesmerizing. After looking at her once, I'd already committed every feature of her face to memory—the slope of her nose, the roundness of her eyes, the way her full lips pulled into a smile. I wanted to run my fingers through her hair, see up close if her eyes were really that deep of a brown or if it was the lighting. Her lips stayed turned up, her cheeks flushed, even after we'd stopped making eye contact.

I wasn't in the headspace to make a move on her, but I knew I couldn't let GJ.

But, as if knowing what I was thinking and making the active choice to be an ass, GJ got up from the couch and walked over toward them.

Before I could really think up a plan, I chugged the rest of my beer and tailed quickly behind her.

"Were you ever planning on saying something, or were you just going to keep staring at us all night?" GJ asked.

I cringed at the line, wishing I could put up a neon sign above my head that said *I do not endorse this.*

"Not that there's anything wrong with the view, but we were looking for one basketball player in particular. Maybe you can help us," the brunette said. The blonde next to her blushed.

"Maya, it's fine—" she said, tugging on the arm of the brunette—presumably Maya.

Maya.

Maya kept her eyes fixed on GJ while waiting for her response, but I kept my eyes on her. She was shorter than me—unsurprising—but not by much. She was pink from the heat in the house and was down to wearing only a thin shirt. For no more than three seconds, I let my eyes wander.

The grossest version of myself took over, eyeing the way her nipples pressed against her shirt and the thin slice of toned stomach I could see. Something in me stirred alive that hadn't in a long time.

One second.

I'd never thought of myself as someone who was into collarbones or necks, but like someone out of the Jane Austen era, I was completely enamored by the sight.

Two seconds.

Her legs were long, almost as long as mine, even though she was only just tall enough to reach my shoulder. Her loose fitting jeans hung off of her in a way that made it easy to imagine putting my hands on her waist. I was surprised by how badly I wanted to.

Three seconds.

I pulled my eyes away. GJ had completely gotten in my head, and I was going to kill her for it if given the chance. Someone like Maya storming into my life out of nowhere was the last thing I needed right now.

"Maya." Her friend nudged her again, offering me and GJ a polite smile in the process even though she was definitely looking for an out.

I blinked, bringing myself back to reality and shaking off the daze Maya had just yanked me into. I'd managed to go from completely uninterested in dating to fantasizing about someone in literal seconds.

"We can help," I said, unable to let it go. I was an athlete on track to go pro—competition was my middle name. If I saw something or someone I liked, I was going to fight for it.

GJ turned to me, amused and surprised all at once. With a massive and corny grin on her face, she looked between me and the two girls in front of us. I could see her putting the pieces together and I was definitely going to get teased for it later.

"Yeah, I guess we're helping," GJ said. "Who are you looking for? Hopefully, one of us. I'm GJ and this is—"

"We know who you are," the blonde one said. "Both of you." She was so soft-spoken that it didn't come off as dismissive.

"Well, she does," Maya clarified. "I don't watch basketball."

"You know enough to know we're basketball players," I said.

"The height gave it away," she teased back without missing a beat.

"You should come see us play," GJ said. "Theo's our star—absolutely *nasty* on the court."

Maya redirected her attention toward me, her lips turned up in an intrigued smile. I could tell from the slight squint of her eyes that she was evaluating me. I was disappointed that she seemed to be sizing me up more than checking me out. "You're the star player?"

"Yeah, she's got a mouth on her, too, if you can believe it. Court-exclusive, though. You gotta see it in person."

Even as GJ was talking, Maya kept her eyes on me. "Is this true?" Maya asked me.

"I guess you'll have to see it for yourself," I said. "Hope your girlfriend doesn't get jealous."

Maya's eyes sparkled, her mouth twisting to hide her smile. "I don't date," she said. "Maybe you can make me a fan."

I tried not to let her comment about dating faze me, but I was a little disappointed to hear it. The upside was that she was definitely single. "I have no doubt I will."

"Theo can convert any nonbeliever," GJ said.

"Yeah, honestly. I agree," the blonde said with a small shrug.

GJ turned her attention to the blonde. She was always down for competition and always down for the attention of a woman, but she knew better than to go where someone else was clearly trying to go. I didn't exactly consider her *respectful*—she was the worst playboy of the bunch—but she understood our team code. I appreciated that she was intuitive enough to know I was trying my hand with Maya.

But I was only trying for a few minutes. That was it. That was all I could afford to give Maya, all I wanted to risk giving her.

"You're a fan?" GJ asked.

"Lifelong," she said with a small smile. "My dad went here, so I grew up watching the games. Professional basketball, too, but I've always preferred college."

"And you're sure you weren't looking for me?" GJ asked.

"She doesn't bat for our team, unfortunately, which is a huge loss," Maya said. The mention of *our team* didn't get past me. "We're looking for a basketball player from the men's team."

"Well, our loss is his gain," GJ said. "I don't know if I've seen any of the guys tonight."

"Shit," Maya said, sighing.

"Some of them come to our games when they can, especially the guys who swing by here. We're not close with a lot of them, but we know a handful of them. They'll probably be around for the first game," I offered.

"Sounds like you just want me to come to see you play," Maya said.

"I might have an ulterior motive," I said. My flirting was usually not so explicit but it was easy with her. Even though I was genuinely flirting with her, it didn't feel like anything serious. It was like it was a game to her, so it felt like a game to me, too.

Maya was quiet for a beat. "Okay. Maybe I'll see you there, then."

"I'll be looking for you."

"You better," she said. She then turned to her friend. "You wouldn't happen to know any tall, muscular, hot men here for my friend Iris, would you? To make up for her handsome but MIA basketball player?"

"We are not the audience, but we'll keep an eye out," GJ said lightly.

"Appreciated," Maya said.

"Thanks," her friend said to us genuinely, but definitely with an overtone of wanting to end the conversation. She turned to Maya. "Home?"

Maya nodded in agreement. "Home."

They headed off toward the front door together and disappeared into the crowd. I kept my eyes on the back of Maya's head the entire way until they opened the front door. Before Maya exited the house, she turned back and gave me one last look over her shoulder. I stared after her, logging the memory of her in that exact moment as if I was looking at a photograph.

I was disappointed she was gone already; she was the kind of girl I would've spent the whole night looking for at the party, always aware of where she was and hoping we'd find each other when the night ended to go home together. I already knew I'd inevitably look for her in the crowd of every game this season.

"Dude, that was crazy," GJ said and laughed as soon as the girls were gone. She punched me in the shoulder. "You fucking *dog*. I had no idea you had game like that."

I fought off a smile. "Alright, alright—"

"Damn. I mean, it could use some work, but—"

I shook my head. "It's not happening. She's never actually going to come to a game."

GJ shrugged, raising her eyebrows with it. "You never know. She just might."

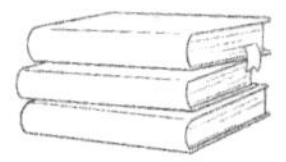

Chapter 3

MAYA

I tapped my closed highlighter against my textbook, restless after staring at it for so long. I felt like I'd been sitting in the same spot for at least twelve hours—it'd been closer to three—and my eyes were seconds away from falling out of my head.

I picked up my phone, craving some kind of distraction, and then immediately put it down. Once I got sucked into its vortex, it was impossible for me to put it down. My study session would be effectively over, and I couldn't let that happen—not yet, at least.

I looked at the clock on my open laptop, willing the time to go by faster. I still had another half of a textbook chapter to go before I was done, but I'd also promised myself I'd get back home no later than seven-thirty because I had an early class in the morning. The longer I stared at my computer, the more time passed and the less time I spent studying.

But that also meant I'd just have to come back here tomorrow and finish what I didn't do tonight.

I groaned, the sound blending in with the bustle of students sitting in every corner of the eatery. I'd found a spot in my favorite section of the student center and camped out, a tradition I'd held onto since I was a first-year here.

This—the Feinberg Student Center, or just *the Berg* to most of us—was my favorite place to study on campus. I'd tried my room (too risky, I was prone to falling asleep), the library (far too quiet), and a coffee shop near campus (too busy with no seating). This place—filled with its aroma of fried foods and salad bar toppings and one very shitty grab-and-go coffee counter—had become somewhat of a study safe haven for me. I loved the obnoxiously bright green leather booths and the sound of laughter blending in with the sounds of people talking and typing. The windows allowed in so much natural light, and there was ample seating and a sense of time never really feeling real, like I was at a casino.

I forced myself to dive back into my textbook, the noise around me allowing my brain the room to actually focus on the words in front of me.

I'd always been naturally good at school—good at testing, good at studying, good at writing papers—and I'd always liked it. Despite the vibe I tended to bring to any room I was in, I didn't *mind* structure and routine; I was just particular about it. My routine for getting my coursework done was a little intense, even by Iris's standards. But it felt good; every finished assignment, every stellar grade, tapped into my internal reward system in a way nothing else ever had.

It was the reason I was looking into graduate school. I didn't necessarily come to school with a dream job, but I'd discovered it over the time I'd been here. My dream job was *this*—writing papers and teaching and reading and learning all the time, for the rest of my life. I hadn't talked about it much with anyone, only ever thrown it around with Iris a few times to see if she thought it was the right path for me. She'd always been unequivocally supportive, but it was scary to admit my future was riding on my ability to complete yet another degree before I'd even finished this one.

Part of me didn't feel like I was smart enough to pursue a PhD. Social science felt so obvious to me that it barely felt like school. I didn't feel like a budding expert in my field; I felt like someone with common sense. But as Iris had told me at one point when I mentioned it to her, it probably just felt like common sense because I was naturally good at it. There were people out there who also felt the same way about things like chemistry, a trait I unfortunately did not inherit.

I was excited and ready to apply, but I was also nervous about it. PhD programs were typically small and competitive, and I wasn't sure I would make the cut. I sometimes felt too silly, my personality too big, for something like that—like I'd be the Elle

Woods of whatever school I went to but in a less charming, more *smudged mascara* way.

Fortunately, my professors believed in me, seemingly even more than I believed in myself. They allowed me opportunities as a research assistant—usually just cleaning data for graduate students, but it was something—and talked me through how they structured their lectures. Meeting with professors during office hours and working on research projects with them was a dirty little secret that I shared with the entire sociology department. And Iris. But that was it.

After working through one section of the chapter in front of me, I gave myself a second to drink water and reset. I'd already begun drafting an essay and worked through a textbook chapter for another class today, so I was at the tail end of my ability to be productive. My breaks were no longer helpful and were instead only delaying the inevitable, which was my brain short-circuiting.

I suddenly stopped, my heart jumping into my throat and my water bottle nearly falling from my hands, when I caught a flash of what looked like a familiar face. I looked away as quickly as I could and then turned back to see if my gut feeling had been right.

In the week and a half since I met Lakeside Green's star point guard Theo McCall, I'd been seeing her face everywhere. I'd see tall people, people with her same long sandy hair, people in fucking *sweatpants*—she hadn't even worn those to the party,

I'd only ever seen her wear them in photos online—and think it was her. I felt like I was losing my mind.

But no one ever actually looked like her. No one had her honey blonde hair, her natural sun-soaked highlights catching even in dim light. No one had her warm, deep brown eyes that crinkled when she smiled. No one had her full lips that seemed to reveal every emotion she was feeling and every thought she was having with just the tiniest upturn.

I accepted that some of the obsession was my fault. The night after the party, I went home and googled her. I'd searched her name using an incognito window and everything, as if she was somehow going to know otherwise.

I'd stayed up for hours obsessively combing through her social media and online presence, ending up on stats pages I couldn't completely make sense of and basketball fan pages that spoke in sports terminology that might as well have been German. Through that, I'd definitely developed a strange and borderline problematic fascination with her. It felt almost parasocial, even though we'd met before.

The entire walk home that night from the party, all Iris had been able to talk about was how cool it was she'd finally managed to meet Theo. We'd both heard she'd occasionally go to the parties at The 151, but we'd never actually crossed paths with her. I'd always known of her because everyone did, but I'd never confidently put a face to the name because of that.

But now, apparently, she was all I could see. In everyone. Everywhere.

I tried to focus on my textbook, but it was impossible. I'd unlocked the Theo part of my brain, something that had been firmly planted and did not seem to have any interest in being uprooted. Theo would slip in there, and I'd find myself completely zoned out in class, losing track of time during my walk home. Despite thinking I was seeing her everywhere, not one person could compete—no one had the same arms, the same build, the same warm brown eyes and curious smile.

It'd become a huge hindrance to my day-to-day life. I had to get it out of my system somehow. The best solution I could think of was finding someone else for my brain to latch onto, but I'd had zero luck so far. Not one person on a dating app or around campus seemed even remotely interesting compared to Theo.

I bit my lip, thinking back to the fan edits and photos I'd been looking at of Theo just last night. I didn't know what my fascination was; I'd never been into sports. My mom didn't watch sports, and none of her boyfriends were ever allowed to bring sports near me because of my own rules that I'd set. I didn't think I'd ever sat through an entire game of any sport in my entire life.

But Theo suddenly had me watching basketball clips, learning about whatever the fuck a triple-double was.

Admittedly, watching the clips did paint a picture as to why everyone seemed to like watching her play so much. GJ hadn't just been hyping her up to get her laid; Theo really was that good. She was quick and smart on the court, obvious to even the untrained eye. And according to my research, she'd already had several major shots go viral. One half-court three-pointer—language I freshly learned at about two a.m. that night—got a feature as one of the best plays of the week across all sports—men's and women's, college and professional.

I couldn't help it—I was fascinated. I'd spent what felt like every second since we'd met wrestling with if it was really worth it to go to the first game of the season or not. When I was feeling really bold, it seemed like a great idea. I could go and have fun. It would be casual, cool, easy. I wasn't going *for* Theo; I was going because Iris wanted to go. And it didn't matter if Theo didn't follow through on looking for me.

But late at night, as I was looking at all of the attention Theo drew online and all of the talk around her going pro, all I could think about was how I was setting myself up for embarrassment. I wasn't so naive to believe I could go and not be at least a little bit hurt if Theo didn't acknowledge me.

I didn't know what it was. Something truly horrible was happening to my brain chemistry, and I wanted it to stop.

"Jeez, you look like you're in *distress*," Iris said as she threw herself down in the seat across from me. She lifted my open textbook to look at the cover. "*Applied Methodology for the Social Sciences* is really getting to you, huh?"

Iris shoved her backpack off and leaned onto the table with her elbows. We'd developed our routines around each other, a habit we started our freshman year in our dorm and never stopped. Iris had an evening class one night a week this semester, while I only had one class the entire day, so I used that as my uninterrupted study time. We always met up and walked back home together after.

"Very funny," I said. I closed my textbook and my laptop, suddenly very grateful for the break. Anything to get myself off the Theo McCall train.

"You about ready to start walking home? This place is making me hungry, and I promised myself I wouldn't eat here again after I got food poisoning that one time."

"The burger had only been a *little* undercooked. It happens. You can't write this place off forever because of it."

"Oh, I can, and I will," Iris said. "But come on. I want to make pasta tonight, and if I don't get it started in the next, like, twenty minutes, I won't be able to go to bed on time."

"You are such an old lady."

She shrugged, smirking. "I love my six a.m. workout class."

An unwelcome—but very, *very* hot—image of Theo at the gym flashed into my mind. A familiar feeling zipped through me. I was definitely attracted to her, whether I really wanted to be or not. The body wanted it what it wanted, and mine was apparently really into athletes now.

I didn't even have to imagine what Theo looked like working out; there were videos all over the women's basketball page. Her lifting weights, dribbling balls, running drills. The clips weren't just of her, but it felt that way when I was scrolling through. Every time I watched one, I'd have to put my phone down and think extremely modest thoughts to keep myself from forgetting how to breathe.

"Trust me, I know you do," I said, shaking my thoughts of Theo away. "I, unfortunately, do not like that I can hear your alarm all the way in my room when you have to get up for them."

"At least we're not sharing a room anymore."

"Grateful every single day," I teased, even though Iris had been a textbook perfect roommate the entire time we'd been in the dorms.

I slid my laptop and textbook in my bag and forced myself up from my booth, groaning the entire way mostly for the drama of it. It felt good to be standing up and no longer confined to my seat.

"What's been going on with you?" Iris asked as we headed for the door. We both bundled ourselves up as we walked—gloves and hats on, scarves pulled up to our noses. We'd done decently well at adjusting to the dropping temperatures, but it was still surprising every year when the cold started to really kick in. Despite still being sensitive to the weather, I'd definitely become one of those people who say things like, *It was only twenty-three today, it wasn't that bad* while on the phone with friends from back home.

I took bundling up as an opportunity to think on Iris's question—and also hopefully brush it off long enough that she would forget she asked me.

"Hellooo," Iris drew out, her voice partially muffled by her red scarf. She looked over at me. "I've known you long enough to know when you're acting weird."

We stepped outside into the biting air and folded in on ourselves, shielding our faces from the abnormally windy evening we were having. The sun had already set, so our walk to our off-campus housing was illuminated by sidewalk lamps. There were patches of snow still in the grass, lingering from earlier in the week.

"I'm not acting weird," I said, still avoiding her question.

"You totally are," she said. She nudged her shoulder into me. "C'mon. You can tell me."

I took a deep breath. "I don't know. School. Senior year stuff." I felt bad for lying, but it also wasn't a particularly convincing lie. Knowing Iris, she'd most likely accept what I was saying at face value, but know something more would come out later.

"Fair," she said, confirming my suspicions. "Well, we're *almost* to the weekend. And if you need an excuse to drink before then, the women's basketball game is tomorrow..."

I brushed off the sing-songy tone to her voice. She'd been trying since the party to get me to agree to go, but I kept giving her all kinds of excuses as to why I didn't want to.

As far as I knew, Iris had no idea that Theo McCall had managed to completely consume my every waking moment. She'd never been good at subtlety or keeping secrets, so it was hard for me to imagine she knew and wasn't saying anything.

The only reason she was asking me to go was because she genuinely wanted to go. I felt like a shitty friend for blowing her off when I had no alternative plans, but the thought of going made my stomach turn with a never-before-experienced type of anxiety. It was like my brain equated showing up to the game as the same thing as proposing to Theo.

"I don't know, Iris."

"Please," she said, grabbing onto my arm as we walked. "Please, please, please, please."

"Iris!" I said, laughing.

"Come *on*. Just one game. I know sports are so not your thing, but I really think we should go. The team is expected to be really good this year, and Theo is supposed to be on fire," Iris said, and then her eyes lit up. My body instinctively stiffened. For a brief moment, I was worried she'd actually been able to read my mind this entire time. "Wait, we *have* to go. I forgot the most important detail of all in convincing you—*the* Theo McCall literally invited you to go. You can't leave her hanging."

I waved it off, my heart pounding as I came down from my rush of anxiety. "She didn't actually mean it. I'm sure she says that to everyone she crosses paths with. And it wasn't really Theo. It was mostly GJ."

"I don't know if you were too drunk to remember properly, but Theo was very much part of that conversation too," Iris said. "Do you not think she was flirting with you? I kind of think she was. No, actually, I like, *definitely* think she was."

"She's an athlete, Iris. It's par for the course for her," I said, not exactly denying that I was pretty sure she'd been flirting too. There wasn't really doubt in my mind she'd been interested; the bigger question was everything else, like how much she meant all of it. My gut feeling was telling me I was being naive if I thought it meant anything more to her than a casual social interaction she'd immediately forget about. I was sure she hadn't thought about me again after we met.

"Since when have you cared?" Iris asked. "You told me in very explicit detail what happened with you and that DJ that one time, and we've *all* heard the stories about her—"

"Okay, okay," I said.

"I'm just saying. Not slut shaming anywhere in this scenario, it's just an objective truth that you've never cared about if your partners were flirting with you for sport or not—mostly because *you* chronically flirt for sport."

My mouth went dry, and it wasn't from the cold wind. I felt suddenly very caught and exposed, like Iris had pulled an accidental truth out of me. She kind of had; I hadn't even thought of that, how part of combing through Theo's online presence was to see if there were any women in the picture. It didn't seem like there was one, but that was part of the issue. If there wasn't one, that probably meant that there were many.

But Iris was right to point out the obvious—I'd never cared about things like that before. I'd never wanted to be someone's only, so it never mattered if there was anyone else. I never saw a girl flirting with my friend with benefits or another one of my fling's casual flings as competition, only ever as a guarantee that things would always stay casual. My favorite people to go after were the ones who would never want commitment from me.

It was official: something really was wrong with me.

"I *don't*, I just…" I shrugged and forced myself to think up some kind of lie. "I don't know. I've never gone for the athletic type. I don't know if that world is really my thing."

"They're *everyone's* thing. There's a sport for any ideal body type, and I seem to remember that your preference has always been tall women."

"Yeah, me and everyone else in the world."

"Exactly my point," she said. "*Come on*. Even if Theo didn't catch your eye, I'm sure there's another basketball player you'll like at the game. Mags is infamously the hot one on the team, and everyone is pretty sure she's gay. She's never actually denied it."

I chuckled softly. "You really want me to go?"

"I *really* want you to go."

I sighed a little bit as Iris clung to my arm again. "Okay. I'll go," I said, and Iris cheered, making me laugh again.

Chapter 4

THEO

Sweat dripped down my face and back, and my shirt clung to me as if I'd been standing in the rain for hours. Any part of me that could sweat was drenched in it. I'd never wanted a shower so badly, but I also couldn't get enough of it. I liked the physical manifestation of how hard I'd been working.

Our practices were always intense, but Coach Darlene had been making us hit it extra hard leading into our first game of the season. Based on the way she'd been berating us, she didn't think we were in the shape we should be. Our team was predicted to be good this year—even better than last year, and we'd made it into the division tournament then. The hope was that we would at the very least make it to the championship this time around. Our players who were good last season—including me—had only gotten better during the offseason.

"Two-a-days are killing me," Nia, our best small forward, huffed out from next to me. We always had some kind of workout at least twice a day, but it was typically conditioning in the morning and then drills in the evening. Just before the start of the season, Coach liked to transition us from conditioning to doing drills both morning and evening, usually followed by a pick-up game. Conditioning was tacked on in the middle of the day instead, usually done as individual workouts; we spent what felt like half of our waking hours in physical motion.

It didn't matter how in shape we were—it was always an uphill battle. I loved the high that came from working out more than anything, but it never got less tiring. We'd had a full day already, and pushing through the last twenty minutes was the hardest.

"We're almost done," I said. I squirted water into my open mouth, my chest still rapidly rising and falling.

After a water break, we jumped into doing three-man weaves on rotation. As soon as I was back in motion, the part of my brain that was protesting against physical activity shut off. The hardest part was always starting and getting back into it; when I was in the middle of it, all I knew was that I loved it. I loved using my body, loved running, loved being out there with my teammates. It was the best feeling in the world. The only thing that was better was actually playing in a game and having a crowd there to cheer us on.

I tossed the ball over to Gemma, who sent it to Ellie. Ellie shot it, effortlessly dropping it in.

"Nothing but net, baby," GJ said, clapping her hands togeth er as we jogged off the court and let the next group of three go.

We stood on the sideline and Ellie wiped sweat from her forehead. She was bright pink up down to her chest and her red curly hair was falling out of her hair tie. She looked like she was bordering on vomiting.

This was her first year playing for a major program; she'd always been good but not good enough to get recruited for a school like ours. But after initially playing for a much smaller D1 team last year as a freshman, she put up a hard fight and ended up transferring here. When she'd first introduced herself to me, she told me that it was an honor to be my backup. I didn't think there was anyone else in the world with that kind of mentality, and I didn't get it at first, but I'd grown to appreciate it.

She was the baby on the team—she wasn't the youngest person we had, but she was the youngest who got time on the court. She was also the greenest in just about every area of her life. We didn't engage much socially; she tended to stick by the side of some of the other girls on the team who I wasn't as close with. And the few one-on-one interactions we'd had suggested she had one of the more sheltered upbringings of anyone I knew, meaning she and GJ usually just stared at each other blankly whenever they tried to speak to each other.

"You good, Ellie?" I asked.

"Totally fine," she said between hard breaths.

"Good work out there." I clapped a hand to her shoulder, her shirt wet under my palm, and she nodded with appreciation.

Our group went up again, this time switching out the order. Gemma started us off and Ellie sent it to me. When I sank the ball, we sprinted off the court to let the other groups go.

"Good! Good!" Coach Darlene shouted, her voice echoing off the gym walls.

After finishing off another few rounds, Coach blew her whistle. We sprinted across the gym to circle up around her. GJ threw her arm over my shoulders and then laughed as I shook her off.

"Keep your sweat to yourself," I grumbled, pushing her away. Her dark skin glistened under the fluorescent gym lighting.

"There are women out there who would kill to be in your shoes," she said back.

"And I'm not one of them."

Coach gathered us up. Everyone was ripe and breathing hard, but Coach Darlene had been in the game a long time, both as a coach and a player, to be used to it.

"This was good. I can tell you're all working hard. Gemma, I want to see more from you—Holden University's defense was strong in the pre-season. They're going to blow right through you if you don't guard on your left. Mags, your threes weren't as consistent today. Need you to get your head in the game. Work with McCall tomorrow."

Mags shot a look in my direction, clearly not thrilled with that proposal. She was the least likely on the team to take any kind of advice and she spent more time bitching about Coach's orders than anyone else.

Coach then let us go, and we headed off to gather our things.

"McCall!" she called out before I could get too far, and I stopped, turning back toward her. She and I had a different relationship from everyone else on the team. Our team had gone through a pretty significant transition last year; after having a starting line-up of mostly seniors, she was left with me and GJ. Our team right now was young and still learning, but the combination of our skills was promising.

Mostly, however, people were looking at me to anchor it.

"How are you feeling? Head on straight?" Coach asked, dropping her usual coaching voice into something softer and more human. We'd always had a good relationship; I respected her coaching and her playing style. I'd idolized her growing up—she'd played for thirteen years professionally before going on to coach at a college level. She was a celebrated player when she was on the court, a four-time WNBA All-Star and division champion when she played in college. She was exactly the kind of player that I wanted to be, if not better. She'd been coaching here for years with not much to show for it other than a love for the sport and her players. But she was determined to make this program something special, and I was right there with her.

"Ready," I said with a nod. I forced out an image of Maya sitting in the crowd, watching me play. My palms got sweaty just thinking about it. But I wasn't about to let my coach know that there was something—*someone*—that made it feel impossible to keep my head on straight.

"We've always done well against Holden, but don't let that get to your head. Every second of this season counts," she said. "There's a lot of pressure on you, but I know you can handle it. Make us proud."

"Will do, Coach."

"Okay, good. Now shower and go home. You smell terrible," she said, and I laughed.

After showering and getting my things together, GJ and I headed back home. We lived with two other senior girls on the rowing team who needed rooms filled. Because of our schedules, it felt like we never crossed paths with them. It was cordial, which was about as much as I could ask for.

"I am so fucking ready for this game, bro," GJ said as we cut across the street. I could see her breath in the cold air. Our house was as close to our gym as we could possibly get, so we rarely bothered with throwing on coats or changing after practice.

The cold air usually felt good after being stuffed into a gym for so long.

"Coach was right that their defense is good."

GJ waved me off. "I'm not worried."

"You're never worried."

"Because we're gonna kill it this year. No one is ready for us," GJ said. "Did you see the pre-season panel about us? You're going to be all over ESPN again this year."

"You know I don't pay attention to that stuff," I said, and it was true—I had zero interest in seeing what anyone was saying. I preferred to keep it objective, basing my feelings on the number of wins and broken records and the occasional award. But things like articles and panels and social media comments were of zero interest to me. People having shit to say didn't ruin my game; they were just annoying. And usually wrong.

"That's *inconceivable* to me. People are obsessed with you; I'd want to see it. And I will see it, once I'm no longer competing with you for the spotlight," she teased.

"I get enough attention when I play and see the people there to watch me," I said. "And I know they're there to watch me specifically because no one would ever come just to see you play."

GJ threw her head back with a laugh. "You know, maybe I should DM that Maya girl on your behalf just to see you sweat it out a bit. Maybe I'll be the star this season since you don't seem to want it."

My heart thudded at the mention of Maya, like she was some secret that wasn't supposed to be let out into the world. She wasn't exactly a secret—GJ refused to let it go and kept pestering me about her. But GJ seemed to mostly enjoy having something to torment me over. It didn't seem like she realized exactly how much I actually *thought* about Maya. With the way she was messing with me, it was obvious she viewed it as a fleeting moment with a random hot girl on campus, but I'd found it hard to stop thinking about Maya.

I'd tried to find her online, but I didn't have a last name and she wasn't close enough with anyone on the team to be followed by anyone. And I knew Maya had introduced her friend, but I'd been so focused on Maya that I couldn't remember her name, either.I felt like I was losing my mind, knowing that there was this girl out there literally on my college campus that I couldn't find. It seemed like every person ever had an online presence, and I'd never cared much about any of it. Now, I was desperate to find anything I could on the one girl who didn't seem to be online at all.

GJ, however, didn't know any of that. And I preferred to keep it that way. The easiest way of doing that was letting GJ relentlessly tease me about having seen me flirt with someone and never letting her get near the actual truth.

"Yeah, for sure," I said, brushing it off even though my stomach knotted at the thought.

I'd convinced myself that there was no way Maya was actually coming to the game. In some timeline out there in some part of the universe, maybe. But not in this one.

I hadn't been able to completely figure Maya out, but during the brief interaction, she'd given off that she was uninterested in something serious. She was fun and bold and confident, but not looking for anything. She was a girl who *didn't date.* The kind of person who flirted so frequently that she knew how to get herself out of anything, including the exact right response to appease me and GJ when we mentioned coming to our game.

I also couldn't bank on Maya even remembering that we'd met. I had no idea if she was drunk or high or both. Maybe all of it was fuzzy, and she didn't remember that she'd said she wanted to go. Or even worse—she regretted that she'd spoken to us. Being a basketball player had associated clout, but it didn't guarantee that people thought we were actually *cool.* Most of the athletes I knew, especially the men, tended to be a lot dorkier and a lot less impressive when they weren't playing. We didn't exactly have much time growing up to flirt and fuck around; most of us were away at camps and practices and games, too busy to actually talk to our crushes. I wasn't going to pretend I was above having zero game as a consequence of that, even if I did get featured on ESPN.

I took a deep breath. I couldn't let myself go there. I was many things, but I wasn't the kind of person people got embarrassed they spoke to or flirted with. If anything, GJ was right—I was a campus icon. If I were playing it cooler, I could act like I was the kind of person who invited girls to my games all the time.

But I wasn't, so instead I was worried that I'd embarrassed myself by flirting with her. As if she'd known that I didn't normally do that and was giggling to her friend on the way back about how badly I'd fumbled my chance.

"Don't worry, dude—I'm sure she'll be there," GJ said, still teasing me. "You could pull even the biggest non-basketball fan."

"Are you still hurting over the blonde wanting a man over you?"

"I'd be jealous, but I don't think there's a single man on that team who deserves her," GJ said. "And the team sucks. They didn't even make the cut for the first round. At least we made it to the Sweet Sixteen."

"You nervous she might go to the game?"

"I never get nervous knowing someone is there to see me play," GJ said, and I nodded, forcing myself to start feeling the same way.

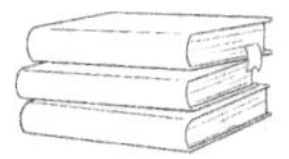

Chapter 5

MAYA

The door handle to my bedroom jiggled and then opened.

"I'm coming in," Iris said as she was already standing in my room. Her arms were full of green and white shirts, all of them school-related. "I know you don't have a single item of school spirit clothing, so I thought I'd help."

I smiled a little bit. Iris was right; school spirit had never really been my thing. The only time I'd ever worn something proudly promoting our university was borrowing a shirt from a one-night-stand.

Iris, on the other hand, was fully decked out. I knew how serious she was about college sports, but I'd never paid enough attention to *actually* realize. She even had eyeshadow on that matched our school colors.

"You're the only person who can wear that shade of green like that, I hope you know," I said.

"The green will look great with your eyes," Iris said as she dumped the shirts onto my bed and dug through them.

I put down the book I was reading and sat up, knowing I was about to check out from my quiet evening. Ever since I'd agreed to go, Iris had been over the moon. She'd been playing down her excitement pretty well until now, knowing she'd probably scare me off if she was too enthusiastic too early in. I really wasn't feeling it—I mostly just wanted to be home tonight—but Iris was so excited that I couldn't back out on her.

"Wearing a men's basketball shirt on opening night feels like a betrayal," Iris said. "Maybe this one?"

"Whichever one you don't want to wear, you can give me," I said. "I'll wear anything."

"The shirt I want to wear is already pulled out. It's my lucky shirt."

I didn't even try to hide my amused smile. "You have a lucky shirt?"

"Yes, but you don't pay attention to sports enough to realize I wear it when there's a big game," Iris pointed out and I resisted the urge to tease her. "I usually don't bother when it's going to be an obvious blowout, but games like today we definitely need it."

"I probably know more about sports than we think I do," I said. "We go to a school with a massive D1 sports program. Some of it must've crept in."

"Do you know when the basketball season is?"

"Well *now*, duh."

"When does it end?"

I picked through the shirts, wracking my brain. There was no harm in guessing incorrectly, but I did feel a little bit like I had a point to prove. "Um. February?"

"Close, that's football."

I bit my lip, genuinely trying to think of what it could be. "December?"

Iris shook her head. "Think March Madness. Think spring. Think draft in mid-April." She moved her hands as she talked, trying to get the wheels turning for me.

"What's March Madness?"

"Oh my god." She looked simultaneously offended, surprised, and full of pity. I'd pulled a lot of different reactions out of her over the years, but that was the first time I'd seen all of those at once.

"My mom wasn't exactly a sports person! That's not my fault!" I said. "Okay, so March Madness is a big deal. I'm jotting this down."

Iris looked at me like I was a lost cause. "You need to learn at least a little bit of this if you're going to be WAG."

"I don't know what that means."

Iris snorted and then finally dug out a shirt from the pile, tossing it over in my direction. "I think that'll work. It gets hot in the arena, so dress appropriately."

"Yes, ma'am," I said. Iris scooped the rest of her shirts up into her arms and headed for the door. Before she left, I said, "I swear I'm not *not* into sports. I just have to be exposed to it. I'm learning. No one's ever taught it to me before."

"You should have Theo do it. She'd be an even better teacher," Iris said over her shoulder with a smirk as she exited my bedroom.

Annoyingly, I could tell I was spending far too much time on my makeup. I was using my most delicate hand when it came to my mascara, and I used more setting spray than I usually did just in case my makeup started to melt in the heat of the arena.

I wasn't totally sure what I was walking into. I knew what a basketball game *looked* like—I'd seen One Tree Hill—but I didn't know what a game at my specific university looked like. The clips made it seem lively, at least.

I smoothed out my borrowed shirt in my bathroom mirror. Iris was right—the green was flattering.

And, much to my own chagrin, I hoped Theo would feel the same way—if she even looked for me in the crowd. If she even *remembered* that we'd talked about me going.

I scoffed at myself, trying to physically force out the embarrassment I was feeling. I knew I was going to have to be as unaffected as possible later when there wasn't even so much as a passing glance from her before I left the arena. I hated that there was even the tiniest bit of hope sitting in my chest that she would, at the very least, look at me.

I repeated what had become my favorite mantra leading up to the game: *You are cool. You are smart. You are hot. You are funny. People like you. It doesn't matter if Theo does. You don't even like basketball. Who cares if you get the attention of one of the players? Who cares if you don't?*

I cleaned up the bathroom, putting all of my makeup away and unplugging my Airwrap. It wasn't like I was going *for* Theo, anyway; I was going for Iris. She'd been the obvious basketball fan of the two of us. It wasn't like it'd be a surprise if she went, and I tagged along. I was just being a good friend, engaging in her interests.

"You ready? We should start walking over now," Iris called out from her room.

"Yeah, I'm ready." I shut off the bathroom light and went to join her.

Iris and I met in the living room. Her face lit up like a proud mom when she saw me. "You look so cute!"

"Thank you for the shirt," I said. The one she'd picked out for me was simple—all it said was *Lakeside Green University* with our logo on the bottom. It felt perfectly neutral. Not the wrong sport, but also not attempting to convince anyone I was more of a fan than I was.

"Of course," Iris said. She threw her arms around me. "I'm *so* excited you're coming. I never want to invite you to these things after that time freshman year when you said following a sport is like being in a cult. I know you have ulterior motives around coming, but I'll be selfish about it either way."

For the entire time we'd known each other, Iris had been going to games with a handful of her friends from the nursing program. She looked forward to it—the perfect combination of girls' night out and her favorite sport. She'd invited me a few times, but I was usually off getting dinner or drinks with someone, already booked out for the evening—and also not particularly motivated to change my plans around for a basketball game.

Iris having her group had always made me happy but now, I was feeling somewhat neglectful. I'd never once bothered to just go with her and see if I liked it. I'd completely written it off.

"No ulterior motives—I'm many things, but being the kind of person who uses my best friend to get closer to an athlete is not one of them," I insisted. "It's our last college basketball season as students. I should go at least once."

Iris smiled. "I really do think you're going to like it."

I was skeptical. "We'll see," I said.

From there, we grabbed plastic water bottles full of vodka and lemonade, threw on our coats, and started walking.

We weren't far from the arena and it turned out, the walk was really beautiful. We cut through mostly green space on campus, with benches scattered throughout and lovingly tended to patches of garden flowers that bloomed in the late spring.

Once we cut across the street closest to the arena, though, things looked a little different.

"There are so many people here," I said. The parking lot was almost completely full, and there was a line of people waiting to get their tickets checked. Cars were lined up for what felt like forever with people trying to get into the parking lot.

"It wasn't always like this," Iris admitted. We tossed our now-empty water bottles of alcohol into bins outside. She turned to me, clearly thinking about how she wanted to phrase her next sentence. "Theo is kind of a big deal. She's been a huge draw for the program. We used to barely fill one-quarter of the stadium for a good game, but she's been pulling in massive crowds. This game and the next four home games are already completely sold out. It'll most likely be her last year here, since I can't imagine she'll delay announcing for the draft until next year. Everyone wants to see her before she goes pro." She paused. "I swear I'm not just talking her up because I think you should go for her."

"Kind of a big deal?" I asked because it was the only thing I could force out of my mouth that sounded somewhat normal. The more I learned about Theo, the harder it was for me not to be mortifyingly nervous.

"You'll see," she said.

After braving the line to enter, Iris and I were quickly enveloped by the heat of the arena. We slipped off our coats, and I followed her through the crowd. She was moving with the expert navigation skills of someone who'd been here a thousand times before. I, however, was moving like a toddler who was scared of losing their parents in a grocery store.

Iris headed off toward our designated section. The building, as far as I could tell, was basically a giant circle. It was packed with people, all of them humming with excitement. There were long lines waiting for food and merchandise, and people pushing by to get to their seats. A couple of the stands had t-shirts on sale with player names and numbers on the back. When I spotted *McCall* with the giant 25 underneath, I was hit with a combination of being starstruck and a little overwhelmed by Theo's impact.

I'd seen the clips of her playing online, found her featured on the social media pages of sports news outlets and fans. I'd seen how many people followed her online and the number of comments she'd get that were people talking about flying out from all over the country to see her.

But seeing her shirt in person made it all suddenly very real. I was in way over my head with her.

Iris waved for me to follow, showing off our tickets and our student IDs to some guy in a vest checking them by an entrance to our seating section. He let us through and Iris cut down, heading closer to the court.

"This is the student section," she said, raising her voice over the noise of the arena. There was music pounding and everyone's voices echoed and carried through the whole building. I wasn't sure I'd ever been in a room with nearly fifteen thousand people before but it was overwhelming to say the least. "No assigned seating, so we had to get here early."

"Early?" I asked, looking at how many people were already in their seats and walking around. The student section was less crowded, but it was obvious who the superfans were—people were mostly crowding down by the court, leaving the upper row seats of the section empty.

Iris found a spot only a few rows up from the court. She waved at a group of people. "Oh, Tamara's already here!" she said.

"Go say hi, I'll hold our seats."

Iris smiled appreciatively. "Thank you." She climbed up from the seat and hurried over to a group of people to say hi.

I turned my attention back to the court and the people filing in. The energy was like nothing I'd ever felt before. Maybe I was just buzzed, but I could see why people liked coming out to games so much. There was something intoxicating about the excitement bubbling up in everyone.

Not much later, after doing some googling with my phone screen dimmed to understand what exactly a point guard was, Iris came back to greet me.

"It's about to be showtime," she said.

"Did you want to sit with everyone? We can move over there," I offered.

"No, it's okay. I don't want to overwhelm you," she said. "It'll be all basketball speak over there. You need to at least learn the basics first before I start throwing out assist-to-turnover ratios and field goal percentage."

"Thank you for that," I said.

"I'm realistic with who I'm teaching," she said. "I'm going to grab a soda before the game. Do you want anything?"

"I think I'm okay."

Iris got up and headed back up the stairs, leaving me alone again—and leaving me with my thoughts in the process. As I sat there, I reminded myself that I was here with Iris, and Iris was so excited that I came with her. I wasn't here to see the rising basketball superstar on the team or to shoot my shot with her. I was here for my friend, so there wasn't a reason to be embarrassed.

But even so, I felt a little bit like I had a glowing sign hanging over my head that said, *This idiot is here because she thinks the basketball captain actually meant it when she asked her to come.*

The lights suddenly dimmed, and the court was lit up with streaks of green and white, completely pulling my attention away from my pity party.

"Coyotes—make some noise!" The DJ shouted, and the crowd erupted, making me jump. It felt like the walls and stands were practically shaking from the sound alone. I knew with confidence I'd never been in a room that loud before. "Okay, enough. Let's not get too excited because before we can bring out our team, we have to introduce Holden University."

The crowd booed, and my lips perked up in a small smile. Scattered throughout the arena, I could see orange shirts floating in the sea of green. Their cheers were swallowed by the booing.

The announcer then took over the DJ. "From Holden University, we have senior Naomi Rich, junior Margot Vega…"

The players jumped up from their seats one-by-one, running onto the court. They clapped hands with coaches and players standing in rows on either side of them.

"Here," Iris said as she sat down next to me again. She had two cups in her hand and handed one off to me. "I got you one too so you won't drink all of mine like usual."

"Your drinks always taste better than mine."

"Amazing considering we always order the same exact soda."

I shrugged. "Some people get all the luck," I said and then took a sip from my straw. "Thank you."

"Of course, my treat—since I convinced you to come in the first place," she said.

The crowd suddenly got loud again, cutting off our conversation. I realized all of the Holden players were out on the court now, which meant the announcer was about to introduce Lakeside Green.

The players were huddled in a way that made it hard for me to see the details of their faces. I knew Theo was there, hidden in the mix of bodies and in the shadows away from the flashing lights, but it was like I couldn't process that she was really there until I saw her.

My mouth went dry. For the first time since the party, I was about to see Theo McCall in person. And actually in person this time, not just someone who vaguely looked like her from a distance.

Nervous was unfortunately and annoyingly an understatement.

The announcer went through the team, the players running from their chairs to the court to the sound of everyone cheering and stomping their feet. The entire student section rose, and I rose with them. Iris, who was normally pretty soft spoken, was cheering so loudly that I couldn't help but laugh in surprise.

Just like with Holden, the players ran out to their names, lit up by the lights of the arena. We were now close enough and the lights were bright enough that we could see the details of everyone's faces—the excitement and determination.

With every name called, I knew we were getting closer to Theo. Every single time someone new was about to come out, I braced myself for seeing her live and in person again.

Part of me hoped that maybe when I saw her again, I'd realize that I'd made it all up in my head. There was no way she was as hot in real life as I remembered her being. I'd seen pictures and videos, but I blamed it all on the uniform effect; I was inevitably going to think she was hot because she was any kind of uniform—basketball included—was hot. It didn't require me being a sports fan to admit that to myself.

"And our captain, our multi-time All-American, our top scorer of all time here at Lakeside Green—Theo McCall!" the announcer called out, dragging out Theo's name.

I inhaled sharply and watched as Theo ran out in all her glory. Initially, I could only see her back, but as she turned back toward the student section, it was confirmed—she was one-hundred percent, without a single doubt in my mind, as hot as I remembered her being.

The crowd was going absolutely nuts over her. I'd never seen anything like it before. And unlike the version of Theo I'd seen at the party—somewhat more reserved and laid back—this version of Theo fed into it. She lifted her hands to her ears and waved them up and down, encouraging everyone to cheer even louder.

"Three-o! Three-o!" the crowd sang out.

"What are they saying?"

"Three-o, it's Theo's nickname," Iris explained over the roar of the crowd. It suddenly clicked for me—I'd seen people commenting that on her social media posts.

I couldn't take my eyes off of her. From rows back, I could see the cocky smile her face had broken into. Her eyes were lit up with a specific kind of fire.

And it was so, *so* incredibly hot. With the way my body was responding to her, just looking at her might as well have been foreplay.

Even after Theo had gone over to join her teammates, the crowd was still going. I looked around at all of the signs and t-shirts. My body fluttered at the realization that all these people were here for her. It was partially in awe, and also partially the sinking realization that she was essentially a budding celebrity. Not only did she probably meet a million people in passing a day, but she also definitely didn't have any reason to mean it when she invited people to games. It was probably a reflex for her. She wasn't actually inviting *me*, she was just inviting a new random person who she could maybe get to buy merch with her name on it.

My stomach knotted. It'd been obvious from her social media how big she was, but this was something else entirely. Unlike anyone else I'd been attracted to before, I didn't feel like I was just competing with people in my immediate vicinity. It felt like I was competing with anyone who vaguely liked the sport and knew her name. Everyone wanted a piece of her.

Eventually, the crowd calmed down, and the game was able to start. I tried to stay in it, but it was hard to shake the crushing feeling that I'd known was going to be inevitable—I wasn't anything special to her.

But when I turned to Iris and watched her shout and groan and cheer as the game progressed, I refused to let Theo get in my head. I could think Theo was hot, and that it was. That was how it had always gone. She was just any other hot person—someone for me to flirt with. No harm, no foul. No hurt feelings.

The game moved surprisingly quickly. I knew only about as much as I'd ever seen in pop culture about basketball, but the rhythm started to make sense to me pretty quickly. I liked that it was quick—the players never stopped running, the ball never stopped moving.

Every time Theo got her hands on the ball, it was like the entire stadium held their breath to see what she would do. As she hit effortless shots that even I knew were impressively far, she'd spin to look at the crowd with a look of fiery hot determination. It was hard to imagine the soft-spoken, gentle-natured girl I'd met at a party could transform into the player in front of me. It almost felt like two completely different people.

GJ hadn't been kidding. I had to see Theo on the court to start to really understand her.

At halftime, the Lakeside Green Coyotes were up 40-32. The game was close, like Iris had told me it would be, but based on the reactions around us, she—and everyone else—weren't expecting it to be this close.

The teams raced off the court, slapping low-fives to each other. As the teams jogged to their respective locker rooms, Theo was held back.

"What's going on?" I asked.

"Halftime interview."

"Wait, seriously?" I asked, leaning forward to get a better look. A woman in a nice pantsuit with a microphone was standing courtside next to Theo. A man holding a heavy, very legitimate-looking camera was pointing it at them.

"Yeah. This is serious business. People love Lakeside Green basketball—they're watching it all over the country right now."

"She's talking to, like, ESPN?" I asked. "Actual ESPN?"

Iris chuckled. "I'm surprised you even know what ESPN is."

"Hey!" I laughed.

"But yes, she's talking to ESPN. The games usually get aired on major networks. You can watch your eye candy on live television during her away games if you want."

I rolled my eyes but logged that information in the back of my mind for later.

Iris bounced her leg next to me. "I don't know where the defense is. It's like everyone wants to run the score up. They're letting it turn into a close game. This is ridiculous."

"That's what I was thinking too," I said, teasing her slightly.

Iris broke into a smile. "It's fine, you can make fun of me."

"No, I think I get it," I said. "I feel kind of bad for all of the times I told you to stop talking to me about sports."

"Oh my god, hell has actually frozen over."

I snorted. "Whatever."

"I'm glad you're enjoying it. This is a good game to get you into it—I'm actually kind of nervous for them," she said. "Most of the games aren't really like this. There are the programs with money and recruitment reach, the programs that don't have any of that, and then ours is somewhere in the middle. We've historically gotten crushed by the Wildcats, but I think Theo might be what changes our fate."

"Right," I said.

"They're from Point Brook University," Iris explained, and I nodded, now understanding. I'd heard their name before in passing in relation to other sports. "Cam Kerr—"

"*And another three for Kerr,*" I said, imitating the announcers from the games Iris would watch in the living room. I was usually fucking around on my phone and never actually paid attention, but the occasional piece of basketball knowledge would get committed to memory in the process.

"Exactly. Kerr is one of the other major college superstars right now. She's a major shit talker—she's already made it pretty clear she's over the Theo talk. This season will be the determining factor in where everyone ends up in the draft. It's not really a question of if they'll go pro at this point; it's who they'll end up with and how good they'll be when they get there."

I nodded. The players came back onto the court, ready to go into the second half of the game. "And for us, we have…?"

Iris smiled a little bit. "Nia Adams, small forward. She's wearing twenty-two over there. Fast and versatile. She's good, not a stellar shooter, but good glue to get a play done. And then next to her is Gemma Doherty. She's the center. She and Mags are good friends."

"And Mags is the hot one?" I asked. When Iris threw an amused glance at me, I rethought my sentence. "You know I'm not into femmes. The one who everyone says is the hot one on the team?"

"Yeah. She gets all kinds of brand deals. People love her. I'm sure she's by far the wealthiest on the team. Being good helps, but being photogenic, interested in fashion, *and* good really helps."

"Okay," I said, nodding. I knew their names and the numbers on their jerseys weren't going to be committed to memory, but I wanted to try.

"You already know Theo and GJ," she said, pointing them out as if I hadn't kept half my mind on Theo the entire time we'd been sitting here.

As Iris moved on to the rest of the players, my gaze was fixed on Theo. She was sitting with her legs spread, her elbows propped up on her knees. She and GJ were talking about something, leaning toward each other; Theo's expression suggested

It was something deadly serious, but GJ's expression suggested their conversation was something playful.

Part of my fascination with Theo had definitely led to an interest in her relationship with GJ. Their dynamic was, unfortunately, very sweet. There were so many clips of them together online, and it wasn't hard for me to see why people liked them so much. The more digging I did, the more charmed I was, and the more I felt like I was basically already friends with them. I had to keep reminding myself that they were two random people I'd met at a party and nothing more, no matter how nice they seemed.

My eyes traced over Theo's long legs, her muscular arms. Her jaw was a hard straight line. Looking at her, I didn't know why anyone would ever suggest that Mags was the hottest one on the team.

As if finally feeling eyes in her direction, GJ glanced over at the student section. She scanned the crowd and then landed on me and Iris. She nudged Theo, who pulled her attention over to the student section, too. She scanned the crowd and then, finally, I saw the recognition in her face as she registered who she was looking at.

I quickly glanced away, mortified. Part of me had wanted to be seen, like I was Gabriella in High School Musical, and a spotlight was going to land on me at some point to let Theo know I was there. But another part of me had hoped we were far enough away and so hidden in the crowd that she wouldn't *actually* see me.

But I knew myself and couldn't deny the truth. I kept staring over there as if I'd been hoping to finally get them to see me. But now that I had, I wanted to run from the arena altogether.

I quickly turned away and then looked back, unable to resist checking if they were still looking over at me. I had way too much pride to be the girl who shied away from their eyes on me. Theo might make me uncharacteristically nervous and completely shake up my aloof, no-strings thing, but I didn't need to make that obvious to her.

GJ waved and nudged Theo, laughing. They said a few words to each other, but it was impossible to lipread from so far away. Based on their expressions, it looked almost like GJ was teasing her. My stomach sank, and I wondered if there was a chance that they'd invited me here just to see if they could get me to come, like the popular athlete asking the nerdy girl to prom.

But I shook that thought away immediately. We weren't sixteen, this wasn't some shitty high school movie, and nothing about GJ or Theo suggested that they were bullies.

At the very least, they were people I could consider acquaintances. They were friends with my friends. And that's exactly what this was—a friend thing. It had never been suggested to be anything different, and based on my behavior, I couldn't be trusted trying to pursue anything more than that with her.

But it was fine. Because I could totally handle being just friends with Theo McCall—even if she was the most beautiful, most incredible person I'd ever seen.

Chapter 6
THEO

I didn't have to think about it for even a second. As soon as my eyes landed on her, I knew I was looking at Maya. It'd been almost two full weeks since I'd seen her, but I'd had a photo of her face permanently ingrained in my head just in case we happened to cross paths again.

And sure enough, there she was.

She was sitting with her blonde friend, who was animatedly talking to her about something she was looking at on the court. Maya didn't seem to be listening to her; instead, her attention was directed fully at me. Or maybe GJ. But based on the way our eyes stayed locked on each other, I could only assume she'd been looking specifically for me.

For the first time ever in my basketball career—even going back to when I was a kid, a preteen, a teenager—my heart skipped a beat on the court.

Maya actually came to see me play.

I didn't get nervous out here. I'd gotten nervous before games before, and I got nervous about games, but the second I was on the court, every worry turned to white noise. Anxiety turned into the excitement of getting to play the sport that I loved. And I was *good*; I'd always been good. I had no reason to ever feel nervous out here.

Maya gave me more than enough reason, however.

We held each other's gazes for what had to have been an eternity. I couldn't bring myself to look away. I wanted to go run up to her, wanted to say hi. I thought about waving, but I didn't want to embarrass myself like that, especially not when I knew everyone in the stands was looking down here at me and my team.

I desperately wished there was a way to get her to stay and make sure she came down after the game to see me. I needed some kind of signal, some way to let her know that I was happy to see her beyond just a passing smile. I couldn't let her go again.

She was somehow even more beautiful the second time around, so much better than the mental image I'd had of her in my head. It was hard to make out the exact details from so far, but I could see bits and pieces. Her makeup was different this time, a little lighter, and she was wearing a Lakeside Green t-shirt. Her hair was down and less wavy than it had been at the party.

GJ nudged me, and I snapped back into reality. Even though it felt like I'd been staring at Maya for a lifetime, we'd only been on the court for a minute or two.

"You ready for this, McCall?" GJ asked, clapping her hands together. She stood up and shook out her body. "Your girl is here. You need to put on a show for her."

I shook my head. "Not my girl."

"Right. Like you're not staring longingly up at the student section. Or maybe you're just eyeing the fat heads of my beautiful face."

"Why would I do that when I can stare at the real thing right here?"

GJ threw her body forward as she laughed. "Funny as hell, McCall. I do not give you enough credit for that."

The starting lineup—Coach Darlene wasn't taking any risks today with who was on the court unless she had to, the game was too important—got up and took position on the court.

Reasonably, we'd all been ripped a new one when we were in the locker room. The game was a lot closer than anyone wanted it to be, and our ability to pull this off would be an indicator of what the rest of the season would look like. The last two quarters needed to be tight.

And even though GJ had been teasing me about Maya being there, she was right—I wanted to impress her. If I had any shot of getting to know her more, I couldn't let her think I was all talk.

The game started up, all of us practically frozen in place until the ball was tossed in the air to signal the start of the game.

When I was playing, nothing really existed anymore other than the court and the ball. I saw it all happening nearly in slow motion; I knew who needed to be where, how to get the ball where it needed to go, and who could take an assist to get the ball in. I prided myself on being an excellent shot, but also someone who knew we were playing a team sport. It wasn't all about me, even when people who critiqued me tried to make it that way.

"Come on, baby. Let me see it," GJ yelled. I knew from her tone she was trash talking the other team. She was an expert at avoiding technicals and the decibel of her natural speaking voice was that of a professional stage actor. Few people were as loud as she was on a court. I fought off a smile listening to her.

Mags started with the ball, throwing it hard in Gemma's direction. From there, we were off to the races. There was awareness in the back of my mind that Maya was watching me, but it didn't throw me off my game. If anything, I played with more pride and more fun than I usually did. Rather than occasionally stepping back and sticking to something more basic and less risky, I went for half-court threes.

I could tell I was showing off, and the crowd could, too. They loved it. Every time the ball was in my hands, everyone waited to see what I was going to do next. I could see it in their faces, hear it in the way they all cheered when the ball dropped into the net.

The sound of everyone cheering for our team was the best kind of high. I let myself get lost in it, quickly bringing the score from only being a few points away to gaining a solid eighteen-point lead toward the end of the third quarter. I'd probably feel bad after the game for being a showoff, but I had nothing to feel bad about right now.

As the clock ticked down, I went for a hook shot that landed just as the buzzer went off. The crowd went to their feet as if it'd been the game-winning shot, and I turned to see if Maya had stood up, too. Across the way, I saw her standing with her friend, both of them clapping and cheering.

As the quarter wrapped up and the team ran for their huddle, I took my moment to enjoy it. I threw my arms up, encouraging the crowd to cheer even louder than before. It was exactly the kind of love that the team needed to hear to close out the game.

When I turned and saw Maya again, her eyes still locked on me, I flashed her an easy smile over my shoulder. Deep in the throes of a game, I wasn't nervous about what she thought. This was my arena, my stage, my sport. I had no reason to second-guess myself out here.

We breezed through the fourth quarter. I loved to win but I hated the end of a game; I wanted to be out on the court for as long as I physically could. There were practice days where I found myself unable to leave, wanting to push myself harder and harder not because anyone asked me to, but because I wanted to. Basketball was my passion, hobby, and career. It was the one true love of my life.

The game closed with an easy 80-68. It was about as close as everyone imagined the score would be, and the stats for our team looked good. I knew Coach Darlene was still going to have a fuck ton of notes for us and was never going to let us get off easily, but it was a strong start to the season.

"Yeah, baby! That's what I'm talking about!" GJ said, slapping her hand to my back. "We're getting a motherfucking ring this year!"

I laughed, wiping sweat from my forehead with my jersey. "One game at a time."

"Nah, I am not taking that." She shook her head. "Come on. Let me hear it."

I rolled my eyes but didn't really mean it. I smiled as I said, "We're getting a ring this year."

She threw her arm over my shoulder, pulling me into her chest. "We're getting a fucking ring this year!" she cheered. As she launched into a round of singing "We Are the Champions," I got pulled to the side to talk to a commenter about the win.

I never minded doing a post-game interview but today, I was feeling antsy about catching Maya before she left. I didn't want her to think I wasn't going to say anything to her. I didn't have a phone number or any of her social media to reach her. I'd just have to hope she'd keep showing up. And if I didn't catch her after this game, there was no way she was coming to any of them in the future. I couldn't risk her thinking that I didn't care that she came.

The interview was fast, the same usual talk of plays in the game, what the season was going to look like for us. Despite the media training and practice we received, I never really knew what to say. I was always proud of my team, even when we lost. And I didn't really know how to explain what plays we did when or why I went for something; the sport was purely instinct and muscle memory at this point. I didn't know how to explain my decision making to anyone else. I went for the three because I knew I could make the three; it was always as simple as that.

When the interview wrapped up, I headed over to the student section. Despite wanting to play it cool, I knew there was nothing cool about being the person looking for someone else. I didn't need to see my face to know I probably looked a little desperate.

"Maya!" I yelled when I spotted her. She'd been in the process of putting on her coat; I'd caught her at just the right time. She looked around, trying to find the source of my voice. "Maya!"

She finally looked down at the court and saw me standing by the metal divider between the bleachers and the courtside seats. It was the closest we could get without me taking the steps up into the bleachers or her coming down onto the floor. Her friend looked down at me and smiled before pushing Maya off toward me.

Maya brushed past people and floated down the steps, closer to the barricade. When she made it down to the lowest level, she put her hands on the metal and leaned toward me. She was even more beautiful up close. Her hazel eyes flashed with green, reflecting off the green of her shirt. Her cheeks had the tiniest bit of pink to them from the heat of being in the packed arena.

"What'd you think?" I asked and wiped sweat from my forehead. It was an unfortunate reminder that I was, of course, drenched in sweat while talking to the girl of my dreams.

"That was pretty incredible," she admitted. "Congrats on your first triple-double of the season."

I broke out into such a stupid grin that I had to turn my face away from her. I knew I didn't have long—I had to meet with Coach Darlene and our team in the locker room, prepare for our post-game press conference, shower. And then the team usually did something together after a game, so my entire night was booked out. But I wanted whatever time I could get here with her.

"I didn't think you were a basketball fan," I said.

"I'm not, Iris told me to say that," she replied. "I still don't really know what that means. But it sounds impressive."

My lips turned up in a smile. "It's something."

Maya cracked a smile. "I want to say you're going to be the next big thing, but I think you already are the big thing. National celebrity status."

"Just here to play ball."

"Of course."

"Yo, McCall! Get over here!"

"Shit," I muttered under my breath. I turned to see my teammates heading off. GJ was already getting corralled for the panel. I turned to Gemma, who'd been the one to call out for me. "One sec!"

"Busy bee," Maya said.

I didn't have time to play coy; I had one shot with her before she might be gone again. "You coming to the next one?"

"You want me to?"

My lips perked up into another smile as I started backing my way toward my team. I wanted to ask for her number, or at the very least some kind of social media account, but I didn't have my phone on me. "I don't have much time to talk now, but DM me. I want to see you."

"I'll consider," Maya said, which was about as much as I could hope for from a girl who said she didn't date. At least we both knew I wasn't afraid to compete for something; I always liked a challenge.

I smiled at her before turning back toward my team, jogging to meet them. As I was about to get moved through the tunnel and toward the locker room, I turned back to see Maya still looking over at me as she headed back up the stairs toward her friend.

Even if she didn't DM me or come to any of my other games, I'd at least always have that mental image.

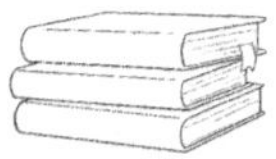

Chapter 7

MAYA

I had no idea what kind of DM I was supposed to send to a superstar college basketball player.

Theo had asked me to message her so casually that it had initially been fine. I was cool, collected. I knew what I was doing. *She'd* been the one to ask, so the ball was technically in my court, so to speak.

After the game, Iris had relentlessly teased me about being a future WAG—which I'd finally learned was *wives and girl-friends* in relation to sports—all the way home, and I'd spent the whole time insisting that it wasn't anything. And there were points when I almost convinced myself that it was true, that everything with Theo really wasn't that serious to me, and this was all for the story, the bragging rights.

The buzz of the alcohol had helped significantly in keeping me sane and confident. I felt like the coolest version of myself.

I had basically the female college-level LeBron James telling me to DM her. That was the definition of hot girl shit.

But it was much easier to be confident immediately after the game, when there was still alcohol coursing through my bloodstream and I hadn't gotten in my head yet. I'd even kept the high going when I'd gone out after the game with Iris, hitting up a house party down the street hosted by some of her friends. The whole night, I thought about Theo in passing—her arms during the game, the confidence of her playing. The way she moved around the court like she knew everyone was there to see her perform. The game had been fun to watch, but it'd been impossible to keep my eyes off of her when she was playing—and I wasn't even sure if that was because she was hot or if it was because she was just that enjoyable to watch.

I'd carried the warm, intoxicating buzz that came with being around Theo close to my chest all night. I wasn't such a cool girl that I was going to wait days to reach out, but I couldn't bring myself to send something immediately. I wanted to keep the feeling going, and I was scared it might go away as soon as I messaged her. I wasn't sure I was ready for the bubble to burst yet. It was such a fresh, fragile feeling I'd never experienced before.

I'd also clocked that I was the only girl she'd spoken to in the stands—other than the people who wanted autographs—but that didn't mean I was the only girl on her radar.

Not that I cared.

But either way, I didn't want to come across as too eager. I wouldn't be surprised if she was tired of people being excited to meet her, excited for their chance to be with a star player. I had to find a balance in there somewhere—genuinely glad to be talking to her, but not too into it. A normal amount of excitement, whatever that meant.

It wasn't until I got home, hopped in the shower, put on my pajamas, and was left alone in my quiet room with no Iris to keep my mind busy that reality sank in.

Thinking about DMing Theo was a hell of a lot easier than actually drafting a DM to her.

I rolled over onto my side. It was rounding on three in the morning, and I was sobering up from the game and the party after. Not a single DM idea I had felt right, and I was starting to get in my head about it now that the alcohol was leaving my body. Was a simple *hey* good enough? A *remember me*? I didn't want to completely embarrass myself right off the bat with the first message. I could absolutely still fuck this up.

But I didn't even know why I cared so much. She was hot, but lots of people were hot. She was a basketball player, but I didn't even like sports. None of it made sense. There was no reason why she was the specific person who caught my eye.

I put my face into my pillow and groaned. I didn't even know Theo McCall, and she was driving me crazy.

I turned over again, staring at the streak of moonlight coming through my curtains. I had to get over this somehow.

And maybe getting over it needed to include getting to know her. Part of my identity at this point was never wanting to get too close. I loved to flirt and loved the game of getting someone's attention. But I never wanted to actually keep it; it was never that serious. And it was usually because there were things about them that I couldn't get around, tiny icks that ruined the whole thing—the way they ate, their hobbies, their opinions on completely minute things. I was quick to get into something and quick to leave.

I just had to find something that would make me want to leave Theo McCall.

I woke up to my alarm the next morning, groggy and confused. I didn't remember falling asleep, but I knew I definitely didn't get enough of it. My phone was still in my hand, and I panicked for a moment, wondering if I'd sent Theo something in the midst of being exhausted. But when I unlocked my phone, there was nothing—only Theo's Instagram page.

Just as I was about to say fuck it and roll over, Iris knocked on my bedroom door.

"Maya! You up? We should get moving soon. I have a smoothie made for you already."

I debated on telling her I couldn't go anymore. It was so much easier to agree to go out for an early morning workout when I was sober and not exhausted. But right now, I was experiencing a hangover and my body felt like a bag of sand. I couldn't workout under these conditions.

But I also didn't want to leave Iris high and dry. And it'd been too long since I'd last been.

"I'm getting up," I said, mostly to myself.

"I'll be in the kitchen!" she responded, way too chipper for the circumstances.

"Okay," I said, half-groaning.

I dragged myself out of bed and pulled on workout clothes. By the time I had my hair up, I was back in the swing of things. Despite being exhausted, it felt good to get up and actually get myself moving instead of moping around and letting my hangover win.

I met Iris in the kitchen where she was drinking a green smoothie. Her blonde hair was tightly braided, and she was wearing her favorite matching set. "How are you feeling?" she asked.

"Sickly."

"Sorry," she said with earnest empathy. "I would've let you stay in bed if you wanted to."

"This is good for me. I should get up," I said. "I had a hard time falling asleep."

"Up all night messaging Theo?"

My face went hot as I poured out my portion of the smoothie into a cup. I leaned against the kitchen counter. "No, I haven't messaged her yet."

"Up all night fantasizing about your lover-to-be? Decided to play hard to get?" she teased. "I wouldn't blame you for being into her. She's a lot of fun to watch on the court. Totally different meeting her than I thought it would be based on how her games go. But she only bickered, like, once with the refs this game, which is low for her. Maybe she's mellowing in her old age."

"It was cool to see her out there," I admitted.

"Would you wanna come to another game with me?" Iris asked, practically fluttering her eyelashes at me.

The thought made me surprisingly uneasy—the thought of seeing Theo again in general made me uneasy. But it also excited me. The flutter in my chest was something new and I liked it and was scared of it in equal measure.

I just wasn't sure it was worth it to really lean into. I could easily run from it all before it actually turned into anything, leaving it so Theo was never anything more than a memory.

Then I remembered: *find something that would make you want to leave.* I had to hold myself to that promise; otherwise, I was going to waste my senior year of college away pining over some random athlete I wouldn't remember in two years.

"Yeah, I'll go with you," I said.

Iris cheered. "This is the best early Christmas present I could ever ask for. I would say I'm surprised watching Theo play was what did it for you, but she tends to have that effect on everyone."

My stomach knotted. Little did Iris know that was exactly my fear.

Because Iris and I were up early on a Friday morning—by design, neither of us had morning classes on Fridays—there weren't many people at the student gym. Since we'd been coming here around the same time for a few weeks, we'd gotten used to seeing most of the same faces and knew the general routine of what equipment would be open.

But as I was wandering around, I couldn't help but feel pairs of eyes on me. I glanced down and patted myself, making sure I hadn't somehow forgotten a shirt or pants or something. My period had ended last week, so I knew it couldn't possibly be that.

I looked around, eyeing the curious faces. Maybe I had something on my face or my hair looked like shit.

"Do I look weird?" I whispered, leaning toward Iris.

"No, why?" she asked, completely oblivious to what I was seeing.

"I feel like people are...looking at me," I said.

Iris looked at me, surprised and visibly weirded out. She playfully pressed a palm to my forehead. "Are you feeling okay? Not that I think people even are looking at you, but you've never once been the kind of person to shy away from attention."

"I'm not shying away, it's just…" I looked around, catching the eyes of a girl nearby who'd been looking at me. I felt like a teenager who'd smoked a bunch of weed and then been dropped in a grocery store. I leaned in even closer to Iris. "I really think they're looking at me."

"Maybe you being a weirdo who's frantically looking around is catching people's attention," she teased. She put her headphones on. "Everything's fine. Go workout."

I nodded, trying to convince myself that she was right. Even though something in my gut was telling me this wasn't normal, I didn't have any real evidence other than a feeling. Irrationally, I wondered if there was somehow a way that everyone knew Theo had hit on me last night, but that didn't seem right. Theo was a big deal, but she was a big deal in basketball; I doubted anyone cared about her personal life.

And beyond that, there was no reason for anyone to care about *my* personal life. I wasn't some major influencer or even a small-time campus celebrity. People didn't know my face and name like that, especially not enough to stare at me in the gym because of a brief interaction with a college basketball player.

I brushed it off and went to the stairmaster while Iris headed off to the rowing machine. I forced myself to focus entirely on the audiobook in my ears, pushing out every other thought in my head.

The distraction was helpful for more than one reason; I needed a reprieve from thinking about Theo, and thinking everything came back to Theo. I was driving myself insane, always wondering if I was going to run into her and what she was up to and if she thought about me even half as much as I thought about her.

And I still hadn't even come up with something to say to her. All of that time spent thinking about her, wondering about her, and stressing about her, and I still hadn't found the right introductory text.

I tabled it all for now, getting lost in the story playing out in my ears. I could deal with Theo later.

I moved between machines at the gym in my usual routine, minding my own business as I went, and no longer looking to see if anyone was looking at me. As I got my body moving more, it was easier for me to forget that I'd been feeling so paranoid earlier. I quickly got back in the rhythm, letting my mind wander to the sounds of my book and the steadiness of my breath. Despite my best efforts, Theo's arms and smile and gentle off-court demeanor would pop back into my head at random, but I would shut it out as quickly as I could.

The only thing that made it actually possible to relax was that I probably wasn't going to run into her here. The team was successful enough that I doubted they worked out in the student gym.

But even as I convinced myself this was a Theo-free zone, it was still hard not to think about her working out here. I imagined her confidence on the machines, the weights she could probably lift. Iris was right; maybe athletes *were* everyone's type. I'd never thought much about arms, but that was before I'd seen what Theo's looked like when they were flexed.

By the time I was sweaty and hungry enough to justify leaving, I'd completely forgotten my concerns that people had been looking at me sideways. And I'd half-managed to push thoughts of Theo out of my head.

Or, at the very least, I was doing better controlling my spiral out here than I was from bed last night.

I texted Iris to see if she was ready to go, and she responded quickly with a *Yes!!!* I wiped down the leg press I'd been using and then headed off to find her near the lockers at the front door of the gym. We lived close enough to the gym that we didn't have to bother with the locker room.

"I'm so ready to eat," Iris said. "And nap. I need to lie in that one specific spot on the couch in the sun for a while before heading to work."

"I know exactly what you mean," I said. The only things on my agenda for the day were one class and then a long study session preparing for an upcoming exam. I usually liked that my Fridays were easy, but today was one of those days when I needed a distraction. Iris was usually perfect for that, but she didn't get home until the late evening. I was coming up on crunch time for needing to message Theo if I didn't want to look like a complete asshole who was blowing her off.

But I wasn't exactly itching to message her too quickly; the feeling that would come after texting her was the only thing worse than trying to figure out what to say to her in the first place.

And I still hadn't thought of the perfect thing to say. Not that I was worried about that.

"Do you want to go to The 151 tonight? I think they're hosting something again—Amelia texted me about it. But I think Stephen's has drink specials." Iris kept her eyes fixed on her phone as we walked. I held the door to the gym open for her and was greeted by warm sun and frigid air that pinched the parts of my skin that were exposed. The layer of sweat sitting on my skin was slowly sucked away by the dry air as we walked.

"I don't know which one yet," I said. "I'm kind of down for whatever. Stephen's might be fun—I feel like we haven't been there much so far this year."

Stephen's was the local dive bar a couple of minutes from campus. It didn't usually get that busy, but it was still a lot of fun. There was a pool table, and the drinks were surprisingly good for the price. I could also unapologetically fuck up their tater tots any day of the week.

"Let me check in with everyone and see what they're up to. I should know what the plan is before I get off work, so I know how quickly I need to eat and get ready—" Iris suddenly stopped dead in the middle of the sidewalk.

I turned and looked at her. "Hello?"

She put a hand gently to her mouth and looked up at me. "Oh my god."

"What?" I asked and walked back toward her.

"Um." She looked down at her phone again. "I think I know why you thought people were staring at you. I think they actually might've been."

My heart raced thinking over anything I could've done to deserve a public callout online. I didn't know if I had any previous hook-ups bold enough to share stories online about me, but maybe it was my time to shine in the lesbian gossip circles. I hadn't exactly been careful about my reputation around campus.

Iris turned her phone toward me. She'd gotten a text from Tamara, one of her friends from the basketball game. *Is this your friend from the game last night?*

Attached to the text was a screenshot from a social media app that included a picture of me and Theo talking. And based on the body language, I couldn't even blame the person for captioning the photo: *Looks like Theo McCall is off the market—sorry ladies!* Based on the amount of interactions the post had gotten, it'd been making rounds way beyond just our campus. It'd already gotten more likes than the entire size of our student population.

My heart raced, taking in every detail. For the first time in my life, I was speechless. I'd never posted much about myself online and didn't have aspirations of becoming an internet personality. It didn't feel real that so many people had seen a picture of me.

"Shit, dude," Iris said.

"I guess I have something to DM Theo about now," I said.

Chapter 8

THEO

Class was, as usual, too long.

I prided myself on avoiding the major athlete stereotype of having zero interest in school—GJ was unsurprisingly the worst offender on our team—but that didn't stop me from getting antsy. An hour and a half into my three-hour lecture, and all I could think about was how badly I wanted to be moving my body. Now that the season had officially started, I felt like someone had started me up like a wind-up toy. Everything was about getting to the next game.

We played around two games a week throughout the season and our next one was on Sunday. We had two away games next week and it would go on just like that—back and forth between home and somewhere else in the United States—for the next couple of months.

I felt like the luckiest person alive every time I thought about how I got to play D1 basketball. All of the flights, the time spent playing, the winning alongside my team. This was what I'd spent my entire career working toward. It was all worth it now—all of that time as a kid in the car and at practice instead of out, the parties I skipped out on in high school because I had a travel game the next day or was out of town for a game.

And as much as I wanted to have a contingency plan with a decent degree and professional connections, it did not feel worth sitting through a mandatory Friday morning lecture.

I tapped my foot, looking around to see if anyone else felt as restless as I did. As one of the only seniors on the team, I was the only person from my basketball team in this class. It wasn't usually like that; we typically moved in packs, especially when it came to summer and winter session classes. We all tended to be in similar majors with similar attitudes toward school.

Normally, it meant I had at least one ally in having the urge to run laps after sitting for too long. But it was just me in this class.

I stood up to go stretch my legs. The professor usually gave us periodic five-minute stretch breaks, but I couldn't wait for the next one. I had to get up now. We were in a small, theatre-style classroom with so few of us that we could all keep two or three seats between each other. I cut easily through my row and then down the steps, acknowledging my professor on the way out.

Once I was out in the hall, I paced and shook out my shoulders. I reached for my phone, chewing on my lip.

Now that I was off the court and no longer riding the high of playing and winning, I wasn't feeling so confident with Maya. She hadn't messaged me all last night—not that I'd noticed—and I still hadn't seen anything from her this morning. It could've been for any combination of reasons, like she got busy or forgot. I'd been resisting the urge to check every couple of minutes to see if she'd sent anything.

I didn't have my notifications on because my phone would be unusable, which then forced me to actually open the app and see if she'd sent anything. I'd slept like shit last night, my brain resisting the urge to sleep just in case Maya happened to message me at two in the morning. I'd spent the entire party last night sneaking glances at my phone, willing her to send me something. Or at least follow me.

I'd been unsuccessful in fighting off my growing social media addiction; if anything, the more time went by, the more frantically I was checking, like I was worried her message had slipped by me. I was certain my screen time for Instagram had never been so high.

I went into my messages from accounts I didn't follow—doing it with the same anxiety levels and discrete approach of someone doing something illegal—and nearly dropped my phone when I saw I had a new message from a girl who looked just like her.

My heart raced as I clicked on it. *Maya Healy*. That was her name. She was unsurprisingly photogenic. The picture she'd chosen for her profile picture was cute; she had a giant smile on her face, and she was bundled up and out in the snow, probably in the mountains around here. I scrolled through the pictures she posted. Most of her grid was made up of group photos, but she occasionally posted pictures of just herself. I couldn't deep dive now, but I knew I was inevitably going to when I had free time later.

I followed her before even fully reading her message. I so badly wanted to see more of her—see her friends, where she was from, what her interests were. I wanted to find something we had in common, or something I could learn more about.

Anything to keep the conversation going with her.

After sending my request, I went back to her message and looked at the preview: *Wow, we move fast.*

I blinked at it for a second, wondering what she meant. My heart sank. It couldn't possibly be that she was worried me asking for her to DM me would be moving too quickly. To me, it felt like we were doing everything at a glacially slow pace. I'd been dying over here wanting to talk to her, but maybe the feeling wasn't mutual.

I clicked on the full message and saw that she'd sent an image with the text. But the image was blurred, probably as a security measure. My heart raced as I clicked *accept* on the message so I could see what she'd sent me.

When I saw what it was, I almost burst out laughing from surprise.

When was someone going to tell me I was off the market? I wrote back, not wanting to overthink it. If I started stressing, I wouldn't respond to her for another couple of hours at least, and then I would probably talk myself out of responding at all. Or I'd respond with something like *lol* because I talked myself out of any other type of response.

I looked back at the picture. The person who captioned it wasn't wrong; it really did look like I was off the market. Maya and I were leaning toward each other, our eyes and attention completely focused on each other. Despite the obvious commotion around us, we were deep in conversation. I was grinning at her in a way I'd never seen myself grin before, and I was mortified I was capable of looking that down bad.

But Maya also looked completely invested. If I was down bad, Maya seemed to be too.

I dug around on Twitter to find the original tweet and scrolled through the responses. I was surprised to see how many people had something to say about the photo and how far it'd gone online, mostly because my teammates hadn't said anything to me about it, and they spent way more time on social media than I did. I would be shocked if none of them had seen it based on how big it had gotten literally overnight.

The comments were admittedly hilarious: *That should be me. Theo, I can treat you better than she can. I can't believe my wife has a girlfriend.*

There were a handful that referenced not realizing I was gay, which was fair enough since it wasn't a secret, but it also wasn't super public information. I'd never had a public girlfriend, and everyone on the team, including the straight players, did things like publicly celebrated pride month. I felt like it was obvious just by looking at me, but people must not want to be presumptuous.

I glanced at my phone clock and realized I'd been out here for way too long. I took one last glance at the photo, wanting to memorize every detail of it, before I headed back to class.

I spent the entire rest of my class wondering if Maya was going to respond and how long it would take to hear back from her. Class somehow moved at an even slower pace than before. I'd never been so tempted to sneak glances at my phone, but I refused to let myself develop that habit.

When I got out of class, what felt like a year later, I had another message from Maya waiting for me. *I was supposed to tell you, but everyone spoiled the surprise.*

I bit back the world's stupidest grin on my face and put my phone in the pocket of my sweatpants. I was going to respond to her, but I wanted to sit on this one longer. I liked holding onto the feeling for a second of knowing I could respond to her, and I wasn't waiting pathetically for her response, wondering if each one was going to be her last.

Before heading home, I grabbed a coffee from the coffee stand outside my classroom. As I waited for my order to be ready, my phone started blowing up—vibrating once, then twice, then too many times to possibly know how many messages were coming in.

I fished my phone from my sweatpants pocket and checked. As usual, it was the team group chat—the only reason my phone ever went off like that. We had a couple of different chats between the different social groups on the team, but the main one between all of us was the one we all used the most. We were fortunate to have a strong sense of camaraderie. I didn't think anyone could top the high school team I'd been on, but the relationship I'd built with the Lakeside girls was something else entirely.

Before I even opened the messages, I could already guess what it was going to be about. It seemed the photo was finally making its rounds; everyone had probably just woken up from how hard we'd all partied last night. Coach Darlene had been generous in giving us the morning off since it'd been the first win of the season, the exchange being an extra-long workout this evening. It seemed like everyone other than me had skipped class to relish in the rare late morning.

Get it, McCall!!

Since when do you have a girl?

Y'all fucking??

I nearly rolled my eyes, fighting off a laugh. The group chat went on and on, teasing me about the dramatic responses people were posting about the picture and the amount of buzz the photo had gotten.

I was, admittedly, surprised by it too. I knew I had some pull—our games were aired on TV, I'd been in nationally aired commercials, been featured in sports articles, and praised as the present and future of the sport. But I didn't think people actually cared about *me*. I assumed it'd always been about the game. And that was how I preferred it to be. Mags wanted to be a personality, and she wasn't shy about it. Players like Cam Kerr made it their entire brand to be as publicly visible as possible.

But I'd never wanted that. I'd always kept it strictly game-related. I never talked shit in a press conference, never ragged on people on social media, never talked about my own personal life online. Every once in a while, I'd post a picture of my parents to celebrate one of their birthdays or their anniversary, but nothing was ever about dating. The most I posted about was basketball from the official Lakeside Green social media accounts, followed by reposted pictures of the team my teammates shared.

That had been intentional to a certain extent—no one needed to know my business— but it had also felt stupid, like everyone who saw me post about my parents would be like, *Okay, and? Give us another highlight.* I posted about basketball because people cared about basketball. They wanted to see me play and practice and wanted to follow me from college to—hope-fully—the pros.

But I was realizing now that might not actually be the case. Maybe people wanted more of me than I thought.

"Order for Theo," a barista said from the coffee cart. I walked up and grabbed it, quietly thanking her while keeping my head down. Unfortunately, it was hard to hide as someone who had an obvious basketball player build—I was six feet tall and pretty much always in athleisure.

As I exited the building, I looked down at the coffee in my hands and weighed my options on responding to Maya. I was already in this shit; I might as well see it through. No use in pretending anything between the two of us could ever be normal now.

I pulled out my phone and wrote, *Tell me more over coffee?*, attaching my phone number to the end so I could avoid social media as much as possible for the rest of the day. I was surprised by my own boldness, but also couldn't deny that I felt I had a good reason to be bold. I probably needed to start acknowledging that I was someone who could take big swings, even though I mostly felt like I was still just some girl trying her best to follow her dreams. I wasn't *actually* there yet.

My phone vibrated in my pocket, and I took a deep breath, hoping it would be Maya. But instead, my mom's contact photo popped up.

I pushed through the exit doors and headed outside. For a moment, I wondered if she was calling because she'd seen or heard something about the picture with Maya. But then I remembered that it was my mom who I was talking about, the same woman who could barely figure out how to post on Instagram. Her last update had been from one of my high school games, and I'd had to coach her through the whole process. I don't think she even knew what Twitter was. "Hey, Mom."

"Hey, sweetie. Congrats on your game. Your dad and I wished we could've been there for it," she said.

I smiled at the sound of her voice. One of the hardest things about basketball season was that my parents were pretty much entirely off-limits to me. We not only lived in different states right now, but I was constantly either practicing or out with the team or traveling somewhere for a game. There was no real downtime to justify them coming to visit, especially from a flight away. "I wanted to call you last night, but we all know how post-game goes."

She was right; as much as I tried to make time to talk to my parents after my games, it was hard to find the time. I was shuttled from one thing to the next, and by the time I could call my parents, they were usually already settled in bed for the night. I'd never been able to get into the swing of calling them to talk through a game immediately after; we've had to settle for the tradition of them calling me the day after, my mom usually trying to catch me just as I was leaving a class so she knew I was walking around campus and wasn't busy.

"Oh, it's okay. I know you guys will see me when I go to a closer game," I said. My parents still lived in the neighborhood I grew up in, a little town a few hours outside of Ann Arbor. There'd never been much to say about my hometown—there weren't a lot of kids and there wasn't much to do. Basketball offered an escape, especially during the winter when I couldn't shoot basketballs in my backyard because of the snow. It allowed me to travel and be with more kids my own age other than the faces I'd known since kindergarten.

By the time college recruiters were looking at me—as young as middle school, in some cases—I was ready to get out and go just about anywhere that would give me an offer. There were bigger and better-funded programs than Lakeside Green's, but the two options had been clear: Either be the big fish in a small pond, or be a small fish among a lot of other talented fish in a much larger pond. It didn't feel worth it to go to a school with a basically guaranteed ring if I didn't get to play.

And either way, getting to build Lakeside Green into a reputable women's basketball program was an honor. It'd been the best kind of ego boost I could ask for, knowing I was leaving behind a legitimate legacy at this school. After nearly two decades of nothing of note happening and mostly losing records, things had finally started to turn around. It'd been fun getting people excited about the sport for the first time in a long time here.

"Your dad was yelling at the TV like crazy," Mom said.

"I can't believe twenty-four didn't get a tech! Refs should've been on her!" Dad said from offscreen. He'd raised his voice so I could hear him; he was probably sitting across the room from her. I could picture my parents so easily—my mom reading from her favorite spot on the couch, and my dad on his phone after messing around in the garage.

My parents had been in their thirties when they had me and were fortunate to be able to retire now that I was leaving school. Once they realized that I was competent enough to take care of myself—either through basketball or whatever other means I could find—they both eased out of working full-time and work mostly on an as-needed basis now in consultant work.

Despite the flexibility of their schedules now, I was insistent from the beginning that they didn't need to be the kind of parents who flew out for every game. If anything, I was sure they didn't really want to. We had too many games throughout the season for them to be roadies, or to consistently see me play without basically relocating to Colorado for the season.

And, as I liked to tease them, they were getting too old to be on and off airplanes all the time. They were still spry and took great care of themselves, but it was way more fun to tease them about how their jetsetting years were behind them.

"I get hit like that all the time, it happens," I said. My memories of the games were always like watching a sports reel. I rarely remembered the interpersonal stuff—accidental shoves, fouls. I was used to my body getting knocked around, and I never took it personally or thought about it beyond the game. Adrenaline made it possible for me to bounce back up like nothing happened.

The only thing I took care in remembering was the game itself, strengths and weaknesses of the other players, who liked to play dirty, plays teams liked to run. That was the stuff that really mattered to me; not technicals and off-court beef.

"Never gets less scary," Mom said.

Mom and Dad had never been quiet about how proud they were of me. Sometimes, it didn't seem like they understood how they'd raised someone like me—someone so competitive, so driven, so *loud* about how much I loved basketball. I wasn't afraid to raise my voice on the court where needed and my mouth would get me into hot shit regularly. Growing up, my parents were usually the ones to reel me in from the sidelines. Now, it was mostly my coach. And my teammates, other than GJ, who encouraged it.

Both of my parents had been athletes, but for much smaller programs and with much less drive to do it professionally. They knew they'd give up basketball after college graduation; I knew from as young as third grade that I was going to do everything it took to play professionally. It'd been obvious to everyone that I was something special; I had that right combination of natural talent and drive to see it through. My feelings on it had never wavered. But their concern for my well-being and making sure I knew I wasn't expected to be the best had also never wavered.

"I have huge muscles now, Mom. I can take care of myself."

Mom snorted. "But you're good? You have money for food? Sneakers don't have holes?"

"Yeah, everything's good here. Ready for the game on Sunday. And I'm excited to start traveling again next week for games. We have one in Florida that I'm looking forward to. It'll be nice to be somewhere warmer than here."

"Yeah, tell me about it. You getting much snow?"

"The usual," I said.

"Same here," Mom said. "Okay, well, I won't hold you too long. Your dad and I have a very exciting day ahead of us of grocery shopping and grabbing some things from Home Depot."

"Sad I'm missing it," I said, mostly as a joke but also partially because it was true. I wished it was easier for them to be here with me sometimes, even just in passing. It wasn't that I wanted a lot of time with them; I just wanted to be able to have a random Tuesday night dinner together or spend a Sunday watching football together.

That was one of the things that had changed the most in me as I'd grown up. When I was a kid, I didn't mind all of the time on the road—and I also didn't realize how lucky I was to have parents who were so patient and available. They drove me wherever for games and practices, paid up whatever money they could find to make sure I could play year-round. AAU basketball had never been off the table for me and I was grateful for that. Most of my time with my parents growing up had been spent going to or from practice or a game. I'd never thought that much about what a sacrifice that was for them; I just wanted to play.

But now that I'd moved out and moved so far from them, I realized how little time I actually had with them because of basketball. All of the driving around and weekend tournaments were quality time, but I didn't have that anymore. What used to be the thing that would keep us in the same room and car had taken me to a different timezone.

"We're sad you're missing it, too," Mom said. I could hear in her voice that she really meant it. Neither of my parents had really wanted me to move out. At the very least, they'd held onto hope that I would stay within the state for them, preferably driving distance. I was their only child and my mom had told me from day one how quiet the house was now that I wasn't there anymore.

But the stars hadn't aligned that way. The programs I wanted were all too far for that. My parents had barely even wanted me to push for my dream school—Point Brook University—so when I didn't get recruited there, they'd really been crossing their fingers I'd stay close to home. But Lakeside Green offered the best program otherwise; the only downside being I was even further from home than Point Brook would've been.

I continued my walk across campus, both of us staying on the phone for a touch too long. We silently played the game of *you hang up, no you hang up.*

"Alright, honey. Time for us to get moving," Mom said.

"Okay, I'll talk to you later," I said. "Love you."

"Love you, too."

When I hung up the phone, I saw a text message from an unsaved number. My heart nearly stopped; I was certain I was misreading it. But when I read over it a second time, I confirmed it was real. *Hey, it's Maya. I'm at the Berg if you're free at any point today.*

I had to lock my phone and put it at my side for a second to take a deep breath and avoid embarrassing myself publicly. I had never forced a smile off my face so quickly, but I knew it was probably still peeking through. I couldn't help it.

I cleared my throat and unlocked my phone again. In response, I wrote, *Cool, just got out of class. See you in a few.*

The Berg was one of the mid-sized student centers on campus. It was closer to the freshman dorms, so I hadn't been in a long time. And even then, I hadn't really gone when I was a freshman. I needed absolute silence to study, and a casual, noisy dining area was the exact opposite of that. School wasn't *hard* for me, but it wasn't exactly my favorite thing. I'd much rather run a bunch of suicides and drills than sit down to write a paper.

It was surprising to me that Maya hung out here. But I'd be lying if I said this wasn't the most excited I'd ever been to go to a student center. She might as well have invited me to a five-star restaurant.

When I stepped inside, it felt like being brought right back to freshman year. For just a second, I was the scared eighteen-year-old who wasn't sure what college was going to look like. I wasn't nervous to play basketball and get into the swing of the game in college—my skills had never wavered, and I'd been waiting my entire life to play in front of huge crowds—but I *was* nervous about having a new team and new coach. There was so much learning that had happened so early into college—my first dorm parties, a poorly-planned and executed crush on a girl on my floor, the realization that being away from home was hard and exciting all at once.

But the nostalgia wore off almost immediately when I realized that people were definitely staring at me. I hadn't gained any type of name or face recognition, even on my campus, until closer to the end of my sophomore season. All it had taken to go from faceless to the face of the program was a few major wins against schools typically considered better than us. From there, it was easy to keep their attention.

It'd never been a secret who'd changed the momentum for us. Coach Darlene always gave me credit where credit was due; she trusted me enough to let me do what I needed to do and play big. As soon as she gave me the green light, I started pushing my team in whatever way I could. I tried new approaches to playing, new ways of keeping them ahead of everyone else on the court.

Even though I'd spent my whole life waiting for this exact moment, it felt like it'd all happened so fast. One moment, I was a girl playing basketball, hoping to get recruited some-where—anywhere—decent so I could play. The next, I was doing post-game interviews for the biggest sports networks in the nation and selling out our arena. I never took sole credit for a win because basketball was a team sport, but there wasn't one person who could deny that I'd been the reason attendance numbers went up so much.

By this point in my senior year, people were coming to games for me specifically. I didn't let it get to my head, but I acknowl-edged it. And that meant I tended to pull way more attention in public places on campus than I used to. Most of my classmates and people my age had gotten used to it. But it seemed like freshmen hadn't yet gotten the memo that staring at me and turning to their friends to say, *Wait, is that Theo?* wasn't exactly subtle.

I pretended not to see any of it as I looked around for Maya's familiar head of brown hair. Eventually, I found her sitting in a back corner near the windows. She was positioned comfortably and set up like she'd been here for hours—her laptop was open next to a notebook, two different textbooks, and printed out pages of articles she'd gone to town on with a highlighter. She was deeply immersed in her laptop, her eyes never drifting from the screen like mine did when I was doing schoolwork.

"Hey," I said as I approached.

Maya blinked up at me through her glasses like she'd forgotten I was coming. She lifted her legs from the booth seating across from her and sat up straight. She was dressed down today—her hair was in a claw clip, her glasses were on. She was wearing an oversized sweatshirt for a high school I didn't recognize the name of, probably from her hometown.

Just looking at her made me blush.

"Hey," she said and gestured for me to sit down. "Welcome to my office."

"Spacious," I said.

"It's certainly something."

"You can really study here?" I asked. It was so noisy that we practically had to raise our voices to speak to each other.

"Oh, I love it," she said. "I can't focus anywhere else."

I nodded, looking around as if trying to find our next conversation topic on the wall. I caught a few people looking over at us and immediately looked away. I hoped that Maya didn't catch it, but she definitely had.

"Sorry, upon reflection, I probably should've picked somewhere way less public to discuss the paparazzi shot taken of us," she admitted.

"No, it's okay," I said, and I could tell from Maya's face that she wasn't completely sold. I dropped my voice and leaned across the table. "I'm...used to it."

Maya's lips twisted up in an amused smile. "Oh, a true local celebrity."

"It's not like that—"

"It sounds like it's *exactly* like that," she said. "Of course, people would snap a random picture of us at a game. People are really obsessed with you."

"*Obsessed* is a strong word. They just know my name."

"And face, because it's plastered everywhere around campus. The giant banner of you and your teammates leading into the arena is pretty cool, by the way."

"Oh, god," I said, turning away so she couldn't see how visibly embarrassed I was. I knew it was written all over me.

"And I don't know if anyone told you but your jersey is *everywhere*."

From beneath my palms, I said, "So I've heard."

I finally pulled my hands away to see Maya grinning, clearly pleased with herself. "Any reason you picked twenty-five?"

"Lucky number, I guess. I don't really know. It got assigned to me as a kid, and I never let it go."

"Hm," she said.

"Good enough answer?"

"I was expecting something more heartfelt. I thought athletes always had some kind of story for their number."

"What, my story isn't heartfelt enough?" I teased back, surprised by how easily I was falling into rhythm with her. There wasn't anyone in my life who would consider me particularly chatty. But Maya brought it out of me.

"What makes it so lucky?" she asked, closing her laptop and leaning in closer to me. She took off her glasses and put them down on the table. "Or maybe that's a dumb question. I guess your career speaks for itself."

"My ego is loving this," I said. I hoped I was successfully playing off how nervous her direct eye contact was making me.

"I'm honestly surprised you're not more of a nightmare. Or you just do a really good job of hiding it."

I laughed. "I dribble a ball better than the average person. It's not, like, a revolutionary contribution to society. Ego isn't necessary outside of the court."

"It seems like it might be. Revolutionary, I mean," she said. "But what do I know?"

Absent-mindedly, I picked up her highlighter and twirled it between my fingers. "You study here often?"

"Pretty much exclusively. Come find me whenever."

She was so quick with it that it stirred up an unfamiliar feeling in me.

Jealousy.

It took a second to place, but as soon as I had it, it was undeniable. I thought about her going to parties, effortlessly throwing around lines and attention. It was easy to imagine her breaking hearts, fucking people up long after she'd ended things with them. She was genuinely kind and warm, and had a specific magnetism I hadn't seen in anyone else. It had to be her confidence. She walked around with the same kind of aura that people on my team did, but without any kind of stats or ball skills to back it up. She was naturally that self-assured.

I wasn't jealous of the confidence; I was drawn to it. I'd always liked that in someone else. But I *was* jealous of the thought of her using that confidence to charm other people in the same way she was charming me.

I didn't mind the competition; I just had to know where she stood on me versus everyone else. And that was the part that I couldn't get a read on.

"I don't think I can study here with the noise, but I'll come for you."

"You really can't handle the noise? Don't you have, like, literally thousands of people screaming at you during a game?"

"It's different. I need the crowd to play. Noise is distracting everywhere else."

She smiled a little bit. I couldn't figure out what exactly it was that had her smiling at me like that but I didn't mind it. I wasn't going to ask questions. At least, not now. I knew when to appreciate a good thing for what it was.

There was a slight pause in the conversation. A beat passed. Maya kept her eyes squarely on me. "Why did you ask me to get coffee?" she finally asked.

"You're literally my girlfriend."

Maya let out a singular laugh, and I was proud of myself for managing to pull it off. "Right, right. Of course. Stupid question."

"But actually, no, I just..." I shrugged. "I don't know. Thought I'd see what was up. I couldn't pass up the opportunity to discuss the photo in extensive detail. Which, by the way, might be the most intimate photo I've ever taken with someone."

Maya looked amused all over again. "Right," she said. I could tell she didn't believe me, but it was genuinely the truth. There wasn't time to meet people, wasn't time to fuck around. Relationships weren't in the picture for me, especially not to the level of being photographed in public together. I didn't give myself that time, and I didn't really want it.

I saw what love did to my teammates—feeling sick to their stomachs, getting in their heads, worrying all the time about one thing or another. It never felt easy. And I'd see, time and time again, how hard it was for people to maintain something committed when their schedule could be so overwhelming.

It also didn't help that most of my teammates weren't necessarily interested in stability. GJ was entirely uninterested in something monogamous. Mags kept her dating life completely locked down; not even we knew what she was up to. Gemma, Nia, and Ellie all seemed to be doing their own thing, mostly focused on making their game the best it could be than trying to find love.

Our schedules weren't so busy that there wasn't time, but it wasn't easy. Something eventually had to give. The easiest solution was to either do casual or nothing at all. Or to have found their lifelong partner before diving deep into D1 basketball, like some of my old teammates had done.

"I guess the line of women waiting for me after the game gave me away," I said. To my surprise, I could see a look of panic on Maya's face. It passed quickly and effortlessly—if I blinked, I would've missed it completely—but it had been there. "Joking. Sorry. You were visibly the only person in general waiting for me after the game, which was a first. Normally, I don't have anyone waiting for me other than my parents sometimes."

I waited, hoping the sound of Maya's laughter would ring out soon. I tried to read her expression but she'd shifted, a closed book. My heart raced at the thought of potentially having fucked it up already.

"Other than the people waiting for your autograph," she said and I nearly let out a sigh of relief.

I snorted. "Yeah, they were there too. But they don't look at me longingly, leaning over into the court to talk to me."

Her jaw dropped. "I was not looking at you *longingly*—" she protested.

"Everyone online disagrees."

"Okay, well, then you were also staring at me longingly."

"And some would say I was right to do that."

Maya tried to hide her smile, but her lips perked up, giving her away. "I can't believe we're dating now. No one ever told me it could be this easy."

"I don't believe for even one second that dating isn't easy for you."

"You don't even know me!" Maya laughed.

"I'm just saying," I said. Something in the spirit of GJ had absolutely taken over me, but I didn't care. It'd never felt this *easy* with someone before. There was no weirdness or discomfort.

As I'd gotten more and more public attention, people seemed to have lost the ability to flirt with me normally. Everyone would either stare at me from across the room or approach me, looking genuinely nervous. And while I appreciated being the kind of person who was hot enough to make other people nervous, it didn't give me much to work with.

Maya matched me exactly. She understood the rhythm of the conversation. She talked to me like I was someone she found hot—hopefully—but not intimidating. And she definitely didn't see me as some on-the-rise basketball player who could help fulfill her WAG dreams. Basketball and my micro-celebrity status were something she could tease me about. She didn't have the anxiety of someone who worried she might lose me; she had the ego to know she could have me if she wanted.

And it was hot as hell.

"I'm sure dating isn't particularly difficult for you either, Troy Bolton," Maya said.

I laughed so hard I threw my head back. "Troy Bolton?"

"That was the best basketball reference I could come up with," she said, also laughing. "I don't think you're either of the Scott brothers. Maybe you're one of the Space Jam characters."

I was laughing so hard now that I could feel my face flush. "Oh my *god*. Even if I don't manage to get you into the sport itself, I'm happy to offer the public service of introducing you to other basketball-related media. Everyone would benefit."

"I think I need that." Her voice was so earnest, her laughter so real, that it felt like I was seeing behind the curtain. Her facade had dropped the tiniest bit. It wasn't to say that she was faking her friendliness or flirtiness, but I was sure there was more depth to her than quick lines and looking at people through her long lashes. The cracks were starting to show through; she was warming up to me.

"Call whenever, I'll be there," I said. As soon as I said it, my mind flashed to what my schedule looked like. *Call whenever* didn't carry the same weight it did during the offseason. I'd have to be intentional about making time for Maya, and I wasn't going to get ahead of myself with restructuring my days around her, even if it was tempting.

Maya's eyes met mine again, and the urge to kiss her suddenly hit me like a truck. It hadn't been the first time it'd crossed my mind—I'd been thinking about it incessantly since we met—but it was the first time I'd felt it when she was right in front of me.

Based on the way Maya's lips separated and her gaze drifted over my face, I couldn't help but wonder if she was thinking about the same thing.

"What else would a girlfriend do?" she asked softly, and I couldn't tell if we were kidding anymore.

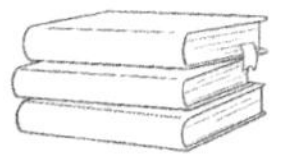

Chapter 9

MAYA

I rode the very scary, very fragile high of talking to Theo for the rest of the day. I thought about her while I was in the coffee line getting another cup mid-study session. I thought about her during my walk home, during my shower, while I was cooking myself dinner. I thought about her while I was getting ready for my night out with Iris.

Iris knew Theo and I had seen each other, but nothing else other than me insisting that it was strictly platonic.

If anyone was going to understand my obsession with Theo McCall, it was Iris. Theo was undeniably hot. She was tall, muscular. Just thinking about her half-crooked smile nearly brought me to my knees. And her voice was so smooth and impossibly sexy. Whenever she spoke, I could practically hear how she would sound whispering in my ear.

But there was something holding me back from saying anything more to Iris, even playfully. I didn't know what it was. I wasn't going to keep Theo a secret by any means, but I couldn't actually *tell* Iris how I was feeling. She would know in a second that something was going on with me. I'd never, *ever* talked about anyone that way before. I'd never even thought about someone else that way before in private.

I was down bad in a way never before experienced and all I'd done was see Theo play basketball and flirt with her a little.

And even then, I had no way of knowing if the flirting was actually reciprocated. We hadn't established anything between us and had barely even talked about the photo. All I knew was that Theo had lightly offered to hang out again in the future, but hadn't given me a definitive date or time. It felt like an expert move from a well-trained player. It was a way to keep me on my toes and keep me waiting for her. I knew the move well because I'd also done it: *yeah, let's do coffee. I'll text you later to figure it out. Not sure what my schedule looks like, but I'll let you know.*

But my gut feeling was telling me that she was flirting back, even if it was just a little bit.

"You are literally walking on air," Iris said as I walked from my bedroom into our living room. She glanced up at me from the kitchen as she poured out a shot for herself.

I stopped and blinked at her. "What are you talking about?"

"I don't know what you're thinking about, but it's all over your face. You look like you're on a completely different planet. If you're not having the best sex flashback of your life right now, I don't know what else you could possibly be thinking about."

I frowned, leaning over the kitchen counter to look at her. I popped a pretzel into my mouth, our favorite pregame snack for the quick carbs. "What do you mean?"

"Dude, look at you," she said. "I'm guessing hanging out with Theo went really well."

"Stop," I moaned, dragging out the vowel. I ducked my head into my hands. "It was nothing. We were just hanging out. She asked me to DM her, and then she asked to get coffee."

"And then you went back to her place and you fucked for, like, six hours straight," Iris said and then sighed dreamily. "I know her stamina must be insane."

It had to be; no one could work out that much and get tired in bed. "Not the point," I said, shaking away my own thoughts about Theo that were very much not appropriate. "Nothing happened. I didn't go home with her. We talked and then she left because she had to eat and change before practice."

"You saying the words *before practice* is hilarious to me. I love this sports era for you, but it's going to take me a second to get used to," Iris said and then threw back her shot, grimacing as it went down.

"There is no sports era for me. Theo and I are just..." I waved my hands around in the air as if that was going to answer things.

"She literally asked you to slide into her DMs. You guys then proceeded to hang out. I don't see what could possibly be confusing about that."

"It's a lesbian thing. I don't know. Like, we were probably flirting. But we also probably weren't. Nothing happened. People will kiss as friends so nothing is really off the table. You have to, like, actually talk about it to get any kind of real answers."

"So just talk to her," Iris said like it was the most obvious thing in the world.

"I can't talk to her because I don't even know what I would want, if I want anything at all," I said, more trying to convince myself than Iris.

My plan of not talking about Theo was quickly disintegrating. I should've known Iris was going to see right through me. She'd always been able to tell when I was bullshitting. Sometimes, she let it go and let me talk when I was ready. Other times, she prodded until my entire story collapsed and the truth came out.

"You have a hot basketball player—arguably, like, *the* female college basketball player of the moment—going after you."

"You know me. I don't do...serious. Or feelings. Or relationships. Or whatever. I don't want to talk to her unless I'm totally sure, and the odds are that in, like, two weeks I'll be over this and move on. It's way too early to even get a *suggestion* on what she's feeling, anyway. I know lesbians are stereotyped to U-Haul, but we're also stereotyped to have painstakingly slow friends-to-lovers arcs."

"The latter of which you're holding out for?" Iris asked cutely, tilting her head and fluttering her eyelashes at me.

"I'm just having some fun. We'll hang out and like…whatever. I don't know."

"I mean, how would you feel if she suddenly popped out with some new girl in, like, two weeks? Honestly?"

My stomach knotted up at the thought. I'd kept everything so logical, purely focusing on what I could see and what the facts were. From what I could tell, she wasn't seeing anyone because no one else had gone to her season opener and waited for her. She also didn't seem to date much because there was nothing online about a previous girlfriend—no pictures, no long-lost posts. Nothing.

Not that I'd been looking.

But Iris proposing that question brought me face-to-face with the thing I hadn't wanted to address, which was that anything could be going on in secret. Girls not showing up to her games just meant that she didn't have a girlfriend; it didn't tell me anything else.

The thought stirred up something weird in me that I didn't like. My insides knotted up.

Jealousy. That was what that feeling was. It was new to me, but I already didn't like it.

"I mean, it'd be…whatever," I lied, as if the thought of Theo looking at someone else like she looked at me didn't make me want to vomit.

Iris raised her eyebrows at me slightly, and I knew she didn't believe me. I rolled my eyes in response.

"You know me, I'll be over it in a week," I said. It was true—I loved a fling with character. DJs, international students, graduate students in town for a conference. I got to experience something new for a fleeting moment and then moved on. Theo fit the same exact formula. It would be fine.

But even as I thought it, my gut was telling me it wasn't true. Theo was different; it was undeniable.

Iris and I opted for Stephen's instead of a house party. Drinks were pretty cheap because it was a dive bar, but it was really only fun to show up already pretty plastered. Otherwise, we started thinking too much about how the floors looked like they'd never been cleaned, and the tables were always sticky.

When we arrived, we realized Stephen's was doing some kind of discount night for a Lakeside Green football game they were playing in California. It was busier than either of us expected it to be, but the crowd was lively and a lot of fun.

"You really are trying to turn me into a sports girl," I teased as we walked in. The game was playing on a huge projector. We were there for the very tail end of it but the score was close, so the crowd at Stephen's was still going nuts.

"You know I wouldn't drag you to football without a heads up," Iris said. She'd always been more of a basketball girl than a football one; she only went to football games when she was invited by other people.

"Find us a place to sit, I'll get us drinks," I said. With the specials the bar was offering, I was happy to pay.

Iris headed off to find an open seat, and I went to the bar to get us drinks. As I waited for a space at the counter to order, I glanced around to see who was here. I was surprised Iris and I had never accidentally overlapped with a sporting event here before; I didn't even realize they hosted nights like this here, even though it made sense. But we tended to bounce between house parties—it was a huge thing on our campus—and only went to bars when we wanted a change of scenery.

As I looked around the room, taking in the green jerseys and face paint and spray-on hair dye, I felt the same way I had during the basketball game. Before Iris had introduced me to a game, I'd seen all of it as a nuisance and kind of overdramatic. But now, I could see the sense of community that came from sports like this. It was hard for me to ever imagine going as hard as even owning sports merchandise, but I could appreciate it for what it was now.

I smiled a little bit, thinking about how there were people who got this excited about Theo playing. I imagined people sitting around their TVs and going to bars just like these to see her play. So many of them were probably wearing her name and number, too. I was sure it was exactly what she'd always dreamed of for herself.

"Didn't realize there was a game going on?"

I turned and saw a woman standing next to me. I did the usual scan out of habit—short nails, no wedding ring, but silver rings on her other fingers, tattoos winding up her arms. Her long hair was tied back off her face. It was obvious what she was here for.

"No, I guess I should've opted for green," I said. She was wearing a cut-off Lakeside Green shirt. It was black instead of the usual green, very much fitting with the cool girl, motorcycle vibe she was giving off.

"I don't know, I think I like the shirt you're wearing," she said.

I nearly rolled my eyes, half expecting her to launch into some variation of *and I'd like it even more if you weren't wearing it.*

Even beyond already knowing every line in the book, I found myself uninterested in her. Normally, I could overlook the corniness—and I would've on any other night. She was hot, and she was flirting with me. I was single, she was presumably also single. There was nothing holding us back.

But there *was* something holding me back. As she was talking to me, all I could think about was Theo.

As the girl in front of me picked up her beer to take a sip, all I could think about was how Theo's hands looked when she was fiddling with my highlighter at the table. It'd taken all of my willpower not to stare at them the entire time we'd been together. It was so easy to imagine those same fingers intertwined with my own, tangled up in my hair, traveling over my body.

And then there was the way her arms looked under her short-sleeve t-shirt. I wanted to run my hands over her biceps, squeeze them, kiss them.

Suddenly, I was itching to get out of this conversation. For the first time, maybe ever in my life, I was passing up the opportunity to flirt and doing so willingly.

And most surprising of all, I was doing it with zero label or confirmation from someone else that they actually liked me and were interested in me in return.

"Thanks," I said, hoping I was still being polite but firm enough to get out of this. If I stood here any longer, I was at risk of saying something out loud about how attracted I was to Theo and how she was the person I wanted to be seeing tonight.

Alcohol seemed to be having the opposite effect of what I'd intended it to—it highlighted my feelings for Theo and made everyone else seem entirely unappealing.

"Not much of a football fan, then?" the girl asked, still trying even though I wasn't giving her much. Her effort was starting to feel grating rather than admirable.

"Not really," I said. "But my girlfriend is."

She nodded with acknowledgement and backed off. It wasn't my first time using the line, but it was my first time using it because I was genuinely interested in someone else. Normally, I would use it whenever the person wasn't really my type or I wasn't getting any kind of spark. This time, though, it actually felt like it meant something.

I ordered drinks for me and Iris, the process uninterrupted by anyone else attempting to take me home. I ordered Iris and me two rounds each to save time and avoid having to brave waiting at the bar again. I couldn't tell if the crowd was going to clear after the game or not, but I wasn't taking any chances.

"Drinks on drinks!" Iris said as I walked over. She'd found us a tiny round table toward the back that had barely any view of the screen; it seemed like this side of the bar was mostly non-sports fans looking for a night out.

As I placed the cups—expertly balanced in my hands like a practiced barmaid—down onto the table, the crowd erupted.

"Overtime," Iris said.

"Fuck," I said. I settled into the chair across from her.

"Sorry, I didn't realize the crowd was going to be like this," she said. She took a long sip of one of her drinks through her straw. "Did you get her number?"

"What?"

"The girl at the bar. I saw her talking to you. She was radiating gay from all the way over here."

"Oh," I said, having already brushed the thought of her away. It was nothing she'd done, and I hoped her all the best, but I had someone else who was taking up all of the real estate in my head. "Yeah, I did. We might get a drink sometime," I lied.

"You're scarily good at this," Iris said, shaking her head.

"Yeah," I said and tried to quickly think of a way to pivot the conversation. "I promise we'll find your basketball player. It's meant to happen."

Iris waved me off. "I'm more worried about *your* basketball player."

"I don't have one," I said, and it almost sounded convincing.

Iris and I called it a night earlier than we usually did—she wanted a full night of sleep before heading into work, and I wanted to get up early to finish a paper that was due.

After showering sticky dive bar air off of me, I curled up in bed in the biggest, softest t-shirt in my closet and a pair of loose-fitting women's boxers. I leaned over and cracked my bedroom window open just the tiniest bit so I could get some fresh air into the room, one of my worst vices. I loved sleeping with the window open, even when it was nineteen degrees and the heat was blasting in the house. I only ever cracked it so it wouldn't get too cold, but I slept better with the fresh air.

I picked up my phone and scrolled through social media, only half paying attention to what I was looking at. It was all the same—party updates, people taking vacations, trips back home to visit parents. People from high school posting updates from the local bars. Every once in a while, someone would have a picture to share from an engagement or a baby, which still threw me off whenever I saw it. Even though some of the people posting were seniors when I was a high school freshman, it was hard to believe I was anywhere near old enough for that kind of commitment.

Then, a picture of Theo crossed my feed. My heart stopped as soon as I registered the familiar colors, the basketball court behind her. It was a picture from the first home game of the season. I zoomed in on her face, taking in her easy smile. My heart fluttered.

We hadn't texted since coordinating plans to meet up. I didn't know if that meant we were never going to speak again, if I was supposed to reach out, or if Theo wanted to reach out first. I didn't want to appear overeager, but I also didn't want to come across as aloof. It was the stupidest, most childish game ever invented, but I wasn't used to playing this way, so I genuinely didn't know what to do. It turned out it was a lot easier to text first or go a few days without texting when I didn't care much about the other person.

I clicked onto her profile, unable to help myself. There was another post that was a series of stills from a recent practice, promoting that there was a game this weekend. At the end, she attached a short video of her tossing the ball from halfway down the court. Her teammates exploded into cheers as the camera cut off, catching the tiniest, cockiest smile from Theo.

God, she was so hot it was disgusting.

It had to be the ego; that was what I really liked about her. She was so confident, so certain that she was going to go places. And she was so *good*. I didn't have to know anything about basketball to know that she was something special. People didn't talk about just anyone like that, giving them features in magazines and coming from all around the country to see them play. Everyone knew what she had—including herself.

I paused the video, taking in the details of her face. Her jawline was sharp and defined, her lips so full I knew she had to be a good kisser.

I closed out the app and put my phone down. I couldn't keep doing this. I had to figure out how to be normal about her. We could be friends or less than friends, but I couldn't keep torturing myself like this.

I picked my phone up and went into my app store. Slowly, as if someone was forcing me to do it, I typed in the name of the first dating app I could think of. I clicked *search* and then, when it popped up, stared at the download button for a long time, debating on if it would be worth it.

It wouldn't be to look for anything serious, which was ideal for a dating app. I just wanted to find someone who stirred up even half of the mess of feelings I felt toward Theo. Someone who was as attractive, as compelling, as magnetic.

I bit my lip, my thumb hovering over the download button. It could be so easy. I could force myself to get over all of this, running from one issue to the next just like my mom always did.

There was no use in facing anything head-on when moving on and pretending it never happened was an option. I could push Theo to the back burner, playing impossible to get until she gave up and left me alone. I could block her, and in a couple of months, Iris would bring Theo up, and all I'd say in response was, *Who?*

It was what I'd always done. Maybe not to that extreme, but I had always found ways of keeping myself out of anything serious. I would push away, run away, pretend things never happened or were never as serious as they might've seemed. I kept my feelings in such a tightly locked box that I wasn't sure I'd ever allowed myself to have a genuine, sweaty-palms, heart-racing, capital-C Crush.

But then, Theo came along. And Theo made it so I didn't even want to flirt with a random girl at a bar. She made it so all I could think about was her. I was suddenly the kind of person who waited by the phone and wondered if she was supposed to text first or if I was.

I exited out of the app store and dropped my phone onto my bed. It wasn't going to happen. A dating app wasn't going to fix this. I wasn't sure anything would. I had to find a way to get over it; it was the only option.

I woke up the next morning to my phone vibrating with a text from Theo. My heart raced as I opened it, checking to see what she said.

Just got out of practice, if you want to come see me.

I thought it over for about half a second before making the executive decision to go. I had some pride, but not so much pride that I was going to pass up the opportunity to see Theo again. At the very least, I needed to keep seeing her for now so I could get her out of my system.

She shared the address of where she was, and I got up, throwing on something cute and flattering enough. I didn't want to think too much about it; if I spent too long fixating on an outfit, I'd inevitably start to make myself nervous. If I pretended that this was nothing—the equivalent of hanging out with Iris—then I wouldn't overthink it. Obviously.

I headed out and trekked across campus toward her. She'd led me to some kind of workout facility. I entered without an issue and headed in to find her.

Locker room on your right.

A feeling stirred in me. I hadn't imagined that Theo would be bold in that way when we first met. Theo gave quietly confident in her day-to-day life; she didn't pursue and she definitely didn't pull any fuck-boy adjacent moves.

But maybe that'd been naive of me to think.

Either way, I was intrigued enough to go find her. I wandered through the building until I found a door clearly marked *locker room*.

"Theo?" I called out from the door, not wanting to intrude in case this was the wrong room.

"Maya, hey," she said. She came out from around the corner. She was wearing a shirt that was clinging to her sweaty body, her hair pushed away from her face. Her sweat glistened in the low lighting of the room that looked suspiciously like the locker room from my old gym back home.

"Hey," I said.

"Come here."

I didn't even attempt to protest. My feet carried me over to her, not wasting a single second. She made it so easy for me. No games, no questions about her intentions. It was obvious why we were both here alone.

Theo and I stood together, only a small distance between us. She brushed a piece of hair from my face and then pulled me in for a kiss. Neither of us hesitated or waited to explore; we both knew exactly what we wanted.

My hands traveled over her firm arms. They were slick with sweat, but in a way that was weirdly hot, especially considering I'd never been someone who was into athletes. I'd also never played sports or done any formal athletics outside of dance, which I quit when I was nine. I didn't necessarily dream of sticky, sweaty sex. I wasn't interested in working out with someone else. I didn't like sweat, period.

But god, was it hot when Theo was drenched in it.

Her hands found my hair as mine trailed down her abs. She was so strong and lean. Everything about her was chiseled in a way I'd never experienced before. It left me breathless.

"Fuck, Maya," Theo whispered as she moved to kiss my neck. My entire body was on fire. All of my blood rushed south, and I knew I was going to let her take me right there in the locker room. I didn't care if anyone walked in; I had to have Theo. I wasn't giving her up.

I suddenly opened my eyes, jolting awake. I was in my own bed, in my own room. Completely alone. It didn't take long to realize that the entire thing had been a very stupid, borderline porn-like dream.

I groaned. This was unbelievable. I needed to get myself out of this bullshit I was feeling for Theo as quickly as possible. I picked up my phone and looked at the screen. I let out a small sigh as I looked at it.

Even worse than having a vivid sex dream about Theo McCall was realizing that I was disappointed she hadn't actually texted me while I was sleeping.

Chapter 10

THEO

Saturday morning, just like every Saturday that wasn't a game day, was busy. Practices were less formal on weekends; they were usually dedicated to personalized training and pick-up games. But because I didn't like to let myself take it easy, I didn't view weekends as a breather. If anything, I loved weekends because we could usually rope some of the men's team into playing with us.

Depending on the mood we were all in and who was playing, we would either do mixed teams or men's versus women's. If we were all really having a good time—meaning the guys weren't being assholes about how we could keep up with them—we'd play multiple games against each other. Since we were all riding the high of winning on our respective teams, everyone was excited to be on the court and put in the work. Usually, especially as the men's team's willpower started to dwindle and the losses started to stack up, there was less motivation to play casually like this.

"No chance you're getting that in, McCall," Danny from the men's team said. We were both seniors and had been keeping an eye on each other's careers for as long as we'd been students here. Unlike me, Danny hadn't gotten a huge amount of attention when he'd been coming up through middle school and high school. His stats were also—admittedly—not nearly as good as mine. But men and women tended to play differently when it came to technical skills and approach to the game, so it was hard to compare. We felt evenly matched enough on the court to play a decent game without either of us having to go easy on each other.

Other than Danny, I didn't really bother with retaining the names of the guys on the men's team. They all blended together, a mix of nicknames and last names. They weren't particularly exciting to watch and none of them were expected to get drafted.

Not remembering them was mostly an act of pettiness, though; it hadn't been until me that the women's team had gotten any decent attention. People only seemed to want to pay attention to the men's team here, even though they'd historically always been worse than us.

Some of the guys, like Danny, were cool about it and recognized where our team was in comparison to theirs. Others were not so cool and usually did mental gymnastics to explain why we weren't actually that good and why they were technically still better than us, even though their overall team record and individual records were worse.

"Oh, yeah?" I challenged. I dribbled the ball, my eyes dancing around the court for one of my teammates. I played out all of the potential moves in my head like everyone on the court was a chess piece. I could go left to GJ, but she had two guys who could move in quickly on her. Mags was in a decent position, but she was prone to dropping passes and could be a liability from this far away.

Even though time felt like it was moving at a glacial pace and I was taking forever, only a few seconds had passed. We didn't have a formal shot clock when we played casually like this, but we all knew when someone had held onto a ball too long.

"I have, like, six inches on you," Danny said as he hopped and held out his arms.

"But can you run?" I asked before crossing him, ducking just out of his reach. No one on my team was in any position to take the ball from me, so I went for the basket. Even though I was tall, Danny was right that he—and most of the men's team—had several inches on all of us. They were bigger and stronger, but that just meant that we had to play smarter, and we always did.

I spun off of nineteen on the men's team and went for a hook shot, dropping it through the net with ease. Before the ball even hit the court again, we were cheering. I tried not to let myself go too big with celebrating during games—mostly to avoid technicals—but I had no issue with doing it here. This was where I really let myself go, getting as mean as I could be on the court. I didn't care if it wasn't a real game; it was impossible to turn the competitive part of my brain off.

"Jesus Christ!" Six shouted. "Not one of you could get to her?"

GJ shrugged, always ready to come to my defense. "You think you can stop Theo McCall?"

A few of the guys threw their arms in the air and wiped sweat from their foreheads, signaling that they were calling it. They walked over to get water as GJ jogged over to me.

"I can't wait to see Cam Kerr humble you," one of the guys yelled, clearly half joking from his tone but still half meaning it as well. Men didn't tend to take well to my success. But it was also an athlete thing; everyone wanted to be the best. Everyone was always trying to *find* the best. Cam Kerr was my most obvious close competition, someone who might not get drafted first—I was holding firm that she wouldn't beat me out on that—but would definitely make it onto every top ten list.

"They're just mad because you got that three on them," she said. "You guys are all a bunch of cowards giving up this easy!" she then shouted, laughing.

"You are such an asshole."

"They should learn not to be sore losers."

We walked over to get water for ourselves, and the rest of the girls joined us.

"Can we call it a day altogether? I'm cramping so fucking bad from my period," Nia said as she squeezed water into her mouth. She gripped her side. "If I'm not horizontal in the next thirty minutes, I think I'm going to vomit."

"Don't let Coach Darlene hear you say that," Gemma said. "She'd have you running laps in a heartbeat."

"*Pain is in your head, ladies*," GJ and Mags said in a near-perfect imitation of Darlene's voice.

"I have a paper to write," Ellie said quietly with a small shrug, always the neutral one. When she was on the court, it was easy to believe she'd been recruited. She was the youngest on our team, and she probably wouldn't start in any of our games this season, but it was clear why Coach Darlene had wanted her. She was tough, clever, and quick on her feet.

She also never had much to say to anyone about anything. I thought her quiet approach to playing was related to wanting to keep her head down, but I realized quickly she was quiet everywhere. While the rest of the team was loud and rowdy with each other, Ellie usually didn't have much to say.

She didn't know it, but I'd made it my personal goal to take her under my wing. I wanted to see what she was capable of and what we could pull out of her. My hope was that by junior year, she was able to match up to the stats GJ and I were pulling—and maybe also learn the art of shit talking along the way.

"I might hit the gym if anyone wants to go over with me," I said.

"Do you ever take a break?" Mags asked.

"I'm only going for a little bit," I said. But the truth was that I didn't really take a break. I was always giving myself an excuse to work out—I needed to work on my arms, I should get some cardio in, I could run a few more drills. It was hard for me to pull myself away from all of it sometimes, even when I was tired and drenched in sweat.

"Good game, fellas!" GJ yelled as the men's team started shuffling out of the gym. One of them turned back and flipped her off before leaving. "They're always so rude."

"You told one of them that their height was wasted on them," Nia reminded her.

"And I was right to say it. If I was 6'6", I wouldn't be fucking around like them," GJ said. "Embarrassing."

I snorted and packed up the rest of my things, ripping open a protein bar in the process.

"Bye!" Mags called out as she headed out with Gemma. Nia followed closely behind.

"Good game, Ellie," I said as she was gathering up her things.

"Oh! Thanks," she said, sounding somewhat surprised.

"Your fadeaway could use a little work, but it's almost there."

She smiled, taking the critique with zero ego. Her full cheeks flushed slightly. "Thanks. I'll keep that in mind."

Ellie then headed off, leaving only me in GJ in the gym. GJ had taken a seat on a bench and was going to town on the orange she'd brought.

"If she doesn't go pro, I'll be so sad."

"Yeah, she's promising," I said.

"Oh, no. I just meant with a name like that. *Ellie Allison.* That's cool as fuck," GJ said with her mouth half-full.

I rolled my eyes, and GJ gathered up her orange peels so we could head off together to the gym down the hall.

I spent my session working on my arms, music blasting in my ears as I lifted my hand weights. GJ was across the room from me, the two of us the only ones in here. The ability to coexist well in a gym was always one of my favorite things about GJ. We understood when we could fuck around and when we both wanted a quiet moment to focus on working out.

The upcoming game was on my mind when my phone vibrated next to me with a text from Maya. My eyebrows lifted with surprise. We hadn't spoken since we'd hung out, and she didn't strike me as someone who would really put in the effort to reach out first to initiate a conversation. But then again, she *did* strike me as someone who was bold and straightforward. If she didn't want to hang out with me, whether platonically or not, I wouldn't hear from her. It was definitely a good sign she was texting first.

Nothing between me and Maya had been made particularly clear. I was still riding the very thin line of going in whatever direction she wanted to go in. I was worried I might overstep or make her uncomfortable. I was also worried about my ability to make time to foster something new in general. Even if we both liked each other, finding time to spend together was hard. The last thing I needed was to drag out the courting phase until graduation, only to realize it was never going to be anything in the first place.

Some people liked the companionship and didn't mind the idea of having a fling or two on the side to keep them busy. But I'd grown up an only child; I didn't need the company of anyone else. My team was enough social interaction for me.

After finishing my reps—suddenly motivated to do them a little faster than usual—I rewarded myself with checking my phone.

Any recs for someone looking to get into basketball media?

I cleared my throat, turning my music down so I could focus on the text and read it over and over again as if committing it to memory. Even though we'd only met a handful of times, I read the text message in her voice. I could picture the way her mouth would form each word, practically hear the slight, ever-present smile she always had on her face.

I put my phone down and finished the rest of my workout before responding. I wanted to take my time thinking up a response, and also didn't want to get in the habit of throwing everything to the side as soon as a girl texted me. Even if that girl was Maya.

Finally, as GJ and I were both rounding out our usual workouts, I picked up my phone again.

Have you seen Love & Basketball?

I bit my lip and then sent it, refusing to sit on the message for too long.

"What's got you staring at your phone?" GJ asked.

"You're addicted to living up my ass."

"I see everything. Especially when you've been making intense eye contact with that phone like you've been wanting to ask to take it home."

"I haven't been looking at it for that long."

"You were looking over for the last twenty minutes. It's not going to run away, I swear," GJ said as she wiped her sweat from her forehead. She lifted her shoulder-length locs off of her neck, deep in thought, and then looked at me. "Are you texting that girl?"

"I...yeah," I said, half-shrugging to try and force myself to act casually. I was the coolest person alive, so incredibly chill.

"Dude!" GJ shouted. She put her hands on my shoulders and practically shook me around. "Holy shit. She got you *bad*."

"It's nothing, we're just texting."

"And you hung out one-on-one."

"Yeah, to like...talk about that photo of us everyone is sharing. But that's it."

"Oh, sure. I basically never see you with a girl *ever*, and all of a sudden there's one popping up everywhere. Definitely means nothing. Could never be something serious," she said. She punched my shoulder. "She literally came to our game, dude. She wouldn't do that if she wasn't at least thinking about it."

I'd been silently telling myself the same thing. Maya was probably at least a tiny bit interested in me. She didn't even like basketball; there'd been no reason for her to go otherwise.

But that didn't mean I'd be able to actually *maintain* her interest. It was hard when my entire life revolved around bas-ketball. I had a completely different college experience from everyone else. And a lot of it—the dedication to practicing and working out, brand deals, being ready to move anywhere based on who signed me—was stuff that I didn't expect someone who wasn't a basketball fan to understand or care about.

"I...I don't know, man."

But as I said it, my phone vibrated again. *That should've been the caption of our photo. Missed opportunity.*

I fought off a grin so GJ wouldn't see it as GJ slapped a hand to my shoulder. "Don't let the fear of striking out keep you from playing the game. Or whatever the saying is. I don't play baseball."

Once GJ and I wrapped up our workouts, we headed back

home. GJ went off to do whatever the fuck GJ did outside of basketball—definitely not classwork—and I sat down to study.

After getting some of my reading for one of my marketing classes done, I leaned back into the shitty second—and probably third, fourth, and fifth—hand couch in my living room. I pulled out my phone and looked over the messages between us, something I told myself I was only allowed to do when I finished my work.

Keeping that in mind for when we hard launch, I wrote in response to her joke about how our viral photo should've been captioned. It'd taken me a few drafts to get to a message that felt right and it was when GJ and I were walking home that I finally thought of that one.

As much as I hated to admit it, GJ had been right. I needed to lean in.

Unlike with our other responses, Maya had been quick to get back to me. I'd barely made it to my front door by the time my phone was vibrating again. *The girls are gonna hate me for this. Someone who doesn't even watch basketball bagging the future first draft pick? I'm their worst nightmare.*

Maya teasing me about it was the only time I didn't mind someone talking to me about getting drafted. It normally made me anxious and uneasy, like everyone was jinxing it for me. But when Maya said it—even in writing—I suddenly felt like the hot shit I was probably supposed to feel like all the time, not just on the court.

They'll never know you don't watch basketball. I'll be sure to show you the ropes.

I'd forced myself to put my phone down after that point. I was stupidly nervous to see what she was going to say in response, and needed the distraction of school work, so I didn't stare at my phone until she responded. I'd even silenced my phone, hoping it would cut back on my temptation to pick it up.

But that had been two hours ago; I hadn't heard from her since. I sighed. Maybe the text had come across as too forward, and I was never going to hear from her again.

I nearly rolled my eyes at myself. I needed to take a deep breath. It wasn't that serious.

But even though my brain could process the situation logically, I couldn't seem to get my body to agree. Throughout the rest of the late afternoon into the evening, I kept glancing over at my phone and hoped a text would pop up. I reminded myself that it was the weekend and she could be out doing anything. Her priority probably wasn't texting me; it was fine. We didn't know each other.

But even so, I kept looking at my darkened phone screen as if I could get a response out of her that way.

Finally, as I was about to head out for a quick evening run and then go to bed early for the game tomorrow, my phone vibrated. When I saw that it was Maya who had texted, I tried to force myself not to immediately pick up my phone, but failed miserably.

All this talk and no action, she wrote back. It took me a second to figure out what she was saying. But the second I understood, I had to resist celebrating in a way that would probably get me an unsportsmanlike tech on the court.

And then I remembered that getting Maya to want to hang out—not only *want* to hang out, but initiate the conversation around us hanging out—was only the first part of the battle. The second part, which was finding the time to hang out, was much harder.

I weighed my options, mentally going over my calendar in my head. I had the game tomorrow at three in the afternoon, meaning there would be a pre-game locker room meet-up and a pre-game warm-up before then to make time for. Afterwards, I'd probably spend time with at least a few of the people on the team, so Sunday was pretty much a wash. I was traveling a few days next week for games—Texas on Wednesday and Iowa over the weekend—and would have to spend time in between that in classes and tutoring, and making up classwork.

There were places I could fit her in, but I wasn't sure it would be easy. If Maya's schedule didn't have any flexibility, it would be nearly impossible. And besides that, I didn't want Maya to base her schedule around me.

GJ's voice and her stupid cliche popped into my head, reminding me that I shouldn't throw in the towel. Just because it seemed impossible to figure out now didn't mean it wasn't possible. The best I could do was cross the bridge when I got there—even if it was hard for someone who was used to a structured schedule and rigid routine.

I took a deep breath.

Are you free tonight?

As soon as I sent it, three little bubbles popped up on Maya's end. They disappeared and then reappeared a second later. A text then popped up.

What time?

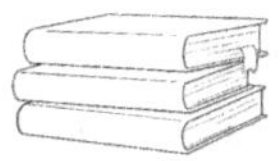

Chapter 11

MAYA

It had all happened so quickly. One minute, Theo and I were texting, and I was teasing her about not asking me to hang out. The next, Theo was coming over to my house.

I didn't really know what had taken over me in asking her to come over here. Maybe it was the way she'd so playfully texted me, *I'm not sure I want you to see my living room, I don't want you to get the ick.* Or maybe it was just that I had so much fun texting her that I couldn't resist wanting to see her again as soon as possible.

I had friends who rotated around me—people I got drinks with, people I met up with after class, people I saw at parties—but it'd been a long time since I'd had someone new around that I was excited about. Despite my best efforts to hide it, I knew I had a little extra pep in my step. It was someone to change up the routine; someone to offer me something new. It was impossible to resist the story of it all and the grip Theo seemed to have on me. I wanted to know as much as I could about her and permanently store it in my memory. In ten years, I'd tell my friends over drinks, *remember when Theo McCall was texting me?* and it would be worth it.

I looked at myself in the mirror; I had to be realistic. Despite the undeniable thrill I felt over Theo coming over, I was doing everything I could to push it down. I didn't really want to talk about Theo as a vague memory ten years from now; she deserved better than to be used for a story.

"Just get her out of your system," I mumbled to myself as I put on mascara—enough makeup to feel put together but not so much that Theo would think I put it on just for her when our only plans were to hang out at my apartment.

I headed out into the open floor plan living room just as Iris walked in with bags of groceries from Trader Joe's, our local spot.

"I got you a four-pack of those elderberry blueberry acai seltzer water things," Iris said.

"None of those are the right fruits, but I know exactly what you're talking about," I said. "Thank you so much. How was work?"

"Oh, you know," she said. "Same stuff. One of my clients thinks I'm her daughter this time instead of her sister. Another one keeps talking about needing to take the dog out for a walk, but she had the dog in, like, 1983."

"Jeez," I said. Iris didn't like it when people talked about her work as if it were something saintly, but I really respected what she did. I tried my best to mince my words and not go down the path of either praising her too highly or dragging details out of her when I knew her work could be a lot to handle emotionally. She'd had clients who couldn't remember their own names, clients who passed from old age or illness. It was a tough job. But she handled it well, talking weekly with a therapist and taking breaks when she needed.

"I gave everyone some of those candy bags you helped me make, though. They were very excited," she said, and I smiled, always happy to help her out. We'd binged reality TV while putting them together; it'd barely felt like work.

"What's the rest of the day look like for you?" I asked as I reached into Iris's grocery bags and helped her stock the fridge. I hadn't told her about Theo yet, but considering she was coming over in less than an hour, it was going to have to come up.

"Probably not doing much. I'll have to see. I obviously don't get my period anymore, but I feel vaguely PMS-like," she said. I'd never been on birth control, so Iris was my educational resource on what the experience felt like. "Very luteal phase right now. Or maybe I'm just depressed because the basketball player has been impossible to find. It can be hard to tell."

"Sorry," I said, sympathizing. I didn't necessarily understand the longstanding unrequited crush part, but I definitely understood the luteal phase downswing. "I invited someone over, but I can cancel if it feels like it'll be too much having someone here."

"I think it should be fine. Maybe don't keep them here too late but I'll probably just be hiding in my room, anyway," Iris kept moving, loading her veggies into the fridge. "Who's coming over?"

"Um," I said, dragging it out. "Theo…?"

Iris, who'd been previously unfazed, nearly dropped the oat milk in her hands. "You're lying. Theo McCall is coming over?" She paused. "I guess I am going out after all. I do *not* need my favorite sport ruined by the sounds of—"

I cut her off before she could go any further. "We're just watching a movie. It's chill. Nothing major."

Iris turned to me, as if trying to piece together if this was a really weird and elaborate joke. When I didn't back down, she realized I was being serious.

"Dude, what the fuck?" she stood by the open fridge, totally dumbfounded. "Have you guys been texting? Or was it, like, a random invite?" She turned to me. "Did Theo McCall booty call you? Or no—even more likely, did *you* booty call Theo McCall? She's, like, a superstar basketball player. You can't just booty call someone like that!"

"No one is booty calling anyone," I clarified. "We're just hanging out. We've been texting. Kind of a lot, actually. But whatever. She's coming over and we're going to watch a movie, and it will be *chill*. Everyone is going to be normal about it."

"Oh, watching a movie?" Iris asked with air quotes. "Since when have you ever actually had anyone over to watch a movie? Everyone knows what that actually means."

I flashed back to the very realistic dream of me and Theo making out in the locker room. I'd be lying if that hadn't been flashing periodically through my head as we'd been texting. But that wasn't *the* reason I'd invited her over.

"It means something different this time."

"Oh, does it really?" Iris asked playfully. "I mean, I don't blame you at all. Theo's hot. And cool. And definitely seems interested in you."

"It's just a movie," I said. But as Iris was talking, the more I realized she was right. I'd been so caught up in watching a basketball movie together as an excuse to hang out again that I'd completely forgotten the phrase *Netflix and chill.*

It was a total rookie move. I was an idiot.

Even if I didn't mean it that way, Theo probably did. And while I wanted to get Theo out of my system, I wasn't sure having sex was the way to do it. In fact, I worried it might make it worse. The last thing the chemicals in my body needed was to be drawn to her even more.

In a weird way, Theo felt like more than that, too. She seemed genuinely nice. And interested in getting to know me outside of sex, which wasn't particularly common amongst the people I'd met on campus. Everyone always wanted casual, always exploring, always looking for the next best thing. And the people who craved stability felt too stable for me in a way that was off-putting.

Until Theo proved herself to be otherwise, I was going to assume she was a genuinely nice person. And she offered just enough unpredictability with her schedule and pending professional basketball career to keep things interesting.

But if she stepped out of line and made it weird, coming into this assuming we were hooking up, I was nixing the whole plan. We'd fuck once and then never speak again and that would be that. She *was* hot, so I wasn't going to completely pass up the opportunity. But she wasn't so hot that I was going to completely lose my sense of self in her and hold out for a crush on someone who was secretly an asshole.

"It's just a movie," I reiterated, mostly to myself this time.

Theo arrived exactly on time, which felt on brand for her even though I didn't know her that well. The knock on the door also felt on brand for her—direct, to the point. No musicality to it.

"Go get your girl," Iris said as she stood up from the couch. Despite not feeling great, Iris had stuck it out and offered emotional support. Unsurprisingly, I was nervous for Theo to come over. It was out of character for me, but it'd been a consistent theme with Theo. The nerves seemed to level out when we were together, but the anticipation each time was killing me. It was so unlike me.

I brushed off Iris's comment as she went off to her bedroom. I headed to the door of the apartment, smiling to myself as I thought about Theo's text: *I think I'm here, someone let me in. They made it clear they thought I was very tall.*

Did they ask if you play basketball, or is that offensive to assume of someone tall? I had written back, unable to help myself even though I'd see her in a second.

I walked to the front door of my apartment and opened it. Theo stood in front of me, looking almost sheepish in her sweatsuit. She had a grocery bag with her. "I brought snacks," she said. She phrased it almost like a question, and I knew immediately from her tone that she wasn't here for any of the reasons Iris—and now I—had started to suspect. No one who wanted to get laid that badly would look so shy. Or so *cute*.

The bravado that I'd been approaching the situation with melted away instantly. I didn't have to hardball her. The pep talk I'd given myself in the shower, reminding myself that I was too hot to get tugged around by someone—even if she was a star athlete—felt silly in retrospect.

"Come in," I said, stepping aside. "What'd you bring?"

"Kind of a mix of everything," she replied, peeking into the bag. "Sorry I didn't ask before coming. I was already running behind, but I saw the corner store and thought I should grab something since you're hosting."

"No, it's okay. I appreciate the effort," I said. I decided against teasing Theo for her 'running behind' still getting her to my place exactly on time.

I followed a few steps behind Theo and felt like I was seeing my apartment for the first time again, except this time through Theo's eyes. My neighbor had been right; she was tall. I didn't consider myself or Iris to be particularly short—we were probably taller than average, if anything—but suddenly, everything in the house felt small in comparison to Theo. I wasn't sure anyone over 5'6" had stepped foot in our apartment, except the occasional man Iris had had over, who I rarely actually met.

Theo put the bag of snacks on the counter and started pulling them out so I could see. She then stopped. "Is this okay?" she asked.

That triggered a visceral reaction in me unlike anything I'd ever experienced. I stiffened immediately and forced out any thoughts of where else I might want to hear those words. But it was impossible. I could practically hear it; Theo's breathy voice asking me, *Is this okay?* after sneaking off to my room, pulling off my clothes...

Focus.

"Yeah, that's fine," I said, hoping Theo couldn't tell I was thousands of miles away.

Theo got a lot of the classics—microwave popcorn, a mix of chocolate and fruity candy.

"It's my own movie theater concession stand," I said.

"Nothing but the best," Theo said. "I'm partial to Reese's, personally. But to each their own."

"Any Twix in there?"

Theo looked up at me, panic in her eyes. "No. I'm so sorry."

"No Twix?" I asked, feigning heartbreak. "It is my favorite, but I'll survive without it."

"I'll walk back and get you some."

"You absolutely do not need to do that," I said. I responded so instinctively that it took me a second to register what Theo had even said. I couldn't remember the last time someone other than Iris had offered to do something that nice for me. I softened a little bit. "It's nice of you to offer."

Theo shrugged. "I'm the one who bought the snacks. I should've asked before coming over. Easy solution to the problem."

I waited for some kind of side comment or bitching to follow—something I'd gotten used to with the types of people I usually dated—but there wasn't anything. No indication that I was ruining the night or unappreciative, comments that they'd slip in so easily it'd barely register. I wasn't someone who let comments like that throw me; I just kicked the girls to the curb instead.

But it appeared Theo was passing the test I didn't even know I'd been giving.

"A Crunch bar is perfect," I said, and plucked it off the counter.

"Are you sure?"

"Oh, yeah. I'll eat basically anything with chocolate in it, anyway," I said.

Theo's lips perked up in a smile. "I feel you," she said and then clapped her hands together. "Okay, so. Which movie? Love & Basketball? Coach Carter? White Men Can't Jump?"

"What? No Air Bud? Not factually accurate enough?"

"No, actually. Dogs are infamously good at basketball. Every team has one that's pulled out for special occasions," she deadpanned.

My lips perked up as I spun on my heel and slowly moved toward the living room. "I don't think I have a preference. I didn't realize how far behind I was in like...sports pop culture until recently."

"What made you realize? Anything in particular?"

My lips perked up in a smile. "Ha-ha."

"Basketball specific? Not interested in watching people ball on film?"

"Ball on film is a wild way of putting it, but no, it's every sport," I said. "My mom was more interested in her hair and her boyfriends than sports. And her boyfriends were more interested in, like, their jobs and my mom to worry about introducing me to sports."

"Damn," Theo said.

I waved my hand. "It doesn't really feel like you're missing anything if you've never been around it."

Theo gathered her candy and followed behind me. I sat down on one end of the couch and Theo sat down on the other end, not so far over that it felt weird, but not so close that we were touching.

I curled up on the couch while Theo got comfortable, her long limbs spread over the couch that usually felt much more spacious when it was just me and Iris.

"So, you've never just, like, seen a football game? Wait, have you seen Remember the Titans? Or Miracle?"

"I'm assuming these are sports movies."

"Oh my god," Theo said, like I'd just told her I'd never tasted sugar before. "Sorry, that's just so hard for me to imagine. Basketball has been my thing forever. My parents' thing, too. I don't know life without sports."

"Do you like it that way?"

"I wouldn't want it any other way," she said. "Basketball is it for me. I love playing. I'm just lucky I'm good at it; that doesn't always happen. You can love a game that refuses to love you back."

I nodded as if I understood. "I don't think I've ever loved anything passionately enough to feel that way," I said. "School is the closest thing, but I wouldn't consider that a hobby. Or interest. Or something I'd do for fun."

"I think you can learn for fun," she said with a shrug. "School's never really been my thing, so the thought of picking up a book outside of class is totally unappealing to me. But based on the books you have around, it seems like you feel the opposite."

Her comment made me look around the room as if it was the first time I'd realized there were books scattered throughout the apartment. We had a Smart TV and didn't play video games, so the console our TV was on was only stacked with books and nothing else. Pretty much every surface of the house had at least one book on it—not for decorative purposes, but because Iris and I tend to leave them around by accident. I was the queen of literally putting a book down with the intention of going back to it and then never finishing it.

"Fair point," I said.

"Do you have a favorite genre you like to read?" she asked as she leaned forward and picked up a book from the coffee table.

"Non-fiction."

Theo's eyebrows raised. "Really?"

"It's not, like, historical non-fiction or anything. It's purely sociological. I like the study of people. It feels like reading a fiction novel most of the time."

Theo looked at me skeptically. "I don't think most people would agree with that."

I nodded in reluctant agreement. I hadn't thought about it that way before, but it made sense. "I'm thinking about going to graduate school," I said, almost like I was admitting to something embarrassing. I hated that it was a sore spot for me, but I knew I had a complex. I gave that I could shotgun a beer and flirt my way into any party; I didn't exactly give budding academic.

"Oh, shit," Theo said, impressed. My heart surged involuntarily from the subtle praise and the way she accepted that information without question. No looks of *are you sure?* or questioning my intelligence. "Really? Any schools picked out yet?"

"A few," I lied. I'd had a running list of potential programs for years ever since a professor initially brought it up with me and told me it seemed like a fitting pathway for me. "We'll see, though. I don't know. There are only so many spots available."

"You're talking to someone who's *definitely* getting drafted to play professional women's basketball. Odds don't mean anything when you're good," Theo said. "And based on what I've seen, you study your ass off."

I blushed, embarrassed. "Oh, god. Stop, please," I said, hiding my face.

"No, I'm being serious. Look at these books you have around. And I've seen your study set-up."

I bit my lip to stop my grin from splitting my face open. It felt so seen and understood in that moment. Theo and I had only just gotten to know each other, but it was like she knew all the right things to say to me.

It didn't help that the person saying them to me was the hottest person I'd ever seen in my life. It was almost overwhelming to have her approval, like I was living in some kind of fantasy.

It was impossible to keep my eyes off of her. I watched her move like I was going to write a report on it. I probably could've. I could write pages and pages about the way her lips turned up in an easy smile, the way she sat so confidently on my couch, the ease of our conversation. All of the anticipation was gone, and now I was completely relaxed, enveloped by the warmth that Theo brought with her into every room.

"Is it weird I have a hard time viewing you on the court as the same person I see off the court?" I asked.

Theo shook her head, seemingly not surprised at all by my question. "Nah. That sounds about right. My team teases me about it, too. I'm a lot...bolder on the court."

"Yeah, the person who thinks showing up to my house on time is showing up late isn't exactly giving 'yells at refs and talks shit to her opponents.'"

"I guess I've just never felt like I've had to talk a big game off the court. My ability to play speaks for itself. Always has," she said. "And my timeliness is important to me. I like routine. It's the only thing that makes balancing sports with everything else possible."

"It seems like you're kept busy. Did you get the sweatsuit from the brand deal you did?" I asked, teasing her.

She chuckled. "Oh. Yeah, I did. It's comfy, though, I swear. I'm not just wearing it because they paid me to at one point."

"We live such different lives."

"It becomes a lot more normal once you get used to it," Theo said. "But wait, I feel like we've skipped over the most important part of all of this. You really haven't seen *any* of the classic sports movies?"

"I've seen some, I guess. But not really. I don't exactly seek them out," I said. "It's not just basketball, though. I'm generally uneducated when it comes to sports, movies included."

"You've seriously been missing out."

"I've seen One Tree Hill, at least. It doesn't get much more factually accurate than that, I'm assuming."

"I haven't seen it."

I turned to her in shock. "You're lying."

I'd completely forgotten that we'd decided to hangout to watch something instead of just talking the entire time. But there was something about Theo that made it hard to stop. I genuinely *wanted* to talk to her. I'd always been chatty and Iris and I could go for hours if we didn't have class or work pulling us away. But with everyone other than Iris—truly my platonic soulmate—I'd eventually get bored.

But conversation with Theo was genuinely fun, and texting her was the same. It was new for me to feel that way. Most of my interest in previous flings began and ended with them giving me attention and having a story to tell. Once the initial *who are you? What do you want to do after college?* questions were asked, there wasn't anything else to say.

Part of me was waiting for the other shoe to drop. We'd only just gotten to know each other; surely, there was something in her that I would grow to dislike.

Our plans to watch a movie got pushed further and further into the background as we talked. Theo let me talk for far too long about the dynamics about the One Tree Hill characters, while Theo contributed occasional vocabulary assistance when I talked about the games and team.

Mostly, though, she just let me talk.

When her phone suddenly vibrated in the middle of us chatting, it seemed to break both of us out of a trance. I had no idea how long we'd been sitting on the couch for, our candy mostly untouched.

"Oh, shit," Theo said when she checked her phone. "Sorry. It's later than I thought it was. I need to get back. There's a game tomorrow and I have this kind of routine I like to follow the night before."

"Oh," I said, hoping I sounded more surprised than disappointed. Part of me wanted to protest, saying it wasn't that late or that we hadn't been there that long but Theo was right—*four hours* had somehow slipped by like it was nothing. I couldn't believe it when I looked at the time; I was convinced somehow all of the technology in my house had been set to the wrong time. "So much for watching a movie, I guess. Got a little sidetracked."

"Yeah, a little," Theo teased. She got up and I followed, both of us heading toward the door in small steps as if waiting to see what the other person was going to do.

"Do you want your candy back?" I asked.

"Oh, no. I bought it for you," Theo said.

I tried to think of a smooth response but I was so surprised by her direct answer that I threw me off my game. I'd never had anyone buy me something like that before—flowers, candy. I never let it get that serious. But Theo made it sound like the most casual thing in the world. "Oh. Thanks," I said, the best I could come up with.

We headed to the front door and paused in front of it as Theo slipped on her shoes. For the first time since she got here, the silence between us felt a little weird—and heavy.

Probably because, for some reason, kissing her right now felt like the most natural course of action.

Even though this wasn't a date.

And even though we weren't actually interested in each other. Not romantically, at least.

Obviously.

"This was really fun," I said quietly, unable to come up with a better way of describing it. It felt like such a simple word for the expansive feeling that being around Theo evoked in me. But she *was* fun. She was running in the sprinklers in the summer as a kid, getting tipsy and silly with friends over drinks on a sun washed patio during happy hour, kind of fun.

We'd only crossed paths a handful of times, but she managed to leave me with a warm ball of light in my chest just at the sight of her smile and the sound of her voice. I was growing to really appreciate her easy going personality, no longer seeing it as a front to seem cool and laid back but as who she actually was.

The front hallway entrance of my apartment had never felt so compact. I had my back practically against the wall with Theo standing so close to me I could feel the heat radiating from her body. She was a whole head taller than me, forcing me to look up at her from what felt far too close. My heart thudded, my body going haywire.

"Yeah, thanks for inviting me over." Theo looked at me and I looked at her, the feeling passing between us something I'd never felt before. It was the adrenaline of knowing a first kiss was coming after a date combined with the uncertainty of if it would really happen combined with the confusion of if I really *actually* wanted that to happen.

"Yeah." I knew I was stalling. I was waiting to see what she was going to do and follow her lead.

I locked eyes with Theo and my lips parted. My attraction to her had been undeniable from the beginning, so the logical part of my brain was hardly putting up a fight. Fuck worrying about a mess and what would happen next; I wanted Theo now.

The only thing I didn't know was if she wanted me just as badly.

Chapter 12

THEO

I was about an inch away from doing something so incredibly stupid.

I had to leave Maya's house as soon as possible. The longer I stood there, the closer I was to throwing caution to the wind and kissing her. We were already standing so close we were nearly touching and I was pretty sure she'd been flirting with me throughout the night.

But I didn't actually know any of it for sure. And if I asked, I risked asking too soon and scaring her off. I had to play smart with her, as someone who hadn't exactly given me the impression she was looking for anything serious.

My uncertainty definitely wasn't because she turned me into a coward who could barely remember my name when she looked at me like that, with her brown eyes on mine and her cheeks all flushed.

I could just kiss her. I could.

"Am I going to see you at the game tomorrow?" I asked instead, the one thing I could think of to say that didn't make my palms slick with sweat.

"How am I supposed to know what's going on when the person who's supposed to teach me didn't show me a single basketball movie today?"

I laughed. "Fair point."

"But yeah, I'll be there. Iris will keep feeding me basketball-related lines to say to you at the end," she said. "Maybe we can go viral again."

"Oh, we can only hope," I teased.

She paused for a moment. "Maybe we really should keep it going. It's kind of funny," Maya admitted.

"Do you really think people would care that much?"

She shrugged. "It seems like they do. And most of the campus probably thinks we're already dating—sorry to all of the other women in your life."

"There aren't any, so no one's feelings can be hurt."

"Except maybe your millions of fans who've all been holding out hope they'd get a chance with you."

"Millions feels like an exaggeration."

Having an online presence was one of my least favorite parts of the attention I'd been getting. I had no issue with posting stats or clips from a game or practice, but I wasn't sure I really wanted anyone to know anything about me beyond that. It wasn't their business.

But then again, knowing a woman like Maya—so beautiful and warm that it literally glowed through in a random picture of her—wasn't such a bad thing to be known for. And if keeping it going meant that I'd have more time with Maya, I'd take it.

Maya raised her eyebrows playfully. "Come on. Do it for the story. Do it for the bit. It doesn't have to be anything crazy, I'll just show up to your games every once in a while. And then when we get bored, you can have your post-breakup glow up where everyone compliments you on how well you've been handling it."

"I guess it is funny," I said, because that was the only plausible reason why I'd agree to something like this. I didn't really need a relationship to help boost my public image, and I wasn't sure it even would boost it that much. But I couldn't say *yeah, I'm down to do it only because you—the prettiest woman I've ever laid eyes on—are asking me to. Do you also want me to run through fire? I'd do it for you.*

"What about all of the other women in your life?" I asked, because I realized I might not be giving up anyone for this, but Maya definitely was.

"There aren't any," Maya said a little too quickly. "Sometimes there are. But it's never been anyone serious. It might be good for me to take a break, honestly. I've been in a bit of a slump lately."

I tried not to latch onto *sometimes there are* because Maya was a single, autonomous adult who was allowed to do whatever she wanted. But the thought of anyone else with her made me sick to my stomach. I'd never considered myself possessive, but she was enough to bring it out of me.

Maybe I was just as competitive off the court as I was playing basketball; I'd just never had something I wanted that badly before.

Continuing to be photographed in public together might not lead to any professional gain for me, but it definitely had one major benefit: Having Maya to myself. It was impossible to deny that I was feeling greedy about her time. If she wanted someone else, I'd respect it. But now that I had the chance to temporarily take her off the market—even in the context of pretending to date—I was absolutely going to take it.

"And you really get something out of doing this?" I asked.

She nodded. "You have no idea."

All of my teammates would confirm that I was someone who was strict about my pre-game rituals. I thrived on structure, so it made sense. But there was also the tiniest bit of superstition behind it, just like with most athletes. I ate the same meal the night before and the same breakfast the day of. I always got a full night of sleep and restricted how late I would stay out, depending on how late in the day the game was.

I didn't like to stray from it. I'd been keeping it up for as long as I'd been in college, and certain parts—like eating the same breakfast before every game—I'd been doing since I was in middle school.

But Maya was tempting me to break the routine.

I knew even going over to her house in the late evening was cutting it close. And that was before I'd accidentally spent four hours at her house, chatting with her as if there was no one in the world except for us.

And I didn't want to leave.

It'd taken everything in me to get myself up from the couch and actually leave her apartment. I was pretty sure from the time I said I would leave to the time it took me to physically open the door and exit was at least twenty minutes.

I didn't know how it happened. It was like time wasn't real when I was with her, and I could never have enough time with her. It wasn't a feeling I was used to. I was pretty sure it was a feeling I'd never experienced before.

The high of a game was the closest I'd ever gotten otherwise, and even then, this was different. It was the kind of thing people would write songs about—the thrill of seeing her, the nerves around when I'd see her next. The way it was impossible to get myself to leave, and all I wanted to do before I left was kiss her.

It was like I wanted to stay just to see if I could get more from her. I wanted as much time as I could possibly have next to her, hoping that at any point, maybe things would shift and she'd make a move on me. Or maybe she'd open the door for me to make a move on her.

Unfortunately, it was still nearly impossible to figure out where things were. I could say that it was a good sign that we were fake dating and able to talk so much, but it also could mean that it was a good sign for friendship. Maybe that was all this was. She was comfortable with me because there were no feelings at all on her end.

The entire walk back to my apartment, I was cycling through it. I would convince myself one second that she was into me; the next, I was certain that it was just the stereotypical lesbian experience of thinking a girl is flirting when she was really just being friendly.

It wasn't until I started my usual routine of prepping my usual dinner, stretching, taking a hot shower, and taking a quiet evening for myself that things started to level out. I approached it like a game—force out the noise and focus on what mattered.

And what mattered was that I'd gotten time at all with Maya—who was amazing and smart and funny and still worth getting to know no matter what happened between us.

I just couldn't help but also wish I could kiss her, too.

The next morning flew by. I got out of bed quickly for the game and got ready, warming myself up with pushups before heading downstairs for breakfast.

"Game day, baby!" GJ yelled, always with way more energy than anyone needed to have in the morning.

"Yeah," I agreed with way less enthusiasm.

She slapped a hand to my back. "This is gonna be a good one. You ready for a blowout?"

"I don't know if blowouts are really that fun," I said. I didn't mind winning, but there was something depressing about winning against a team that everyone knew didn't have the kind of money or players that we did.

College basketball tended to be that way—there were the huge, big name teams that everyone knew, and then there were the smaller schools that were still in our division but were rarely ever championship-bound. Sometimes, they'd surprise everyone. But mostly, the games wrapped with a record of 85-36, and the crowd leaving early.

I preferred the challenge of playing a game that was intense to the very finish. A buzzer-beater, the rush of pushing to the final second. I loved that feeling more than anything in the world; the uphill battle was irresistible.

Our morning and then afternoon moved through the same pre-game motions they always had. We focused on light workouts, getting our bodies warmed up and ready to play. We didn't want to practice too hard and risk being fatigued before the game even started.

"Okay, ladies—let's see some action," Coach Darlene said in the locker room. "You already know the drill."

"Suicides if we don't blow them out as hard as we should've," Mags mumbled from next to me, making a couple of other girls on the team giggle. It was fun to tease Coach Darlene about the predictable punishments she'd enforce upon us, but not so fun when we actually had to see it through.

We huddled, heat and adrenaline radiating off of everyone.

"Lakeside!" The team shouted and then erupted into cheers. We ran out from the locker room onto the court to warm up and then took our seats to wait for the game to start.

The other team was announced, met with scattered cheers and applause but mostly with boos. Then, it was our team.

The starters ran from our chairs to the court one after another, greeted with loud applause and hollering from the crowd. Our team's hype up song pounded through the arena as lights flashed.

I shook out my muscles, getting myself ready for running out.

"And the name everyone's been waiting for—our two-time All-American and all-time leading women's scorer...Theo McCall!" the announcer's voice boomed through the arena.

I lightly jogged past my teammates, high-fiving everyone as I ran onto the court. Every single nerve I'd been experiencing earlier melted away completely. There was nothing but me and the game out there.

When I looked over the crowd, I was surprised by how many people were there. Usually, our first home game pulled some of our best numbers, followed by a bunch of pretty dull crowds until the next big ticket game.

This game, however, was still just as high energy as our first game of the season. It wasn't as packed, but it was still busier than I imagined it was going to be before coming in. We'd sold out games last season, but no one had known if the momentum was going to keep up. It looked like not only was the momentum there, but it was even more intense than it had been last season.

People were really starting to care.

It was impossible not to be energized by the crowd. I jogged out, throwing my hands in the air to get everyone to cheer even louder. It was my favorite move to pull on the court. I didn't feel like I had that much power in day-to-day life—I was mostly just a college student who was told what to do by my professors and coaching staff and parents—but out here, I was able to command an entire crowd of fifteen thousand. Just me.

I looked over toward the student section and scanned for Maya's face. The lights of the area flashed over everyone's faces, illuminating them. But there were way too many faces to sort through to find her. I kept hoping I'd somehow be drawn to her, like I'd be able to find her face in a giant crowd no matter the circumstances. It seemed like maybe I didn't have that superpower after all.

Or she just wasn't there for the game.

I brushed the feeling away without a second thought. I'd never needed anyone there for me at a game—my parents came when they could to support me, but there were a lot of times they weren't able to. It was just me and my team and the stands filled with people. That was what mattered the most to me.

It wasn't difficult to lock into the game from there. I immediately jumped into my game day headspace, the same one I'd been able to access since I was a kid.

The game had always made sense to me. I saw where the plays fit together and how everyone moved around on the court. I could confidently play off of people's strengths and knew where to get the ball and when so we could score. Basketball had always felt as easy as breathing. The older I got, the more I'd hear things like *basketball IQ* get thrown around. Recruiters especially, even as young as middle school, knew what I had, usually even before I understood how good I truly was. Mostly, I just knew I was crushing my standard competition growing up, and it wasn't until I started playing seriously against other teams across the United States that I felt challenged.

And even then, I usually found a way to come out on top.

The roar of noise—music, people yelling, players talking shit—all became white noise. Occasionally, something would break through, and I'd engage, usually throw a few choice words out. But the harder we shut out a team, the harder it was for them to come up with anything to say to us.

Even so, it didn't stop GJ from getting technicals left and right.

"Oh, that was bullshit!" GJ shouted.

"An elbow's an elbow," one of the referees said and shrugged. "Watch your limbs, Mitchell."

When the ref turned around, GJ scrunched up her nose. "Watch your limbs, Mitchell," she said back in a quieter, mocking tone, knowing exactly how loud she could be to avoid getting in trouble.

I snorted. "Avoid an ejection, GJ. How about that?"

GJ waved her hand at me and Gemma and I laughed.

After coming back from halftime, the score was 75-30 in our favor. It wasn't expected that the tide would turn anytime soon, and the other school would come back, but I wasn't about to let them off easy. Coach Darlene would most likely keep me in until late in the fourth quarter, once she felt like the score was confidently in our favor. As wide as the gap was now, I wasn't going to fall back.

"Jesus, McCall—let them breathe a little," Mags said later after I hit my fourth three-pointer of the third quarter. It'd only been a few minutes, and I felt a little bad for showing off—I knew that I was—but I couldn't resist.

"Can't keep a dog from biting," GJ said, and we slapped our hands together before running into position for the next play.

We kept the momentum up, bumping the score to nearly 90 points while the other team had only gotten four the entire quarter. Even though the scoring was low on their end, I knew Coach Darlene wasn't going to be happy about letting any points at all slip. There was no reason our defense should be weak enough that we're letting points by.

"Keep the energy up, ladies! Let's make it happen!" Coach Darlene yelled from near the bench.

At the start of the next play, GJ sent the ball flying to me, crossing past two players and effortlessly bouncing the ball past another. I couldn't help but smile a little bit. She'd always matched my playing style—going big and bold wherever possible. We were more prone to turnovers and mistakes because of it, but I'd rather take the risk and fuck up my stats a little bit than always play safe.

I loved playing with GJ because of it; it was going to be hard to have to leave Lakeside Green, mostly because of her. I loved the entire family I had here, but GJ had taught me so much and done so much for me on and off the court. She was without a doubt my best friend, and I felt good knowing the team would be left in her hands when I graduated.

I dribbled the ball, running through my play options in my head. I was usually right in guessing where people were going to go and when, which direction they'd run based on how their feet were positioned or where they'd been consistently going all game. I logged their strengths and weaknesses, only getting better as games progressed.

There wasn't anyone around from my team who could safely take the ball. The player in front of me attempted blocking me, moving side-to-side and eyeing my every move. I quickly moved around her and sent the ball flying, shooting it from nearly half-court. It swished through the net effortlessly.

Even though it wasn't a game-winning point by any means, the entire arena stood up like it was. A low hum of people chanting my name started up, growing louder and louder. I couldn't help but laugh watching the sea of people go absolutely nuts over me. For the first time—at this low-stakes, washout game of all places—I really understood how much people at this school cared about me.

"Three-o! Three-o!" the crowd cheered, stomping their feet and clapping.

I'd seen it over the years and I knew the fans viewed me as special. The number of jerseys with my name and number on it were higher than every other player on the team. But I was really seeing it now.

I looked back over at the student section, throwing a glance that way before getting into position for the next play. As if spotlighted, I finally saw Maya. I smiled at the audience, half playing it off like I was smiling at everyone while keeping my eyes focused on Maya. I didn't know if she could tell from so far away that I was looking at her, but I hoped she could.

The rest of the game went by without much fanfare. The other team eventually got tired of putting up a fight and seemed to realize they were never going to win it. Toward the end of the game, Coach Darlene finally pulled me and let me rest.

"I can't believe how many people are still here," I said and wiped off my forehead as I threw myself down on the bench. I took long pulls from my water bottle.

"They're here for you, McCall. You manage to make a one-sided game exciting," she said, slapping a hand hard on my back. The pride in her voice was evident. She'd told me when she recruited me that getting to coach me was going to be one of the biggest honors of her life. I'd been one of the only female five-star recruits Lakeside Green had ever had in their program history. She'd always made it clear that they didn't have the prestige or the money, but she would still coach the hell out of me—and hopefully bring the rest of the team with us.

So far, it seemed to be working.

After the game, we did our usual handshakes with the opposing team, and I ran through a post-game on-court interview. I'd received pretty significant media training, but all it'd done was give me enough cookie-cutter ways to get through interviews that I barely thought about them. It was my biggest flaw; I loved playing the sport and talking about the sport, but I didn't really want to talk about *me* playing the sport.

After spending far too long talking about the half-court three-pointer I hit, I excused myself and headed over to the student section. I tried to keep it subtle, knowing that I didn't have much time. Most people waited to see significant others and family after the entire circus of the game was done—the locker room talk, the post-game panel, the debrief with teammates as we all talked shit and showered. We'd most likely all be going out together tonight.

But I had to see Maya before I got sucked up into all of that.

I looked around for her up in the student section, trying to spot her hair or smile.

Maya and I locked eyes as I cut across the floor toward the student section. She made her way down the bleacher steps and joined me. She was wearing a Lakeside Green University shirt again, a different one from last time, but just as flattering. Every single time I saw her, I was completely floored by how beautiful she was. It was impossible to believe that she was single, that she was even *real*. It was devastating to me that we'd been on the same campus for so long and had never crossed paths before now.

We met in the same spot as before, the metal barricade separating the court and the stands the only thing between us.

"Congrats on the win," she said.

"I didn't realize you had so many Lakeside Green shirts."

"Me? I bleed green, you know me."

My lips twisted into a smile. "Right."

"Iris let me borrow more clothes from her. Getting me to two basketball games has been the win of her life. I don't think anyone has ever been so excited for anything; she's about to buy me a jersey."

"It'd look good on you," I said before I could fully realize what I was saying. But it was fine because this was what we were doing anyway—we were supposed to be flirting, supposed to be all over each other in public. I wasn't going to take advantage of it and was going to pretty much exclusively follow Maya's lead, but one or two flirty comments wouldn't hurt anyone. It was all plausible deniability.

"I'll make sure it's a twenty-five," Maya said.

I tugged at my own jersey, twenty-five on my chest. "Represent. I'll sign it for you."

"Please do. It'll be what makes it possible for me to buy a house in the future. I'll sell it when you retire in a couple of decades and go down as the greatest to ever do it."

"Bold words from someone who doesn't watch the sport."

Maya shrugged playfully. "I'm a quick learner."

I glanced up at Maya's friend, Iris, who was talking to a couple of other people. I waved when Iris looked down our way and then spotted that she was wearing a Lakeside Green men's basketball shirt.

"Wait, did you guys want to go to a game? Men's basketball, I mean," I asked. "We can probably go out with the guys after. You said Iris had a crush on one of them, right?"

Maya's eyes sparkled as she put her hands on my arms. I stayed as normal as I could, but it was impossible when any part of her was touching me. It was the most physical contact we'd ever had; I was going to relish in it, even if it was embarrassing for me.

"You're a *genius*," she said.

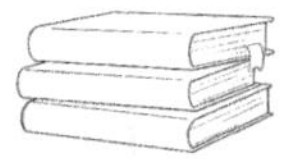

Chapter 13

MAYA

Even though Theo had invited me *and* Iris out, my body was responding to her invitation as if it were an invitation to a solo date. I had butterflies like crazy and was already thinking about what I was going to wear to the game.

"Three basketball games in *two weeks*!" Iris squealed as we walked home from the game. "Thank you for your service, Theo McCall!"

When I told Iris that Theo invited us to a men's game, I made the executive decision not to mention that Theo knew she had a crush on a player from the men's team. I'd also made the executive decision not to mention to Iris that Theo and I were definitely going to be seeing more of each other because of my stupid fake dating idea.

I couldn't believe Theo had actually gone along with it. I'd expected her to be entirely uninterested in how much public attention she had already received. But I wasn't going to question it.

Iris had been begging me for details from the hang out, but there wasn't that much to say—just that I'd had a great time and it seemed like Theo did too. I didn't need to give an elaborate *I have to get closer to her in order to get over this* speech that would just end with Iris going, *Oh, so you* really *like her.*

"Happy to go," I said, because trying to explain any of the other eight million thoughts in my head would've been a lot for both of us.

"I know you're getting into this because of Theo but I'm taking advantage while we have it," she said. "Next, I'll drag you to a Cedar Creek Blizzards game."

I'd heard enough from Iris over the years to know that the Blizzards were the professional women's basketball team in the area. Lakeside Green was the college town just outside of Cedar Creek, so she would go to see the Blizzards whenever she had the chance. During their season—May to October—Maya was always in frosty blue and white instead of our school's deep green.

"We'll work our way to it," I said as Iris looped her arm around mine and pulled me in for an excited side-hug.

Back home, I did my usual routine of showering and then digging through Theo's social media. It'd become an unfortunate habit. I wouldn't say I was *obsessive* about it, but it was definitely a considerable part of my evening.

I just couldn't help it. I didn't know what the pull was, but it was like I needed to be as close to her as I possibly could. I wanted to know everything she was doing, hear her explain it in her slow, even timbre, see her mouth pull up in a permanent half-smile while she talked.

It was my dirty little secret, which I'd gotten surprisingly good at hiding from Iris. I'd found the in between of how much to talk about Theo so she didn't get too tipped off to how I really felt about her. She was definitely close to piecing it together, but I had my own personal history on my side. There was no one less likely to develop a long-term crush than the girl who had never had a long-term crush before.

But it was difficult to maintain that track record when my opponent was Theo McCall.

I scrolled through anything I could find on social media related to her—tagged posts, new posts from her, posts from the team. A video popped up of one of her shots from the game; it was already going viral. All of the comments were hyping her up, talking about wanting to drive out and fly out to see her. Students from Lakeside Green were joking that they'd start selling their tickets to people at a starting rate of two hundred or three hundred dollars each—and people were genuinely considering it in the comments. *DM me, I'll legit take those*, one person wrote.

It was the most peaceful side of the internet I'd ever seen. Theo was managing to unify everyone. And make them come to our small town in the process.

The video after that was a clip of Theo at a post-game conference. It was clearly from today, kicking off with a reporter asking her about her half-court shot.

"It's very impressive," the reporter said from off-camera. "And you've done it a couple of times now."

Theo shrugged. "It's basketball. All practice."

"Theo—how are you feeling about playing Point Brook later this season?" another reporter asked. "Cam Kerr has had quite a bit to say in the press."

The press chuckled, and GJ rolled her eyes, making me think there was more to the situation than I knew. I didn't just have to learn the mechanics of basketball; I also had to learn the dynamics between everyone.

Theo was more diplomatic in her response than GJ. She leaned in close to the microphone, leaning her weight on her forearms. Her biceps flexed as she put weight on her arms. "Point Brook has a lot of really great players—I know it'll be a fun game. I love getting to go up against Cam, we've been playing each other since we were pre-teens. I'll let the game speak for itself."

I had to lock my phone to take a deep breath. "God, she is so hot," I whispered to myself.

My mind flashed to my hands pressed to her arms earlier, and I nearly swooned thinking about it again. I'd seen my moment and taken advantage. I'd been desperately wanting to touch her, be close to her, in any capacity I could. And I was a touchy person with people I was close with, so it wasn't entirely out of character.

I just maybe didn't necessarily mean for the touch to come across as entirely platonic this time.

It was all for the audience, though. I'd done it because it was for the bit, and it was funny. Obviously.

Theo was still the tiniest bit sweaty from the game, and her arms were *firm*. I'd never been someone who was into muscle; I'd always leaned more toward the artist type. The people who liked books and music and drawing. People who looked like they'd never even seen weights or the inside of a gym outside of school requirements.

But I was suddenly *really* understanding the appeal of someone strong. It was easy for me to imagine her arms wrapped around me and how safe I'd feel.

There was the tiniest part of me that craved the kind of predictability that I felt like Theo could offer. She seemed like someone who had a nice, loving family and probably wanted to have a nice, loving family of her own. Her muscles were like the physical manifestation of that. I trusted that she could build me bookshelves in a theoretical home, or fix the dryer.

It also didn't hurt that the mental image of her building furniture for me might as well have been pornographic. I needed to come up with a way to see her holding a hammer as my next grand plan.

I shook my head. Something was seriously wrong with me. I'd *never* felt this way before—ever. Growing up, I'd been the girl who nobody could ever pin down. Boys were interested in me because I wasn't interested in them. And then when I came out, nothing serious ever came of anyone I met. I didn't have the tragic first lesbian heartbreak that left me curled up and crying on the floor like it did my friends.

I was always the person who broke things off and always the person who'd never really wanted more to begin with. I'd roll with the attention I had, liking someone for long enough until I'd get bored and crave something else. I never knew exactly what that something else was. But I'd also never met someone like Theo before, who was making it very hard for me to imagine what else I could want in a partner that she couldn't provide.

I picked up my phone and called the only person I knew who could fix this for me.

"Mom," I said as soon as she answered. I was surprised I'd been able to catch her—she was usually off doing something. She was always on a date or at the gym or at work or out with friends. She had the kind of hustling social life even I envied sometimes.

"Hey, honey," she said, and I could hear the treadmill going in the background. She'd turned one of the spare bedrooms into a home gym and preferred working out in the early mornings and late evenings when it was cooler out. Unlike Colorado, Arizona stayed hot into October most of the time and didn't feel remotely like fall until close to Halloween. Our air conditioning was good, but it wasn't so good that we'd want to workout in it when it was nearly ninety-degrees outside.

"Did you need something?" Mom sounded only slightly out of breath. In classic *hot mom* fashion, she took great care of herself and took a lot of pride in being fit. The only thing keeping her from wearing *my* bikinis to our backyard pool was childbirth.

"I think I have a crush and I need your help," I said. I dropped my voice to a low whisper like I was telling her a secret.

In a way, I kind of was. I knew Iris wasn't going to overhear the phone call, but voices sometimes traveled in our apartment, and I didn't want to risk her hearing me bare my soul in this way. Iris knew me, but she didn't need to know the most deeply pathetic parts of me.

"Oh, it'll pass," Mom said. "It always does for you."

"This one is really bad."

"Why are you whispering? Is she there with you?"

"No, I just…" I put my free hand to my forehead. "Can you, like, tell me something about how I shouldn't let my girl-friend stop me from finding my wife or whatever? I need your live-and-let-live advice right now."

"I don't know if I have that, baby. Love is a beautiful thing. Most people would be thrilled to have a crush. It makes life more exciting. I remember when I met Ray, and it felt like the entire world opened up in a way it never had before," she said.

"Which boyfriend is Ray again?"

"Oh, stop," she responded lightheartedly. The one thing I really appreciated about my mother was that she was self-aware. "I don't think you met Ray. He was the boyfriend from your…sophomore year to junior year. Yes. Yeah." She was quiet for a beat. "Yes, because we went to Vancouver for his work trip in the spring."

"Right," I said. Sometimes, it felt a little bit like I was the mom and my mom was the one with the ridiculous early-twen-ties schedule. I was always asking her what happened to a boyfriend or a friend, and saying things like, *Wait, I thought you were dating Sam? Who's Nick?*

"Anyway. I don't have anyone on my radar right now, and I *love* it, don't get me wrong. But I miss being wined and dined. It makes me feel like a teenager again. I'm suddenly a six-teen-year-old girl waiting to get picked up by the senior boy—"

"Okay, alright," I said, not needing to get into her wild teenage years again. Anyone who thought I went hard with partying and meeting new people had never met my mom.

"Who is this new crush? Can you tell me anything?"

I weighed my options quickly, thinking through the pros and cons of telling her. A major pro was that my mom was normal about crushes, so if I told her I was over Theo, she'd let it go and never bring it up again. A con—probably *the* con—was that I'd have to verbally admit that I was *really* into Theo.

"She's a basketball player," I said, a comfortable middle ground.

"College?"

"Yeah. I met her through a mutual friend, I guess. Or mutual friends. At a party."

"An athlete is different for you."

"Exactly."

Mom was quiet for a minute. I listened to the soft whirr of her treadmill and the sound of her feet hitting the belt. "Is she nice?"

I thought about Theo bringing snacks to us hanging out, the way she offered to go get me Twix. She was considerate about time, about making a move. I loved that she'd waved at Iris when I saw her at the game instead of pretending my best friend didn't exist. And then offering to take us to a men's game, all because she knew Iris had a crush on a basketball player.

I nearly groaned. It was even worse than I thought. Not only was she nice, but she was just as nosy and invested in setting Iris up with her crush as I was. She was shaping up to be my ideal match.

"Unfortunately," I said, defeated.

"I think you might need to see this one through, baby."

I groaned. "Don't give me your Pisces Venus advice right now. You're no help."

"I want what's best for you. Find the person who loves you the way that you should be loved," Mom said. "And find someone worth bringing home to me, whether it's this crush or the next one. I'm dying to finally meet one of your girlfriends."

I half-rolled my eyes, but smiled. "Miss you, Mom."

"Miss you, too, baby. I'm gonna get back to my workout—I'm doing a lap around Central Park right now and I'm close to being done."

We hung up, and I sprawled out on my bed with my phone to my chest. My mom had unfortunately given me the advice I'd secretly wanted to hear, but had also hoped she wouldn't give me—I had to keep sticking this thing out with Theo.

I needed to get her out of my system, needed to find *something* that would make me not like her. It was the only way.

Theo texted me the next day while I was in class about which men's game we'd want to go to. Scheduling was tight, mostly because Theo was going to be in and out of town for away games, and Iris had work. My schedule was slightly more agreeable, but only because my time was spent on social outings—getting brunch, drinks, dinner—and studying. Anything on my calendar could be theoretically rescheduled.

We eventually found one that lined up after Theo came back from the away games. There was one specific Thursday when the men's team was playing, Theo didn't have a game and wouldn't be out of town, and Iris didn't have to work.

"I'm trying not to be offended that I'm somehow the one here with the least intensive schedule," I said when I told Iris what day we were going. I threw myself down onto the couch next to her as she turned on Theo's away game that was on that night.

"Someone has to be the one who's easy to plan with. It works well with Theo. If I were trying to date her and we had our current schedules, I'd see her, like, once a month. She'd be my permanent *no, guys, I swear she's real, she just goes to a different school*," she said. "I also benefit. It's made our friendship sustainable. I appreciate it."

"It doesn't make me lame that I'm not busy every single second of every day?" I asked, even though I kind of was. I didn't *feel* as busy, but I had plans or the option of something to do most evenings.

"No," Iris said as she dunked her hand into the bowl of popcorn that was sitting in my lap. "It's refreshing."

"That feels like a—"

"Shh, it's tip-off," Iris said and sat up straighter. She slapped my hand on my thigh to silence me, nearly knocking over the popcorn bowl in the process.

I bit back a laugh and settled back into the couch. I was nervous watching the game—partially for Theo because I wanted her to win, but also partially because it felt so strange watching her on TV. It felt like an invasion, like this was what would give away that I had a crush on her.

But then again, Theo had been the one who'd texted me just before the game, *Bummer you're not here to flirt with me after the game, now I don't have a way to make the girls jealous,* so maybe it wasn't just me fighting off feelings.

I responded back quickly with, *Don't worry, the real fans know about me.* I hadn't heard back yet, probably because she was busy preparing for a nationally televised basketball game.

The photo of me touching Theo's arms had, somewhat surprisingly, caught on online. The primary fan page that had been following her through her career—given the uncreative but still sweet name of *Theo McCall Central*—had even given it some attention. They usually kept their updates strictly about basketball, but the Theo McCall fans were hungry for whatever they could get. It was obvious how charmed everyone was by how her easygoing attitude contrasted with the competitive, borderline mean edge on the court. I couldn't blame them for it; I was feeling exactly the same way.

Surprisingly, however, was that it seemed like fans were starting to piece together who I was. It made sense—Lakeside Green was a large university, but it wasn't so large that no one would be able to place me. A couple of people had responded to posts about Theo and her *mysterious lady-friend* with comments about how they were pretty sure they'd seen me in their psychology classes or a freshman year math class.

One girl I knew from parties at The 151 responded, *oh shit, that's Maya!!!* which was a consequence to my actions I stupidly hadn't anticipated. It was one thing for my face to be everywhere, but my actual name—which would inevitably show up in a Google search conducted by potential graduate school admissions committees—was something else.

"Oh, shit," Iris sat forward on the couch, her eyes glued to the screen. I blinked, bringing myself back to reality.

"Arlington with the ball. Number twenty-two hurrying down the court," the announcer said.

"And Arlington is good?"

"Pretty good. They had a really good run, like, five years ago, and haven't really been able to get back into the swing of things, but they have a new coach, so we'll see." She looked over at me. "Your girlfriend is going to be fine. It should be an easy win. She'll definitely get some flashy plays in. I think the media attention is boosting her confidence on the court in a good way."

"Not my girl—"

Iris waved me off and pointed to the screen.

I did my best to stay quiet while watching, trying to piece together the times that Iris groaned or cheered with what was happening on screen. She did the best she could with explaining everything, but if she tried to break it down for me play-by-play, she would be talking from start to finish.

Every single time Theo flashed on screen, I felt a tug in my chest. I didn't get to see her up close during the games usually; she was kept at a distance, running up and down the court, blocked by other players.

But on TV, she was right there. They'd zoom in on her periodically or show a replay. Her celebratory yell after landing a shot—one that had Iris literally jumping up from the couch—was shown on the screen repeatedly before commercial breaks.

"I can't believe she's on TV," I said. "Like, that's the same person who's been on this couch."

"How do you think I feel?" Iris asked good-naturedly. "I've been watching her play since freshman year. I've watched her go from niche celebrity status to like...kind of legitimately famous in the basketball community. People are really starting to pay attention, not just to her but to the sport as a whole. Viewer numbers are up all around the country. It's so exciting."

"And she's just hanging out on your couch," I teased. "Maybe I should start saying that she's *your* girlfriend. It feels more appropriate."

"I can only name her stats; you've actually had conversations with her," Iris said. "And while I can admit she's hot, she's not exactly my type."

"Yeah, you want Mr. Basketball."

"Oh, that is the *worst* nickname you could've possibly come up with for him. He deserves better than that."

"It's not my fault—you won't even give me his first name!" Iris shook her head, miming locking her lips and throwing away the key.

"I'll figure it out eventually," I teased and Iris shrugged in response before stuffing her mouth with more popcorn.

Chapter 14

THEO

Maya quickly became part of my routine. I didn't really mean for it to happen and I was assuming she didn't mean for it either. We went from the occasional joke text to texting pretty consistently. Our conversations flowed just as easily on screen as they did in person, so it made sense why it was hard for me to put my phone down sometimes with her.

The conversations were never anything meaningful, usually little quips or small updates about what we were doing throughout the day. Maya teased me about all of the time I spent at practice or in the gym and I tried my best not to text her something like, *Do you have a crush on me too?*

"I didn't even realize you texted," GJ said after getting out of the shower in our shared hotel room. We'd just wrapped up our second away game of the week—a win against a smaller school with decent defense but zero shooting game. It felt like the hoop and the ball were repelling magnets—for them, at least. It'd been smooth sailing for us.

"What do you mean? I text," I said. I put my phone down on my hotel bed, which was admittedly an upgrade from my bed on campus. Everything in my room was pretty plain—basic IKEA furniture, the first mattress I could find online. The rest of my apartment matched the vibe, hence the shitty living room couch. Our NIL money paid us decently well, but my roommates and I didn't feel particularly motivated to use it on our student housing.

"Dude, I've been talking to you for, like, five minutes and you haven't responded once. I don't even think you've heard me talking."

"I'm just…"

GJ looked at me. "Are you still texting the girl from the party?"

"Maya," I said. "Yeah. We're going to a men's basketball game."

Her brown eyes lit up. "A date?"

"Her roommate is coming too."

GJ waved me off, clearly annoyed by my answer. "*Man.* What the fuck?"

"I invited both of them to hang out!" I said defensively. "Maya's trying to set her roommate up with one of the guys on the team."

"Right," GJ said, remembering Iris now, and sighed. "Can't believe she'd go after one of those losers."

"They're nice guys."

"Okay, some of them are nice. *Most* of them are losers."

"Do you want to come to the game? It's an open invite."

"Dude, this is like the worst date ever."

I rotated on my bed to face her as she came to sit down. She was wearing a shirt from her old high school team, her black hair pulled off her neck. Our hotel room had come to smell like what I now thought of as home—shea butter and coconut-based hair products. Since GJ joined the team, we'd been travel game roommates. We'd spent more time together than I'd ever spent with any other friend outside of seeing people at practice. Our friendship had transcended into something that felt closer to what I imagined siblings felt like. She and her sisters joked that I was their bonus white sibling whenever they came out to see us play.

"It's not a date," I reminded her.

"It *should* be."

"I already invited Iris."

"Some guidance—don't do that next time," GJ said and threw herself onto her bed. "And no, I'm not interested in third wheeling your not-date. Or I guess fifth-wheeling, since you're also trying to set her friend up." She paused. "You have to let me know what basketball player it is. I know I'm a lesbian, so I can't speak to it, but none of those men seem worth chasing down."

I shrugged. "No clue. Maya doesn't know either yet, so it'll be new information to everyone. I'm guessing Danny. He's the nice one."

GJ nodded in reluctant agreement. "That would make sense. I still don't get it, though."

I snorted. "When are you going to start dating, huh? Where's the girl I can tease you about?"

"I got a few. None I'm telling you about because none of them are anything," GJ said.

"Man, you are such a nightmare. You're giving us all a bad rep," I said, laughing.

"What, worried Maya's going to think she's one of many?"

I shook my head. "I'd be surprised if she really thought that. My dating life is so bleak that people are photographing us in public together, thinking that we date and it's actual *news*. She told me people found out her name and her Instagram, and she gained so many random followers, she had to make her account private. It's so stupid."

"Yeah, I saw the last picture of you guys. It's cute. People are thinking it's really serious," she said, giving me a sideways look. I hadn't told GJ about me pretending-but-not-really-pretending to date Maya for the cameras for obvious reasons.

"Stop," I groaned.

"Is it serious?" GJ asked, leaning across our beds and smacking my knee. "Come on. You have to tell me. We can be honest here. I know you hung out with her at her apartment."

"And nothing happened, just like I told you."

"Mhm."

I paused, the two of us staring at each other. I knew GJ wasn't going to let me off easily. "I mean, I guess I wouldn't be mad if something did happen—"

"Thank god you're finally *admitting it.* Jesus. I never thought I'd hear the words come out of your mouth. You guys would be walking down the aisle to each other, and you'd be like, *yeah, I mean, she's pretty cool.*"

"I don't think that's how a wedding works."

GJ shot me a look. "You know what I mean. And trust I remember what a wedding looks like after my sister made me be a bridesmaid that one time. I thought she was going to have an aneurysm over me insisting on wearing a suit."

"I loved the pink," I admitted with a nod.

"I did too! At least I matched the other bridesmaids! Like, what? I was gonna wear *black* like the groomsmen? I might not care that much, but I do care enough about my sister to not ruin her photos."

"Maybe one day you'll meet someone who makes you want to care about your wedding."

"Skeptical. I'll get married if you do."

"Bet," I said.

Later that night, I fell asleep thinking about Maya in a wedding dress, her walking down the aisle to me wearing the same pink suit GJ wore to her sister's wedding.

I spent most of my time on the plane ride back preparing for my classes and catching up on work. Maya gave me a renewed motivation to whip through work as quickly as possible, utilizing the tutors where I could and focusing harder on my work than I'd ever focused before. I didn't necessarily need the work to be any better than it was—I was happy to graduate with anything above a 3.0 with how intensive my basketball schedule was—I just needed to do it faster.

It was a feeling I'd never experienced before. It caught up to me in unexpected ways—wishing I could see Maya after practice, rushing through workouts so I could text her again. It wasn't enough to negatively affect my playing, but it was unusual for me. Suddenly, all of the pressure I'd been putting on myself had been lifted. I was learning how easy it was to work someone into a routine if you wanted them there, and I wanted Maya there more than anything.

In the lead up to meeting up for the game, Maya and I kept texting. We were still trapped somewhere between flirty and platonic, but I was just happy to be talking to her at all. I loved her wit and how she seemed to have a response for everything, how she was supportive without ever overdoing it. She could turn around any kind of day I was having.

I looked forward to hearing from her and was disappointed when my phone vibrated and it wasn't her. I had a diagnosable crush, and I was worried that the more I felt it, the more difficult it would be for me to hide it.

But I wasn't about to give up my time with Maya in order to keep my secret crush from her. If anything, I was tempted to bring it up with her the second she gave me an indication that there was a green light. It was still too early, and I was nervous I'd scare her off, but I wasn't so much of a coward that I'd continue on forever keeping my feelings a secret.

Before leaving for the game, I threw on an easy outfit. I had a moment of second-guessing myself as I headed out the door, but I refused to let myself get in my head about it. I didn't need to wear anything special.

I spent the entire walk to the arena telling myself that I needed to be normal, that it wasn't a date, and that I couldn't forget Iris was there. I repeated it over and over again in my head: *be normal. Not a date. Iris will be there.*

"Theo!"

I looked up and saw Maya waving at me. She was standing at the front entrance of the arena, a flood of people walking around her. Iris was next to her with a smile on her face.

Going to a basketball game here sometimes felt a little bit like willingly walking into a cage at a zoo. I knew everyone was staring at me. And it wasn't in a way that assumed I was more important than I was; anyone who watched Lakeside Green basketball, whether men's or women's, knew who I was. Every single person there knew my name, even if they hadn't ever seen me play.

But I still enjoyed going to watch it. I loved the sport as a whole, not just playing. If going meant I had to endure thousands of people looking my way, I could force myself to handle it.

"Hey," I greeted them. Maya and I shared a smile that made my insides turn to mush. I turned to Iris. "Good to see you again."

"Yeah, you too," Iris said. Something in her eyes told me that she was sizing me up a little bit, probably trying to get a sense of my intentions. I didn't blame her—athletes didn't exactly have the best reputation of being loyal, dependable partners.

Part of me hoped that she could tell I had a crush and would push Maya in that direction. But another part of me hoped that not one ounce of my feelings was obvious. If Iris could tell, that meant Maya probably could, and I didn't need that.

"Should we head inside?" Maya asked. Iris and I nodded, and I braved the herd of people walking in. I was a head above most of the people in the room, and inside, I caught the eye of even more people who definitely recognized me.

"Theo! Mom—Theo is here!" a kid nearby shouted. I kept my eyes straight ahead so we didn't make eye contact with them, but I could feel everyone else looking my way.

"Oh my god, you are famous," Maya said with an amused laugh. She dropped her voice low, her arm brushing against mine as she leaned in to talk to me. It was impossible to focus on the words she was saying with her skin on my bare arm.

"I'm not, it's—"

"Yo, Theo! Can I get a picture with you?" a male student asked, stepping in front of us.

I was used to this, but I wasn't used to navigating in front of Maya. And I definitely wasn't used to navigating it in front of Maya *and* one of her friends.

"Oh, um. Sure, man," I said easily. I glanced over at Maya and Iris. "Sorry."

"Take your time," Maya said, and then turned to the guy who had stopped us. "Do you want me to take the picture?"

"Yeah, that would be great," he said and handed his phone to Maya. "Thanks."

He walked over and stood next to me, throwing up his hands in a low peace sign. I appreciated that he didn't bother trying to touch me; there were some people who weren't great about personal space. It was a bold choice considering I was stronger and taller than most of the people who stopped me to ask for photos.

"Smile," Maya said, holding up his phone and snapping a few pictures. I couldn't get a read on her expression. A gripping fear in the very back of my mind—from the deepest place of insecurity—worried that she thought it was annoying.

But the unfortunate reality was that this was what it was like. This was life for me and for anyone else in it with me. It wasn't this bad everywhere, but there were times when people were going to recognize me. And as much as I liked being around Maya, I couldn't change it for her if she didn't like it.

But even so, there was a tiny part of me that wondered if basketball could actually get in the way of us. Navigating her cool girl, no strings attached attitude was one hurdle. Basketball, and the attention that came with specifically me playing basketball, was something else entirely for us to navigate.

I smiled for the camera, forcing the thoughts out of my head. It was way too early into anything to start worrying about it. Maya and I were friends, and that was that. It wasn't worth reading more into it.

Maya handed the phone back to the guy. "They look great."

"Thank you," he said, looking between me and Maya. "This is so fucking cool."

As he walked away, Maya looked at me. "Did anyone tell him that you go to school here? He can get a photo with you whenever, technically."

"I don't know if I need pictures of what I look like in my nine a.m. lecture on business ethics floating around," I said, and she snorted.

Just as I thought we were in the clear on photos, a group approached, followed by a few more people. The group huddled around me and Maya, and I felt an instinctive urge to protect her from everyone walking our way. I put my hands on her waist, holding her steady so she didn't get swept up in the group. It wasn't a massive number of people, but having ten and then fifteen people approaching out of nowhere had a way of feeling like an ambush.

"Theo, can we get a photo?"

"Can you sign my shirt?"

"Theo! Did you see that Bendr said he's flying out to your next game? So fucking cool, do you think you'll get to meet him?"

Maya turned to me, the expression on her face a split between wide-eyed panic and amusement. It seemed like she didn't really know if she should laugh or run.

"I'll take care of this," I said. "Go stand by the wall with Iris. I'll see you in a second."

Maya nodded, her hand finding my forearm. I wanted to reach out and take her by the hand, offer everything I could to try and check in on her, but that felt too far.

As I signed t-shirts and jerseys and answered random questions—including offering a diplomatic *yes, I like Bendr's music* even though I hadn't really listened to him before outside of house parties—I glanced over at Maya and Iris. They were up against the wall, talking to each other.

I wished in that moment I had the ability to hear from a far distance. Or do a decent job at reading lips. I wasn't picking up on anything they were saying, but I was nervous it wasn't going in my favor. I didn't worry I'd done anything wrong necessarily, but Maya probably wasn't used to attention like this in the way that I was—and even then, I was still getting used to it. Jokingly posing for photos as if we were dating was different from actually being approached in public.

After posing for photos until my cheeks hurt from smiling, I forced myself away from the people still standing nearby. "Enjoy the game," I said and walked over to Iris and Maya again, hoping everyone took the hint that I was done for now. They fortunately did. "Sorry, that was...a lot."

"Sorry to bring you right into the middle of it all," Maya said. "I feel bad. I should've known basketball fans were going to go nuts over you here."

I waved the apology off. "I'm the one who offered to come. I think my social currency has skyrocketed since Bendr, like, shared a clip from one of my games or whatever."

"Bendr? Like, the dance music guy? He has that one song..." Iris hummed out the chorus of it, clearly trying to think of the name.

"Yeah," I said.

Maya and Iris were quiet for a second, exchanging a look I couldn't read. My ego on the court was one thing but off the court, I was realizing quickly I had very little interest in being a public figure like this. I just wanted to play basketball, maybe pose for pictures here and there before and after games.

I wasn't naive enough to think I'd ever get away from it. Part of playing at this level was being famous to a certain degree. But I didn't want Maya—or Iris, for that matter—to think that it was something I actually *wanted*. Maya and Iris didn't seem like the kind of people who'd be charmed by things like a crowd wanting to take photos or getting the attention of a famous rapper.

Walking to our seats from there was fortunately uneventful. I'd never been so ready to immerse myself in watching a game.

Iris sat down first, then Maya, and then me. I maintained a normal amount of distance from Maya, but it was hard to give her space when my legs were so long. As I settled in, my knee accidentally brushed against Maya's and I nearly jumped a foot into the air and moved away from her.

But instead of doing the same, Maya's knee seemed to find mine again a moment later. I kept mine against hers that time, waiting to see if she would move.

She didn't.

Maya looked out over the court where the players were warming up. "Do you see him?"

Iris hid her face in her hands. "Stop, oh my god," she said.

"I'm just wondering!"

"I'm not telling you. You will never know my secret."

"Come *on*," Maya pleaded. "You're no fun. We're already here. We might as well look for him."

Iris shook her head. "No. Absolutely not."

"Can Theo know your secret?"

My heart rate picked up at the sound of Maya saying my name. I was already having a hard enough time being present with Maya's knee against mine. I could barely think straight, my thoughts wandering to how well Maya's shirt fit her and how her brown hair fell over her shoulders.

Iris looked like she was considering telling me for a second and then suddenly looked between us. "This was a set-up. You guys are here to find him."

"Not entirely—"

"Maya!" Iris said, laughing. She turned to look at me. "Ignore her. It's not that serious."

"It is that serious because Iris *never* has a crush on anyone. She had a crush on him before she even knew he was on the basketball team. She just saw the tall hot man with the dreamiest eyes and the softest smile—"

"*Maya!*" Iris was nearly crying now from laughing so hard. Her face was bright red.

"You can trust us with this information," Maya said. "I swear."

"I can't trust you with any information on a crush. You don't even know his name, and you're out here scheming. You even pulled out the big guns to make it look less suspicious."

"Am I the big guns in this scenario?" I asked, and Maya cackled with laughter.

"Can you give me a hint, at least?" Maya asked.

"He's on the basketball team."

Maya threw her head back and laughed even harder. It was the most incredible sound I'd ever heard; I immediately committed the moment to my permanent memory. "I hate you," Maya said.

The overhead lights dimmed, and bright white and green spotlights flashed, signaling the start of the game. The players ran back out onto the court.

Even though I didn't want to acknowledge it, the energy was different at the men's games. There were about one-quarter of the fans there as there were for women's games, and it was noticeable in the volume of voices.

My guess was that they struggled under the weight of not having a true star player. Danny was carrying them as far as he could, but it'd been years since they had someone who had major name recognition. And in a program like ours that was always decent but never *the* team, we were quickly forgotten by anyone who wasn't a dedicated fan. I couldn't remember the last time a men's game had sold out. Coach Darlene had told me yesterday after practice that the women's had been sold out for the entire season so far, home and away—the first time ever in program history.

"Wait, so they always start the game like that?" Maya asked.

I nodded. "It's the tip-off."

"I promise I've been trying to teach her things," Iris said.

I laughed. "It's okay."

Down on the court, the opposing team—the Jaguars—got a handle on the ball first. They sprinted down the court, and the Lakeside Green boys found their positions. They set up man-to-man, each person playing hard to stop the ball from moving. But twelve on the Jaguars shot the ball up in the air and dropped it easily through the net.

When the ball made it into Danny's hands, the crowd sat up straighter. It would most likely be the Danny show all over again, mostly because it had to be. I felt bad for him, more than anything. He was genuinely a very talented player. But he didn't have the infrastructure to get anywhere. Unlike my team, which stepped up and matched my skills, his team seemed to fall back and let him take control. Some people might like being the star in that way, but it'd only hurt Danny's game overall. He'd already been pretty explicit with me that he probably wasn't even going to try for the NBA—he might try for G League, but even that was variable—so it was a bummer to know that this was how his last season ever was shaping up for him.

It was like that sometimes, though. We spent most of our lives training, practicing, pushing, ignoring that it would all eventually have to end, until one day, it was just *over*. Sometimes it was in a big way—championships and the promise of a professional future in the game. But sometimes, it was unceremoniously. The whole point of sports was that not everyone could win, which meant someone had to lose, even during their last year of college ball.

I was preparing myself for the possibility of that feeling that I would hear people talk about. Waking up and not having practice or a team. Having a normal job. Basketball would turn into a lifelong fun fact—*did you know we made it to the Elite Eight one year?*—and memories.

I knew that the odds of my never playing again were incredibly low. The odds of me not being drafted at all were also incredibly low, at least based on rumors I'd heard and knowledge of my own stats. But it wasn't just about my own abilities—I could get injured at any time, or I could lose the mental game when I attempted to transition over to playing professionally.

A ref blew the whistle down on the court, pulling my attention back to the game. The scoring was keeping pretty even; based on what I'd seen, the defense was lacking on both teams.

"What was that for? The whistle, I mean?" Maya asked, and then her cheeks flushed. "Sorry. You totally didn't come here to have me nag you with questions the entire time."

"No, I don't mind," I said, partially because the game was a little dull, but I was never going to say that out loud. "Blocking foul. It was a stupid move—I don't know what he was thinking."

The guys lined up so the Jaguars could do their free throw attempts. The first one made it in but the second one didn't, giving the Coyotes a chance to maintain their thin lead.

The refs blew their whistles again and I shook my head. "Traveling," I said, trying not to sound too annoyed.

The game went on like that for what felt like forever. It would stop and start, both teams fouling for dumb reasons. Danny was unsurprisingly the glue keeping them together—he'd scored nearly every point Lakeside Green had on the board by the end of the first half. Maya periodically asked questions throughout the game, but it was so slow-moving that even she seemed to be getting the hang of it and no longer needed to ask. Or she'd zoned out completely.

There was no media coverage for this game; the teams ran straight back into the locker rooms, and the cheerleaders replaced them on the court for halftime.

"Are you finally going to tell me who he is?" Maya asked, turning to Iris. "Do you not want to admit it because he's on the bench?"

"He's not on the bench," Iris protested and then realized her mistake.

Maya's eyes lit up. "Oh, that is *very* good to know. I hope it's the one who keeps scoring. I don't know if I could support you pursuing a man who's one of the worst on his college basketball team."

"I'm ready to sign myself up for a lifetime of rec league games," Iris said, resignation in her voice. "At least one of us won't have to."

Maya turned to look at Iris. I couldn't see her face, but I knew based on Iris's reaction that she got exactly what she wanted. I fought off a smile, understanding exactly what Iris was implying. A burst of hope fluttered in my chest. Maybe Maya really had been thinking of me the same way I'd been thinking about her this whole time.

The cheerleaders finished their routine and ran off the court. Mag's twin sister—Leah—moved with the group, smiling and waving as she went back to the court end line. It was jarring to see someone with such a similar face to Mags on a completely different body.

The second half of the game picked up some momentum—I could only guess both teams had their asses handed to them by their coaches. There were occasional bursts of energy on both sides and quick-thinking plays, but it faded out quickly.

The score started to space out further and further as the other team lost their handle on blocking Danny. Some of the other players started to catch up, too, and finally got the ball into the net, so it wasn't just Danny. By the end of the game, there was hardly any fight left, and the Lakeside Green boys pulled through.

The crowd cheered and celebrated, still excited about the win. We sang our school's fight song, and the boys started gathering their things to head back into the locker room. Before they could leave, I went down to say hi—and test my theory that Danny was the guy that Iris was into.

"Danny!" I yelled, cupping my hands around my mouth so he'd hear me over the noise.

He looked up toward the student section to see where the noise was coming from. When he saw me, he waved and walked over. I waved for Iris and Maya to come down with me to meet him.

"Good game," I said as Danny dapped me up.

"It was alright."

"Twenty-two points is killer, dude."

"You know how it is," he said and I did. Just because the stats from a game were good didn't mean the game itself was good. Their defense had been weak and most of the players on the team who were able to match Danny's shooting abilities hadn't woken up until the second half. It'd felt a little bit like a one-man show and not in a good way.

"You guys doing anything after the game?"

"Uh, yeah. I think we're going to Devonte's tonight. He and James offered to host something at their house."

I wrinkled my nose. "That place is disgusting."

Danny shrugged and wiped sweat from his brow. "Best and final offer."

"Alright, I'll let you know," I said and glanced over at Iris and Maya. Maya looked like she was interested in going; Iris was looking at anything other than Danny. *There it was.* I wasn't reckless enough to be a gambler, but I would've put money on Danny being her guy if I were.

"You guys are welcome to come, too, if you want," Danny said, looking between Maya and Iris.

"That's sweet, thank you," Maya said. "Good game."

"Yeah, good game," Iris said, and Maya looked at her like she'd grown a second head. Based on what I'd seen during the game, Iris loved basketball. She'd had a lot to say about how the Coyotes sucked at rebounding just a few minutes ago. Either she had a personal vendetta against Danny, or he was the guy she'd been secretly crushing on.

I fought off a smile thinking about how Maya had gotten me completely wrapped up in her roommate's personal life. It was so unlike me. I stayed out of drama and personal shit on every front that I could—team drama, dating drama, conference drama. There was a reason I never had much to say about Cam Kerr when her name came up.

But this felt like a way of getting closer to Maya. And maybe a way of helping Iris out, too, if she really was that serious about the crush she had on her mysterious basketball player.

"Thanks," Danny said. "Alright. I gotta get back but maybe see you tonight."

"See you, D," I said.

Danny winked at me and then nodded his head at Iris and Maya. When he walked away, Maya looked at me. "He was sweet."

"He's alright," I said, clapping my hands together. "So, you guys want to go tonight?"

Chapter 15

MAYA

Theo had been right to call Devonte and James's place—whoever they were—a dump. It felt like a frat basement had thrown up over an entire house. Every inch of the floor was sticky, the couches looked like they were picked up from the street, and their wall art was a tapestry with an internet reference I hadn't heard since I was a freshman.

It *was* disgusting. But admittedly, I loved it.

The music was blasting so loud we could hear it from the sidewalk, so it wasn't surprising that it was nearly impossible to hear each other once we got inside.

"I'm gonna grab a beer," Theo yelled over the music. The bass practically shook the walls. "You guys want anything? Good for now?"

Iris and I waved our water bottles of liquor, and Theo nodded as she headed off. There'd been a couple of hours between the game and the party, so Iris and I had gone home to change, eat, and pregame. We met in the middle with Theo, who said some of her teammates might also come by.

"I didn't realize how good we had it at the 151," Iris said over the music.

I laughed. "I guess our frat days aren't behind us yet."

"God has abandoned us."

I spotted Theo from across the room chatting with Danny. I didn't think I was that tipsy, but with the way it was impossible to take my eyes off of her, I knew the alcohol was setting in.

Despite my best efforts, I kept finding myself right back in Theo's orbit. I waited for her to do something that I didn't like, anything that could give me the ick, but nothing had come up. Normally, it took so little for me to stop being interested in someone—their laugh, the way they spoke to others, the way they texted. Things that always made me feel mean, but I knew were only rooted in the fact that I'd never actually liked them.

It was different with Theo, like she couldn't do anything wrong in my eyes. Everything she did was cool and confident and sexy.

Even the way she'd handled the people coming up to her before the game was cool. She handled it like a pro—kind but firm, posing for pictures but also putting a stop to it when she got tired. She kept me and Iris out of the way as much as possible. And the way she'd put her hands on my waist had nearly made my knees weak.

Theo might've taken away my desire to sleep with anyone else, but she had also managed to amplify my sex drive in the process. The more time I spent with her, the more time I spent thinking about her hands and her arms and the way both of those felt on my skin.

My plan of getting close to her so far had only backfired and made me want her more. I was starting to think that my only way out of it was attempting to sleep with her, but that felt extreme and risky, even for me. I had a feeling once I had Theo, I was never going to want to let her go.

Danny and Theo walked back over toward us, and I averted my eyes, attempting to look like I hadn't been staring at Theo the entire time.

"Hey," Danny greeted us. As we formed a small circle, Theo moved to my side, and every inch of my body felt like it was on fire. I'd never been so aware of another person's presence.

"Hey," I said over the music. "Thanks for the invite."

"Yeah, of course," Danny said. He looked at Iris. "Heard you're a basketball fan?"

Iris's face flamed up, and I looked between Danny and Theo, wondering what was going on. I didn't want to make any assumptions, but I had a feeling Theo had something to do with it.

"I am," Iris said, and based on her body language, I knew my cue.

"We're gonna go dance," I said and grabbed Theo by the arm, moving her away from Iris and Danny. Danny roped her right into a conversation involving player names I didn't recognize, not wasting any time at all.

Theo and I found ourselves in a corner of the room where I was still able to keep my eyes on Iris without being in the middle of the conversation. The alcohol temporarily took over my body, and I leaned against the wall, looking up at Theo.

Theo took a swig from her beer can, standing over me. She'd done a lot in making me realize how much I liked being around a tall woman. It was hard for me to ever imagine having a crush on someone who wasn't at least four or five inches taller than me going forward—which limited my dating pool to basically her and her teammates.

"How did you figure it out?" I asked.

Theo leaned in closer to me so we could hear each other. A cloud of light cologne followed—a scent I couldn't place that was sexy and not overbearing. She was so close that if I turned my head, I would be able to put my lips to the skin of her cheek.

I wanted to. But I knew I couldn't.

"What do you mean?" she responded, her voice low in my ear. She put her hand on my waist as she ducked her head, and I nearly blacked out.

"Danny and Iris," I said, trying to sound as normal as possible. "I'd had a feeling when she was being weird with him, but I couldn't tell if he's the mysterious basketball player or if she was nervous being around one of his teammates. She also gets shy around you, so I didn't write off the possibility."

"Shy around me?" I asked.

"Oh, yeah. She *worships* you, dude. She's a legacy Lakeside Green basketball fan."

Theo chuckled. "I can't tell if that makes me more or less nervous talking to her now."

"Why would you be nervous talking to her?"

Theo opened her mouth to respond before stopping herself, blushing and looking away in the process. She backed up, creating physical space between us.

The sight of her blushing was so *cute* that it took everything in me to not to comment on it, gushing about how everything she did was simultaneously so cute and so fucking hot. The words were on the tip of my tongue, the alcohol making it impossible to keep my thoughts to myself.

"Wait, do you want to impress Iris?" I asked, suddenly broken out of my haze of staring longingly at her as her words—and then following silence—registered. "Be honest—do you have a thing for straight blondes or is this for my benefit?" I teased.

Theo rubbed her hand against her jaw, her eyes directed away from me. "Pleading the fifth on that one."

A feeling surged in my chest that reminded me of spring weather and standing in the sun and laughing with my friends during a perfect night out. It was a welcome change of pace from how I felt any other time I was sure someone was flirting with me. I'd been starting to think it was impossible not to be at least a tiny bit bored by someone's moves.

But I was never bored when it came to Theo.

I stood up from the wall, closing the gap between us. I tilted my chin up toward her. Adrenaline coursed through my body, but the alcohol numbed it. It turned out it was much scarier to flirt with someone I actually had a crush on, even with the help of liquid courage.

"I can't believe you want to impress me," I said, externally still teasing her, but internally feeling like I was jumping off a cliff.

Theo looked down at me. I held my breath, waiting to see how she would respond. I couldn't tell if she was going to take the bait or not.

"Why wouldn't I want to impress you?" Theo asked, her eyes on mine. The blushing and the coyness I'd seen in her earlier completely melted away. She meant what she was saying. I didn't know her well, but I knew her well enough to know the silent game we were playing.

My stomach swooped. "You're *the* big basketball star. I should be the one trying to impress you."

"You don't like basketball. I have to prove my worth some other way."

"And that is?"

"By setting up your friend with a basketball player she's had a crush on forever," she said.

I didn't bother to fight off my smile. I grabbed her by the arms, leaning in close to her. "Did you have a feeling before today, or did the way Iris was acting give her away?"

"I didn't know for sure, but I know Danny, and he seems like one of the more likely candidates for someone to have a crush on. The rest of the team are kind of assholes anyway, so even if she wanted one of them I don't think I'd set her up."

"God, you are so hot," I said, a phrase I'd picked up to say under just about any circumstance—Iris getting me coffee in the morning, the grocery store clerk loading my groceries just right. But as soon as the words left my mouth, I saw my mistake.

Theo let the comment slide off, her eyes flickering with something, but quickly letting it go. The party shrank down to just being us, everything else melting away into the background.

I wondered if this would finally be it. That we would finally kiss, finally see what was actually going on between us.

Theo McCall had turned me into the kind of person who got antsy and impatient about being kissed. Rather than being the person who would just make the move and get it over with, I was now the girl who stared at her crush and waited for her to say something, to do anything.

As my eyes flitted from her eyes to her lips to her jawline to her hands that I desperately wanted to weave my fingers through, I knew I was done for. I wanted her more than I'd ever wanted anyone in my life. And not because it was a game, not because I was forcing myself to push her away or get close to her.

I just wanted her. Simple as that.

The realization hit me like an emotional breakthrough that usually came to someone in therapy. It was a punch to the gut and a rush of relief all at once. It'd been so obvious—to me, to Iris, probably to Theo—but it'd never felt so clear.

I had a crush on Theo McCall, and I knew it for certain because if she wanted to kiss me right now, I would let her. And I would enjoy it. And I would absolutely want more from her.

We inched together, my back getting pushed closer to the wall as Theo got closer to me. I didn't even attempt to stop it, to question if this was really the right thing for us to do.

I wanted this—the heat from her body, the closing distance. I'd been trying so hard to fight it and intellectualize it and push it all away, but this was exactly what I'd been hoping for the entire time.

Theo's brown eyes met mine, and I wondered if I should just do it. I only needed to lean forward, probably stand on my toes. If it was a misread of the situation, I could blame the alcohol in my bloodstream.

I leaned against the wall, and Theo stepped forward, getting even closer to me. Our bodies were nearly touching now, only the tiniest bit of air and thin pieces of clothing between us.

I just *knew* Theo would be good to me in bed. I could feel it in the way she carried herself, in the way she looked after me. It was easy to tell when someone would be selfish or lack finesse. But Theo didn't seem like she would be like that. She was kind—the kind of person who set my friend up, who gossiped with me and hung out with me and texted me for hours about nothing.

She also had really great hands.

"Would it ruin everything if we kissed right now?" I asked.

Theo didn't look surprised. If anything, she seemed like she'd been waiting for me to bring it up. She didn't verbally respond; she shook her head and brushed my hair behind my ear. Her thumb trailed down my skin, so gentle it almost made me shiver.

I stood up taller to meet her, and we got closer than we ever had before. We both stopped just as our lips were about to touch, and I worried for a beat that Theo might've been pulling out. But she didn't move away.

Only a breath apart, I leaned forward and finally kissed her.

Kissing her didn't activate the reward part of my brain, the part that celebrated being successful in taking someone home or getting hit on. Instead, it activated something else entirely. For the first time ever, things started to make sense. Crushes made sense, love songs made sense. All of the big, gigantic, swirling feelings that make romance so appealing suddenly made sense.

I'd been right to think that going any further with Theo than talking would be nothing but trouble. Sex was never going to fix this. I couldn't fuck her out of my system and get over my crush on her that way.

Theo's hands found my jaw, and mine found her waist. She pressed me completely against the wall. Her lips were soft and warm and tasted faintly like beer. She kissed me exactly how I imagined she would—firmly but sweetly, careful and courteous. She easily took the lead because that's what she did in every other area of her life, but she wasn't pushy about it.

The only difference was that it was even better actually kissing her than it was thinking about it.

I slipped my hands under her open button-down shirt and then under her tank top, tracing along her lower back. I felt safe and held and turned on in equal measure, in a way that I'd never felt before ever in my life.

Our kiss deepened. We opened our mouths, letting our tongues explore and our bodies naturally respond to each other. I moved without thinking, letting my hands travel. Theo was more respectful, keeping her hands in places that felt modest. I'd never kissed anyone so tall before and it was throwing off the rhythm I was used to, but I liked it.

I could've kissed her forever. I *wanted* to kiss her, exactly in this spot and exactly in this way, forever. No more classes or post-graduation plans or basketball games or talking. Just this.

I didn't know how long we'd kissed like two teenagers who were too nervous to go past first base. Neither of us let our hands or our mouths wander *too* far. It wasn't the wildest makeout I'd ever had in my life, but it was—without a doubt—the sexiest. I was so wet that we might as well have had rounds of hot, out-of-control sex.

When we broke apart, we looked at each other for a long beat. The music and the loud voices and the flashing lights of the small townhouse all came rushing back at once, and I remembered where I was.

I didn't know what there was to say. *Thanks? That was, without a single doubt in my mind, the best kiss of my entire life?*

I hadn't only kissed someone in a long time—at least since I was a teenager—and I didn't know what to do afterwards. Normally, there was a kiss with a goal or a purpose. It was after a date, and it felt like the natural next move. Or it was at the bar with someone I was going to go home with.

But this wasn't a date. And for the first time in my life, I was at a loss for words. I didn't know how to invite Theo back, if I was ready to take that step with her.

"Maya!"

Iris suddenly broke through the crowd and grabbed my arm. I jumped, yanked from the dazed state Theo and I had entered.

"I need to talk to you," she said breathlessly.

"Oh," I said and looked over at Theo, unsure of what to do. The kiss felt like the kind of thing Theo and I needed to talk about, or at least planned to talk about together.

"Sorry, this is urgent," Iris said, turning to Theo. Based on how she was acting, I could only assume she had no idea what had just gone down between me and Theo.

Iris pulled me away before Theo or I could say anything to each other. We moved through the crowd together, further and further away from Theo and closer to the front door. It wasn't until we were outside in the biting cold that Iris finally stopped.

"What's going on?" I asked her. "You're being so weird."

"I completely embarrassed myself," she said, and hid her face in her hands. She flung her arms around in distress. "Theo got me a chance with Danny and I screwed it up and now it's over. I have to find a new crush. Or maybe transfer to a new school in a new state."

"Whoa, okay," I said, grabbing her by the shoulders. "I don't believe it could've been that bad. I'm sure it was fine."

"No, it absolutely wasn't. I just...I made this offhand comment because I thought we had that kind of rapport going and I don't think it landed well at all."

"You're literally *the* nicest person I've ever met. I seriously doubt you messed it up that badly. What kind of joke was it?"

"I just...I made a comment about the men's basketball team here and the women's team. It was so stupid. He seems like such a nice guy, too, and he's one of the only players on the team who's actually keeping it together. He doesn't need to be reminded that the women's team is literally lapping them." She smacked her hand to her forehead and cringed. "I don't know what I was thinking."

"Okay, honestly, a man who can't handle being told that the women's team is better than the men's—an objective truth from a records standpoint—isn't someone worth being around. Men with egos suck."

Iris nodded with the same kind of passion as someone getting hyped up before a game. She took a deep breath.

"It's totally fine. It sucks when a crush doesn't line up but you don't need him anyway," I said, feeling a little bit like I was talking to myself even though my crush seemed to be lining up just fine. Now that the high of the kiss was behind me, reality was sinking in hard, and all I could think about was how I felt like I needed to prepare for the end. The relief of finally kissing Theo had been replaced with crushing anxiety of what was going to come next—and none of the scenarios I was coming up with had a happy ending. "You'll be fine on your own. You always have been."

Iris groaned. "I know. He's just *so* cute. It's so different when the guy is a jerk. But now I feel like I'm the one who was an asshole."

"How did he respond to your comment?"

"It was just like...kind of awkward. I don't know."

"You didn't even let him *respond*?" I laughed. "Dude!"

"I don't even want to hear it from you! You have a crush you refuse to admit to having, and it's so obvious," Iris said and crossed her arms. "You guys were hardcore flirting the entire game. You can't deny it."

"Okay, yes. Maybe," I said.

Iris tilted her head and looked at me, her expression changing. "Something happened," she said, and then she groaned again. "Oh my god, I fucked things up with my crush *and* I ruined your moment with yours. This has to be one of my worst runs I've ever had—"

"Iris, it's fine," I said, fighting off a laugh. "Seriously. It's okay. We just...kissed."

"*Just* kissed?" she screeched, and I shushed her so other people who were standing outside wouldn't start looking. "Holy shit. How was it? How did it happen?"

"It was..." I brushed her comment off, but then realized what I was doing. My instinct was to act like nothing had happened, but in my gut, I knew what it was. I couldn't pretend it was nothing. I could still be anxious about it and certain it wasn't going to end well, and also acknowledge it was the best kiss of my life. My expression softened. "It was really great, Iris. It was a perfect kiss. I'm even more into her than I thought."

Iris, who was normally a ball of energy and enthusiasm, met me at my level—most likely so she didn't scare me out of having a crush. She dropped her voice slightly, pouting her lips. "That's *so* cute."

"Not to take away from your crisis. That's the most important thing right now."

"No, I'm glad there's some good news," Iris admitted. She shivered from the cold, and we both started heading back toward our apartment, synced up after all of these years of friendship. "So, you haven't talked about it?"

I shook my head. "Neither of us really seemed like we knew what to say."

"Do you think you'll kiss again?"

I fought off a sigh. "I hope so," I said, feeling shy in a way I never had before when it came to my feelings. Theo was the only person who'd ever brought it out of me.

"I hope so, too," Iris said gently.

Chapter 16

THEO

I had no idea what to say to Maya. I wasn't a talkative person in most areas of my life, but I was usually able to find the right words. I was the captain of my basketball team—all I did, day in and day out, was make sure my team knew what was going on. I gave them guidance and direction, I worked on building relationships between every member of the team.

But all of a sudden, I had no idea what to do. I had no next step, no direction. It was like my team was looking at me during the fourth quarter, and instead of giving them anything at all to work with, I said, *Actually, maybe we shouldn't push for the win. Do you guys want to? Are you sure you want to?*

It was the dumbest thing I'd ever experienced in my life.

I'd partially hoped she'd reach out first with some kind of quip, but she never ended up texting. After Iris had pulled her away, that was it. I didn't hear from her for the rest of the night. Or into the next morning. Or that evening.

We were starting to reach a critical point of needing to at least say something to each other. It was obvious both of us were waiting to see what the other person was thinking, and I wasn't necessarily *afraid* to reach out first. I did TV interviews. I took on contracts with major athletic brands and had made hundreds of thousands of dollars—redirected into a savings account I told my parents to monitor until I graduated, because the amount overwhelmed me—in NIL money. I navigated the press and fans and school, all in the midst of playing the sport that I loved...

Maybe I was a little afraid of having to reach out to Maya first.

But mostly because I didn't know how she was feeling. I didn't know what the next course of action was. It was the longest we'd gone without texting since we'd started and there was a small part of me that wondered if that was intentional.

But not getting answers in this case was the worst-case scenario. I didn't mind mutual ghosting, but it had to feel actually mutual. If I let Maya go now, I'd spend the rest of my life wondering about her.

Throughout the week, it was obvious during practice how off I was. I was making my shots, but I fumbled through plays and kept overshooting or undershooting during assists. After messing up yet another drill, I groaned.

"I'm taking five," I said, and one of our assistant coaches waved me off the court.

"Dude, you're sucking ass," GJ said from the court as I grabbed my water. Mags bounced her the ball, and GJ shot it from the back corner. I'd always been jealous of her range. I could shoot far—I'd always had theatrics to my benefit; people loved big plays—but GJ was better at tougher close-range shots than me.

"Thank you for the supportive words."

She turned over her shoulder and looked back at me. "What's been up with you? Not that I don't mind the reminder that you're human like the rest of us and have off days. I just don't like seeing it."

"I have a lot on my mind."

GJ caught the ball from Mags again and tossed it up, an endless, effortless loop. It swished easily into the net. "Girl related?" she asked. There was a beat of silence between us, squeaky shoes and basketballs bouncing filling the void. "I know you don't get shaken up by basketball shit, so it has to be a girl."

I put my water bottle down. "Yes, fine. Girl related," I said, unsure if I wanted to talk about it or pretend it didn't exist.

"The girl from the pictures?" Mags asked from down the court.

"A and B conversation," GJ shot back at her.

"Yes, the girl from the pictures," I said. I didn't really want everyone in my business, but everyone already was in my business—they'd been in it since that very first picture made the rounds in our group chat.

And no matter how Mags seemed to feel about me, we were still family at the end of the day. I saw my team more than I saw anyone else. Having Mags ask me about Maya was better than the whole of the internet—which still hadn't loosened its grip on me. GJ teased me about it periodically, keeping up-to-date on new headlines popping up or clips that were doing well online.

"You like her?" Mags asked, ignoring GJ.

"Of course, she likes her. Who else would be capable of making Theo McCall play like shit than the girl she has a crush on?" GJ said.

"I was just wondering. Damn," Mags said and GJ casually flipped her the bird, just out of sight of the coaches.

I snorted. Mags and I played differently and didn't always see eye-to-eye, but I was usually diplomatic about it. Both GJ and Mags had personalities that were too big for that. They got along and played well together, but they bickered like siblings most of the time. GJ tended to keep me out of it because I asked her to, so I never knew what they were doing to piss each other off so badly. Sometimes, it didn't seem like they really needed a reason; they just needed someone to pick on. I didn't understand it, probably because I'd grown up as an only child and both of them had siblings.

"You should text her," GJ said.

"I didn't even tell you what happened."

"You don't need to. You should text her and figure it out. Get it out of your system before you go insane. Or squash our chances at making it to the finals."

"If there's anything keeping us from the finals, it's your inability to get a rebound," Mags said to GJ. Neither of them missed a beat in the drill they were running; the ball passed between their hands and the net as easily as breathing. We'd been practicing these shots for most of our lives to the point that we could probably do them in our sleep if we wanted. At our level, the challenge usually wasn't making the shots at all; it was making the shots while we had a bunch of six-foot-tall women trying to steal the ball from us.

"Try hitting a three *ever* in your college career and then come talk to me," GJ said. She turned back to look at me. "Seriously though, dude. You should talk to her. Just like...invite her out or something. Doesn't have to be anything crazy. Just vibe check her. The worst that happens is she says no."

GJ was right but it didn't make it any easier to think of something to say. I spent the entire rest of the day thinking through variations of texts I could send. All of them either felt too forward or too passive. I was halfway to texting *that kiss rocked!* just to get it over with.

It was so weird not having anything to say to her. Since we'd met, it'd been impossible to shut us up. And now, when it really mattered, I was stuck.

I took a deep breath, thinking back to the kiss. It'd been so unexpected. I'd picked up on a little bit of something during the game, but that was who Maya was. She was fun and flirty and had a bigger personality than me. I didn't think she'd actually go for it.

But I was glad she did. I kept volleying between embarrassment it wasn't as good for her, nervousness she didn't want to hear from me again, and the undeniable truth that I wanted to kiss her again.

By the time I got home, I knew it was time. I couldn't put it off any longer. We'd already been down this road once of waiting to see who would text first, wondering what the other person was thinking the whole time. I needed to nip it in the bud; it was fucking with my routine.

Hey—would you want to hang out again? I have One Tree Hill at the ready.

I cringed. It was the dumbest text I'd ever written in my life. It was so bad that I wouldn't be surprised if Maya blocked my number altogether in response.

But after almost a full day of thinking it over, it was the best I could do. And it was better than nothing. At least this would get me an answer about how Maya was feeling.

I put my phone down and paced, then dropped to the floor to do push-ups to keep my body busy. I didn't know what I was going to do if she didn't respond—probably keep doing push-ups until my arms gave out.

My phone vibrated and I got up immediately to check. *Let's do it.*

I let myself celebrate for only about a second before I realized she didn't give me an actual plan. The only thing worse than having to text to initiate a hangout was having to follow up and say, *Okay, so, when are we doing it?*

My phone was quiet for another beat, but her text bubbles reappeared. I watched the screen to see if she was going to send the follow-up for me or not. After a few more seconds, another message appeared. *When are you free?*

That was the million-dollar question. I never knew when I was free. Or, I knew *exactly* when I was free, it just didn't feel particularly flexible. I had the girl I had a crush on basically standing in front of me—virtually—and agreeing to hang out again. There was a very good chance we might kiss again in the process, or possibly do something even more than that.

This was not the time to hit her with a two-hour time block suggestion, which was about what I was visualizing in my head. Between classes, training, games, and travel for away games, there wasn't much room for fooling around all night. There was nothing that could kill a mood like, *Are you free from exactly 5-7 p.m. on Tuesday? What about 8-10 p.m. on Friday?*

I didn't really know what to expect, other than that I offered *One Tree Hill* as an activity. It was too broad to know exactly what to expect of hanging out again post-kiss. But in anticipation of the possibility, I wanted to pick a night where we could theoretically stay up together and it wouldn't completely throw off the entire next rest of my day.

The biggest issue being that I was someone who liked my schedule and had maintained basically the same one the entire time I'd been in college.

I mentally thought through my calendar and then sighed. I had to volley it back to her. It would be easier for me to move things around based on her than try and find time I already had free in my calendar.

I have away games coming up again. When are you free? I'll base my schedule around you.

Where are the away games? she wrote back.

Utah and Kentucky.

My heart thudded in my chest, my palms sweaty. We were slowly back in our old routine, but it felt fragile. Saying the wrong thing could ruin it all, but I didn't know what the wrong thing was. I didn't know if I should be implying the kiss was a mistake or leaning into it. Or maybe we were supposed to pretend it didn't happen at all. I wished I could somehow telepathically communicate with her that I was following her lead, that I would do whatever she wanted me to do.

Did you want an audience?

My lips turned up in a smile. *I love an audience.*

Her text bubble popped up and then went away. I waited to see what she meant, wondering if she was actually asking for the reason I thought she was asking.

I'll come see you play. It's been a while since we've gone viral.

The fame is getting to your head.

Sorry, it's the aspiring WAG in me. You're my new means of retiring. Already looking forward to becoming a housewife.

You'll have to go NBA for that. W rookies don't even make low six figures most of the time.

I'm investing early.

I smiled at my phone, unable to help myself. The rhythm was there like it always had been. Everything was fine between us, even if I still had questions.

I thought back to Maya leaning in toward me at the party. The way she'd asked if I thought a kiss between us would ruin everything. The way she'd kissed me.

Her perfume had been light and sweet and her hair was soft in my hands. I didn't just want to take her home to see her naked; I wanted to be with her. Hold her, take care of her, somehow find the time to spend days in bed together.

See you in Utah? I wrote, the best I could offer for now. It wasn't exactly a big romantic gesture or the promise of time alone, but it was time together.

See you in Utah.

Chapter 17

MAYA

The road to Utah was long and boring, but occasionally beautiful. When I said that out loud to Iris on hour four of our drive, she turned to look at me through her sunglasses.

"That's kind of poetic," she said and then turned back to look out over the road that had looked the same for most of the drive. The shortest route took us through Wyoming—something that didn't make sense to me, but I wasn't in charge of the roads—which was quiet but surprisingly flat and uninspiring.

"I thought Wyoming had mountains," I said, my hands on the wheel and eyes on the road despite there not being a single obstacle in front of us. We hadn't seen a genuine highway in hours; it'd been us and a handful of other cars for long stretches since we'd left the city.

Iris had gotten bored with our collective Spotify playlist, so we were toying around with FM radio and seeing what played on the local stations. We'd mostly found static. *For ambiance,* as Iris said.

"Further north. I think the Tetons are, like, three hours from here. Maybe four," she said. "I'd look it up, but my service is garbage. I googled it up before we left because I was hoping we might see something more than...grass."

"I think we're the only people in the world who overestimated Wyoming."

Iris stretched in her seat, rotating her torso left and then right. "As fun as this is, I think I miss using my legs."

"Two hours to go," I said. The timing of Theo's game had worked out well—it was on a Saturday evening, so we could leave Friday, stay the night, watch the game, and then drive back Sunday morning. When I told Iris that I wanted to go, she nearly dropped to her knees and started crying. She was one more basketball game invite away from forming a religion around Theo McCall.

I didn't know what kind of attitude I should have going into the game. I didn't know if this was romantic or not, if I was going with the expectation we'd kiss again, or if we were going to pretend it didn't happen. I was choosing actively—and fighting hard, especially late at night when I was alone—to not feel embarrassed by my decision to kiss her.

She'd *definitely* kissed me back, there was no denying that. But she could've kissed me back for any number of reasons without thinking about it. Maybe she'd realized later it was a mistake, or it wasn't a good kiss.

I shook my head. There was no way it wasn't a good kiss. No kiss in the history of the world could be *that* good and only be one-sided.

"Should we go to a soda shop while we're there? I've heard Swig is actually pretty good," Iris asked, and then turned to me. "Maybe Theo can take you to a Swig."

"You already know Theo won't have the time for something like that. She might not have the time to see me at all while we're out there," I said. "And I don't think she's ever had a sip of soda in her life."

Iris was quiet for a moment and then nodded. "That's fair, actually. No wonder her abs are so...like that."

"Yeah," I said and then wandered off into thinking about Theo shirtless. It was an incredibly welcome visual, one that had made the drive feel much faster than it actually was. My daydream about Theo and I fooling around in a bathroom at a party had gotten particularly detailed while Iris napped earlier.

Theo and I had gotten back into the swing of things effortlessly once she'd broken the ice. We were back to texting as if we were physically unable to stop. I wasn't addicted to my phone exactly, but it was enough that Iris practically had to peel it away from my face while we were watching the newest season of Love is Blind.

Iris and I had booked a hotel based on Theo's recommendation via text, and I didn't know if that implied it was the hotel she was staying in or if she was one she knew from the area. It hadn't escaped me that we might end up in the same hotel, which for some reason felt way hotter than our arrangement on campus. If anything, it was more inconvenient considering we'd both have actual roommates here; it was like living in the freshman dorms all over again. But there was something about the proximity with both of us in the same building, but unable to be together, that was really hot to me.

Not that I actually knew anything was going to happen with her. I wasn't going to text and ask something like, *Hey, were we planning on fucking on this trip?* I was bold, but I wasn't that bold.

I was, however, just bold enough to invite myself to one of Theo's away games. I was playing it off as part of my craving for adventure and new experiences—that wasn't unique to Theo. But I knew that I mostly just wanted answers from her, which I had to see her in person for. I wanted to know what was going on, what to think and feel.

Or, as only admitted to myself, I wanted to know if she felt the same way about me. I already knew how I felt; how she was feeling was a mystery to me.

The last hour of the drive seemed to drag on for a lifetime, but we eventually pulled into the hotel just off the university's campus. Based on what Theo and Iris had told me, this wasn't a massive basketball school. Their program was D1, so they were decent. But compared to some of the larger powerhouse schools, their record wasn't very good, and their arena was a lot smaller.

The hotel was cute and generic, and the parking lot was only about half full. I parked the car and got out, taking the time to stretch and shake out my limbs. The air was crisp, and we could see the suggestion of mountains from here in the distance, just like back in Colorado. It was already dark out, the transition into winter kicking our asses, so it was hard to see the details of our surroundings.

Iris and I grabbed our bags from the car and headed inside. The receptionist was an eager woman who looked like she wasn't much older than Iris and me. She made eye contact with us immediately upon walking in, and her smile was almost unsettlingly large on her face.

"Hi! Welcome!"

"Hi," I said, my energy seeming almost miserable compared to how chipper she was.

"Checking in?"

"We are," Iris said and walked toward the desk.

"Name?"

"Maya Healy," I said and pulled out my ID. Iris did the same.

"Coming for the game?" she asked, nodding to Iris's Lakeside Green University shirt.

We nodded. "We are," I said.

"Very exciting stuff. It's been *so* busy around here with tourists. Everyone's here to see the number one team in the conference do their thing." She leaned toward us and dropped her voice like she was telling us a secret. "Did you know the team is staying here? You might run into them."

I didn't know if she was legally allowed to tell us something like that but I would let it slide this one time. I fought off a smile, wondering if I might run into Theo. I couldn't help but be charmed that she'd intentionally given me the name of the hotel she and her team were staying in.

"I sure hope we do," Iris said, playing along. "That Theo McCall sure is something, right?"

"Oh my goodness, yes, absolutely," the receptionist responded, her eyes practically starry at the mention of her. I picked up on it immediately, my radar going off. I desperately wanted to say *she's just as good at kissing as she is at basketball,* but resisted. I was surprised by how hot my jealousy was burning, but I'd also never been faced with someone who was into Theo. The comments online were nothing compared to seeing someone in person who *definitely* watched the same Theo fan edits I did and wanted her just as badly.

The receptionist went to work on her computer, oblivious to me clocking her, as she talked, inputting our information from our IDs into her system. "All of my friends are going out to see her play; we've been looking forward to it all season. And she was *so* nice during check-in. I wanted to ask her to sign something for me, but she was busy," she continued on. I was half-charmed by the positive review of Theo—I'd never been involved with people who'd be considered kind by strangers; most of them were, frankly, assholes—and half feeling suddenly *very* possessive. "You're so lucky that she goes to your school." Iris glanced over at me, a small smile on her lips. "You have no idea," she said and then turned back to the receptionist.

The receptionist—her name tag read *Allie* with a hand-drawn smiley face—clicked around on her computer a few more times and then slid our room keys in the reader to activate them. "Okay, here you go," she said and handed them over the counter. When she looked up again, her attention was pulled toward the door instead of us. Her eyes widened. "Oh. Oh, wow."

Iris and I looked at each other, wondering what could possibly be happening. We glanced over toward the door and saw the entire Lakeside Green basketball team climbing out of a travel bus. Theo hopped off toward the end of the line, chatting with GJ.

I took a deep breath, trying to calm down my heart rate. But there was something about just seeing Theo that had a way of making my senses go completely out of control. It was like I had to resist the urge to touch her, to leap into her arms.

The sliding doors opened automatically for the team, and when they looked over at us, they flashed easy smiles of acknowledgement. I didn't know if any of them recognized me, but if they did, they were doing a decent job of keeping it quiet.

GJ saw us before Theo. She nudged her and pointed over at us, making Theo look up in our direction. When Theo's eyes landed on mine, the world seemed to stop for a second. She broke out into a smile and walked over my way.

That definitely caught the attention of her teammates, who turned to look.

"Is that the girl?" one of them whispered, and I knew that the gossip definitely hadn't just stayed online.

It also seemed to catch the attention of Allie, who was blushing so hard that her face was red all the way up to her hairline.

"Hey," Theo greeted me. It was the first time we'd been in the same place since we'd kissed, the moment I'd been mentally preparing myself for days. I was ready for it to be awkward or tense or weird, because that was how it had been immediately following our kiss.

But instead, all I felt was an intense desire to kiss her again right here and tell her that I'd missed her. Because it was true—I did.

"Hey," I said. She looked so good in her team-affiliated athleisure that I almost couldn't look at her. Her smell was still the same, so she must've brought whatever shampoo or body wash she used back home. I wanted to burrow my face in her neck and live there forever.

"How was your drive over? I'm glad you could make it."

"McCall, come on," an older man said, probably one of the assistant coaches, waving her down the hall toward the hotel rooms.

"Sorry, one second," Theo said, and he gave her a knowing look. I was sure the coach had navigated all kinds of interpersonal relationships—people sneaking out to see their girlfriends, overbearing families who won't leave their kid's side. I was a tiny bit flattered I fell into the category of people he was wary of. I would never aspire to be a distraction, but I kind of liked that I seemed like I could be one. I had to mean enough to Theo for that to be the case.

"It was good," I said.

"Quiet," Iris agreed, and I remembered she was there for the first time since making eye contact with Theo.

"Did you need anything for your room?" Allie suddenly asked, and we all turned to look at her. "Towels? More pillows? We want to make sure your stay is comfortable."

I could tell immediately from her expression what was going on. She wasn't trying to edge me out—there was no bad will toward me; if anything, I wasn't sure she even really saw me anymore, now that Theo was there. Her approach to flirting was about as indirect as it could be, but I knew what it was.

I was surprised by my urge to grab Theo's hand. Whereas before, I'd almost be relieved when I saw someone flirting with the person I was with in public, I felt the need to pull Theo away as quickly as possible. It turned out the one time I didn't appreciate a woman taking charge and shooting her shot with someone was when it came to Theo.

"Oh, no. Things are great, thank you," Theo said, completely oblivious. She turned to her team members who were slowly filtering back to their rooms. I had a feeling based on their pace that they were hanging around to see what was going on between me and Theo. "You guys need anything?"

They all shook their heads, a chorus of *all goods* ringing out through the otherwise empty hotel lobby.

Theo turned back to me. "Coming to the game tomorrow?"

"Of course," I said.

"I know I'm technically not supposed to be rooting for you but I am," Allie said, stepping in again.

"I appreciate that," Theo said. It was clear just how often she had interactions like this based on how easily she responded. She sounded genuine and polite but distant. I respected it, but I would also cry into my pillow if she ever spoke to me in that tone. She turned to me and Iris again. "All good for going up? What room are you in?"

"213," Allie offered before Iris or I could answer.

"Thank you," Theo said and reached out to take my and Iris's bags from our hands. The three of us walked down the hall toward the elevators. "I'll be back in my room soon," she said as we passed the assistant coach from earlier.

"You're lucky I trust you," he responded. "I'm keeping my eye on the clock."

"For sure."

We walked down the hall to the elevator. Most of the other team members had dispersed by now, so the hotel was quiet and still.

"Intense," I said as I pressed the button to go up.

"Games are serious business," Theo said, which somehow felt like a simplification of how good her team was and how much money I was sure the school pumped into them.

The elevator dinged and we went inside, Theo in the middle of me and Iris.

"I think you might've been her gay awakening," I said, hoping she'd get what I meant, as the elevator doors closed. Theo laughed but didn't say anything else; it was stupid how relieved I was she didn't bring her up or want to talk more about her. She'd clearly just been another passing interaction for Theo, one of a thousand fans she ran into when she was out.

I pressed the button to go to the second floor, brushing against Theo's firm torso in the process.

When we made it to the second floor, I realized our hotel room door was about ten steps away from the elevator. I tried not to be disappointed I had to say goodbye to Theo already for the night.

Iris looked between me and Theo. "I'm going to check out the room. Make sure there aren't bedbugs or whatever. Thanks for carrying our stuff," she said. She took our bags from Theo and unlocked the door, a satisfying *click* sounding out as it opened.

"Yeah, no problem," Theo said.

Iris disappeared into our hotel room, and the door shut behind her.

"She's going to be listening from inside, I hope you know," I said.

Theo laughed again, and all I could think about was kissing her. I missed her lips, her body against mine. I hadn't thought about kissing anyone else since kissing her—I hadn't thought about anyone else, *period,* since we'd met. I barely remembered I'd kissed anyone else in my life before her.

There was life before Theo and life after Theo, and the life after Theo included zero memories of exes or flings or crushes. I knew with full confidence I'd never felt this way about anyone before.

"What are you worried she'll overhear?" Theo challenged with a playful smile.

I smiled back at her, wondering if there was any way at all we could sneak in some kind of quickie in the hallway without getting arrested.

"Thank you for coming," she said, her voice lowered.

"I'm looking forward to seeing you play."

"I hope I don't suck."

I snorted. "I don't think that's possible for you."

We were so close together that I wondered if we were going to kiss again—if it was appropriate to and if that was what we both wanted. I wasn't going to go for kissing her first on two separate occasions back-to-back, but it was tempting.

I would if she asked.

"I'll look for you in the stands," Theo said, and it felt almost as good as being kissed. A warmth spread at my core that didn't just feel like a carnal desire for her to fuck me—that was there too—but something more.

"Okay," I said, because I didn't know what else there was to say.

We lingered by the door of my hotel room for I don't know how much longer. Time passed so slowly, but also too quickly. I didn't know if I should bring up the kiss or not, and I didn't know if I wanted to.

"I'll see you tomorrow," Theo finally said, and the weight of crushing disappointment fell on my chest.

"Okay," I said, even though all I wanted to do was ask her to stay. Maybe I needed to take it as a sign that she wasn't actually interested. But Theo—grounded, practical, kind-natured Theo—didn't strike me as someone who played games. Everything she did was with thoughtful consideration. There was always a chance she just wasn't as impulsive as I was, that kissing again right now—just before a game and without talking about our first kiss—was a bad idea.

But it didn't mean I didn't still want her to do it.

"Okay," she said and started toward the stairwell. She glanced back once and then twice, and I offered only a small wave each time. It wasn't until she disappeared down the stairs that I finally went into my hotel room.

When I opened the door, Iris jumped back and leaned against the desk nearby, her phone in her hand but not lit up. She pretended to look down at it.

"I'm not even going to bother giving you the scoop because I know you were listening," I said.

"I'm nosy!" she said. "I'm guessing no kiss. Unless it was just like, really quiet and you didn't acknowledge it at all."

"No, no kiss," I said with a sigh and then threw myself down on the hotel bed. "We didn't talk about the last kiss, either. I don't really know what's going on."

"It seems like it's going okay, though," Iris said. "I mean, she invited you here. She acknowledged you were here. She lingered by the doorway. That doesn't feel like someone who's running from you or the possibility of whatever you guys might have." She walked to the bathroom and turned the water on. "Plus, she carried our bags," she said, raising her voice over the sound of running water.

"She's a nice person," I said.

Iris stepped out of the bathroom to look at me, shaking out her hair from her claw clip in the process. "Okay? And?"

"Maybe she's just doing all of this because she's a nice person. You know? Like letting me down easy."

"I know I don't have as much experience with dating as you do, but that would be really weird. And out of character for her. And also just generally probably not what she's doing. I know how I act when someone is pursuing me and I'm not interested, and it's definitely not hovering by a door, seeming like you want to kiss them."

"I don't know—"

"Look, I'm going to be honest with you. I care about your well-being probably more than you care about your own. If I didn't think there was a chance Theo wanted you, and you doing all of this was setting yourself up for embarrassment, I wouldn't agree to it. I'm not just excited that you're agreeing to go to games with me. I'm doing all of this with you because I think you and Theo like each other and need a little bit of handholding to get there."

"I don't need hand holding—"

"Dude, you like *just* finally admitted that you had a crush on her."

I was quiet for a moment. "Okay, fair."

"I'm going to shower, but no more spiraling out while I'm gone," she said.

"Yeah, yeah," I mumbled to myself. I rolled on my side and went on my phone, hoping I could distract myself from the crushing doubt that Theo might not actually be into me.

Because I was nothing if not predictable, my distraction from Theo ended up including more Theo. She'd posted earlier today promoting the game and sharing new photos from practices and travel. Her pictures were so casual—she didn't take pictures of herself and usually just shared whatever the team photographer took of her.

In one shot, she was laughing with GJ on the court. Her face was lit up, her hair pulled into a ponytail. My heart ached looking it—the joy in her smile, the line of her jaw. It took everything in me to not trace my finger along my screen as if it replaced actually touching her.

Iris got out of the shower not much later, and I took her place in the bathroom, turning the water up as hot as I could handle to wash our road trip from my skin. The entire time I was in the shower, Theo was floating around in the back of my mind. She was mixed in there along with remembering I'd left a load of laundry in the dryer at my and Iris's apartment, and that I needed to follow up with professors about graduate school recommendation letters. I'd find myself thinking about where she'd fit into the schedule, thinking of stories I wanted to tell her, and questions I still wanted to ask her about herself.

When I got out, I toweled off my hair and body and then pulled on my softest pajamas. I curled up in the queen bed next to Iris's and relished in the soft hotel sheets.

"I can't believe how big these beds feel," she said, practically making snow angels in her bed.

"I can come snuggle in next to you, make it feel a little smaller," I teased.

"Absolutely not. One luxury to being single is that I sleep alone and always have the whole bed to myself," Iris said. "That almost replaces the comforting caress of a man."

"*Comforting caress of a man* just gave me hives," I said, and Iris cackled.

I readjusted my pillow, and Iris shut the light off. "If you stay up all night spiraling out, I'll know," Iris warned, her voice traveling through the dark.

"I'm not going to," I said, even though the odds of that were likely. I didn't know what happened to my cool girl, emotionally detached demeanor, but I was missing it deeply. I didn't even remember who I'd been before Theo.

Iris responded with a skeptical *mhm* before rolling over. I laid on my back, staring up at the ceiling and playing out what the game might look like tomorrow. And then I thought about how Allie—and other girls like her—were going to be there. Jealousy zipped through me, tightening my stomach and making my heart race.

I nearly groaned. I couldn't believe I'd become the kind of person who got worked up about things like that. Theo had never given any indication that she was seeing anyone else or was some kind of major player.

And even besides that, there was no reason to assume we'd be exclusive when all we'd done so far was kiss. Once. Modestly. And then never talked about it.

My phone vibrated from next to me, and I picked it up, turning my brightness all the way down so I didn't disturb Iris.

It's so weird knowing you're here but not being able to see you, Theo wrote. It was like she'd known I was thinking about her. But then again, I thought about her all the time. It wasn't so much kismet as it was incredibly probable. It would be harder for her to text me during a time when I *wasn't* thinking about her.

I read the text again and then again, memorizing it so I could see it even when my eyes were closed.

I would say you should sneak out to see me, but I think that one coach would actually kill me, I wrote back.

He definitely would, she quickly wrote back. Her text bubbles popped up again, telling me she was sending a follow-up. *He can't stop me from saying something to you after the game tomorrow, though. Even just for a minute.*

I'd take the minute, I wrote back without thinking. As soon as it sent, I realized how explicit that felt. "Oh my god," I whisper-groaned to myself. I pressed my palms to my face as if Theo were able to see me. I had to be the most pathetic person alive.

My phone vibrated again, and I looked at it with one eye closed, scared to see what her response was.

I'd give it to you, she wrote back, and I suddenly felt a little better and a little less pathetic. It didn't completely erase the feeling, though. *I'll see you tomorrow. Goodnight, Maya.*

I could hear her voice as I read her text, see her face as she said it. *Maya.* The way my name sounded in her low, steady voice. The way her lips turned up in a smile every time she hit the second *a* in my name.

My finger hovered over the text, debating on if I should react to it or not. I just wrote back *Goodnight, Theo* instead and left it at that.

When I put my phone down and closed my eyes, I imagined Theo in bed next to me, her arm draped over my waist.

Iris and I burned most of the next day away by driving into the nearest major city. The only item on our list was to get Iris something from Swig, which was tastier than I thought it would be. We wandered between thrift stores and bookstores until it was time to head back.

Theo and I stayed in touch as much as we could. We'd kept up a rhythm of texting on game days, usually up until the minute she couldn't have her phone on her anymore at all. The team was kept busy, so I didn't hear from her as much, but I appreciated that she tried.

Iris and I headed back to the hotel toward the late afternoon and got ready for the game. We pregamed lightly with canned mixed drinks we'd brought from home and then Ubered to the game, a whole six minutes down the road.

"There's a good number of people here," Iris said, sounding surprised when we pulled into the parking lot. "I knew the game was sold out, but I guess I didn't imagine how hectic it'd feel."

"Everyone's coming to see Theo," our driver said from the front seat. He looked at us through the rearview mirror. "I'm sure you guys already understand, though," he said and nodded to our shirts.

"Do the games usually look like this?" Iris asked.

He shook his head. "The girls haven't had decent odds of making it to the finals in years. People only come when there's someone in town worth seeing."

I looked around, trying to conceptualize what the parking lot usually looked like based on what he was saying. I'd gotten so used to the buzz around Theo that I assumed every game looked like they did back home—almost overwhelmingly busy, every seat packed, everyone excited to be there. The same energy had been carried over here.

But based on Iris's expression, this wasn't how things normally looked.

The driver pulled into the rideshare lane. "Enjoy the game, ladies."

"Thank you," Iris and I said in unison as we got out of the car.

I hugged my arms around myself. The arena here was smaller than back home, but seemed just as crowded.

"We get to sit in the normal seats this time, no student section," Iris said as we approached the entrance. "I got us close to the court, though."

"I'll only accept courtside."

Iris's lips turned up in a smile. "I'm impressed you know what that means."

"I've been working on it."

We got our tickets scanned by a bored looking college student and then headed into the arena. It was laid out differently from back home, and the school colors were different here. But the number of Lakeside Green jerseys with the number *25* on the back was the same.

"I didn't realize so many people traveled for away games," I said.

"They usually don't," she said. "And these aren't just Lakeside fans—they're fans from everywhere. People love Theo. It doesn't matter if she's playing at home or not."

"What do you mean?"

"You'll see," Iris said and walked us to the entrance of our section. She followed the row numbers until she found our seats, about ten rows up from the court and right on the half-court line..

"These are good seats," I said.

Iris playfully flipped her hair over her shoulder. "I have my ways," she said.

I looked out over the crowd that was filing into their seats. There was a mix of faces—families, older couples, college students. Everyone looked so happy to be there. I'd never really been exposed to a community like this before outside of starting to go to basketball games. It was sweet to see that Lakeside Green wasn't unique.

The teams were still warming up on the court and I scanned through the team to find Theo. The whole team was warming up in matching outfits—long sleeve Coyotes t-shirts and matching athletic shorts. But then I spotted Theo, dribbling and shooting down the court.

She was so hot, even from a distance, that it made me sick. I still had a hard time reconciling that she was the same person I was texting and talking to. On the court, she felt almost larger than life. The basketball player who argued with refs and threw elbows and kept beating record after record.

"There's your girl," Iris teased, nudging me with her shoulder.

I smiled a little bit, wishing there was some way of being able to get her attention from all the way over here. But the arena was big enough for thousands of people—she wasn't going to know where to look or how to find me. It wasn't like back home where Iris and I always sat in the student section.

The teams slowed down on warming up and huddled together before running off the court. I settled in, now understanding the rhythm of the game enough to know when it was about to start.

When the announcer started with Lakeside Green, I noticed that not as many people were booing the away team as they did when we were home. The student section was noisy, and some pockets of fans in the crowd, but that was about it.

When Theo ran out, however, what felt like the entire arena started cheering—which was very much like home. It seemed like most of the seats were filled by Lakeside Green fans or people who were just excited to see Theo play in person. No one was expecting an upset.

People were just as excited to see her here as they were in Colorado. Fans held up signs around the stands, sharing how much they loved her, making plays off of her name. One read, *All I wanted for my birthday was to see Theo McCall.* I saw more than a few signs referencing *three-o*.

"People really love her," I said over the roar of the crowd.

"It's everywhere," Iris said in between clapping and cheering for the Lakeside players. "Every game has been like this. She'd gotten close to selling out every home game last year, but she did it this year. Same with her away games, too." She turned and looked at me. "I know you don't know enough about basketball to know any differently, but this is big time. It doesn't always look like this."

I smiled a little bit, admittedly proud of Theo. I didn't know if I knew her well enough to have any right to feel that way, but it was true.

After tipping off, the game was off to the races. I was still getting used to the plays, what was allowed and what wasn't, what player wore what number. But I could hear Theo's voice in my head breaking the plays down for me as I watched. It was making more sense than it had before.

Theo went for a three, and when it swished in, the cheerleaders and her teammates on the bench went wild. Iris cheered, too, along with most of the crowd in the arena. Even Theo let herself celebrate for a second, but the moment passed quickly as the game rolled on.

"What was that?" I asked. People normally got excited about her threes, but it was so early in the game that it couldn't possibly mean that much. And it'd been an exciting shot, but nothing she hadn't done before.

"She just broke the record for most points scored by a player in their college career," Iris said. "*Ever*. Between men's and women's." She turned and looked at me, a coy smile at her lips. "What, that never came up during your internet stalking?"

I tried to wrap my head around it but I couldn't. I just shook my head, unable to believe it was Theo who was doing all of that. I understood it but I also didn't. She was just the girl from a party, the girl who talked to me for hours on my couch.

But also, apparently, *the* women's basketball player.

The game flew by. Despite the Uber driver's words about the team not having finals potential in years, they were putting up a decent fight against the Coyotes. One of the players had been able to get a few successful blocks on Theo, which even Theo seemed a little impressed by.

But by the last few minutes of the fourth quarter, it was obvious the Coyotes were going to swing it. When the final buzzer sounded off, the players lined up for handshakes and post-game interviews and Iris practically yanked me down to the barricade between us and the court. After Theo wrapped up talking to the reporter on the court, she ran back to celebrate with her team.

Iris started waving to get Theo's attention, and Theo glanced over. When she realized we were standing there, she broke into a smile and jogged over. Even from a distance, I could see that she was drenched in sweat. But something about her was so effortlessly hot, even immediately following a game. When she realized security was separating us from the court and the court-side seats below, she waved for us to come down, and security let us pass.

"Thank you," Iris said, unable to hide the grin on her face at the special treatment.

Down at the court, Theo pulled me into a hug that nearly lifted me off the ground. I squealed and laughed, not at all expecting that reaction.

"Congrats on the record," I said, still laughing. I knew right then how much I liked her because her sweaty uniform against my skin was deeply unpleasant—but I also would've stayed right there forever if I could've.

When she went to put me down, she pressed her lips to my cheek. She was so close to my lips that I couldn't tell if it was intentional that she'd kissed my cheek or if she'd just missed.

Either way, I felt the sensation throughout my entire body. It was all so much at once—the thrill of being here, Theo wanting to celebrate with me, the privilege of coming down courtside to celebrate all because I knew her.

Even after Theo pulled away from our hug, we hovered physically near each other.

"I think that was convincing enough," I joked, feeling an intense need to play off the interaction. "The fans will love that." I cringed a little bit. I was definitely going to be overthinking that tonight.

"Thanks for coming," Theo said, and I decided not to think too much into how Theo wasn't playing along with the fake girlfriend jokes anymore. I didn't have it in me to guess what that meant.

"I can't believe you didn't tell me about the record!" I said, punching her lightly in the arm. I brushed off thoughts of how firm her muscles were and how badly I wanted to run my hands over her muscles.

"It never came up," Theo said casually and then draped her arm over my shoulders.

"You smell so bad." I laughed, ducking out from under her.

Theo turned and chased me, nearly picking me up in her arms again as I laughed. When we turned around, Theo suddenly stopped and stood up straight.

When I looked over, I saw a white middle-aged couple looking at the two of us curiously, an amused smile on both of their faces.

"Hi, honey," the woman said.

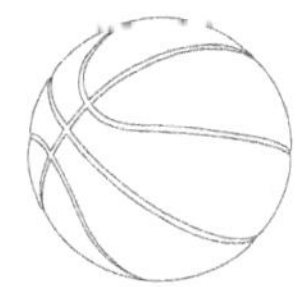

Chapter 18

THEO

My parents had never met anyone I'd dated before, mostly because I'd never had a girlfriend.

There was always basketball to worry about. If I didn't have time to make it to parties, I definitely didn't have the time to maintain any kind of stable, consistent relationship. And more than anything, I didn't really *want* to. There was no point in them meeting anyone if I didn't like them enough to make the time for them between practices and games.

But because the universe had a sick sense of humor, they were meeting the girl I was in a super unclear, very public, not-quite-relationship with.

"Hey," I said, stepping away from Maya. It took me a second to even process that they were here. The embarrassment of feeling like I was just caught fooling around with someone by my parents came first; then, came the realization that they were standing in front of me. I walked over to them, pulling both of my parents into a family hug. They were both about my height, so it was easy to pull them together. "What are you guys doing here? When did you get here?"

"We flew in last night. We weren't going to miss you breaking your record," Mom said.

"We're hands off with you, but not that hands off," Dad joked.

My parents had always struggled a little bit with finding the sweet spot between supporting me and being there for me, and giving me the independence I liked. I'd always been someone capable of figuring most of my own shit out. I kept myself motivated when it came to playing, and kept up my grades so I would never have to sit out. My parents didn't have to do much with me. If anything, they probably wished I would do less.

"We wanted to surprise you but I guess you also have a surprise for us." Mom glanced over at Maya, who was talking to Iris and looking just about anywhere but my family.

"It's..."

"You didn't want to tell us you had a girlfriend?" Mom asked, dropping her voice so she didn't completely embarrass me.

I scratched my neck. "Um."

She shook her head, her round cheeks lifting with her smile. "Always keeping us on our toes. Do we get to meet her, or are you going to insist on keeping her a secret from us from ten feet away?"

"She's not my girlfriend," I said, the gentlest way I could think of to say no to them. I was not emotionally prepared for anything of that sort. If anything, I was still trying to catch up from the fact that I'd very publicly kissed Maya on the cheek without thinking about how there were literally thousands of people around us.

"Oh, is this one of those, like, situation-things. You know?" Dad looked at my mom for help. "Like, the casual...I can't remember the name. Seeing each other but not putting a label on it. The kids are doing it these days. No one wants to be serious."

"I'm going to be sick," I said.

"She's pretty," Mom said.

"She is," I agreed.

Mom stood in place for a moment before leaning forward and pulling me into another hug. "I missed you, sweetie."

"I missed you, too," I said.

She stepped away again. "Can we catch you at some point tonight? We'll buy you a drink to celebrate your record."

"Yeah, that sounds great. I gotta meet up with the team and shower but I'll find you before we have our team dinner."

"Okay," Mom said and looked over at Maya. "It was nice to meet you."

Maya waved back, her cheeks red. I wanted to dig myself a hole and hide in it. This was the exact opposite of cool and casual. I couldn't think of a faster way to scare off someone who didn't do commitment like a run-in with parents.

"I'll find you in a little bit," I said to my parents and then hurried to meet my team, who were all waiting for me. Fortunately, they were being patient with me, most likely because of the new record. They'd also been celebrating just as hard as I had, every success of mine feeling like a success for the entire team.

I glanced back at Maya before walking through the tunnel and mouthed, *Sorry*. Maya smiled: *It's okay*.

As GJ threw her arm around my neck, pulling me into a tight hug that felt more like a chokehold, all I could think about was that I hoped everything with Maya really would be fine.

As excited as I was to go out with my parents that night, I felt torn in two directions—wanting to be with my team and Maya, and wanting to be with them while I had them.

We went over all of the usual things, like how retirement was treating them, how the old widow across the street was doing, how my classes were. It all felt so grown-up, like I'd suddenly transformed into not being a child overnight.

It also made me realize I craved their time and having them around more than I missed actually hanging out with them, which was one of the more bittersweet parts of growing up. There was only so much I could talk to my parents about and joke around with them about before it skirted the line of making things weird.

After long hugs and promises that I would see them when I played in Michigan, my parents headed upstairs to their room from the hotel bar and I Ubered back to my hotel.

"You should let Maya know that we're going out," GJ said when I got back. We had a small window between now and hotel curfew and everyone was planning on taking full advantage of it.

"Do you think everyone would be cool with that?" I asked. "Since it's usually just the team."

"It's only ever just the team because everyone else is single," GJ said. "It'll be totally fine. I think everyone's curious to meet her. She's like the first lady of Lakeside Green women's basketball right now."

"I don't know if I'd say that."

"Like, no one on the team dates, but especially not you. It's a big moment for all of us," GJ said. "I was starting to think I'd be attending your wedding once we were both a million years old. Or you'd be one of those famous people who fall off the face of the earth after a historic run in sports history. The recluse who never gets married and just watches basketball highlights from her mega mansion in the middle of nowhere."

"I don't think I like the expectations you have of my future, actually." I buttoned up the bottom few buttons of my shirt and smoothed down my hair.

"Text her," GJ said, cupping her hands to her mouth like she was speaking into a megaphone.

"Okay, okay," I said.

I pulled out my phone and pulled up Maya's contact. Our last interaction had been from last night in a moment of vulnerability. I felt the tiniest bit embarrassed by it—*oh, it's so weird that you're here but I can't see you, I'm a pathetic loser who can't stop thinking about you*—but after how the game had gone, I didn't know how to feel anymore. And honestly, she'd been the one to kiss me first. We might've not talked about it, but it wasn't completely out of line for me to think there was a chance—even if it was slight.

We're going out tonight if you and Iris want to join us. No bars because pretty much the whole team is underage, but you're welcome to come, I wrote. I sent it immediately, knowing that GJ was hovering nearby and the last thing I needed was her teasing me over how many times I redrafted texts to Maya.

Maya responded quickly. *We're in.*

See you in the lobby in fifteen.

"She's coming," I said, and put my phone in my pocket. I smoothed out my clothes and cleared my throat. The nerves I'd felt around texting Maya were turning into adrenaline instead. I wanted to see her, and the sooner I could see her, the better.

We checked to make sure we had our wallets on us, and GJ got a last-minute charge on her phone that was somehow on fourteen percent. When we were only a few minutes out from our designated meeting time in the lobby, we headed downstairs. We jogged the steps from the fourth floor, racing each other down.

As we pushed open the stairwell door and started our walk to the lobby, we were breathless and laughing. But when I saw that Mags was standing with Maya and Iris, my laughter cut out immediately. I walked over to them. GJ trailed behind, and I already knew I was going to get an earful of teasing from her tonight. But it was worth it—I wasn't letting Mags anywhere near Maya.

"Hey," I greeted them.

"I can't believe you've been hiding Maya from us," Mags said. I could see in her body language that she was intrigued.

"I haven't been hiding her," I said and stepped protectively next to Maya. I resisted the urge to put my arm around her.

"I'd keep her away from us, too," Mags admitted with an upturned smile, specifically in my direction. I resisted rolling my eyes. I'd gotten used to putting up with Mags' shit over the years we'd played together, but I didn't like that she was pulling Maya into the middle of it. Maya wasn't someone for us to compete over; I actually liked her.

I didn't return her smile. "I think Gemma was looking for you."

"Right." Mags looked between us. Iris and GJ had stepped to the side and were looking over curiously. "Nice to meet you, Maya."

When Mags walked away, my blood pressure leveled out, and embarrassment replaced the annoyance and possessiveness I'd been feeling. But before I could explain myself to Maya, GJ started herding everyone to the front door of the hotel.

"Alright, everyone's here. Let's get going. The place is basically across the street," GJ said. "Walk with a buddy, hold hands—"

"Thanks, Mom," Nia said from the back. Nia and GJ had always worked well together. I had a feeling Nia—as the other person on the team who was patient with GJ—was going to replace me as GJ's right hand when I graduated.

"We all know it's daddy, but whatever," GJ said, and I snorted.

I gently brushed my hand against Maya's lower back to gesture for her to walk ahead of me. The team headed down the sidewalk carefully, all of us bundled up against the cold and walking in pairs more to gossip than anything.

Everyone around us was chatting, but Maya and I didn't say anything to each other. We walked in silence, only brushing against each other occasionally as we walked.

I'd definitely fucked up. Maya definitely thought I was some possessive asshole who wasn't going to let her ever talk to anyone else. Maybe she thought that I'd intentionally called my parents down and set up for them to meet.

It was the least cool, least casual combination of events I could ever put upon someone who didn't do commitment. It was the exact opposite way of approaching winning her over. Nothing about that was going to charm her. I was surprised she hadn't already thought of some way to get herself out of this.

Maybe she was waiting on a third strike. She was going to see if I did anything else stupid tonight and then make her decision based on that. By next week, I'd stop hearing from her completely, and then a few weeks from now, I'd run into her flirting with other people at parties.

Or it was too late for a third strike. There'd been so many other things I'd done today that I'd forgotten I'd accidentally almost kissed her on the lips publicly.

I winced. I was having a historically bad run. I didn't even usually rag on myself like that when it came to dating—I *knew* I was hot and cool—but I felt like I really deserved it tonight.

I tried to think of something to ease the silence between us but I couldn't think of anything. Everything I wanted to say felt like the dumbest thing imaginable.

Fortunately, we made it to the restaurant not much later. We'd settled on the diner across the street. Almost definitely, some of the girls had snuck in flasks to spike their coffees and juices, but it was the safest bet that wouldn't make our coaches blow a fuse. We only got so much unsupervised time during away games, and it was because I was good at keeping them on a tight leash.

As the team flooded inside, I grabbed Maya and held her outside with me. When GJ saw that we weren't going in yet, she gave me a thumbs up and walked Iris along with the rest of the team.

The door swung shut, and quiet settled over us. Us not speaking to each other felt suddenly way more prominent—but it also gave me a second to collect my thoughts and think of something to say to her.

"I'm sorry," I finally said, practically spitting the words out.

"For what?" Maya asked, sounding genuinely surprised. It was a relief that it didn't seem like she'd been waiting for some kind of apology and explanation from me.

"Just...everything. I didn't realize my parents were going to be there, I swear," I said. "And then..."

The kiss from earlier lingered between the two of us. I thought back on how it felt to have her in my arms again. It'd been entirely by accident, but I wasn't sure I completely regretted it.

"It's okay," she said.

"And I'm sorry for being weird about Mags. I'd pretend that didn't happen, but I know it did. I'm not trying to be weird—"

Maya stood up on her toes and put her arms around my neck to kiss me. It happened so quickly I didn't realize what was happening until it was. As soon as my brain processed her lips on mine, I pulled her in closer and deepened our kiss. Even though it wasn't our first kiss, it felt like the first one. All of the others had been experimental or accidental or without thinking. But this was something else.

"It's okay," she said softly and casually as if she didn't just make me weak at the knees. She dropped back down onto her heels but I let my hands linger on her waist. "I was weird about Allie."

"Allie?"

"The hotel receptionist," she admitted.

"Oh, she's just a fan," I said.

"That is really cute that you genuinely believe that." She glanced inside. "I also don't think you have to worry about Mags."

"I know, she's just always finding new ways of—"

"Oh, no. I believe that. I just meant I *really* don't think you have to worry about her in that way," she said and nodded inside.

I turned to look and spotted Mags sitting with Gemma. They were laughing together, leaning toward each other. They'd always been close—the teammates who were immediate best friends, always teasing each other and always in the same place. I'd thought of them as similar to me and GJ.

But looking at them through fresh eyes, I realized maybe Maya was onto something. They looked more like me and Maya than me and GJ.

"Oh," I said, and Maya laughed.

She laced her fingers through mine. "Are we good?" she asked quietly. It was a simple question, a vague one, but it carried so much weight and uncertainty. I knew exactly what she was asking.

"Yeah, we're good," I said, and I resisted the urge to scoop her up into my arms again. That was the most confirmation I'd gotten about her wanting anything of meaning with me. I was willing to take it as slow as we needed to go, but I wasn't going to pretend that it gave me a hope that maybe it wouldn't take as long as I'd thought to win her over.

I looked at her and then back at the diner. "I'm not sure I'm that hungry, actually," I said.

Maya's eyes flickered with curiosity. "You know, I don't think I am either."

"Want to walk back with me?"

She nodded. "Yes."

Maya and I walked back to the hotel together and made it back to the room I was sharing with GJ before we heard anything from anyone. I was about to unlock the door when my phone buzzed.

"GJ texted," I said and turned my phone so Maya could see. All she'd written was *Where'd you go??*

She snorted. "Iris texted me too. She was checking my location and could see that I was back at the hotel."

"I'm sure they can tell what's going on," I said, and then my face flushed. I didn't like the implication of that, as if us walking back here meant that anything at all was going to happen. I'd been *thinking* about it and the vibe was definitely there, but that didn't mean anything. We should probably try at least kissing in private for the first time before we aspire to more.

I unlocked the hotel room door and we stepped inside. Maya smiled as she looked over the room.

"I think I know which side is yours," she said.

"What do you mean?"

She gestured to the two sides of the room. One was spotless and one was less so—clothes draped on any surface, the bed un-made, the suitcase half open on the floor with clothes hanging out.

I laughed. "Okay, fair enough."

"Do you keep your room like this at your apartment, too, or is it a travel thing?"

"Everywhere. I've always been neat."

Maya nodded and then, as if speaking to herself, said, "Hot."

My phone vibrated with another message from GJ: *You have until curfew. Have fun you crazy kids.*

I blushed, putting my phone face down on the desk near me. Maya was too busy looking at the room to notice.

I looked at her, just the two of us alone in the hotel room, and was suddenly hit by the reality of what we were doing. I could feel how badly I wanted her—it'd never been a secret—but now that we were here, it was like I'd never touched a woman before.

But maybe that was true to some extent. I'd never touched a woman like Maya before. I'd never liked someone this much before, never wanted someone this badly before. It really did feel like the first time.

Maya glanced at me, and the weight of us being alone in the same room as my bed settled in the silence between us.

She turned to look at me. "Do you want to kiss me or should I do it?"

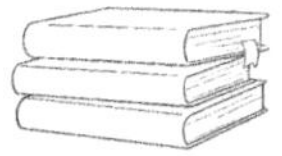

Chapter 19

MAYA

I hadn't felt so nervous going into sex since my first time as a teenager. That had felt like a lifetime ago; I'd learned so much about myself in that time. What I wanted, what I liked, what I didn't like.

Unlike my first time, I wasn't nervous that it would be good. I also wasn't nervous about having to navigate sex with a man—something I'd gone into at sixteen as if it was an item to check off a checklist—or my first time with a woman, something I'd gone into much less reluctantly when I was seventeen.

Instead, I was nervous because sex this time was with Theo. And with Theo came feelings. And I'd never had that wrapped up in sex before.

Theo approached me, an amused smile on her lips. "I've wanted to kiss you since the moment we met," she said. "That hasn't gone away."

Butterflies went berserk in my stomach as she leaned down and pressed her lips to mine. This was the fourth time we'd kissed or almost kissed—not that I was counting—and it was different and new from the other times.

We were alone this time. Really alone. No crowd, no cameras, no party. Just us in a hotel room with the heat blasting to compete with the freezing cold temperatures outside.

Sex had always been about going through the motions for me. I was someone who understood the mission at hand and what we needed to do to get there. It was no-frills; I never wanted to drag it out longer than it needed to be.

But with Theo, I savored every second of it. When her hands found my face, pulling me in closer to deepen our kiss, I really thought I might stumble back like a lovestruck cartoon character. I leaned into her, using her to hold myself up so I didn't fall on my ass.

We matched each other exactly. Our kisses were the same tempo. There was none of the tedious work of having to find a way that worked for the parties involved, making sure no one was making the kiss too wet or too dry or too forceful or too half-hearted.

When I opened my mouth and Theo followed my lead, I nearly moaned from need. Theo had barely touched me, and I already knew I was soaking wet. I'd been waiting for this exact moment with her for what felt like forever. I'd been so, *so* incredibly patient. We both had, considering it'd been obvious how badly we'd both wanted each other from the very beginning.

I pushed her down onto the bed and straddled her, only for Theo to turn us over so I was underneath her. I would be lying if I said it wasn't a turn-on how swiftly she'd been able to do it; her muscles really were no joke. There wasn't a doubt in my mind that she probably *could* bench me if she really wanted to. Iris would be proud.

I moaned, squirming from the sensation of her lips against my neck. She trailed downwards from my neck to my ear, taking her time. When she slid her knee between my legs, I gasped and gripped onto her, my nails digging into her back.

"Oh, *Theo*." We hadn't taken a single item of clothing off between the two of us, and I was certain she could get me to finish right there. Other than the occasional dream about Theo, I'd been uncharacteristically good for her. I'd waited. I'd let myself sit with how badly I wanted her. It turned out it was true that anticipation and being forced to wait did a hell of a lot for someone's libido.

Theo snaked her hand under my shirt, gripping my hip, before trailing upwards. Her tongue slipped up my neck toward my ear, and my back arched.

I held her close to me as her fingers found my nipples. She squeezed the hardened mounds between her fingertips, taking her time with them. Her hands were gentle and firm at the same time—I wanted her to touch me forever.

"Get this off of me," I said breathlessly and Theo sat up, peeling my shirt over my head effortlessly.

She pushed me back down into the pillows, and I let her continue on, wanting her to touch and kiss every single inch of my skin. She took her delicious time, as if we didn't technically have a curfew and she didn't have a roommate who was going to want to come back eventually.

Theo trailed kisses down from my lips to my breasts, moving her fingers over my nipples. I squeezed my legs to her torso, gently rocking against her for any kind of relief. The tension in me was a balloon that was ready to burst.

My pants were pulled away soon after, leaving me in only my underwear. I was suddenly so grateful that I'd actually packed—and worn—the hot ones I had stuffed in my dresser. I'd initially felt stupid for bringing something so sexy to what was literally a road trip to a college basketball game, but the stars had really aligned.

"Do you want me to eat you out?" she asked as she moved further down, kissing from the fullness of my breasts to the flat expanse of my stomach. Her voice was as smooth as honey, thick and slow with desire. I'd never understood the phrase *talk me through it* until now. I never wanted Theo to stop.

"Yes," I begged breathlessly. "*Yes*. Please."

She kissed from my left hip to my right and then moved down, lower and lower. She spread my legs and readjusted so her head was between them. I looked at her—beautiful, perfect

Theo—who looked back at me with so much lust in her eyes I was surprised she was able to wait even one more second to make me cum.

I gripped onto the sheets as she moved from my hips to my thighs. She readjusted up toward the insides of my knees first, teasing me. And then she inched her way back, moving patiently over my body. As she got closer to the spot between the legs—the spot I was so desperate for her to touch—she traced her tongue over my upper thigh, sending a shockwave of pleasure to my core.

She only kissed my slit through my underwear at first but the feeling was enough to make me moan out desperately with zero concern for if the walls were thin. I would've been embarrassed, but I wasn't—anyone else in my position, with Theo McCall doing everything in her power to make sure I had the time of my life, would've reacted exactly the same way.

"Does that feel good?" Theo asked from between my thighs. I could tell from her tone that she wasn't asking because she needed the confirmation. It was starting to look like smugness wasn't just a court-specific trait for her.

I realized how naive I'd been to think that Theo was shyer than me, how I thought I'd have to tempt her into making the first move. When we were standing in the bedroom and the two of us were looking at each other, I'd really thought I might need to hold her hand through this. But Theo had just been playing coy the entire time. She not only knew exactly what she was doing, but she was really fucking good at it, too.

I nodded desperately, and she moved my panties to the side. She flicked her tongue just once against my clit, and then eased her way deeper between the lips of my pussy. I was practically seeing stars from how turned on I was and how good it felt. She followed every rhythm of my body—when I moved against her lips, when I moaned, when it felt so good that I couldn't even get the words out of my mouth. She logged it all mentally, just like how she told me she'd log her opponents during her basketball games. She knew what worked and what didn't.

And when my orgasm was just about to crest, she pulled away—telling me she knew exactly what she was doing when she was reading me.

"Fuck," I whimpered. Theo had reduced me to nothing but a mess of need and desire. Every cell in my body was humming *Theo, Theo, Theo.*

"We still have more time together," she said. "I don't want this to be over yet."

She slipped my underwear out from under me and tossed it somewhere on the floor nearby. When she dipped her face back between my legs, I immediately spiked back into nearly finishing. I tried to think of anything I could to slow it down but it was impossible. The steady rhythm of Theo's tongue, the way she looked in the moon-soaked room, was overwhelming. I couldn't fight it.

"Oh, Theo," I cried out, pressing my hand to my mouth so I didn't disturb the entire hotel.

My orgasm built up quickly, surging through me and leaving me with little regard for how I looked or sounded to Theo.

The stereotype that lesbians were good in bed was often true. I'd had great one-night stands and usually a better track record of successfully finishing during them than what Iris or any of our other straight friends reported back. But it wasn't *always* true. There were people who completely missed the mark and never seemed to find the exact right places. Even after a few times of fooling around with them, I'd still come up feeling the need to fake it or come up with an excuse to get out of being the receiver.

But with Theo, it was a completely different story.

Theo seemed to understand my body even better than I understood it. She was attentive, listening to my every breath and tuned into my every movement. I didn't have to ask her to slow down or keep going because she could read my body before I had to say anything.

"Come here," I panted, pulling her back up toward me. I kissed her deeply, trying to remember the last time I'd orgasmed like that with a partner—if I ever had. I'd seen stars; I'd accessed something new in my body that I'd never felt before.

She kissed me deeply, holding me close to her as she did so. When she dipped her face to my neck, placing gentle kisses back up toward my ear, my hunger for her started up all over again.

I arched my back, hoping she would be able to read that I was begging for more. I didn't want to be greedy, but I also didn't want the feeling to stop. My orgasm had only served to make me hornier, something I didn't realize was possible.

Theo understood. With one hand in my hair, she trailed the other down between my legs. I wiggled desperately against her. When the tips of her fingers finally found my clit, I had to hold myself back from crying out all over again. Every touch made my body flinch with an overwhelming rush of pleasure, but I didn't want her to stop.

She kept her touch feather-soft, sliding her finger up and down my clit at first until I became less sensitive. I tried not to think too much about the fact that it was obvious she was good in bed—*really* good in bed. Like, good enough that I could only assume she was used to working girls up to an orgasm, letting them come down, and then working them right back up. It was practically an art form, the way she was doing it.

Then again—I was here and they weren't. And if anything, I was grateful that she'd learned everything that she had, even if it had to be practiced on other women.

By the time Theo was putting pressure against my entrance, teasing to go inside of me, I was so wet I couldn't even believe it'd all come from my body. No lube, no extra spit, required.

Propped up on one elbow, she looked down at me. "Is this okay?" she asked, her voice. She had to know that it was more than okay. I was practically crawling out of my skin for her.

"Fuck me," I said, not taking my eyes off of her.

She flashed her famous crooked smile. "Needy girl."

"*Theo*," I pleaded, moving my hips and rocking against her hand.

She then slipped a finger inside. The sensation of her so suddenly deep inside me caught me off guard. I gasped, clinging to her. And then my body caught up to what was going on. I felt a warm rush between my legs.

"Oh my *god*," I moaned, throwing my head back. I tried to keep my eyes on Theo, but I couldn't. They closed of their own volition and stayed closed as my body was taken over by wave after wave of need and want and desire. Every nerve in my body was going haywire as Theo pushed and pulled her fingers in and out of me.

She worked her way up to two fingers, effortlessly gliding into me. The orgasms came quickly one after another. I didn't even think it was real or possible to experience sex like this. I was no stranger to a vibrator, but Theo was offering me a totally new form of pleasure. This was the kind of sex that people got hooked on, the kind of sex that made people want to quit their jobs and skip class and not leave their bed for days at a time, even for food or water.

I managed to force my eyes open for a second and looked at Theo, her hair falling over her shoulders as she thrusted her fingers into me. She was perfect. Her muscles were flexed from holding herself up, and her fingers were long and moved with expert precision. I didn't even know how many orgasms I'd made it up to by the time she curled her fingers up and went for my g-spot.

By then, I was seeing stars all over again and was left totally breathless. My legs shook uncontrollably, and my brain went completely and entirely empty. Every part of me was ultra-focused on Theo, unable to think about anything else or feel anything else. All I wanted was her—and the next orgasm she was going to give me.

She built the next one up slowly, inching me closer and closer to the edge. She kept her fingers curled, touching something new that I wasn't sure anyone had ever found in me before. It felt different from the other orgasms she'd already given me, accessing a different set of nerves and giving me a completely different response.

When the orgasm finally started to crest, I bit my lip and pulled on Theo's shirt. "Oh," I breathed out.

"That's it. Good girl," Theo whispered, gently kissing my temple. "Let me feel it."

I whined and moaned and silently begged until finally, I couldn't even produce a sound anymore. When the orgasm finally crashed through my body, it felt like I'd entered a completely different level of being.

My chest rose and fell like I'd just done the most intensive workout of my entire life. I pulled Theo back down toward me, and she pulled me into her arms. It was the safest, most comfortable place in the world.

"How was that?" Theo asked, pressing a kiss to my forehead.

I curled up on her chest, wrapping my arms around her torso. I wanted to sleep in her arms and then never get up. I felt sorry for the version of myself before who had written off athletes and muscles; no one had ever held me like this before. I had to take a moment to catch my breath.

"That was..." I tried to think of something, but couldn't. A laugh bubbled out of me, and I put my fingers to my mouth to try and quell it. The post-orgasm flush kicked in, and I felt the need to giggle and yell out from the rooftops that I just got laid.

Now that I'd experienced it, I knew with certainty that sex with Theo was so good that it made up for years of bad one-night stands and nights spent alone. It'd all felt worth it to get me here.

"Hopefully good," Theo said.

"Amazing," I said, honestly. "Perfect."

"Did you want anything else?"

"I think I'd exit this plane of existence if you touched me again," I said. "My body can't handle another round."

Theo snorted. "You're weirder than you let on."

I laughed and then got a little embarrassed. Theo was right—I had the easygoing persona down for parties and meeting new people. I knew how to be just the right amount of interested and almost neutral to blend in and be agreeable. I had what felt like a million friends on rotation, all of whom I knew and liked and knew and liked me, but I didn't know much more than that. I'd never been opposed to having casual friends; I just didn't speak to them as much as I spoke to someone like Iris.

It was rare for me to let the mask slip and become a real person instead of a miniature version of my social butterfly, perfectly manicured mother. But it felt impossible to keep my true self hidden with Theo so charming and kind and *safe*. I trusted that I could talk to her as an actual person with real feelings and emotions—someone who would break out during her periods, who got frustrated and angry and impatient, who wasn't all chugging drinks at parties and dancing on tables—and I *wanted* to talk to her like an actual person. I wanted her to really like *me*, as a whole person.

"As long as you still find me sexy," I teased, playing off my embarrassment over being so vulnerable with her.

"I couldn't imagine a universe where I wouldn't find you sexy," Theo said, brushing a piece of hair from my face.

I kissed her neck, our bodies molded together. I'd never liked lying like this before, all wrapped up in someone else, but it was the only thing I wanted right now. I didn't feel a single ounce of desire to leave, which was the most shocking thing of all.

"Did you want anything?" I asked. Theo had taken charge in a way that made me want to lie back and see what she had to offer. But now, I wouldn't mind reversing the roles. I needed to see Theo—my focused, driven, hyper-serious basketball star—unravel, just for a second.

"I'm good for tonight," Theo said. When she glanced over at me, she could read off of my expression what it was that I didn't want to say out loud. "Nothing to do with you, I promise. I'm more of a giver than a receiver."

"Stone top?" I asked, not minding if that was the case. I'd never been in the position before of a partner who doesn't want to be touched at all, but I could adapt.

"Not completely stone," she said. "But I've always preferred to be the one in charge. It's more important to me that you have a great time."

"Do you have, like, a ratio?"

"A ratio?"

"You know, of giving to receiving."

"Oh." Theo looked across the room for a second as she thought it over. "No one's ever asked me that before. I guess maybe seventy to thirty? It could change in either direction, though." She looked down at me for a second and then looked away again. "If I'm being honest, I haven't...been around that much. Basketball has always been the first and only love. Makes getting motivated to get out there kind of difficult."

I smiled a little bit, sitting up. I rested my hand on her chest, and my brown hair fell over my right shoulder. "You mean to tell me that Theo McCall, basketball extraordinaire, *isn't* some kind of playboy?"

She laughed. "No, not even a little bit. Not like you, at least."

"Hey!" I said, laughing.

"But yeah, I don't know. It's never been a priority. I've only ever had things here and there. Nothing serious or worth noting. And always during the offseason. I'd never wanted to risk my game by getting into something while I'm playing."
I smirked. "Until me."

Theo pulled me back toward her playfully. Her cheeks were newly flushed pink, definitely related more to embarrassment than to sex, based on her bashful expression. "Yeah, until you. Whatever."

Suddenly, my years of feeling shy and weird about feelings seemed to melt away. I'd spent so long scared of conversations that suggested anything remotely serious. I hated the thought of being *the one* or having someone I thought of as *the one*. The permanency had always scared the shit out of me.

But Theo didn't make any of it feel scary. She didn't say it like a proclamation or like it was going to completely flip my life upside down. She wasn't putting me in a cage, wasn't making me feel like a trapped bird. I just felt...happy. Normal.

I felt like a girl whose crush liked me back.

Theo traced her hand over my bare back. "So, when you said that you didn't date the first time we met...what exactly did that mean?"

I thought back to our first interaction and how much had changed since then. The period of my life when I didn't know

Theo felt like a lifetime ago. Even though it hadn't been that long, I couldn't help but think back on how cute it all was. Meeting each other, going to games. How nervous I'd been going to see her and messaging her.

I felt like a completely different person from then to now, and only in the best ways. Iris always told me that my first significant relationship was going to knock me on my ass—she'd gone through her first big heartbreak as a high school senior—and I'd always brushed it off. I was insistent that I was never going to change and that I'd always keep one foot out the door. There was always someone else who was more interesting, a new high that was worth chasing.

But it was different with Theo.

I'd only known her for such a short time, and we'd only just now slept together for the first time, but I knew she was my first big relationship. Or I wanted her to be, at least. I couldn't argue against it, couldn't fight it.

The only thing I could do was lean in and hope that nothing changed.

"I *didn't* date," I said, choosing my words carefully. "Everything was casual all the time with everyone. My mom was never big on commitment, and she always seemed so much happier when she wasn't attached to someone, and I think I got a lot of that from her."

"Have you ever wanted to date?" Theo asked, and I could hear what she was suggesting. There was such a hopeful and curious undertone.

"Not before you," I admitted.

We both sat in silence, letting my words sink in. I was just as surprised I'd said them as I was sure Theo was to hear them.

As soon as I opened the door to my hotel room, I heard Iris's feet scramble on the hotel carpet. She met me right in front of the entrance.

"How was it? Tell me everything," she said as she grabbed me by the arms.

"Hi to you too," I said, but I couldn't keep the smile off my face. "How was the diner?'

She waved off my comment. "You know neither of us cares about the diner. You're literally glowing." She followed me back toward the hotel beds where I kicked off my shoes and threw myself down. Memories came flooding back—Theo's hands in my hair, her low voice asking me what I liked and what felt good, her sheets against my bare skin. Hotels were never going to be the same for me. Utah as a whole was never going to be the same to me—this place suddenly felt like the sexiest state in the nation; it might as well have been Vegas. "I thought that was a myth that people glowed and looked different after sex, but it's like someone put a lightbulb on inside of you."

"It was...amazing," I admitted. I put my hands to my face, resisting squealing like a little kid. "I really like her, Iris. It was perfect. I've never been treated like that before. She was so...gentle. And attentive. It was like receiving the best massage of my life or something. I don't even know how to explain it. It was definitely the best sex of my life."

Iris sat down on the edge of her bed. "I'm seething with jealousy, but I'm so happy for you. I'm glad you guys were finally able to figure it out. I was worried it'd end up being one of those things where you wait until graduation and realize too late that you were both into each other."

"I'm glad it wasn't," I said. My body hummed with lingering pleasure and the sensation of being with Theo. It wasn't just post-sex glow; it was post-Theo glow. It was perfect. It was storybook sex, porn sex, *feels like the first time* sex.

"I'm assuming you're going to see her again, then."

I nodded. There was no use in pretending that I wasn't going to want to see her. All I wanted was to be near her again. I was relieved she'd only be out of town for one more game this week, and then I'd have her again next week. Days were going to feel like years, but it was worth it to me.

"Who are you and what have you done with my best friend?" Iris teased and then sighed. "I can't believe it really happened.

Someone finally broke down Maya Healy's walls. It was going to happen eventually. I'm just glad it was Theo."

"You want the friends and family of WAG discount."

She held her hands up. "All I'm saying is this is the best-case scenario for me. I don't think there's a partner in the world I'd be happier with for you for a multitude of reasons."

I snorted. "Playing the long game for you."

"You can't even make the jokes properly anymore, I see that smile on your face."

"Whatever," I said, even though I could feel that it was true.

In the weeks following, I kept waiting for the happy little honeymoon bubble to burst but it didn't. Unlike my crushes before, my feelings for Theo seemed to only intensify. What I'd been feeling before we'd gotten together continued to be true—I liked her more the more I got to know her.

To my surprise, she continued to be just as kind and supportive as when we first met. I couldn't find any cracks in the armor, anything that suggested she'd been putting on a show for me. The only thing that seemed to change was rather than waiting for me to make a move, she was more assertive and way more willing to take charge—and I didn't have any complaints about that

"I was thinking about you in class today," Theo said after we practically sprinted from her front door to her bedroom. Our time spent together had flown by over the winter months; we'd accidentally built a routine around each other. She'd barely waited for me to completely shut the door before I was in her arms again, her face buried in my neck.

The feeling of her lips against my skin was so distracting that I could barely formulate a response. It'd been weeks of this—blowing through finals and the holidays. Theo's basketball schedule was intense the entire time. There was no time to really celebrate having time off from classes when her travel schedule was still just as rigorous.

I'd stuck around by association. My mom was off in Cancun with some guy she'd been seeing on and off, and I didn't have any friends from back home I was going to go out of my way to see. Holidays had never been a tradition for me, so it wasn't a loss. I felt worse for Theo, who was on the phone with her parents multiple times a week to check in. It was obvious that not being home for the holidays was hard for her.

"This is how it is every year," she said when I asked her about it, and we left it at that.

Things were similar for New Years—there was no time off, no ability to go out all night and drink when there were games to play. Theo still maintained her pre-game routine, so our time together was limited to random chunks of time and sleepovers where she was usually up hours before me.

If anyone had told me that this would be my life a few months ago, I would've told them that there was no way I'd be down for something like that. The schedule was all over the place—Theo was constantly here and then there, constantly up and out. She was always needed at practice or at a game.

But I didn't mind it. It felt like easing myself into something. It gave me time to miss Theo instead of working myself up and spiraling out.

Theo was also more than worth it. Despite her schedule, she was attentive and kind; she was busy but she wasn't neglectful, and that was all that mattered. She took good care of me and actually listened to my day. There were people I'd met with schedules not even one-quarter as intense who couldn't bother to send a text back.

I dragged Theo toward her bed, ready to get lost in the feeling of being with her.

I was certain that the shoe was going to drop, that something was going to ruin everything, but it wasn't coming. The more time we spent together, the looser the knot in my chest became, and I realized that maybe I wasn't anti-commitment as much as I'd been uninterested in committing to anyone before her.

Chapter 20

THEO

"Shoot from your fingertips," I said as I bounced the basketball back to Maya. She'd sent it flying in just about every direction, making me run circles to get it back before it bounced into the creek at the bottom of the hill's edge.

There was a public outdoor basketball court on campus that was—unsurprisingly—empty throughout most of the winter here. Even though I'd gone to practice and the gym earlier in the day, I still had energy to spare that I wanted to burn off. The air was so cold that it made my skin and lungs sting, but the sky was fading into a perfect pink and purple sunset. It was a nice change of pace to be outside and to be with Maya, who'd managed to keep me grounded during a long stretch of games over the holidays.

Our relationship was starting to feel like someone had hit the gas, and neither of us seemed to have any interest in slowing down. It was even better than I'd been hoping for when I'd daydreamed about her. Even though my schedule felt hectic and completely out of control, there always seemed to be a second to see Maya.

But things were really starting to ramp up. As we rounded on February with only three losses so far under our belt, talks about me not only going pro but being the first draft pick overall felt certain. Barring any injuries, things were lining up exactly as I'd always hoped they would. But that meant that there was pressure—talks of agents, pending deals, contracts. As soon as the season finished, I was able to be off to the races with all of it. I was no longer making NIL money; I was making money as a professional athlete.

The gossip and theories and emails and meetings were all a little overwhelming. It felt like everyone had something to say about me, even if it was good. Hearing that people considered me the new face of the sport was an honor, but it was still a buzzing in the ear that took away from actually playing.

The only thing I didn't mind was the pictures floating around of me and Maya. They'd gone from a joke to something neither of us paid attention to. My teammates still occasionally sent social media updates as a joke, but public dialogue around us had shifted from *are they dating?* to *they're absolutely together*. Maya's new favorite hobby was sending edits made of the two of us online, saying, *Maybe the fans are right? Should we sleep together?*

I was happy to give it a pass, happy to let everyone else in the world break the news that things were pretty serious between us. I wanted everyone to know, but I wasn't about to break my streak of never speaking publicly about my personal life; that was inevitably going to be a can of worms I could never close.

The only people I had to talk to directly about it were my parents, since the rest of the team could pick up on the context clues. My parents had essentially just said *we already knew that* when I told them. I'd spent weeks hyping myself up for the conversation, preparing myself for the worst. But instead, I told them that, no, I wasn't going to bring her home with me to Michigan when I played there in a few weeks, and, yes, they could meet her once the season was over.

The only holdup was that I hadn't talked to Maya about formally meeting my parents yet. We hadn't gotten as far as labels, only confirming that we were the only person the other person was seeing. It meant something, but it wasn't everything. I was still holding back in some ways with her, worried that she might run out on me. As time passed, I started to feel more and more like she really meant it. But any sudden move felt risky, at least until we really talked about what we were doing.

All I knew was that I wanted this to keep going for as long as she'd let it.

"How?" Maya asked. I could see her breath in the cold air. It was warmer than it had been, which wasn't saying much. It felt good to breathe fresh air; it felt like I spent so much time confined to gyms and arenas.

"You know, like…" I said and then showed her, letting the ball spin off my fingertips and straight up into the air.

"You're a terrible teacher." She laughed as I tossed the ball her way, and she caught it.

"It's a light movement. You don't want to put too much pressure on it. It should feel effortless."

"Easy for you to say."

"It's all in the fingers."

"Oh, yeah?" Maya teased, and I had to resist scooping her into my arms and taking her home.

Being around Maya made me feel like a teenager. Everything she did was the hottest thing anyone had ever done. She made even the most mundane things—watching her do the dishes, sort through laundry, do her coursework, talk about graduate school—sexy. It'd been weeks of us unable to keep our hands off of each other and finding it hard to have to leave each other's side. I'd push off falling asleep during sleepovers because I wanted to stay up talking to her for as long as I could.

I'd refused to let her get in the way of anything related to basketball, and it'd been easier than I'd imagined. I'd spent so much of my life worried that everything would come crashing down if I invited someone in, but it was effortless with her. My games and time management were just as good. If anything, I was more on top of my shit than ever because I wanted as much time with her as I could get.

Maya dribbled the ball and shot it up, bouncing off the rim instead of missing completely this time. She reacted like someone who'd just made a buzzer beater.

"I'm getting it!" she cheered as I sprinted off to catch the ball that had bounced impressively far off the court. She was so cute that I didn't mind the light exercise, even if I was optimistic that she'd eventually get better and we could do more shooting and less jogging in all directions.

"You're so close to making your first basket of the evening," I joked.

"My mom could see a video recording of this, and she still wouldn't believe it," she said. "I know sports are everything to you, but me even having a basketball in my hands is crazy."

"You could definitely be worse, all things considered."

"That's what I'm saying!"

I ran back over to her and tossed her the ball. She dribbled it and attempted to go between her legs, but failed miserably. She caught it at the last second before it rolled off the court and down the hill into the abyss, swallowed by bushes and overgrown grass.

"Please don't get the ick."

I laughed. "I could never."

I stepped in front of her as she dribbled, doing a slightly better job than when we'd first started. She tried to dodge me, but I got in front of her.

She threw her head back with laughter. "I'm begging you not to break my ankles. Please show mercy."

My lips turned up in a smile. She'd gotten pretty good with her basketball slang, probably from listening to me talk shop with GJ when we crossed paths in our house. I'd also managed to catch Iris a few times and would do the same with her. She'd been out of the house more often with the holiday season, though, having made the drive back to her parents' house when classes were out of session.

Not that Maya or I minded having the apartment to ourselves.

I playfully snatched the ball from under Maya's hand and moved around her, shooting it in. She chased after the ball and sent it flying back to me. I caught it and shot it up again, sending it cleanly through the metal ring.

"We're supposed to be working on your basketball skills, not mine," I said.

"Watching you shoot is so hot, though. You can't take that from me," she said.

Maya hadn't kept it a secret how much she liked that I played basketball. It'd been somewhat surprising hearing it from her, but it was a welcome one. I wasn't about to say no to her appreciating my biceps or the way I looked in my uniform.

I bounced the ball in her direction, and she caught it as I walked up to her. "You ready to call it a game, big baller?"

"I think so," she said. "Shower?"

I thought about Maya standing naked under her shower head, a mental image that had stuck with me since the first time we'd showered together. It'd come back to me when I was in class, working out, texting her. It'd never gotten old; I didn't think it ever would.

"Absolutely," I agreed.

We wandered slowly back to her place, taking our time as we walked. Maya and I kept our hands laced together the entire way back. I held the basketball in my free arm, dropping it by the shoes at the front entrance of her house. It'd taken up a temporary home there since the outdoor court here was closer to her apartment than mine.

Warmth enveloped us as soon as we stepped inside. The familiar scent of her home—warm and comforting, hints of floral perfume throughout—welcomed me in. I'd come to prefer being at her place more so than mine. GJ had made it clear she missed walking back to the house with me after practice, but I think it'd also given her incentive to get up to whatever fuckboy behavior she liked to engage in. She'd fully come out of retirement since I'd become busy with Maya.

"Hello!" Iris called out from the kitchen as Maya and I kicked off our shoes. We exited the front hallway entrance and stepped into the open floor plan living room and kitchen. Iris was in the kitchen, chopping up some potatoes to throw into a pan she had nearby. Her laptop was open nearby with a show she was watching on Netflix on low volume. "Oh, you guys are *pink*. Run all the way home or something?"

"We were playing basketball," Maya said.

"Oh." She raised her eyebrows. "I never in a million years thought I'd ever hear those words come out of your mouth. Any good?"

"I almost made a basket."

"Your teacher sucks."

I snorted. "Take it up with the student."

"I don't think my hand-eye coordination is very good. Let's all pray that that's something that can be taught," Maya admitted. "We're going to go shower."

"Okay, have fun," Iris half-sang as she dropped her potatoes into the pan.

I followed Maya to her bathroom, her bedroom just down the hall. I'd come to know the layout of her apartment like the back of my hand.

She turned on the water as I shut the door behind us. When she stripped off her clothes, I had to remind myself that I also had to take off my own clothes and couldn't just stare at her.

Maya leaned into the shower to check the temperature of the water, and I couldn't resist the opportunity to stare. She had a perfect ass—round and softer than mine, which had become all muscle from years of hard workouts. I'd never considered myself someone who was more into either ass or tits. I'd never cared enough. Maya was making me realize I was into both; they just both had to be hers.

When the water was hot enough, she stepped into the shower, and I followed behind her. Just like with every shower, I felt the tiniest bit too tall for it. I usually never minded. When I wasn't with Maya, I prided myself on being able to take extremely efficient showers, usually not even letting the water get hot so it'd wake me up or cool me down after playing. And when I was with Maya, I was too distracted looking at her to think about how I felt like a giant.

We'd fallen into an easy routine with showering to the point that showers by myself had started to feel boring. I was surprised by how easily Maya had leaned into patterns of domesticity with me, but I wasn't dumb enough to bring it up until she did. I knew to appreciate what I had.

We handed each other our respective shampoos, cycling out so we both had time under the water. When Maya started rubbing her soap into her skin, my eyes traced over the fullness of her breasts and her clear face, free of any hair falling into it like it did when it was dry. That was one of my favorite parts of showering together. Unlike me, she rarely had her hair up. This was my time to see her face that clearly. I let myself shamelessly stare when she had her eyes closed and head tilted back under the water.

When we swapped, her nipples hardened from the transition into cold air. I pulled her close, letting my hands fall over her wet skin, and held our bodies together. She draped her arms over my neck, the next steps of our shower temporarily forgotten.

"Hi, pretty girl," I said.

She looked up at me. "Hi."

My hands traced further and further down, moving over the curve of her ass. If we weren't careful, I knew we'd end up fooling around in here for hours—or at least fool around until the water got cold.

It was moments like this where I felt the urge to tell her that I loved her. The words were sitting right there, at the tip of my tongue, nearly impossible to ignore. I was seconds away from saying them at any time we were alone together, and it'd only gotten worse the more I'd gotten to know her. She'd look at me a certain way, tilt her head a certain way, say something a certain way.

It felt too soon to say it, but it also felt strangely so right. There were moments when it felt like the most natural thing in the world—like lying in bed with her, our bodies wrapped up in each other. It wouldn't even be related to sex; it was just being around her. That was enough for me. And I knew it had to be love—or at least something close to it—because I'd never felt like this with anyone before. I'd never *had* something like this with anyone else before.

We finished our shower and wrapped ourselves tightly in our towels before heading back to her room to get dressed. We'd been going back and forth between our apartments so often that we'd been accidentally leaving things at each other's places, which slowly escalated into us intentionally leaving things. It made our lives easier, usually, if we had everything with us. I was always in and out of practice or class, and she needed her things for class, too, so it made logical sense.

I also, admittedly, got a small thrill out of leaving things with her. It wasn't just from a practical place. I loved getting texts of her finding my shirts in her laundry, always sending a photo of her wearing it whenever she found it. The shirts were always too long on her and fit her completely differently than they fit me. I loved it; I wanted to make a museum of every photo she sent me of herself.

We got dressed and then headed into the kitchen, where we passed off with Iris. She gave us a small wave as she headed into her bedroom for the evening.

"I don't have much," Maya admitted as she looked through her fridge and the pantry. "Pasta? I can probably find something to add into it. Or I'll make like a white wine sauce of some kind."

One thing that Maya hadn't disclosed to me at any point until recently was that she was really good in the kitchen. I'd never had the time to learn how to cook more than the basics; it also wasn't necessarily on my list of priorities. But Maya's cooking was a completely different story. She'd be modest about it, but watching her move was impressive. I usually ended up sitting back and letting her work, never of my own volition, and only ever because she never had something she needed me to help with.

I sat at the barstools positioned around her L-shaped kitchen counter and watched her work. She was chatting aimlessly the entire time, talking to me about new shoes she was looking at online and how her mom's new boyfriend sounded like an asshole. I was listening intently but I also gave myself the time to admire her while she moved around the kitchen.

I stood up from the barstool that had become my designated spot whenever we cooked here and stepped toward the stove. I wrapped my arms around her waist, pulling her in close to me. Maya's body softened as she melted against my touch, leaning her weight against me. I kissed the top of her head as she put her hand over my arms.

I was about to pull away to let her focus again, but she held me there. "Again," she said, and I let myself smile freely, knowing she couldn't see me. It was hard to believe that this was the girl who'd said she wasn't looking for commitment or anything serious. I obliged happily, kissing the top of her head again and then again. I could never get enough of the smell of her shampoo, or anything at all that reminded me of her.

I felt the urge to say to her, stronger than ever. *I love you*. It was right there, too much too soon, but I knew I felt it. I just had to hold on a little longer.

And I had to hope that nothing between us would change before I had the opportunity to say it.

Chapter 21

MAYA

I was fighting the urge to check my email inbox every couple of seconds.

"It's too early," Iris told me as we walked to the gym. She'd made the executive decision that we were going to go together to get me out of my head.

The start of February meant graduate school decisions were going to come soon. Maybe not *this* soon, as Iris reminded me over and over again, but soon enough. The anticipation was killing me. I'd sent out six applications to different sociology doctorate programs, all of which would offer me exactly what I wanted. I didn't bother with location and instead went purely for what they could offer: what the students said about the program, what the professors specialized in, what kind of opportunities there were for research and training to become a professor.

It was the most excited and nervous I'd ever been for anything. My expectations for my undergraduate degree had been minimal. I knew I wanted out of Arizona, but that was as far as I'd gotten. I didn't fully know what it was I wanted to do or what I could do with a degree. I anticipated some corporate office job, something passionless and with a vague title that only made sense to other people in my industry.

But instead, I started taking pre-requisite humanities classes and discovered the social sciences, and my career aspirations immediately became clear to me. Ever since then, I'd been pushing hard to train for research and teaching positions in the future. My professors had given me opportunities over the years to learn and grow and I felt ready.

Or at least, ready enough. I still felt a little bit like a kid playing dress up sometimes.

And just because I felt like I was ready didn't mean I was actually going to get accepted into a program.

"I'm going to be so sad when you have to leave me," Iris said, playfully frowning at me. "We've basically lived in the same skin for the past four years. It's going to be so weird not seeing your face every day."

"You might not, I applied for that one program in Colorado," I said. The rest were all over the map—east coast, west coast, midwest. I was leaving it all pretty much up to chance. I wanted to say that if no one wanted me, I didn't know what I would do but that wasn't the truth. I knew exactly what I'd do: I'd get a job, I just wouldn't be happy about it.

"If the universe is on our side, it'll keep us together," she said. "I don't want to have to find another roommate. Not that my current roommate is even around that much since she's always over at her *girlfriend's* house."

"Not girlfriends," I specified. We hadn't talked about labels yet and something stirred in me every time I thought about it. It wasn't that I didn't want to be official—we basically were—but I couldn't fight the feeling that something would change between us once we put a label on it. I was worried things would suddenly go south, and I'd spend the rest of my life wishing we hadn't pushed to make things so serious. "And that's part of what's made me such a great roommate. Isn't it the ideal situation to have someone who still pays half the rent but is never around?"

"Not when I actually want to hangout with you," Iris said, ignoring my *girlfriend* comment. She knew better than to pick an argument with me on it. I hadn't budged once on my stance of refusing to talk about it or even acknowledge it.

"I'm not going anywhere, even if I do have to move," I said. I pushed down the feeling that was swelling inside of me at the thought of how a new chapter was coming. Leaving Iris would be one of the hardest things I'd do in my life—even harder than leaving home. I'd never had the kind of attachment to my hometown like everyone else did. I'd been grateful to leave, grateful to meet more people, grateful for the opportunity to make friends who weren't there out of convenience.

I thought I'd always have that somewhere in me, that trying to connect with others was hard for me. But Iris had proven me wrong. And Theo seemed to be proving me wrong, too, which was just as scary.

But graduate school was graduate school. It was what I'd been working for all this time. I didn't want to completely give up on everything I'd been working for.

I took a deep breath. I had to go one step at a time. I'd worry about getting into a program and then worry about everything else.

Later that night, I headed over to Theo's place after I finished my classes and reading for the night, and she finished her second practice of the day. Her coach had been working her hard. Theo didn't seem to ever get tired, so it was hard to tell, but her schedule seemed to keep getting busier and busier. The closer March—and her game against Cam Kerr and Point Brook University—got, the smaller the windows of time Theo had for me seemed to get.

I'd started to get antsy when I didn't hear from her in her usual amount of time, or at the times I usually heard from her.

I was logical enough to know that she was busy and it had nothing to do with me, but it didn't necessarily make her not being around any easier.

But I only felt it when we weren't together. During the times when it was just us, it was something almost magical. Time slipped away quickly, neither of us ever running out of things to say to the other person.

"Hi," I greeted her as soon as I stepped into her house. Her hair was damp from her shower and I could still smell the lingering shampoo and body wash on her. She was wearing athletic shorts and a long sleeve Lakeside Green basketball shirt. I saw her in variations of the same outfit a million times over, and I found it irresistible every single time. It never, ever got old.

She pulled me into her arms, and all of the noise cut out. Every single worry about her not being around and how maybe I was a little bit of a hindrance to her schedule faded away in an instant.

It was only two weeks before what was arguably Theo's biggest regular season game but there we were, pretending that nothing else was going on around us. No basketball, no pending championships, no upcoming draft, no graduate school decisions. We were just two normal people.

She kissed the top of my head. "Hi, pretty girl."

"How was practice?"

"Same old," she said. "I really think this is going to be a good year for us."

"It's *been* a good year," I said, even though I knew Theo was too tough on herself and the team to actually think like that. *A good year* was the closest Theo ever got to talking about making it to the Final Four and then the championship.

The Coyotes were pretty much a shoo-in for making it into the first round of the tournament, but sports commentators seemed to be going back and forth on whether they actually stood a chance. They had a good record, but it would be on the Point Brook game to know if they could actually bring it home against a major star-power team. So far, it seemed like everyone's odds were on Point Brook to win—unsurprising, since they'd won more rings than any other school.

It was still funny to me how basketball so casually came into my life. Theo and I talked about the sport like it was any other job, any other hobby. She didn't treat it like she was about to get drafted into *the* women's basketball league, or that she was *the* top pick and top college player of the moment.

As I played all of this out in my head, all I could think about was how Theo had turned me into the kind of person who talked about playoff odds and who was going to be taking home a ring. The transition had been subtle, and I couldn't help but think it was at least a little funny.

I'd always imagined myself being one of those people who was steadfast in maintaining my own life and interests outside of my partner, but it felt so different in actual practice—and when it came to someone I actually liked. Monotony and listening to someone talk about their day had never felt so comfortable, so easy.

"What are you thinking about?" Theo asked.

"Basketball," I said.

Theo's lips turned up in a smile. "Who are you?" she teased.

I chuckled. "I have no idea."

She kissed my forehead and eased my purse off my arm and then my coat from my shoulders. "No more basketball unless it has to do with the Scott brothers."

I moaned. "Ugh, you are *so hot*."

"I got you something on the way back from practice," Theo said and ducked into the kitchen.

I looked at her curiously. "What is it?"

"You have to sit down with me to get it," she said, and I dragged her over to the couch. We quickly settled in our usual position—Theo sitting upright with me lying my head in her lap. It was my second favorite way she touched me, outside of when we fell asleep together at night, and she had her arms wrapped around me.

"Okay, let me see it," I said, holding my hands out.

She handed off a Twix bar that she'd stuffed into her pocket. I gasped. "I've been craving one of these all day!" My face softened as I looked up at her from her lap. "Thank you."

"Of course."

I sat up and kissed her, the angle definitely as uncomfortable for her as it was for me, but I didn't care.

It didn't seem like Theo did, either. She took her time kissing me. She pressed her lips gently against mine, really kissing me instead of making out or initiating sex. It was so intimate. I'd come to love the soft, kind way she touched me. Rather than wanting to run from her like I did with everyone else before, I leaned into it.

When we broke apart, Theo picked up the TV remote. "Shall we?"

"Of course," I said and settled back into position.

Theo turned on One Tree Hill—we'd managed to make it pretty deep into the second season, which I considered a huge accomplishment considering the schedules we had—and my brain was split between watching the show and thinking about how lucky I was to have this.

As the episode progressed, I traced my hand absently over Theo's bare knee and the lower part of her thigh. To say that we'd actually *watched* the entirety of the first season and part of the second was a slight exaggeration. It had definitely been playing in the background, at least.

Theo's breath changed as I moved my hand further and further up her leg. I was slow and careful, taking my time moving across her surprisingly silky skin. Her basketball shorts were the tiniest bit baggy, leaving room for me to move up her leg without a barrier.

Theo had mostly kept true to her ratio of seventy to thirty in terms of giving to receiving—if anything, she'd overestimated her number. She hadn't asked for anything from me so far. I didn't mind; our sex seemed to somehow only get better the more we got to know each other. I had no opposition to taking as many orgasms as Theo was willing to give me.

But I also wanted to make sure she always knew the option was there.

Theo gently raked her hands through my hair. The further up I moved, the more her gentle touch felt like her gripping my hair. I kept my eyes focused on the screen, but didn't process a single thing that was going on. Knowing what Theo wanted was more important to me.

I kept up my rhythm of moving further and further up her leg. She let out a small, needy sigh, and I bit back a smile. Desire swirled inside of me, my body remembering all of the sex we'd had before. The times we'd snuck in a round before practice or when she'd come find me at my apartment immediately after getting back from an away game.

Theo readjusted, spreading her legs a little further apart, and I kept going. Even if Theo wasn't interested in sex being performed on her, I could at least tease her—something she'd been demonstrated to like.

I sat up and straddled her lap. She rested her hands on my waist and looked at me, the two of us eye level from this position.

I traced my hands over the waistband of her shorts, running my fingers over her skin in the process. She leaned her head against the couch cushion and tilted her jaw up toward me.

"Fuck, Maya," she said, looking over my body. I was fully dressed and in a matching athleisure set that was cute but maybe not so cute that it deserved the same reaction someone might give to lingerie. I was flattered either way.

I kissed Theo again, moving my hand further up her shirt toward her sports bra. She didn't mind touching over it, but she preferred that it stayed on. She had what felt like a million different ones and looked equally as good in all of them, but there was a dark green one that I was particularly fond of.

She pulled me close to her by my face and kissed me even more deeply. Her lips moved across my skin, moving lower and lower. The episode of our show was quickly forgotten; I knew we wouldn't be going back to it. By the time we did, we'd probably be at least a few episodes ahead of where we were.

"Are your roommates home?" I asked. We were in Theo's house, so I knew her room wasn't far, but I didn't want to wait if I didn't have to.

She shook her head. "I don't know when they'll be back."

"We'll be quick, then," I said.

Theo's eyes lit up with need. A smile spread across her lips. She kissed me again, our hands wandering each other's bodies freely. In the background, the Tree Hill Ravens played hard on the court.

Theo slid her hands up my shirt, cupping my breasts in the process. Her hands were warm and familiar; I loved the feeling of her on my skin. She continued kissing my neck, and a shock of pleasure moved from my core upwards. My entire body felt like it was on fire in the best way.

I slipped my hand to her waistband, sliding it underneath to touch her waist.

She looked at me. "Would you want to...?"

My eyes lit up. "Really?"

Theo chuckled. "You're being really cool about this."

"Sorry," I said and then laughed. "I've been looking forward to this. *Not* that there's ever been any rush. Or that we'd ever have to."

Theo smiled. "You've been thinking about me?"

"Always."

"It's okay, I'm also always thinking about fucking you."

My heart raced—adrenaline and pure, unfiltered horniness coursed through me. It was embarrassing and exciting all at once. I felt so weirdly vulnerable being in this position, where Theo knew just how badly I wanted her.

But it was also empowering to know she wanted me just as badly.

I moved my hand further down until I reached the waist of her briefs. Theo's breath changed, and I moved further down. I stayed over her briefs at first, tracing my fingers over the material. She spread her legs further out for me, giving me the room to glide my finger over her slit.

She gripped my waist, and I kissed her neck, letting my breath linger against her skin. Goosebumps erupted over her skin.

I pulled my hand back up and then slipped it into her briefs this time. She leaned her head back against the couch and bit her lip.

I moved lower until I was between her legs. She was already wet to the touch. I traced my finger up her slit.

"*Maya*," she exhaled

"Is this okay?"

"More than okay."

I moved my fingers gently against her clit, testing what she liked. She responded well to gentle, slow movement rather than something more aggressive.

"I don't really like penetration," she said through a haze of lust. "Just something to keep in mind."

"Of course," I said and restricted my fingers to her clit. She lightly gasped, spreading her legs even further apart from beneath me. I readjusted, giving myself a better range of motion. Since no one was home, we could technically get away with taking our clothes off, but this was so hot I didn't want to stop.

I slipped my fingers against her, continuing to move my hand as her clit hardened under my touch. She was so wet there was little friction; if anything, it was hard to keep my hand in the same spot.

I knew the second I'd reached *the* spot for Theo. She let out the sexiest groan I'd ever heard in my life. It hit me in that moment that I was fucking Theo McCall, that this was the same girl who was plastered all over ESPN and sports headlines and our university campus.

Theo turned her head to look at me, keeping her eyes on me as I kept going.

"That feels so good, Maya," she said softly. She put her hands above her head and gripped the back of the couch, leaning further back. Her back arched toward me.

I kept going, listening to Theo's breath change in rhythm. The closer she got to finishing, the needier her movements became. I sped up the tiniest bit and increased pressure. She gasped out again and clenched her thighs around my hand.

She covered her eyes with one of her arms, letting herself get completely swept away. When the orgasm finished running its course, she dropped her arm and looked over at me. Her chest was rising and falling quickly, her cheeks flushed.

"Wow," she said and then laughed. "Jesus."

"Good?"

"Better than good. I don't think anyone has ever gotten me to finish like that before." She sat up, and I leaned in to kiss her cheek. She turned and kissed me on the lips and then the cheeks. I turned my head, letting her kiss every inch of my face until I broke into laughter.

She pulled me into her arms, and I snuggled in.

"I know we're making it work on the couch and my room-mates aren't home, but what if we went to my room?" Theo asked.

I perked up with curiosity. "What are you planning?"

"We don't have to—"

"No, I want to," I said and got up, grabbing Theo by the hand to pull her up from the couch too. It required both of my hands, all of my strength, and some assistance from Theo for me to get her up. "I think I need to do more weights at the gym."

"I can teach you."

"I'd much rather watch you lift weights at the gym than you teach me," I said, and then squealed as Theo scooped me up into her arms. She carried me fireman style up the stairs of her house, walking the familiar halls to her bedroom.

She dropped me down onto her bed and I reached for her clothes, pulling her shirt over her head and then mine. I let myself sink into the comfort of Theo's bed—her green com-forter and sheets I'd come to look forward to sleeping in. Theo's room had really started to feel like a second home not long after we started seeing each other. It was plain and straightforward and so different from mine—some posters on the wall, a rack of sneakers in the corner, a few books, and some basketball memorabilia—but so Theo. I was starting to love anything and everything that reminded me of her, even the simplest things.

Theo climbed into bed with me, her arms on either side of my head. We kissed deeply, our hands roaming without a care in the world. Now that we were in Theo's room, all bets were off. We didn't have to play coy.

My hands traced over Theo's muscled back and her flexed arms. She kissed down my stomach and around my bare chest. When she brought her mouth to my nipples, my back arched, and I dug my nails into her skin.

She removed my pants and then my underwear. Our motions were so fluid; there wasn't much left for us to explore that we hadn't explored already. We'd gotten to know most of our favorite spots and ways to be touched. It was a comforting rhythm.

Theo had raised my expectations around sex. I'd never let anyone get to the point where it felt like they truly knew me that well, even in the bedroom. But I was letting Theo go there and see me for long enough that she was truly learning *everything* about me. It was making me realize how nice it was to have a partner who already knew what I liked. Random hookups were fun for the sake of meeting someone new or for the adventure. But in terms of intimacy and the ability to have fun—and the chances of having an orgasm—consistency was becoming ideal. Now that I knew what I had, I didn't want to give it up and go back to strangers.

I flipped Theo over and straddled her, just below her neck. When she realized what I was silently proposing, her face lit up.

"Oh, hell yeah," she said and moved her arms so we could get into position.

I straddled her face and gripped her bed frame. Theo wrapped her arms around my legs to keep me still and then brought her tongue to my pussy. My knees nearly gave out immediately. A rush of blood went to my clit, making me light-headed.

"Oh my god." I exhaled. I put one hand in Theo's hair, combing my fingers through her roots and gripping on.

Theo continued flicking her tongue against me, and I rocked my hips the tiniest bit to create more friction. She tightened her grip around my legs, and I tilted my chin up, gasping and moaning at the ceiling.

The biggest benefit of all to Theo's roommates not being home was that we could be as loud as we wanted. It reminded me of winter break, when Theo and I basically camped out at my house because Iris was gone for so long. GJ had the same schedule as Theo, she was stuck on campus, too. Iris being away had given us the reprieve we needed from feeling like we always had roommates and friends and teammates around. It got to be just us, cosplaying like two grown-ups who were able to live in their own apartment.

Theo sped up her movements, moving her tongue up my opening and circling my clit. Every time she made contact with my mound, it sent a shockwave of warm pleasure to my core. I could feel and hear how wet I was against Theo's mouth.

She brought her hands up and gripped my ass. I rode her face until both of us were out of breath and red in the face. The orgasm started up slowly—a blooming sensation in my stomach and nipples and clit. When it hit, it felt like a tidal wave. Theo kept going through it, bringing me to the edge again before the first one could even completely finish.

"Oh, Theo," I moaned, white-knuckling her headboard. "Oh my god. Oh my *god*."

When I became so sensitive that I physically couldn't handle it anymore, I readjusted and moved back so I was sitting on her chest.

"All done?" Theo asked, looking up at me. She was so fucking sexy like this, all flushed from sex. I loved the way her hair fell over the pillow and the soft, lustful expression in her eyes.

"Just need a minute," I said and moved again so I was sitting next to her. She stayed flat on her back, draping her arm over my knees. I weaved my fingers through her hair, unable to stop myself from gazing at her.

I wanted to blame post-sex hormones but me staring at her was happening all the time—over dinner, while watching a movie. We'd be studying together and I'd find my eyes wandering toward her instead of my textbook. It wasn't entirely my fault—she just looked *so* good in glasses and so cute when she was immersed in what she was reading.

My pulse quickened at the mental image. I traced my fingers over Theo's bicep.

"Do you want to use the strap?" I asked.

She sat up immediately. "Of course," Theo said.

She reached into her side table and pulled out the strap and harness. We'd been slowly integrating more things into our rotation. I'd become particularly fond of using my vibrator with her over winter break; there were a couple of times I was worried my neighbors might call for help, concerned about my wellbeing, from how loud I'd been.

Theo pulled the harness on and tightened it against her waist. After applying lube, she got on her knees on the bed and sat between my legs.

She leaned over me and kissed me. I reached between her legs and poised the dildo at my slit.

When she slid into me, I felt it through my whole body. Even though she'd only gone in a little bit, my toes curled and my back arched. I gripped onto her back.

"How's this so far?" Theo asked. "Everything feel okay?"

"So good," I said and Theo eased deeper and deeper into me, filling me up. I could feel every inch of her—every *millimeter*. It felt incredible. Warmth gushed between my legs, enveloping the strap.

As I got increasingly turned on, Theo was able to move more freely. When she could feel that I was getting really wet, she started thrusting into me in slow, deep motions. She took her time sliding in and out of me.

"I love fucking you," she said in my ear. "You're so hot, Maya."

I moaned in response, her voice effectively turning me on even more. I held onto her, readjusting my hips so she could get an even deeper angle.

"Good girl," Theo said. "You like that?"

I nodded desperately. I didn't want her to stop—I *never* wanted her to stop. I couldn't formulate any actual thoughts or sentences. Theo moved with the stamina and confidence of an athlete. It was impossible not to get swept up in how good it felt to have her inside of me.

"Use your words, baby."

I moaned again, my chest rising and falling more rapidly as I got closer to finishing. "It's so good, Theo," I said, using every bit of my brain power that I could. "That feels so good."

Theo moved faster inside of me and I matched her pace with the movement of my hips. I cried out as an orgasm burst through me.

I was too sensitive to try going for another round so quickly. Theo eased out of me and slipped the strap off, dropping it to the ground nearby.

"I'll deal with that later," she said and climbed back into bed with me. She wrapped me in her arms and I closed my eyes. Every chemical that got released during sex felt like it was dancing and singing in my body. I could stay exactly like that for the rest of my life and I would never complain about it.

"Did you want anything?" I asked as I curled up on Theo's chest. She stroked her hand up and down my bare back.

"No, I'm…taken care of," Theo said. She looked away. "Did you know that you can orgasm from getting someone else off?"

I laughed, hugging myself to her even tighter. "Oh, that is so fucking hot," I said.

Chapter 22

THEO

I dribbled the ball, crouching low to keep it just out of reach of number thirteen on the opposing team—the Yellowjackets. She'd been riding my ass all game, doing everything she could to attempt to block my shots. Her success had been minimal—I'd sunken thirty-two points, one of my highest games of all time—so her hovering was more like a bug that wouldn't leave me alone than anything else.

I glanced between Gemma and Nia. Nia had never been much of a shooter, but she was good with an assist. I bounced the ball just past the feet of a player on the Yellowjackets and Nia caught it, running hard as she dribbled. I ran on the right side of the court to set up for her to send the ball back toward me.

"Nia!" I shouted.

With a quick chest pass, she sent the ball flying to me. I lined it up and shot it quickly before number thirteen could knock it out of my hands.

I moved backwards, waiting to see if it would fall. When it slipped through the net, the crowd went to their feet. I gave myself a few seconds to celebrate before I was at risk of getting a technical and then continued on.

We played hard, maintaining a consistent lead of twenty-three points. When it reached the last few minutes of the game, Coach Darlene pulled me to give someone else a chance to play—common when it was obvious we were going to win—and swapped Ellie in for me. GJ was also called back to the bench. We sat back, drinking water, as we cheered on our teammates to finish out the game.

"Move those feet, Ellie!" GJ shouted. "Watch your left!"

I squirted water into my mouth and took deep breaths, my heart rate slowly going back to normal after running for what felt like an hour straight.

GJ turned to look at me. "Did you see Bendr is here?"

"Of course I did," I said. I glanced over to look at him. He was a kind of dorky looking white guy—shorter and less muscly in person than I thought he would be. Even so, it was pretty cool that he intentionally came out here to see us. Outside of basketball legends, he was probably the most significant celebrity I'd met so far. And he wasn't a bad one considering he'd had several number one hits and was played on the radio all the time. "Everyone's been talking about it. He posted that thing online, too, saying that he was coming."

"Look at you keeping up with celebrity social media," she said. "I'm impressed. You're a changed woman."

I brushed the comment off and dabbed sweat from my face with my towel. "Maya keeps me updated. She's like my pseudo-social media manager now. She thinks it's funny."

That was maybe an understatement—Maya thought it was hilarious. She'd dig around online and only ever told me information unrelated to my playing and Cam Kerr. She even found the occasional article about us, which usually just referred to her as the *mystery woman* who was presumed to also be a student on campus. A few of them actually mentioned her by name, but there wasn't much online about her so they'd leave those at *Maya Healy is a student at Lakeside Green from Arizona.* The articles always featured the first photo of us together, a random photo from Maya's social media, and then a photo of me playing. There weren't many articles, but there were enough that Maya could make jokes about everyone's lack of creativity and their poor sleuthing skills.

"Are you sure that isn't just another way of saying that she monitors your texts to make sure you're not fooling around with anyone else?"

"Oh, right. You know me," I said dryly and turned to look at her. "I always forget you've dated people who are kind of nuts until you say things like that."

"To be fair, they aren't wrong to be worried. But we're never *exclusive*. We're just seeing each other. And then probably other people, too. Or at least, I am," GJ said.

I chuckled and shook my head. For being best friends, we had opposite approaches to dating. I used to not think too much about it, but hearing her now has made me grateful for Maya. I liked that things were so stable with us. I couldn't imagine wanting anyone else ever again now that she was in my life.

I put my water down and glanced at the clock, then back at the court. "There's not enough ball movement," I said, shaking my head. The Yellowjackets had managed to slow down our lead, bringing it to only thirteen points. I sat forward. "Shoot, Ellie!"

Coach Darlene hovered near me and GJ and I was tempted to tell her to put me back in. But I knew exactly what she was doing—she wanted to see what the team was going to be like without me. It was hard to know when I'd been running the team for so long if they could stand entirely on their own two feet. I believed in them, but it would be a major transition.

Our team, just like any other, developed a rhythm with each other. Adding new people or taking away old ones changed that rhythm, no matter how hard Coach Darlene tried to keep everything exactly the same.

And despite my attempts at being modest, I knew the team had been built around me. Coach had made it clear how much I'd impacted her decisions on where and how people were played. I wasn't the only player on the team, but I was her all-around best. And graduating meant leaving her—and everyone else—to their own devices.

I glanced over at GJ. Fortunately, she wasn't graduating yet, so I knew the team was going to end up in good hands. But filling the void I was going to leave would be difficult. GJ was not going to have it easy next season.

After a few sloppy plays, the buzzer sounded off, and the game was over. The lead had dropped to twelve points after some back-and-forth scoring. It was decent, but still a little too close for comfort. I wasn't going to rag on the team for it too much—they didn't have GJ in, who they would still have next season. And the team was still so young. There was time for them to get stronger and faster. The building blocks were there, especially in Ellie.

After handshakes, I looked over to the student section to find Maya. She and Iris usually sat in the same spot, which made it easy to find them. It was right near a group of Iris's friends. Maya said they were nice, but she hadn't gotten to know them outside of basketball games.

"Theo! Big T!"

I turned and saw Bendr waving to get my attention from his courtside seats. He was with a few of his friends, all of them dripped out like they were courtside at the Lakers instead of a college basketball game.

GJ took me by the arm and moved me over that way further from the student section and Maya. "Yo, Bendr! Huge fan," she said easily, even though I knew she didn't listen to his music. I wasn't even sure she totally knew who he was other than being in music.

"*Sick* game, guys," Bendr said in a thick Australian accent. He clapped his hands together. "You're fucking incredible."

"Thanks, man," I said and then dapped him up with more intensity than was probably necessary. I pushed down any smug feelings I had toward definitely being stronger than him—or at least being able to match him.

"You're both going pro?" he asked.

"Just me," I said. "Hopefully. GJ still has another year until she's eligible."

"Almost to the orange carpet," GJ said.

Bendr laughed like that was the funniest joke he'd heard in his life. "I'll be seeing you again. Definitely," he said. He turned to his friends, pointing at me. "This is the future of the sport right here. Remember this fucking name and this fucking face. Hopefully, she'll remember me when she's making more money than all of us combined from a Nike deal or something."

I smiled, feeling a little bit like I had to play polite, but also genuinely flattered. As much as Bendr seemed like kind of a quintessential jerk, it was still surprising every time I heard adult men praising my playing. I'd spent most of my college career fighting off devil's advocate types who would discuss the technicalities of my stats, trying to say that mine didn't mean as much as someone else's for one reason or another. It seemed to be part of the gig when you started breaking records left and right; everyone wanted an explanation. No one really could believe that I was as good as I was.

But maybe things were starting to turn around. People were hopefully starting to accept my numbers for what they were.

"Can we get a picture, by the way?" Bendr asked.

"Oh, for sure," I said and dragged GJ with me to pose with Bendr and his boys. Bendr and I posed for another one-on-one, and then Bendr called over the rest of the team, who'd been eyeing the interaction from afar. The second they saw their chance, all of them jumped in to say something.

"Huge fan," Gemma said.

"It's true. She's always listening to you at the gym." Mags nodded.

I fought off a smile, thinking about what Maya had told me about the two of them and how flirty they could be—whether by accident or on purpose, I wasn't sure.

Maya.

I looked back over at the stands and realized that it was quickly clearing out. As I scanned over the student section, I couldn't see Maya or Iris anymore. And because I was down on the court, I didn't have my phone with me to ask Maya to stay behind for me. My smile quickly faded, and panic set in.

"I'm honored, ladies," Bendr said, putting his hand over his heart and nodding his head. "Really."

"Shit," I muttered under my breath.

GJ looked at me. "What's up?"

"I think Maya and Iris left," I said. "I didn't realize how long we'd been down here for."

"It's okay. It's not like you were intentionally avoiding them, you have someone who's here to see you. You can explain it when you see her—I'm sure she'll understand."

"I know," I said with a small sigh.

And I did know—it was true that I could just explain it all to Maya and it'd probably be fine. But I wasn't exactly happy about it.

Since I'd started seeing Maya, the most important thing to me was that I maintained a balance between her and basketball. I never wanted to lose sight of what I loved, but I also didn't want to have to give her up—or make her feel left behind—because of my sport and future career.

After getting pulled into a few more meandering conversations with Bendr's friends—who were very nice and supportive but didn't know shit about basketball—I thanked them all again and headed off with the team for our post-game huddle.

True to my word about keeping my personal life and basketball separate, I didn't miss a single word of what Coach Darlene said after the game. My mind didn't wander to Maya or if she was going to be mad at me for getting held up.

I saved that for *after* Coach finished.

When we were set free to shower and go home, I grabbed my phone from my locker. I didn't see a text from Maya, which stung a little bit but I couldn't blame her. She knew I didn't have my phone on the court with me; it would've been pointless for her to try and have reached me that way.

Did you go home? I wrote Maya, knowing there was no way she was still in the arena. Even if she had wanted to wait for me, it'd been too long at this point. The custodians and building staff would've cleared her out. But maybe she was hovering nearby, waiting in the parking lot with Iris.

Yeah, we walked back. The pictures of you guys with Bendr are really cute, she wrote. *They're already up all over social media.*

I bit my lip, guilt still swirling in my stomach. Nothing she said indicated that she was upset, but this felt like the first time I hadn't been able to keep our post-game tradition going. We'd known Bendr was coming, but I wasn't expecting it to turn into what it was. And it wasn't fair of me to expect Maya to wait around for me.

Can I see you tonight? I texted, even though I wasn't totally sure how that was even going to be possible. I couldn't duck out on my team for a girl, but I also didn't want to leave Maya hanging tonight.

Text me when you're free and we can see if I'm still awake, Maya wrote back and I wasn't sure what that meant.

Are you mad at me? I wrote, half as a joke but half genuinely wondering. I appreciated that things between us had felt so normal and stable that I didn't feel like a loser for asking. I genuinely needed to know for us to be able to figure things out together. I couldn't make her feel better until I knew that she actually was upset.

Maya took a little longer to respond this time than she had initially. The longer I waited, the antsier I felt. My text was suddenly feeling less lighthearted and playful and way more annoying.

The little bubbles popped up, telling me that she was drafting something. I thought back on all of our conversations about how she'd never been someone who was into commitment or anything serious. My stomach lurched at the thought that this might be it. We'd been able to get away with being so happy and stable because nothing had been going on between us. But eventually, things would have to get serious and real, and I wasn't sure how a girl who'd never wanted anything serious was going to take that.

No, I'm not. I promise. I'm just disappointed I didn't get to see you, she wrote back and her answer was honest enough that I believed her. It genuinely made me feel better.

"Ready?" GJ asked, clapping a hand to my shoulder. Her duffel bag was hanging over her shoulder. "I think I'll shower at home and then we can meet up with everyone from there."

"Yeah," I said. I tried to muster up enthusiasm for the team—we'd won, we were in great shape for our game against Point Brook, our record was still one of the best we'd ever had in program history.

But even so, I couldn't completely shake off the feeling in the pit of my stomach that it was only going to get harder to balance everything as time went on.

After going out with the team to a house party—a singular beer in my system at the request of GJ—I texted Maya to see if she was still awake. She texted back not much later that she'd just gotten into bed.

Come join me, she wrote.

I'd never cut across campus so quickly to get anywhere. I made it to her apartment in record time, GJ watching my location the entire walk to make sure that I made it safely. Maya buzzed me into her apartment, and I took the steps two at a time to her front door.

Inside, the lights in the apartment were off and Iris's door was closed with no light peeking out from under it. Maya's room had a faint glow coming out from the bottom, telling me she was still awake.

I slowly opened her bedroom door so I wouldn't scare her. "Hey," I whispered.

"Hey," she said. "Come lie down."

"Did you have fun at karaoke?" I asked. Maya had gone out with Iris and some of her other friends for a birthday.

"Yeah, it was amazing," Maya said. I dropped all of my clothes to the floor until I was standing in only briefs and my sports bra, and then crawled into bed with her. She laid her head on my chest. "How was going out with the team? Did you get to party with Bendr?"

I laughed. "No, I don't think the Lakeside Green party scene would really be his vibe. I'm sure he got out of here as soon as he could after the game. It was cool he stopped by, though."

"I should've invited him to karaoke. People would've loved that."

"They definitely would've. Free drinks all night, I'm sure," I said.

I settled further into bed, and Maya readjusted around me. It was perfect and cozy and everything I could've possibly asked for. But I knew I wasn't going to be able to sleep until we addressed the elephant in the room. Or at least, the elephant that didn't seem to exist to Maya but felt like it was crushing my chest.

"Are we okay?" I asked, stroking her hair. "From after the game? I really am sorry I wasn't able to find you."

"Oh, it's okay," Maya said in the most serious and genuine tone I'd probably ever heard her use. It was immediately obvious she wasn't being passive-aggressive or playing it off. Maya and I were still getting to know each other, but her direct communication was a trend I'd noticed. She didn't bullshit—at least, not when it came to me. It didn't seem like I'd have to jump through hoops to get information out of her, which I appreciated.

"Are you sure?"

"Yeah. It happens. Things get busy."

I was quiet for a moment. "I just really like the tradition we had going," I said.

She smiled, snuggling in closer. "Me too."

"My parents tried to do something similar for me. They'd call after games."

"That's sweet."

"Yeah, it is. It didn't really end up working out, though. We could never catch each other at the right times."

"Hm." Maya's response was so easygoing that I could only assume she wasn't as worried as I was.

All I kept thinking about was how hard my parents and I had tried to keep some kind of tradition going, and we hadn't been able to. Things had just gotten in the way, one thing after another. It wasn't anyone's fault, and it didn't change that I knew they loved me and supported me; we really were just busy.

But still. It meant that caring about someone and trying to make time for someone didn't mean there would always be time. And I couldn't help but worry that maybe it was inevitable with a schedule—and future—like mine.

Chapter 23

MAYA

A week after the game against the Yellowjackets, I glanced at my calendar and then over at a sleeping Theo in the bed next to me. She didn't have practice today because she'd just gone through a week of away games, and there were a few days until she had a home game again. She was taking full advantage of the downtime that she had after what had been a busy school year so far.

Time was passing quickly—the regular season was over in only a few weeks. And Theo's game against Cam Kerr was coming up very, very soon, something I seemed to be more stressed about than Theo.

Despite the little hiccup after her home game, everything had been fine. It seemed like we were in a good place. I loved spending time with her and loved getting to know her; she was quickly becoming my favorite person in the world to hangout with—something I was never going to say to Iris, both because I knew she'd hate to hear she was being replaced, and also because she'd make fun of me for it.

Over time, I'd learned that Theo slept like someone who hadn't slept in weeks every single time she lay down. When she didn't have to be at practice, she knocked out solidly for at least eight to ten hours. She didn't move and didn't talk in her sleep, and didn't notice when I got up from bed or was on my phone. She—reasonably—slept like someone who burned a million calories a day and didn't stop moving from the second she woke up to the second she went to bed.

Her sleeping face was so cute. I'd seen a few pictures of her as a kid here and there, and she still had some of the same characteristics. Her hair was darker now than it was when she was a kid, but her expressions were still all the same. I loved the pictures of her in basketball uniforms throughout the years; it reminded me that somewhere in her, she was still just a little girl with a dream.

I smiled a little bit and then looked back at my calendar. Valentine's Day was coming up quickly—as in, three days from now. Theo and I hadn't addressed it all, which was fine. But I'd never been the kind of person who wanted Valentine's Day plans. I'd always been someone who was *scared* of Valentine's Day and everything it implied.

To get me through it, Iris had been offering gentle words of encouragement, usually in the form of *you're an idiot for even asking me if I think you and Theo are serious.*

Theo's eyes slowly fluttered open, and I turned my head quickly away, acting like I hadn't just been staring at her and memorizing every faint freckle across the bridge of her nose.

"Why are you staring at me?"

"I'm not," I lied.

"I could feel your beady little eyes on me," she teased, and pulled me down toward her. My phone dropped into the sea of sheets in the process, and I buried myself in her arms. She stroked my hair. "What were you thinking about?"

"What makes you think I was thinking about something?"

"Because I could feel your beady little eyes on me," she repeated, and I laughed.

"Iris's birthday is coming up at the end of the month. Do you think you'll be able to go to the party, or is your schedule going to be too hectic?" I started there because that felt easier than going straight into Valentine's Day. I was so embarrassed by the entire thing that I wanted to crawl out of my skin. Theo and I had covered a lot of ground, but I hadn't gotten to a point yet where I felt totally comfortable asking for her to make time for me.

"Let me look at the dates," she said. She readjusted so she was spooning me. "That was it?"

"I..." I said with a small shrug.

"What are you thinking about, pretty girl? What's going on in that head of yours?" she asked, her voice low.

I squeezed my eyes shut, as if that was going to make it possible for her not to see me. "Are you doing anything on Wednesday?"

"Valentine's Day," Theo said without having to check. She must've been thinking about it too. "You're spoiling my surprise."

I turned to look at her, our noses nearly pressed to each other. "What are you talking about?"

"I was going to do a whole Valentine's Day thing. Well, not like a whole thing, because I know how you are. But I was thinking about it," she said. "Give me the chance to at least ask you to be my Valentine first."

I had to resist squealing with excitement, my nerves from earlier evaporating. "You are so *cute*," I said, wrapping my arms around her and bringing her in for a hug.

For just a second, I flashed to an outside perspective of me being so affectionate toward my partner, and I didn't recognize myself. But maybe that was a good thing. Maybe this whole time, this version of me had been in here, waiting to come out.

The only holdup was that I was still hesitant to make it official. Every time I thought about it, I felt a tug in my chest that made me feel almost sick to my stomach. Outside of a brief high school thing with a boy I didn't even like, I'd never been someone's girlfriend. Not during a time in my life where it really mattered, where things like moving in together and marriage weren't far down the line.

I was so close to getting there with Theo. I'd dreamed about it and thought about it. My friends liked her and had no complaints about her. She was so sweet to me. She was perfect girlfriend material.

But something was holding me back, and I didn't know what.

Fortunately, Theo didn't seem like she was in any kind of rush. She never brought it up, never made any comments that made me think she was getting impatient. She knew me well enough to know that she'd have to wait for me, and she was willing to do that.

At least, for now. I didn't know if she'd be able to be patient forever.

We eventually got up and out of bed and headed to the kitchen. In addition to how hard Theo slept, Theo was also someone who loved food. It made sense—she wasn't going to be able to build the kind of muscle she had without eating consistently. But it was funny watching her cook because it was obvious she learned a basic set of skills and nothing beyond that. She could roast any vegetable, but got nervous trying to cook anything on the stove.

I went to work on making eggs for us while Theo worked on pancakes. She'd introduced me to the protein-dense kind, which I was trying my best to adapt to. It was a small compromise for being able to eat breakfast together every once in a while. She was never opposed to putting chocolate chips in them, which was as much as I could ask for.

As the eggs cooked, I mindlessly scrolled through social media. There were pictures from the party this weekend at The 151, people who'd fled Colorado for the weekend to get away from the cold, people skiing. Then, a video popped up with Theo's face.

It was never less jarring to randomly see video clips *about* Theo. Pictures were fine, and footage shared of her playing online was also fine.

But when it came to people posting theory videos, gossiping about her career, and talking about her, it'd become jarring. Now that I actually knew her and she wasn't just the basketball player I had a crush on from a distance, I'd gotten defensive.

I was initially going to scroll past it, but when I saw that it was a draft predictions video, my finger hovered over the screen. Instead of sliding past, I let it play.

"Draft predictions are starting to become real now that the season is almost over," a guy who was way too enthusiastic said. He was sitting in a gamer chair and flashed up clips of different major college basketball players of the moment—including Theo—and team logo graphics. "Everyone already knows Theo McCall will probably be staying close to her university after last season's bleak performance from the Blizzards. But Cam Kerr seems to have a lot to say about everyone's predictions putting her second."

"What are you watching?" Theo asked, glancing over at me.

"Shh," I said.

A clip of Cam popped up. She was sitting on a post-game panel, her coach and two other players sitting nearby. "The draft isn't here yet. Predictions are predictions, they don't mean anything. I know my stats and I know my skills."

"Do you think predictions will change once you play Lakeside Green?" a reporter asked.

"I'm not saying I can do it, but I know that anyone who can beat Theo McCall might be an even more valuable asset to a team than Theo herself."

The video cut back to the guy. "Looks like we're about to have a battle ahead. We still have March to know for sure how things are going to shake out, but let me know your predictions for who you think will be going where in April."

Theo peeked over my shoulder. "What are you watching?" she asked again.

"Nothing," I said, trying to play it off as casual. But the swirling in my stomach and the half-whisper in my voice was an obvious giveaway. I'd never been a confident liar.

For the first time, the realization really hit me. Theo was actually going to get drafted, meaning she was going to go where her team was. And that was that.

At least with graduate school, it felt like I had some choice. If I got into multiple programs, I could weigh the pros and cons of each one and decide for myself.

But Theo didn't have that luxury. And April was soon, and then the pro season began weeks after that.

My stomach knotted and I realized exactly why I'd been holding out on Theo. Subconsciously, I knew this couldn't possibly be forever.

Even if Theo did get drafted to the Blizzards and stayed in Colorado, there was no promise I'd get into a program here. And there was also no promise that I would stay here, or that Theo would even be the draft pick who made it on the Blizzards.

"You okay?" Theo asked, looking over at me. I realized I'd been staring into the eggs and watching them get way too crispy.

"Yeah, sorry," I said and tried to shake it off. I thought about what our schedules were going to look like—her continuing to fly all around the US, me in a rigorous program that required me to be somewhere for at least five to seven years.

That was a long time in the grand scheme of things. A *really* long time.

Theo looked over at me curiously. "You sure you're okay?"

"Yeah, I'm fine. Just tired," I said. Part of me hoped she'd see right through it. I so badly wanted to talk about all of it, to get it off my chest. Theo had gotten so good about being the person who would keep me level; she'd listen to me monologue for hours about graduate school decisions and my future.

But I didn't know what to do now that my favorite emotional support person was the reason I was wound up.

We could talk about it. But it wouldn't actually fix anything, wouldn't actually give us any answers. The only thing we could do was wait—just like we'd been doing. Both for my graduate decisions and who was going to take Theo in the draft.

There were so many things that could go wrong. Theo could end up not getting picked first. Or she could end up in Colorado, and I wouldn't get accepted into a program here. Or I would get accepted into a program here and we'd try to make it work, only to realize it was never going to.

There was a chance we'd done all of this just for it to crumble as soon as we left Lakeside Green. It was dramatic, but it was true. We'd made the mistake of meeting too late, becoming serious too late. February was the last month of our routine, and then March would be here with a flurry of championship games and then April for the draft and that was it.

I knew the bubble had to burst eventually, but I'd been hoping it wouldn't have to be so soon.

Chapter 24

THEO

I could tell something was up with Maya, but I didn't push it.

I *was* going to ask. Eventually. If it really seemed like I needed to.

But for now, I didn't want to come across like I was badgering her. I knew she'd talk to me when she was ready, just like she always did. Anything beyond the occasional, *Are you doing okay?* would've annoyed me, so I could only think it'd also annoy her.

It had also become hard to find the time to schedule seeing her to even ask her what was going on. After a few days of a break from playing and being on the road, we were back in the swing of things—and twice as hard as before.

The last few games of the season were coming, and our record was still holding up. If everything went as planned, we'd make it into the championship no problem. But that was barring any injuries or players who crumbled under the pressure. And avoiding those pitfalls was easier said than done.

After wrapping up a morning practice and then classes for the day, GJ and I jogged through campus, keeping pace with each other the entire time. She's been a good distraction during all of this.

Not to say that Maya wasn't also a distraction—Maya just couldn't really be a distraction from herself and me wondering what was going on with her. I couldn't help but think maybe the Bendr thing had upset her more than she'd let on. Or maybe Valentine's Day—we'd just done a modest homemade dinner and a movie together at home—had made everything feel way too serious. I'd even held off on buying her flowers and a card because I was nervous she'd get overwhelmed, something I regretted and planned to make right if Maya would let me.

"You ready to take over next year?" I asked.

"It's not guaranteed that I'll be captain," GJ said, mocking my voice. She chuckled to herself.

"Funny."

The air was cold, making my lungs feel tight as we ran. My cheeks stung from the wind. We cut down into one of the wooded trails just off of campus where students usually went to smoke weed and continued on our way.

"Unlike *someone* here, I can admit when I know I'll be on top," she said. "And I personally can't wait. I don't know if anyone's ever told you but you're fucking hard to compete with, dude. You're taking all of the attention off of *me* and my mad skills."

"You're still getting plenty of attention. You're always referred to as my right hand," I said and GJ made a face. "It's making you look good. People know your name. You're definitely on people's list to keep an eye on next year."

"First round or nothing," GJ said, referring to the draft.

"Yeah, since you've had me as your captain. You better be," I said lightly.

I put very little pressure on my team when it came to next steps. I knew that not everyone was going to make the cut to go pro—and not everyone wanted to. It was usually pretty evident who had the talent and drive to keep playing and I tended to latch onto those people. Most of the starters on my team were aspiring to go pro eventually, which I had to assume was a big part of the reason why we'd been playing so well and why they were able to keep pace with me. Without them, I would've been a Danny, struggling to keep a team alive.

But I meant it when I told them it didn't matter if they decided not to go pro. Any of them could change their minds at any point; Coach Darlene and I weren't going to be upset with them because of that.

"Have you thought much about April?" GJ asked. "You thinking you'll end up with the Blizzards?"

There was a list of reasons why the Blizzards was a great fit for me, beyond them just having the first pick and me most likely ending up with them whether we were actually a good fit or not.

They had a young team and a young coach with a lot of energy. They'd struggled for most of the season and obviously came out the worst team in the league, hence getting the first pick, but there was promise there.

Based on what I'd seen, they needed someone who could be their glue, something I felt confident I could do. Objectively, I knew that I had the star power that they would need.

And they were also close to here, which I wouldn't mind. I'd come to like Colorado, and I hoped I'd be able to buy a house big enough for my parents to stay with me whenever they wanted so I wouldn't have to go so long without seeing them.

But the downsides were also pretty obvious—they were a young team with no veteran players. Most of their players had been drafted in the past couple of years, a lot of them I'd played against already at a college level. They fell behind the other teams who were more experienced, which could also end up being my weak spot.

I was used to playing people who played at a college level and were college age; I wasn't used to people who'd been playing professionally for over a decade, the people whose posters I used to keep up on my wall as a kid.

"It's not really up to me," I admitted. "I can think about it all I want but it won't change anything. I'll probably end up with them, but one bad game and I could end up anywhere."

GJ and I kept moving down the trail, hitting a part with a slight incline. We were gentle on our ankles, careful not to accidentally trip over anything. That was the most delicate part of being an athlete—we needed to train to get better, but there was always a chance of us getting hurt.

"If I wasn't your teammate, I'd be praying for that bad game sooner rather than later," GJ said. "I know people are sick of hearing you breaking records left and right. My ego would never be bruised by something like that, personally. But I feel for them."

I snorted. "I'm sure Cam Kerr is putting in the work, doing some kind of, like, manifestation ritual or something. She's out there praying on my downfall."

"She definitely is. I hope you run circles around her at that game. I want to see you beat her smug ass," GJ said. "I'll be helping but I'm handing the reins to you. This is my personal Super Bowl."

"We'll see what happens," I said.

"I know that's Theo speak for *I'm going to kick her ass*," GJ said. "I believe it."

GJ and I followed the trail back toward one of the basketball courts in the area. It was a different court than the one I'd taken Maya to, the one that was on campus near the freshman dorms. This one was further out and technically a residential one that didn't belong to Lakeside Green, but a public hoop was a public hoop. This was where the basketball players on campus liked to mess around—it was a good place to clear our heads, somewhere we didn't risk people coming up to us while we were just trying to have a good time.

"Danny!" I shouted and waved to get his attention. He was out shooting by himself, wearing basketball shorts and a sweatshirt. As I got closer, I could see the sweat pooling at his temples. It was cold in Colorado, but the sun combined with the elevation could be unforgiving. Now that GJ and I were out of the woods and in full sun, I knew some layers would be coming off.

"Hey," he shouted back and then sank an easy fadeaway. We walked over to him and he hugged the ball to his hip. "Glad you could make it. I needed a break."

"I'd need a break from your imbecile teammates, too," GJ agreed and snatched the ball from Danny's hand. She shot it up, sending it cleanly through. Our shooting percentages were high on the court, so shooting like this—no one blocking us, no game time pressure—was comparatively a breeze. We'd all average nearly one-hundred percent if this was how the game was played on the court.

Danny jogged to get the ball and GJ attempted to block. He sidestepped her and shot it in from the two-point range. It landed so cleanly that the metal hoop barely even made a sound.

GJ waved him off. "You got a couple of inches on me."

"Over here," I said, waving my hand to get Danny's attention. He bounced the ball to me and we easily fell into the rhythm of a pick up game. There was no real structure—there were times it was all three of us playing each other, other times I assisted Danny and then GJ. No one was keeping score.

Playing exactly like this reminded me of how much I loved the sport and how lucky I was to get to play at all. I was worried that as I continued moving up in basketball, I'd feel less inclined to play recreationally. But instead, it was impossible to take myself off of a court—any court, whether it was for a real college game or just playing on a random court outside.

"You ready for next week, McCall?" Danny asked.

"Trying my best to be," I said and hit a jumper. GJ caught the ball and dribbled it back to the equivalent of mid-court to keep the ball away from Danny.

"I'll be there to watch," he said. "I'm glad our schedules worked out. I'd be pissed to miss what is going to be, like, game of the century."

"Everyone keeps talking about it as if odds aren't high we'll face off again in the championship," I said.

"But this is what'll set the *tone*," GJ said. "Someone's gotta win, someone's gotta lose. It's going to be a fucking *battlefield* out there, bro. Whoever loses will get their revenge, possibly in the finals. This is, like, movie-level shit."

"I don't know if it's that serious," I said.

GJ passed the ball to me and I passed it to Danny, who was further up the court. "Cam Kerr definitely seems to think it is," GJ said.

"She's talking out of her ass," Danny said.

"She *is* good," I admitted. "I think she just likes the circus."

GJ stepped in, stealing the ball from under Danny's hand. She sprinted away. "Gotta be quicker than that, Danny boy!"

Danny was unaffected; he played through the rhythm of the game, turning on his heel and attempting to block GJ from shooting. "And how's your girl?"

I smiled, unable to help myself every time I thought about Maya. Even in the midst of the moment she was having where she was a little harder to reach and a little more emotionally distant, I felt confident that she'd come back around. The last couple of months hadn't been made up. The feelings were real—even someone who struggled with commitment had to admit that much.

"She's good," I said as I chased GJ and Danny up the court so they could pass the ball to me. "The schedule has been a lot but we find the time. She'll be there to cheer me on at the Point Brook game."

"That's sweet," Danny said as GJ pretended to gag.

We kept playing until we were all sweaty and tired. None of us wanted to go too hard because we had workouts later in the evening, but it still felt good.

As GJ and I gathered our phones and the sweatshirts we'd abandoned while we were playing, I turned to Danny. "Do you remember meeting a blonde at a party, by the way?"

"That's specific," he said.

"Iris."

He thought about it for a second and then I could see a flash of recognition cross his face. "Yeah. Cute, small? She ran out on me at a party," he said. "Is she going around telling everyone I'm the worst now?" he chuckled.

"No, actually. Kind of the opposite," I said. "She's Maya's best friend. She'll definitely be at my game, too. You should look for her."

Danny smiled and slowly nodded. "Okay. I'll keep that in mind."

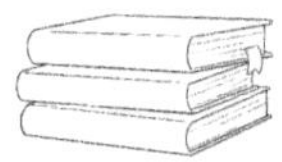

Chapter 25

MAYA

I felt so antsy I was certain I was losing my mind.

If something didn't happen soon—if something didn't *change* soon—I thought I might explode. I'd been trying to be as calm as I could possibly be, but it felt impossible. For days, my brain had been on one endless loop. It felt like the universe was laughing at me for finally figuring things out for myself, for finally attempting to like someone.

I hadn't been able to get back into the swing of things since I saw that video of Cam talking about Theo. I didn't know what exactly it'd set off in my brain, but it'd really stuck and it was impossible to shake off the feeling. I was so nervous about the future, nervous about what was going to come next for me and Theo. It felt pointless to even try when I couldn't imagine it was going to work out in the long run.

My vibe going into March had been pretty abysmal because of it. I'd been coming up with excuses not to see Theo and excuses for why I was in the house and not going to the gym or workout classes as often with Iris.

Iris had been patient with me, but it was obvious she was starting to lose her patience toward the end of day three of me moping around the house.

"You're really killing my mood here, dude," she said randomly while we were settled in to watch TV in the living room. TV had been one of my only escapes from the spiral out I was experiencing. I couldn't use social media because I'd accidentally trained my algorithm to flood me with Theo related things. That was one thing no one warned me about when I started to date someone relatively famous.

"I'm not even doing anything," I protested, which was true. I was sitting on the other end of the couch from Iris, my legs pulled up under me. I was cozy under a blanket and in my softest pajamas.

My days had felt long and boring without Theo, like someone had zapped the light out of my daily activities. But I was struggling to figure out how exactly to work through my feelings. I was scared to see her and sad when I didn't. It was reminiscent of the times I'd avoid seeing someone because I knew I needed to suck it up and dump them. I was worried that was the inevitable next step. It was impossible, though—running would only be a temporary relief; the thought of losing Theo forever made me sick.

"You're like a little rain cloud," Iris said. "And you've been moving around the house like you're haunting the place or something. I practically saw you hovering in the corner the other day."

"That's an exaggeration," I said, even though it was probably a tiny bit true.

She muted the TV and turned to look at me. "I'm begging you to get your shit together. You haven't broken up. Nothing is actually wrong. You're getting yourself all knotted up because of your own worries."

"Yeah, but they're *legitimate* worries."

"Every worry feels like a legitimate worry. That's the whole point. If we didn't care, we wouldn't be worrying," Iris said. "I love you too much to watch you do this to yourself. I'm sorry the timing is weird and I'm sorry a lot of change is coming. But every college senior feels the same way you do to a certain extent. It's a major life transition. It's impossible not to get worked up about it unless you have, like, a guaranteed job right out of school. But even then, it's still change. It's *significant*."

"Normally, I love your *you're not special* talks, but this one hurts especially bad," I said, mostly joking. Iris was the queen of keeping me grounded. Every time I was convinced it was the end of the world because of one thing or another, like not getting into a class I really wanted, she was there to remind me that it wasn't even half as catastrophic as I was imagining.

"I don't think it's worth it to throw away your first real crush without at least trying. You have something with Theo, Maya. Like, it's undeniable. It radiates off of you every time you're together. And that's so scary. But it's also really beautiful."

"But is it really worth it to keep trying if it seems like it's not going to go anywhere?" I asked.

"You don't actually *know* it's not going to go anywhere. You're just assuming it won't work out." She rotated her body to look at me straight-on from across the couch. "Have you even talked to Theo about it?"

"Not really," I said and Iris threw her hands up in exasperation. "I know, I know. But I don't know what there is to say to her. Like, please don't leave me? Please don't trade me in for your basketball team? Take me with you?" I shook my head. "I doubt she's going to want to be put in that position. And I can't shrink myself down like that. I can't. My mother would lose her mind knowing her daughter was saying those things."

"Do you think she might have something to do with this? Like, even a teeny tiny bit?" Iris asked and I knew she was referring to my mom. Our relationship had always been complicated and I could see pieces of my mother—who I'd always known as a flaky, flighty woman—in myself as I got older, whether I wanted that or not.

"Oh, I *know* she has something to do with her. This is all her. Refusing to stick around, running at the first sign of trouble. She always said that stress made her feel wrinkly and aged her too quickly. She drops anything that makes her feel stressed as soon as she can."

"Right. And with zero negative consequences to anyone involved."

My lips turned up in a sad smile. "How embarrassing that it always comes back to our parents."

"Maybe just explain that to Theo as a start. Try to *talk* to her at least. Give her something. I'm sure she can tell you're acting weird too and she's probably trying to be nice and give you space to work through it."

"But what if she doesn't get it?"

"Then she doesn't get it. And you figure it out from there. But Theo has been kind—she deserves better than this."

I sighed a little bit. "I just...I want it to stay how it is. I want this," I said, gesturing to our apartment and campus and little lives we'd built out here. It felt so stable and safe here. It felt like home, especially now that I had Theo.

"I know. But sometimes it's not like that," Iris said. "Things change and we have to be ready for it, even when we're not ready. Mourn the loss and then pick right back up in a new routine."

"I just really like her, Iris. Like, really like her. And I don't know if she can give me what I need from her in terms of commitment. I want her time and attention and availability. I don't want her flying all around the country for months out of the year, leaving me to do my PhD work alone while everyone is able to get married and move in together and see their partner all the time."

"Isn't long distance, like, the lesbian MO? Maybe it's going to find you one way or another," she said. "Maybe instead of thinking of it in terms of the games she'll be away from home for, think of all of the time she'll spend at home when the season is over."

I considered what she was saying. I pictured Theo coming home after games, just like she was doing now. I thought about being able to go to her games and still talk to her even when she was out of town. I didn't know how different professional basketball would be compared to college, but at least there wouldn't be school to worry about anymore—for her, at least. It would take one thing off of her plate.

But then I also pictured the nights when she was away from me. The times when I was stressed from classes and teaching and keeping up with the demands of academia and she wouldn't be able to be physically there with me.

"I like her enough that I think only getting bits and pieces of her might hurt more than not having her at all," I said.

Iris thought it over. "Being totally honest, that really only applies in situations where a partner is inconsistent. I don't know if you can pull that card with Theo. I've seen how you light up when you're with her. And look at how you are now—you don't have any of her at all of your own volition and you're reaching Bridget Jones *All By Myself* levels of...sad. And it's only been a couple of days. I think you think you're protecting yourself but it just looks like self-sabotage."

I crawled across the couch and sat in her lap, wrapping my arms around her neck. "You're the meanest person I know," I said.

"Someone needs to be a straight shooter with you," she said, her voice muffled by my shoulder. She lifted her mouth out from under my sweatshirt. "Maybe a therapist soon instead of me, but we can cross that bridge when you're ready."

"I'll start with talking to Theo first," I said. "And maybe my mom, actually."

"Please do," she said. "I love you but I can't listen to this or see this anymore."

I spent the entire evening emotionally preparing myself to see Theo again. Talking to Iris had leveled me out significantly—it no longer felt like the world was ending and I was starting to think I could handle talking to Theo about everything.

But by the next morning, I was feeling a little less confident. The speech I'd been rehearsing and rewriting in my head all night felt...wrong. I didn't know what to say or how to say it. I had the self-awareness to realize everything I was saying was with the undercurrent of, *we can try, but I don't know if I really even want it to work out,* and *this feels like too much work,* and *is it* really *worth it in the long run? Like, really?*

I hated all of it. I could see what I was doing so clearly. And while bullshit like that worked in relationships that weren't so involved, I knew Theo would see right through it. She might let me go, but she would do it knowing that I was just scared underneath it all—I was scared I'd have to give up my dream or that she'd have to give up hers, that there were too many compromises for us to work through, that we worked best in a relationship that wasn't meant to be anything serious.

But I knew I'd have to talk to her. I couldn't keep putting it off or giving her half-assed answers. I knew she knew she was getting the run-around; I was just fortunate that she was patient enough to not get mad at me for it.

As I was about to leave for class, I grabbed my phone and considered texting Theo. I hated this part—the talking, the big feelings. Even though I knew she liked me, it felt like the hardest part was still yet to come. I wanted to run and hide.

I was about to slip my phone back in my coat pocket, not ready to text her yet, when it vibrated with an email notification. When I saw that it was from one of the schools I applied to, my heart nearly fell to the floor.

"Oh god," I whispered to myself. I stepped off of the sidewalk so people could get by, my heart pounding. I half-closed my eyes as I pressed to open it. When I saw the word *Congratulations!* I nearly dropped my phone. I pressed my hand to my mouth and let out a small squeal. It wasn't necessarily the highest ranked of the programs I'd applied to, but it was one I was still excited about.

The only issue was that it was in Texas. And chances were very high that Theo would be staying here in Colorado for basketball. If this was the only program I got accepted to, we were definitely going to have a problem.

I glanced at the clock. I didn't have time to dwell on this; I had to get to my next class.

"Fuck," I muttered and shoved my phone into my pocket, pushing it—and my pending conversation with Theo—to the back of my mind. Rather than making the decision easier, this seemed to only make things harder.

Because, I realized as I was walking to class, what I really wanted was an excuse to stay here with her.

After talking to Iris again in a panic about my acceptance, she reached the point where she just kept repeating *talk to Theo talk to Theo talk to Theo* and I knew I couldn't put it off any longer. She'd also emphasized the obvious—I'd applied to other programs, so there was always a chance I'd get accepted somewhere else, including the one I'd applied to in Colorado.

In the hour leading up to Theo coming over, I was sick to my stomach in a way I never had been before. I'd been nervous to see her, nervous about where everything might go, but not completely overwhelmed like this. And Iris was out working so it would just be me and Theo; I didn't know if that made it better or worse.

I didn't know what her thoughts were on the situation. Our texts hadn't been anything particularly direct, and it also probably wouldn't be obvious that something was up between us to anyone else. But I knew the way that we talked to each other usually, and our texts were nothing like that. They were drier and more direct, and outside of Theo traveling for basketball, this was the longest we'd gone without seeing each other—and it was entirely because of me.

After buzzing Theo into the apartment, I sat on the couch and waited. And then, because sitting felt weird, I hovered in the kitchen. And then back to the living room. When the front door finally opened, I was relieved that the anticipation part could at least finally be over now.

"Hey," Theo said as she walked into the apartment.

As soon as a I saw her, I crumbled completely. All of the things I'd been telling myself to try and create space—that basketball was always going to be the most important thing to her, that it would honestly kind of suck to be dating to be dating a household name, that Theo's nice persona was inevitably going to fade—disappeared into nothing.

I felt awake again for the first time in days just looking at her. I wanted to crawl into her lap and never get up.

"Hi," I said, fighting off the overwhelming urge to cry for whatever reason. I couldn't believe myself—what the fuck was happening to me? When did I become this girl?

She walked over to the couch and I followed her. When we sat down, we still sat close enough that our bodies brushed each other. I ached to touch her, to run my fingers through her hair.

"How is everything?" Theo asked. She sounded mostly normal, which was somewhat of a surprise to me. Despite her gentleness over text, I'd been expecting she might be less accommodating in person. But there was no underpinning of frustration or annoyance. She was talking to me affectionately, not rudely.

I realized I'd been expecting her to do that—to get mean with me. I'd maybe almost been hoping she would do that so it would be easier to end things right then. I could cut and run from an asshole guilt-free. It was harder when it was someone nice.

"I got my first grad school acceptance," I said softly, picking at the threads of my couch.

"Maya, that's amazing," she said genuinely. "Which program was it?"

"The one in Texas."

"That's huge. Fully funded, right?"

I nodded and smiled a little bit at the enthusiasm in her voice. I glanced up at her. "I didn't know if you'd be excited for me or not."

"Why wouldn't I be excited for you?"

I paused. "I haven't been...super nice."

"We've both had a lot going on," Theo said. "Is it that we celebrated Valentine's Day together? Did it feel like too much?" She ducked her head down to try and catch my eye. "It hasn't gotten past me that we haven't talked about labels. I know we're taking our time."

"No," I said earnestly. It was a surprise to realize that the core of it wasn't that I didn't want to be exclusive and serious with Theo. If anything, I wanted that *so* badly.

"Are you sure? It's okay if you're not ready."

"No, I really think I am," I said. I curled myself up on the couch and looked in her direction. "I think I just keep coming up with a million reasons why we shouldn't."

Theo nodded slowly, taking in what I was saying. "I get that. Tell me what you're worried about. Talk to me," she pleaded.

I fought off the urge to cry again, feeling suddenly way too exposed and vulnerable. "Um. I don't know," I said. "Sorry, that's a lie. I do know. I don't know why I said that." I took a deep breath. "I think I'm worried about what's going to come next. Like, is there really a point in continuing to do this if we know there's a chance we'll end up in different places, doing different things? And even if we end up in the same place, are we really going to be able to see each other?"

Theo sat with it for a second, looking straight ahead instead of at me. "I think all of that is really reasonable."

"Do you have the same concerns?" I asked.

Theo twisted her mouth in thought. "No, not really."

I was surprised and confused, overwhelmed and elated and nervous, all at once. "Why not?" I asked. "You said it yourself—we've both had a lot going on."

"I mean, I like you," she said, like it was as simple as that. "I'll do whatever it takes to make that work, even if we have a lot going on." She turned to look at me. "You can try and push me away all you want, but I'm going to try just as hard to stay. I'll leave if you really want me to and we can let it all go. But I personally don't want that. I never have."

"Even if I have to go to school in Texas?"

"There's a team out there that I'd play against. I'm sure I'd be able to justify a visit to you while I'm out there," she said. "And I'd see you all the time in the offseason."

"It's a big state. I might be far from you."

"I don't know if you've noticed, but I'm kind of a big deal," she said, half-joking. "I have strings I can pull when I want to. *And* unlike college basketball, professional basketball is primarily a summer sport, so your workload might not be as bad because it's outside of the traditional school year. We'll be able to see each other."

"I'll probably still be doing research. And teaching."

"And I'll be playing basketball. We'll just be two people with jobs."

My heart swelled, feeling hopeful for the first time in what felt like forever that maybe we really could figure this out. Theo seemed so serious about making it work. It was hard not to believe her when she made it all sound so easy. We were going to be just two people with jobs, albeit unusual ones.

But then I thought about it practically—flights and Face-Time calls. I imagined watching Theo on TV more than I was able to see her in person. There was a chance I might not even be able to enjoy her early career as a pro basketball player because I'd be so busy with my own work. The first five years *at least* of her playing would be spent with me in school. And then I couldn't imagine I'd ever want to be the kind of girl who stayed at home, no matter how much money Theo was able to bring in. We'd both always be *busy*.

"I can tell there's something going on in your head," Theo said. "You've been quiet for too long."

"Sorry, there's just...a lot to think about," I said.

"I know," she said. "And that's okay. You don't have to figure it all out now. But you're the girl that I want, Maya. The only one. I'm willing to wait for you. I *want* to wait for you."

My eyes finally welled up with tears after threatening to fall the entire time we'd been talking. I'd never had someone speak to me that way, so earnestly holding onto what we had. It was the most special and most cared for I'd ever felt in my life. And all I could think about was how Theo didn't deserve me acting this way. She didn't need someone who was going to make her wait.

"Oh, Maya," Theo said softly as I started crying harder. She moved closer to me and I leaned into her shoulder. She moved her hands up and down my back with a feather-light touch. It was so comforting and exactly what I needed. She was always so good at that, always so tuned into what would help me.

"I think I'm in love with you," I admitted into her neck, the words coming out effortlessly. I'd never really said them to anyone before, other than my mom or Iris. Definitely never to a partner. I didn't feel it easily and I definitely didn't communicate it easily. But just like with everything else, *I love you* felt easy with Theo.

"I know you're in love with me," she said and I laughed through my tears. She gently wiped the tears from under my eyes. "I love you too."

Hearing that Theo loved me was everything to me. As soon as she said it, I understood what everyone meant when they talked about love. It wasn't necessarily fireworks or excitement or rain-soaked confessions—it was a partner fighting to stay even when I was pushing her away. It felt like safety and familiarity and sturdiness.

But love wasn't the only thing that mattered right now. It just made it all the more painful.

"I'm sorry I don't know what to do," I whispered.

"You don't need to know what to do but I understand being careful," she said. "I'm actually surprised you're not jumping headfirst into this and waiting for it to crash and burn like you do with everything else."

"It's because I actually like you."

Theo snorted. "Okay, fair."

I stayed curled up in Theo's arms for as long as I could, trying to pretend that none of this was actually happening. I wanted to live in the happy little bubble we'd created throughout Theo's season. It hadn't been the easiest schedule, but it had been good. We'd found ways of seeing each other.

"You can think about it," Theo said, pressing her lips to the top of my head. "Maybe don't think on it forever, but I'll be here. I'm not letting you go that easy."

I nodded, not knowing what else there was to say.

Chapter 26

THEO

What I really wanted was to go home to my parents' house.

With Maya hitting the brakes and the game against Point Brook looming—along with all of the talk about what was to come *when* I went pro, since no one doubted I would make it—I needed a second to breathe. I didn't really get overwhelmed, but there were more interpersonal and professional things going on in my life than I'd ever had at once.

Basketball itself never felt overwhelming to me. I would get nervous about games, and I was a little nervous that Cam Kerr and the rest of the Point Brook girls would be able to come out on top. I could be as good as physically possible, but that didn't mean we'd win. If their defense was strong, if their offense had a better shooting percentage than ours, it could all be over so quickly.

But I was never nervous about my own playing. Just like I was never worried about having to go on the court and play.

Dealing with girl drama, however, *was* new to me and made a lot of the other major changes in my life feel much bigger than they would otherwise...mostly because I'd already been slotting Maya into what my future would look like.

I'd pictured her helping me move my things in at a new apartment and courtside at my games. I could easily imagine her taking her classes and teaching and then coming home to me during the offseason.

I knew I'd survive without her. A year ago, I'd envisioned going pro without anyone by my side. I'd have my parents to help me move and settle and friends to cheer me on. And that was that. I thought maybe I'd meet someone when I was already pro, probably someone in my general social circle, like a friend of a teammate's partner.

But now, the thought of doing all of that without Maya felt like I was missing something. It wouldn't make it any less special, but it sure as hell wasn't what I wanted.

There hadn't really been a formal conclusion to our conversation, but something about it had felt really final. I couldn't help but think that Maya had pretty much made up her mind, and that was why it was so hard for her to just say it.

But I also couldn't help but hold onto the hope that Maya really *did* want to make it work. She was just scared to.

I was just glad she'd at least come around to talking to me about what she was thinking and feeling. I'd really been worried she wasn't going to say anything at all, and she'd slowly fade out of my life, leaving both of us wondering what could've happened if we'd tried harder or talked more.

Maya and I had still been keeping in touch, and she promised she'd still watch my game. The high of having the girl of my dreams tell me that she loved me kept getting swirled around with the fear that I could lose her.

The game at the university, about an hour from my parents' house, felt like it came at the perfect time. The only issue was that it was impossible to make going to see them work with my schedule. I'd never craved the comfort of my basketball hoop in the backyard more. I wanted to sleep under the comforter I'd slept under all throughout high school and smell the familiar, impossible-to-describe scent of home.

I'd never felt so homesick. The entire flight to Michigan, all I could think about was how the second the season was done and I could get even a second to myself, I was going to fly back to see my parents at their house, instead of making them rent out a room in a hotel.

When it was game time, I was able to push it all to the side and get through playing without an issue just like always. If anything, I played harder than ever, grateful for an outlet for whatever feelings were going on inside of me.

When we won, we took a brief moment to celebrate—along with the acceptance that Point Brook was coming up when we got back home. Adrenaline was high from the win. With our record, we were admittedly feeling pretty invincible. Our team had never been so good, not when I was playing there and never before in the history of the program. It really meant something. And it gave us hope that we wouldn't be crushed by a women's college basketball superpower in the tournament.

"Good game, Theo," Coach Darlene said after the game. "Insane play in the third quarter," she said. "Point Brook is shaking in their boots."

"Thanks, Coach," I said.

It occurred to me how much I was going to miss her when I graduated. She'd become a second mother or an aunt to me—a coach who really listened and cared and believed in me, even if she could be tough on us sometimes. "Go give your parents a hug. I know you miss them," she said.

"Thank you."

"Of course, sweetie," she said, giving my shoulder a squeeze. She looked at me for a moment like a proud mom; it seemed like both of us were realizing the end of the season was quickly approaching, meaning our time together was almost up.

I walked over to my parents, who were sitting courtside. They were looking around, waiting for me. When I walked over, they both stood up and enveloped me in a hug.

"You're so sweaty," Mom said as she stepped back. She half-grimaced, half-smiled.

"I don't know why that could be," I said.

"How are you feeling, sweetie? Are you hungry?"

"Starving," I admitted.

"Come find us when you're back at the hotel?"

"Of course," I said and hugged both of them again. Even though I was sweaty and I could feel both of them partially hovering so I wouldn't get sweat all over them, I was happy to see them.

"See you soon, kid," Dad said and gently shook me by the shoulder before I ran off to meet up with my team.

After dinner with my parents, I went back up to their room for a little bit. The rest of the team was enjoying their free time before curfew, and I was sad to be missing it, but this was exactly where I wanted to be right now.

"I don't know if I like the hardwood they chose," Mom said. She was propped up in bed, the remote next to her. Dad was sitting in a chair across the room, doing something on his phone with his reading glasses on.

"I agree," I said as the home renovation show we were watching played out on screen. It was a little taste of home—something that made it possible for me to almost pretend that I was back.

In a way, just being in this part of Michigan brought back a lot of feelings and nostalgia for me. This was the university my parents took me to growing up. I saw so many basketball games here as a kid, spent so much time hoping that I'd be good enough to play for them. And then after a certain point, I realized I could aim to be even better than that. I could be part of a team that won championships, a team that fostered talent that played in the Olympics and went on to play professionally.

Even though this wasn't the school for me going into adulthood, it was the school that had inspired me initially to stick with playing.

"Their bathroom looks like the bathroom your dad and I had in our first house," Mom said. "I can't believe that style is coming back around."

"It's cute," I said.

The episode passed just like that. Mom would make a small comment, I'd respond with something back. Dad would offer up the occasional grunt or, *Oh, yeah, that is nice* when he looked up at the TV.

It didn't seem like much and it was probably not the most exciting parent visit anyone had ever done, but it felt like home to me. Being on the road so often meant that I had to get creative with finding routine and structure. I liked having GJ as my roommate and I liked that I packed basically the same thing for every single away game. Whenever I saw my parents, it was usually something similar to this—dinner and then downtime. I appreciated the familiarity.

Our conversation during dinner had stayed pretty neutral. They mostly asked me about grades and future plans for basketball. Even though I was legally an adult and could sign my own contracts, I still talked to them and got their approval.

I think they were both ready for me to be able to get an agent, though. We weren't allowed to have them at the college level, but I didn't trust myself to agree to anything without at least some adult in my life reviewing documents for me. My parents had started saying things like, *We trust you on what you want to do* in the past few months, meaning they didn't want the pressure anymore. My contracts kept getting bigger, and the stakes kept getting higher; it was hard for them to keep up.

The expectation was that my career would explode going into playing professionally. There were a lot of things already being teed up or suggested from brands interested in working with me. And I had managers constantly reaching out, practically begging me to keep them in mind for the day I was no longer considered a college athlete.

"Alright, I'm getting a vending machine snack," Dad said and stood up. "You need anything? When are you heading back to your room for curfew?"

"In a little bit," I said. "I'll still be here when you get back."

"Okay." Dad turned to Mom. "Vending machine?"

"Still full from dinner."

"You got it." He got up and left the room.

When the door closed, my mom got up and walked over to me. She slid in the open spot next to me, forcing me over.

"What are you doing?" I asked, laughing.

"I can tell something is up," she said.

"Nothing is up," I lied.

"You can't fool me. You're my only child, my entire job until you moved out of my house was to be aware of how you were feeling. You're sneaky and good at hiding your feelings, but you can't hide them from me."

"I know, it's annoying," I mumbled, and Mom laughed. It was true—she always knew what kind of mood I was in. I didn't find it particularly funny or helpful when I was a moody sixteen-year-old whose mom refused to leave her alone. But in this moment, it was kind of nice.

She was right about me keeping things close to the chest. Even GJ, who was always on my shit, couldn't tell I was having a moment. It was partially because I rarely ever was; anything I was feeling, any frustrations around school or personal life, could be let out on the court and never felt that serious after long enough.

But there were times when I wasn't completely my normal self. I'd had a brief meltdown after I didn't get recruited to play at Point Brook, another brief meltdown when I was worried that Lakeside Green was never going to lead to anything. My mom was the one who'd been there for it.

"Is it basketball related? It's okay to feel overwhelmed by all of the changes coming," Mom said from next to me on the bed. I laid my head in her lap and she combed her fingers through my hair.

"It's not basketball," I admitted, knowing there was no use in lying about it. It felt better to really talk about it than to keep it to my chest. I hadn't talked to anyone about everything that was going on with Maya because I didn't think it was any of their business. Until a decision had been made—mostly on Maya's end—there wasn't anything to say to anyone.

Except for my mom, who could always tell when I was off—even when I did a really good job at hiding it.

Mom was quiet for a moment. I didn't think there'd ever been a point in my life where I was really upset about something that *wasn't* basketball related. I'd had my fair share of school-yard bickering, friendships that fizzled. But nothing ever meant much compared to basketball.

Until Maya, at least.

"Is this about the girl that your dad and I met?"

I nodded, knowing there was no use in lying.

"I'm sorry, sweetie," Mom said. She combed her fingers through my hair. "What happened?"

"I think it's too much for her," I said. As soon as I said it, tears threatened to flow. My throat became tight, reality sinking in. That was absolutely what it was. I'd known it; I just hadn't wanted to admit it. And now that I was saying it out loud, it was impossible to keep pushing down.

"What is? Basketball?"

"All of it. Basketball, dating," I said, gesturing with my hands. "There's not enough time."

"There's always time, you just have to be thoughtful in finding it," Mom said, always the optimist. This wasn't the first time she'd had to pick up the pieces, but it was the first time it was girl related.

As much as I valued my career, losing Maya definitely hurt more.

"I don't know if it would be enough for her," I admitted.

"Did you try talking to her about it?"

I replayed our conversation in my head, just like I'd been doing for days. I kept wondering what she was thinking, what direction she was leaning. I wouldn't blame her for not wanting to go down this path.

Inevitably, basketball and my career were going to be a huge part of our relationship. There were going to be a lot of things I was wrapped up in and a lot of busy scheduling-related things that were going to come up. There would be times I wouldn't be able to be around for her because of work.

But I genuinely did want to try. And I hoped she knew that.

"I did," I said. "I really did."

"Then that's all that matters," she responded.

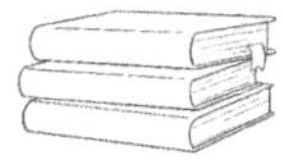

Chapter 27

MAYA

True to my word, I watched Theo's games while she was out of town. I didn't think she really expected me to but I couldn't bring myself to skip them—it made me feel guilty, like I was letting her down.

But I was also sad—it was hard to see her face knowing the distance that had grown between us, literally and emotionally.

And mixed in there was me being proud of her for having accomplished so much. Every time I watched her play, all I'd hear was commentators talking about her like she was performing a miracle.

The amount of time we spent talking had decreased pretty significantly to the point that I barely knew what she was up to. There were no plans to see her when she got back into town after her away games. I couldn't tell if it was her trying to give me space, or if she'd finally hit her breaking point and she didn't want to bother trying with me anymore.

"Jesus, what was that call?" Iris shouted at the screen. When it cut to commercial break a moment later, she turned to look at me. She frowned. "Dude, are you okay?"

"I'm fine," I said, even though I felt a tiny bit sick every time Theo popped up on screen, even in passing. Part of me hated her for it—I couldn't help but feel a little bit like I'd been set up now. My entire life was going to be dictated in phases—Before Theo and After Theo. And there were a lot of feelings that came from both of those things.

Either way, I could never go fully back to Before Theo. She would always be part of me now. I'd remember her as the first person I said I love you to, the first person who had somehow gotten through my desire to keep everyone a distance away.

It felt like there was no winning. I could either have her or not have her and both came with downsides.

"We don't have to watch this," Iris said. "Or you don't, I guess. I still want to."

My lips turned up in what I was sure was a deeply pathetic smile. "It's okay. I told her I'd watch."

"Have you spoken recently?"

"Not really," I said. "I watched her Michigan game and we texted a little about that. But we never really talked about this one."

Iris was quiet for a moment and then we went back to watching, Iris shouting at the TV and me in complete silence.

Theo and I didn't speak when she got back from the away game. I assumed she was probably waiting for me to say something first, but I didn't know what to say. And I knew that my silence was going to mean something to her. The longer I went without giving her something to work with, the easier it would be to figure out what answer I was implying. It was a game I'd played before, just never with someone I'd actually developed a connection with.

It sucked a hell of a lot more when you actually liked the person. The guilt swirling through me was making it impossible to do anything. As more graduate school decisions came in, I found it hard to be excited about them.

And then I did what I did best—I moved on.

Or at least, I attempted to. I dove into work, pushing Theo far from my mind. It was difficult with the buzz around campus leading into the Point Brook game. But I was doing everything I could to avoid it. I knew where the posters of Theo were hung up around campus, so I tried my best not to look at them. I avoided social media so I wouldn't have to see pictures of her. Looking at her was too painful and brought up too much in me—it made me think of breakfast together and time in bed together. The secrets we'd told each other about crushes growing up and stupid things we did as kids. The feeling of being wrapped up in blankets with her, or held in her arms.

I didn't know how anyone navigated a breakup. It felt like a boulder hanging off of me all the time. I didn't have a second of peace; Theo still showed up in my dreams, talking to me, asking me why I didn't try harder, why I didn't trust her.

Despite how much I loved Colorado, I debated on how nice it would be to cut ties and go to a different program, even if I made it into the PhD program here. The urge to run was annoyingly strong and I hated my mom for ingraining it into me, just like I hated Theo for making me want to run in the first place. It felt almost easier for us to have never met in the first place, so I didn't have to navigate all of this.

But then I remembered the sound of her voice, her laugh, the way she looked in glasses when we were studying together. I thought about how we'd talked about both wanting a dog and for just a moment, I could envision us in our own place, a dog or two running around.

Maybe that was the point of all of this. I was scared and I could leave to avoid all of the bad feelings that came with that—or I could figure out how to embrace that the fear of diving headfirst was the point of all of this. Maybe I could get to a place where I could admit to myself that there was no Theo if I wasn't willing to take an initial leap.

By the time Theo's game against Point Brook came around, I still hadn't figured out how to say what I needed to say to Theo. I still felt stuck—and a little bit like it was on me to figure it out. I kept cycling between wanting to reach out to her so badly to fix everything and begging for her to come back, and wanting to push her away even harder for not continuing to come after me.

I knew it was irrational; Theo had been the one who told me she'd wait for me. She'd already made her opinion on everything clear. But part of me hoped she'd run after me even after making a declaration like that.

Iris walked into the living room, all dressed up in green and ready for the game, and spotted me on the couch. I knew I looked pathetic—I was wearing the same sweatpants I'd been wearing for days, I had three different types of chips open in front of me, and I'd gone to town on a bag of Twix Minis. It wasn't pretty.

"You're not coming?" she asked, taking in the sight in front of her. I could see her eyes bouncing between the open bags in front of me and the stain on my sweatpants.

"I don't think I should," I said, my stomach knotting. Iris and I had been going back and forth on it here and there, but I could tell she'd been trying to be gentle with me. That was what Iris did best—she was gentle. And kind. And considerate. But she was also someone who deeply cared about the people she loved, which meant she wasn't going to let me get away with anything.

I could see in her face that she didn't like that answer. Her patience had been dwindling over time and it was exactly why I'd been nervous for any kind of confrontation with her. I'd had a feeling it was coming down the line, but I didn't know how long I was going to have to wait for it to finally happen.

Part of me hoped that Iris would just let it go and let me ruin my own life, but she seemed determined to not let me. It was obvious how much she cared about me, even if I found it annoying right now.

I muted the TV and turned to look at her. "Just say it," I finally said. "I know you've been wanting to."

"I don't think I want to." Iris crossed her arms. "I don't think you actually want to hear it."

"If you're going to be all weird with me, you might as well just let it out. I know you're disappointed—"

"Of *course* I'm disappointed," she said, throwing her hands up in the air. "And this isn't even about the future friend of a WAG stuff. I just can't believe you're doing this when you finally like someone. Like, you have it! It's there for you! You watched me fumble Danny and completely embarrass myself and you *still* can't admit to yourself what it is that you want. It's okay to like Theo and want her and want a life with her. And it's okay if you end up screwing it up. It's better than moping around and pretending you've already lost her when she's practically standing outside your bedroom window with a boombox."

"I already know all of this," I said. It was impossible for me to get actually mad at Iris, especially when she was correct. She'd always gotten me in a way that it felt like no one else had. It wasn't until Theo that I realized someone other than her could actually get to know me—all of the gross, annoying, weird parts that I didn't want anyone to see—and still love me. It felt safe with Iris, like I knew she was never going to leave. But it was the scariest feeling in the world with Theo.

"You think you're going to end it?" Iris asked. "Like, genuinely? That's it?"

"I don't know what else to do—"

"That's *dumb*, Maya. Like, really dumb," she said. "You obviously like her. If you do end things with her, just know that I'm not endorsing it."

"You've already made that clear," I said, feeling a little defensive. Even though Iris's tone was still gentle, her words definitely weren't. "That feels like a complete disregard for my feelings, which are valid."

"Your feelings are based in fear. You're the single most fearless person I've ever met in my *life*. I don't understand why you're acting this way."

"Maybe I've never really been all that fearless," I admitted. "Maybe this whole time, I've just been really good at pretending that I do all of this because I'm not scared of anything. But

I'm the girl who is scared of commitment—point blank. We've always known that about me. I'm scared I'm going to lose my independence and my sense of self. There's nothing actually fearless about me."

Iris looked at me. We were both quiet for a second. We never really ever bickered, so I didn't know where to go from there.

"I don't think you should give it up."

"I don't want to give it up," I said. "I don't want to give her up. But I'm scared. I see what's waiting for me down the line and I'm having a hard time imagining that being a future that works for me." I tossed my words around in my head for a second, thinking it over. "I'm scared I'm going to go through all of this just to get bored. Or that it'll end up being more stress than it's worth. I can think of, like, one thousand reasons why I shouldn't do it."

"What about the reasons you should do it?"
"What do you mean?"

"Like how you feel when you're with her? How you feel heard and understood and supported? How she's the only other person you can spend all of that time with consecutively besides me?" Iris asked. She sat down on the chair next to the couch and turned her body to look at me. "At least come to the game. Don't completely disappear out of her life like this with no explanation."

"I don't know if I can handle looking at her."

"I feel like that should tell you something," she said. "Most people would kill for that exact feeling of having feelings so intense they make your head spin. The magnetic pull between you guys has always been obvious. I think you're going to spend the entire rest of your life chasing this exact feeling if you give it up now."

"What if the head spinning part feels like a bad thing instead of a good thing? Like it's horrific, vomit-inducing, hangover-esque head spinning?"

"I think it's supposed to feel kind of good and bad all at the same time. And then once you've found the right person and let yourself go, it starts to feel only good."

I curled up on the couch, bringing my knees to my chin. "Can I have a little more time?"

"I don't know much more time you'll have," she said. She was quiet for a beat and then stood up. "I can wait for you if you want to come. Just say the word. I'll even risk missing tip off for you."

I thought about it—*really* thought about it. I could just run right back into Theo's arms, tell her I was sorry for the way I was distancing myself, make everything feel good again. But no one ever showed what came *after* the big movie moment. The fights and disappointment and annoyances that added up. The boredom of doing the same things with the same person over and over again. I enjoyed it with Theo but we'd only been in our routine for a few months. After a year, and then a few years, I was sure I'd feel suffocated by it. I knew myself. And I knew the woman who raised me.

"I can't," I said, practically whispering.

The air between us was heavy. Iris was too quiet, to the point that I knew I was at least a little bit in trouble even without her saying it again. "Okay," she said. She got up and grabbed her purse. "I'll see you after the game."

"Okay," I responded, matching her slightly passive tone. It was no use pestering her about it—I knew why she was upset and I wasn't going to be able to give her the answer she wanted.

She left a minute after that, shutting the front door behind her. The apartment was silent from when I'd muted the TV and felt almost suffocatingly still. It was so quiet it was overwhelming.

I turned the TV sound back on it but that didn't fix it. Everything still felt sideways, my body knowing that something was wrong but my brain refusing to admit the truth.

I switched the channel over to Theo's game. The pre-game chatter was already going, switching between the panelists and clips from various Lakeside Green and Point Brook games.

"I think we'll be seeing a lot of scoring from both teams tonight," one of the panelists said. The screen showed four women sitting together, none of whom I recognized but I had a feeling they were probably a pretty significant deal to women's basketball fans. "Both teams are heavy on shooting—it'll come down to whose defense will come out on top."

"I think Lakeside Green might surprise us. Nia Adams is quick on her feet and Gemma Doherty has a lot of energy out there. She's able to match Theo McCall's aggressive style of playing, which is exactly what the team needs."

"And don't forget GJ Mitchell," the panelist next to her said. "We all saw the way she kept Ivy Hill College in line in Michigan."

A third panelist shook her head. "I don't know. I think part of the Point Brook legacy is that the players can do anything. They have defense, shooting—as much as I want to root for an underdog, I don't know if Lakeside Green can pull something like this off. Theo might not be enough, especially up against someone who has demonstrated to match her skill level."

The women went back and forth from there on stats, discussing games, and specific plays that I didn't understand. It seemed like the same kind of conversation I'd always heard in relation to sports—people trying to convince everyone else of who's the greatest of all time.

A clip of Theo from a few games ago popped up and my body couldn't tell the difference between looking at her and someone squeezing my heart in their fist. I wondered if she was nervous, if she was thinking about me. If she'd been tempted to text me before the game or if she was starting to accept that I was successfully pushing her away.

I muted the TV again and pulled out my phone, hoping my mom might still be awake. If there was anyone who was going to understand me and ground me, it was her. She might've not done a great job of talking me out of seeing Theo initially, but I was sure she could remind me of the eight million reasons why her preference was to be single. I needed to hear that right now before I did something stupid.

"What are you doing, calling me late on a Thursday night? You should be getting ready to go out to the bar," Mom said. I could hear the bustling of people around her.

"Are you at the store? Sorry, I can call you later."

"It's okay, I'm just at Fetterman's," she said. Fetterman's was the local organic market around the corner from her house. I'd never liked it there—a container of strawberries cost three times as much there compared to anywhere else—but Mom loved it. She became a loyal shopper once I moved out and she was only feeding herself. It was part of the long list of things she couldn't wait to do once she was an empty-nester, a list that usually felt more like a *I can't wait for my daughter to move out already* list.

"Oh," I said.

"Do you need something, baby? I have you in my headphones, I can still shop."

"Oh, I just..." I suddenly felt ridiculous for calling her, like I always did. But I knew that I needed to do this. If there was anyone who could make me feel less alone in this moment, it was her. "Do you remember that crush I was telling you about?"

"Of course. What happened?"

"Things are getting...complicated, I guess. With graduation coming up. And a lot of other things. And it sucks really bad."

"Okay," Mom said, as if she was waiting for more.

"How do I get over it? How can I just, like, cut and run like you do?" I asked. Tears welled in my eyes and I took a deep breath to calm myself down. I didn't need her to know I was crying. "It just sucks so bad."

"What part of it sucks?"

"All of it. I have to end it but I don't know how. I don't want to have this...*feeling* anymore."

Mom was quiet for a moment. "Honey, you know that I don't just cut and run, right?"

I stopped, sitting up straighter on the couch. "What do you mean?"

"The break-ups, the boyfriends...it's not that I'm just leaving them and feeling nothing. Maybe sometimes, when I really don't like them and I'm over it. But relationships aren't usually that simple, even for me."

The world suddenly tilted on its axis. Years of watching my mom navigate the dating world and singlehood flashed before me through a different lens. I realized that I'd been watching her but I'd never really *talked* to her about it. I'd been a child for so much of it; I didn't know any better, didn't know the actual truth behind what I was seeing. All I knew was the show my mom was putting on for me. But maybe, all this time, she'd just been a convincing actress.

"But the boyfriends," I said, as if that was some kind of point. "You always left so easily. They'd just disappear from your life basically overnight. You would be back to normal the next day, like nothing happened. You were always so detached."

Mom was quiet for so long that I wondered if I'd lost her. The only reason I knew she was still on the other end was because I could still hear the soft sound of other people's voices and music playing over the grocery store radio. "Is that really what it seemed like?" she asked, her voice the softest I'd ever heard it.

My stomach knotted with guilt. "I'm sorry, I shouldn't have brought this up while you were at the grocery store."

"No, no, it's okay." She went quiet again. "I was trying my best to protect you. That was all."

"What do you mean?"

"I tried to make everything feel as normal as possible for you. I carried a lot of guilt around getting impregnated by a man who didn't want children. And there were so many men who promised to be there for you but it was obvious they didn't really want to be fathers. And I didn't want a man around who treated you like a burden," she said. "You were right that I'd cut and run, but it wasn't because I was emotionally detached and could move onto the next thing no problem. I was just the first one to leave."

"Oh, Mom," I said, bringing my fingertips to my lips. For the first time in all of my years of being alive, I understood what it meant to see my mom as a person. She'd lived a whole life before me, did things without me. She had thoughts and feelings, crushes and heartbreak. It felt like the most basic and selfish—and obvious—revelation a person could have, but it was suddenly smacking me across the face.

It was also the closest I'd ever had to my mom telling me that I wasn't a burden to her like I'd always imagined. She wasn't a perfect mom and her actions had always communicated to me that I wasn't the biggest priority in her life most of the time. But it wasn't absurd to think that maybe she was just human and I needed to give her the benefit of the doubt, at least try a little bit to explain to her how her actions made me feel.

"I don't think you want to follow in my footsteps. And I definitely don't think you want me, of all people, talking you into anything," she said. "Or I guess, talking you out of anything. Especially when it sounds like things are going well."

"But what if they don't go well in the future?" I asked, my voice small. But the more I was saying it out loud and the more I was thinking about it, the dumber I felt. I was so caught up in what was going to happen, all of the factors I couldn't control. There wasn't a single thing in life that I was going to be able to predict. And I could definitely be wrong, as demonstrated by how I'd completely misunderstood my mom's entire dating history—and frankly, her as a person. As much as I was convinced I knew everything and could see how things with Theo would turn out, there was always a chance I didn't know nearly as much as I thought.

"I think you already know what you want to do," she said. "You wouldn't have to be talked out of something if you didn't want to do it, at least a little bit." I could almost hear her smile through the phone. "I haven't forgotten our initial conversation about her."

I thought back to practically pleading with my mom to help me get over the small crush I had on Theo. It'd bloomed into something so much bigger than that and something so much more overwhelming.

But also something really beautiful.

Mom was right that I'd already known how I felt. It was exactly what Iris was trying to tell me—and Theo, too, in her way. I wouldn't be agonizing over it like this if the decision was the easy one, the unscary one. But I wanted Theo and I wanted to make it work. And I needed to start being okay with not being able to predict the future if that was going to be the case.

"Oh god," I said. "I think I know what I have to do."

"Go make things right," Mom said.

I smiled a little bit. For the first time since I was a kid, I felt the urge to hug her. "Thanks, Mom."

"I love you, sweetie."

I took a deep breath. "I love you, too. I'll see you at graduation?" I asked.

"Of course," she said, her voice warm.

When we hung up, I looked up at the TV screen. There were only a few more minutes until tip-off. I definitely wasn't going to make it in time for the start of the game—but I could at least try to make it before halftime.

I bit my lip, wondering if it was really worth it to do this. Maybe trying for some kind of big movie moment was a huge mistake and maybe I'd regret it and maybe I'd be mortified for the next few months for even trying.

Or maybe it would be the best thing that had ever happened to me.

Chapter 28

THEO

It was hard to believe that we'd finally made it to what was *the* game of the regular season. We'd spent all season preparing for Point Brook—learning their plays, talking strategy, keeping up with their shit talking.

This was *the* game.

Instead of going into it nervous, every nerve in my body was lit up with adrenaline. I knew I needed to go into this game ready for a fight. It wasn't going to be an easy win, no matter how much we prepared. But I knew there wasn't a single chance I was letting Point Brook and Cam Kerr get bragging rights—mostly because I knew Cam would be insufferable about it.

GJ had been keeping everyone's energy up from the locker room to warm-ups. By the time we were out on the court to warm-up, it was obvious we were buzzing. It made me optimistic the game would be a good one.

Once warm-ups were done and we had to start clearing the court, GJ threw her arm over my shoulder. "Are you ready?"

"More than anything," I said.

One of Point Brook's practice balls came flying in my direction and I caught it. I was about to bounce it back when Cam approached me instead, closing the gap between us.

"Not too close," GJ threatened and I snorted.

Cam was just as effortlessly cool as I'd always remembered. We were about the same height and same build, the brunette to my dark blonde. We were two sides of the same coin in a lot of ways—she was just as loud and competitive on the court as I was, just as prone to collecting techs and picking fights with refs when we were certain we were right. She just brought it off the court in a way I preferred not to.

We hadn't been physically in the same room in a long time. I could see in her face that she'd grown up, but also she looked just like how I remembered from last season—and from when we used to play against each other as kids.

I thought about her going through a similar trajectory as me—a little girl growing up with dreams of getting to play in the big leagues. There were pictures of her floating around online as a child wearing Point Brook T-shirts, posing with Point Brook players after watching them play. She was the girl who'd gotten exactly what I'd always wanted, the girl I'd spent my entire childhood trying to be.

When it was announced she was going to Point Brook, I'd spent a lot of time wondering what it was that she had that I didn't. I still didn't know the answer. But in a lot of ways, it felt really fucking good to know that I'd still come out on top, even after everything.

"You ready for the game, McCall?" Cam asked, her voice deep. Her cocky half-smile was firmly planted on her face as always.

GJ waved her off. "We're going to the locker room."

If Cam was offended, she didn't show it on her face. "There's no beef here. I just gotta put on a performance. People like a show," she said. "You're good, McCall. Looking forward to playing against you."

GJ was about two seconds away from sticking her tongue out at her or doing something else equally as childish. But I thought the words were nice. And it was true—I was looking forward to playing against her, too. Even at our level, it sometimes felt like we were running laps around a lot of the other players we went up against. We didn't make it to being considered first round picks for nothing; we *were* the best. And playing against the best and being challenged in that way was a hell of a lot of fun, even if it was also a lot of pressure.

"You too, Kerr," I said. Cam two-finger saluted me as I tossed the ball back to her. She jogged away to join her team, who was heading back to their locker room.

"I hate everything about her," GJ said.

I laughed, throwing my head back. "Be careful, you might end up becoming teammates in the future."

Just as we were about to head down the tunnel to the locker room, I glanced up at the student section. The stands had been quickly filling with people as we'd been warming up. It was obvious how excited everyone was about this particular match-up. Point Brook was a huge draw; getting to see the two top picks of the WNBA draft duke it out was going to inevitably be a lot of fun.

I scanned through all of the faces, looking for one face in particular. There were so many people here, but there was only one person I really cared about watching my game.

But I didn't see her in her unusual spot in the student section.

When my eyes fell on Iris and an empty seat next to her, my stomach dropped. There wasn't time to be genuinely upset about Maya not coming, but I knew I'd feel it at some point after the game, once the adrenaline wore off.

I didn't know what to do next when it came to Maya. I'd already said my piece; I didn't know at what point I was supposed to accept defeat and when I was supposed to push harder. I'd never really had to chase a girl before. And honestly, it didn't really seem like she wanted to be chased.

I shook all of it away, knowing that I'd have to deal with my feelings later. My quote for the foreseeable future would have to be: *There's no crying in basketball.* Especially with the tournament buzz going from a theoretical, near-future issue to an immediate, right now issue.

After hyping each other up in the locker room and running through our approach and game plan going into the game, we waited to be called out onto the court.

I tried not to get emotional as the stadium lights flashed and the music pumped through the arena and the announcer called out the names of the starting line-ups. But I really was so lucky to have this. This was everything to me, it always had been. All of my hard work had led up to a season like this and the guarantee that I'd be going pro.

It was hard for me to accept—or want to accept—that Maya wouldn't be with me for the next part. She'd only been around for one season of my college career, but it'd been my best one. It'd always felt impossible to have a busy schedule and be seeing someone, but Maya made it feel effortless—the early nights in because I had practice, the late nights meeting her back at her place after an away game. The times I was tired in class, the times I couldn't text her because it was hard for me to find a second between games and school and travel and brand deals and whatever else. She never made it seem like it was too much for her. It seemed like we'd found a routine that worked.

But maybe she'd just been a really good actress.

GJ went up for the tip-off and I brought myself back to the game. Nothing else existed to me right now—it was all about the chess pieces on the court.

GJ got her hand on the ball and sent it toward Mags. Unsurprisingly, Coach came out with all of the big guns. For a game like this, she was going to go with her strongest starting five, the same one we'd had pretty much all season. Me, GJ, Mags, Gemma, Nia—we were a well-oiled machine by this time in the season.

Point Brook was able to keep up, though. Every time we scored, they seemed to come immediately back with the same momentum. Balls were rebounded and sent flying down the court, shots were landing left and right. Even though it was nowhere near the end of the game, the crowd was already practically on their feet, watching every single move carefully. We were playing the kind of game where no one wanted to leave to use the bathroom or get more snacks; there was nonstop, blink-and-you'll-miss-it action.

And it felt fucking incredible.

When I had a rhythm like this going, I was certain I could play forever and my body would somehow never get tired. It was like the most incredible runner's high of my life; this feeling was what made playing so addictive for me growing up. I loved the competitive energy and the excitement from the crowd and how I felt when I was playing. I never wanted it to stop.

By halftime, the score was a tight 34-31, with Point Brook holding a slight lead over us. Cam Kerr had been making us work; our defense was having a hard time locking her down and she was killing us both on points and assists.

"It's annoying how fucking good she is," Mags said shaking her head as we stood by the bench, ready to run onto the court again for the second half. She squeezed her water bottle into her mouth and tossed it back. "She's running laps around us."

"It's refreshing to have you directing your attitude toward someone else," I said.

Mags turned to look at me and we exchanged small smiles. "You know I'll miss you," she responded.

"You sound almost genuine," I teased and she punched my shoulder. "I'd say I'll miss you but I'll be around. Our seasons won't overlap so I'll still have plenty of time to coach you from the stands."

She groaned. "Okay, never mind. Sentimental moment over."

I laughed as we headed back into position for the start of the second half. There'd been a few substitutions throughout the game, but we were back to our starting lineup. We had to get back out on top; the score was close and I imagined the gap would never get that wide, but being even one point down meant we'd lose it all. And while this wasn't *the* game that would determine if we'd make it to the tournament, it was the game that would decide how we'd fare if—*when*—we made it that far.

Rolling out into the third quarter, it was obvious Point Brook had gotten a talk in the locker room. They had a renewed sense of energy and were coming out swinging. Cam was dropping three-pointers left and right, creating an increasingly wide-point deficit.

But I refused to give up momentum or write my team off. I kept us pushing ahead, trying riskier shots and bigger plays to get around Point Brook's defense. We were catching rebounds where they weren't and, after long enough, were able to get a handle on blocking Point Brook's shots. Cam was still difficult to slow down, but everyone else we were keeping locked down.

I kept the ball moving as much as possible, keeping it out of the hands of Point Brook and passing it to my teammates in whatever way possible. The difference in our scores suddenly went from twelve to two.

When GJ sank the ball that brought us to tying with them, the arena went wild. The quarter wrapped up, leaving us with only ten minutes of playing time between us and winning. After huddling and getting a supportive, tough love pep talk from Coach Darlene, we prepared to head back out to the court.

"Let's fucking go!" GJ shouted, clapping her hands. "Close this bitch out!"

I turned to the crowd, waving for them to get louder as we moved into the last part of the game. I loved having home court advantage—there wasn't a better fanbase in the world than mine.

The fourth quarter stayed significantly closer in scoring than the third. As the clock ticked on, time rapidly disappearing, neither team allowed more than a four point difference. I'd never played so hard or thoughtfully in my life.

When we were down to single digit minutes, I knew we'd have to play smart. This was where dumb mistakes would hurt us. The larger the gap in our scores, the more difficult it would be to make up for lost points.

With only two minutes left, Point Brook was maintaining a lead. They wanted it just as badly as we did and they were making it obvious. We hadn't been able to get any decent shooting in.

Needing points on the board, our approach became obvious—get me the ball and get me to score. Despite Point Brook having decent defense, they'd still been having a hard time stopping my shots. I was hitting an even higher percentage of good threes than I normally did, having them land one after another with ease.

I just needed a few more decent ones, and we'd be in the clear. Just one more point than Point Brook was enough.

For a moment, I didn't even hear the crowd. I was so focused on getting the ball where it needed to go. I could see plays before they happened, predicting how to spin away from defense and where I needed to shoot from on the court to make it.

It barely registered that the game was almost over. When I dropped another three, the crowd went to their feet, and the cheerleaders waved their pom-poms. The entire bench started shouting and cheering, too; even Ellie was red in the face with how loud she was getting, and she never raised her voice above speaking level.

"*Three*-o, *three*-o," the crowd sang out, cupping their hands to their mouths to make sure I could hear them.

I kept my reaction to a minimum so I wouldn't get a tech, but it was exactly what I needed to close out the game.

With the crowd behind us, we were quick to rebound, sprint, shoot. We kept the ball between each other, doing everything we could to keep it out of the hands of the Point Brook players. The score was 85-78—a gap that Point Brook could close if they had enough time.

But when I glanced over to the clock, I realized that was it—we were down to seconds left, long enough for us to hold onto the ball and close it out. No more blood, sweat, and tears. An entire season of prepping for this game, all for it to be over just like that.

I dribbled, keeping my face neutral and surveying the court as if I were planning my next shot. The crowd was on their feet, cheering louder and louder as the time ticked on. Our bench got to their feet again as the Point Brook players dropped their game faces, the realization that they lost hitting them.

The second the buzzer sounded and the game was over, my facade dropped. The entire Lakeside Green team—bench and all—ran to meet each other, hugging and celebrating.

"We did it! We fucking did it!" Mags shouted.

"We're getting a fucking natty this year!" Nia said, jumping up and down.

Coach Darlene wrapped her arms around as many of us as she could, her clipboard brushing our backs. "I'm so proud of you, ladies. This was really something special."

The team continued celebrating, laughing and jumping into each other's arms. A massive weight lifted from my chest—and genuine hope replaced it. This was the push we needed to get through the tournament. There was no chance we weren't making the cut to play in the Round of 64—not with our ranking and a win against Point Brook under our belt.

We lined up to high five the other team, a couple of the other players doing the best they could to avoid eye contact with me. When I made it to Cam, she held my hand for a second.

"Good game, McCall. I'll see you in the finals, I'm sure," she said.

"I'll see you at the draft either way," I said and Cam winked, the two of us exchanging a small smile of understanding.

"Don't befriend the enemy," GJ whispered behind me.

"She's not the enemy. She's a few weeks away from being a rookie, just like me," I said. And it was true—Cam might've been annoying to deal with throughout the season, but she wasn't a villain. If anything, I kind of appreciated the hustle of using my name and shit talking to bring attention to her game. We were both good, but a rivalry sold tickets and pulled in even non-basketball fans. It was clever, more than anything.

I looked up toward the crowd, waving my hands to get them loud again. The crowd cheered back, waving their posters and swinging their t-shirts. People were clearing out more slowly than usual, taking their time before leaving so they could get pictures and wait for autographs.

As I scanned the crowd, realizing I only had more game here and I wanted to enjoy every second I could, my eyes drifted over toward Iris again. Danny was sitting next to her now and I smiled to myself, glad he took my advice. When Iris and I locked eyes, she waved at me with a decent amount of urgency and then pointed down to the guardrail.

My heart went double-time. I didn't want to get my hopes up, but it was impossible not to. There was only one person Iris could be pointing at. And there was only one reason why Maya would be here.

Maya stood by the metal barricade, trying her best to hold her position even though there were people pushing to get the attention of players down on the court.

I jogged over to her, not hesitating for even a second. I wasn't interested in being coy with her or protecting my feelings. I wanted to hear her out. I told her I'd wait for her and I was. I wasn't going to go back on my word until she told me to back off.

As I got closer, I realized she was wearing a creased t-shirt with my number on it. She held another shirt in her hands.

I couldn't help it; I jogged the rest of the way. Maya leaned toward me and I reached up for her, pulling her into a kiss. It was the most impulsive thing I'd maybe ever done but I didn't care. I wasn't missing my chance with her.

People around us cheered like something out of a movie. I could see a few confused faces and even more people going, *Wait, is that the girl she keeps getting seen with?*

I didn't care. They could look all they wanted.

When we separated, I took a closer look at her shirt. "Did you just buy that and change in the bathroom?" I asked, laughing.

"What gave it away?" Maya asked sheepishly and it felt like no time at all had passed between us. There was no stiffness, no rebuilding. Just two people who genuinely wanted to be together. Maybe we weren't going to have the easiest time with our schedules and the changes to come, but we were going to do everything we could to make it work.

She smiled at me and seeing it felt like taking the first deep breath I'd taken in a long time. My body flooded with joy, every muscle relaxing. I couldn't take the smile off my face, even when I tried. "Good game. Congrats on the win," she said.

"I'm glad you came."

"I'm glad I did, too." She was quiet for a beat, a thought clearly passing over her. "Fuck it," she said and leaned down, grabbing me by the jersey so she could kiss me again.

Our second kiss was somehow even more perfect than the first. It said everything I knew it was hard for Maya to say—that she also wanted to try and make this work, that she didn't want to lose me. It was gentle and modest, and with full awareness that everyone around us was looking at us, but it didn't matter. The entire crowd melted away, and it was just the two of us. None of this was for them, and none of it was under the guise of being some kind of inside joke between me and Maya. It was a real kiss.

"I missed you," she said when we broke apart. We leaned toward each other, the magnetic pull still there.

"I missed you."

"I'm sorry I didn't know how to say what I wanted. I was just so scared," she admitted.

I locked my fingers with hers, wishing I could pull her over the metal bar to be closer to me. "It's okay. I'm just glad you're here."

"Is now an embarrassing time to tell you I leaned into the whole fake dating thing because I was hoping it'd help me get over my crush on you?"

I threw my head back and laughed. "No, that makes a lot of sense. I agreed to it because I was hoping you'd realize you wanted me if you got to know me more. Under any other circumstances, I would've run screaming from someone who wanted to create *more* press about me."

Maya smiled knowingly, as if she'd had the same thought at one point. "I didn't have to get to know you more—I already wanted you." She leaned further into the railing, closer to me.

"Good, because I already wanted you, too," I said. "I've wanted you since I first laid eyes on you at that house party."

"Me too," Maya admitted.

Behind Maya, I could see Iris and Danny staring down our way, talking to each other. They were still up in the stands, but the arena was clearing out now, making it obvious they were definitely talking about us.

"Danny and Iris?" I asked.

Maya shrugged. "I actually don't know what happened there. He saw her and came over to sit with her. They were together by the time I got here."

I smiled a little bit. I knew exactly why they were sitting together, but that wasn't my business to share. The truth would probably come out eventually.

"You almost skipped the game?" I teased. "What changed your mind?"

"Stop." She snorted and then smiled shyly. "Do you still want to be my date to Iris's birthday party?"

"Yes, absolutely."

"And you don't regret asking me to be your Valentine?"

I fought off a smile. "Never, in a million years. I'm already planning our itinerary for next Valentine's Day."

"You still love me even though commitment is hard for me and it took me a minute to realize you're everything I've ever wanted?"

My chest filled with light. I wasn't going to pretend everything was *perfect*—we probably both needed to work on our communication, and we still had to actually talk about Maya icing me out. But I also knew that something was different. She was here and present. She really wanted this. I could see it in the way she was looking at me, talking to me. This was a woman who really meant it when she said she wanted to try. "Yes, absolutely," I said.

I glanced back to see my team leaving the court. I knew I didn't have much time with Maya—there was never enough time with her. But I would take what I could get.

"I'll see you after this? Come out with me and the team?" I asked.

"Yes, please. I'd love that," Maya said. "Don't be gone too long."

"You know I'll try not to be," I said and then snuck in a kiss, then another, before running to meet the last of my teammates who were waving me over to catch up with them.

As I walked toward the tunnel, I turned to look back at Maya, who'd been watching me walk away. A smile spread across her face when she realized I was looking at her.

That sight—Maya standing by the court while wearing my number, a smile on her face, her hand poised for a small wave—was exactly what I wanted to see at every game for the rest of my career.

And I felt like the luckiest person alive to know I'd have it.

Epilogue

MAYA

"This is so heavy, what could you possibly have packed in this? It feels like rocks." I asked, huffing out a breath of air as I carried the box into Theo's new townhouse.

"You're making me look bad," Theo said, carrying her box practically one-handed, and turned to Iris. "We have actually been going to the gym together. I wasn't making that up."
I put the box down on the kitchen island, needing a second. Theo's new place—in a cute, trendy neighborhood of Cedar Creek, the biggest city in the county—was gorgeous. She'd still kept it modest because she was Theo and even a seven-figure shoe deal wasn't going to make her live lavishly, but it felt very *big city* compared to what had been available on our campus.

After going on to lose in the championship game—against Point Brook, which Theo accepted with grace while everyone else was furious—there hadn't been much time for her to mourn the end of her college career.

She pretty much immediately had to fly out for the draft—toting me and her parents along for the most whirlwind vacation of my life—and ended up being the first pick of the first round, her major personal victory against Cam Kerr. She suddenly had a manager and a public relations team and very important meetings with very important people, pretty much overnight. The team had wasted no time coordinating ad space to get her face all over the airport and the arena.

Fortunately, Theo didn't have to move far because the Cedar Creek Blizzards were only about an hour away from Lakeside Green, but it was still a lot of change all at once. And going from a college town to a city, even in the same state, was still an adjustment.

"Dude, this place is nuts," GJ said, walking up behind Iris. Theo and I had managed to rope the two of them into helping Theo move. Danny had offered, but GJ had shut him down with a quick, *Oh, so you think four women can't handle moving some boxes?* He didn't take offense; he knew he was going to be the person on call to help Theo build her furniture when it arrived. GJ offered muscle but wasn't someone anyone would consider patient enough to build a bed frame.

Not that Theo had much for Danny to help us with, anyway—she'd left behind a lot of the communal furniture for GJ in their old house and purchased new things instead. Everything was in the process of being delivered, however, which meant

Theo's apartment was as empty as it had been when we toured it.

"Yeah, the price was great for the square footage and location," Theo agreed.

"I just meant it looks like something out of HGTV, but go off," GJ said.

"Where do you want the boxes?" Iris asked.

"You can put them anywhere for now, I'll figure it out," Theo said, and we stacked them against one of her walls.

GJ didn't hesitate to explore, taking the steps two at a time to see the second floor. "This makes our old place look like a dump," she said, her voice echoing through the empty rooms.

Iris also wandered, taking a look out of Theo's ground-floor living room windows. "Please let me host a dinner party out of this apartment," she said.

"Of course," Theo said.

I walked over to Theo and hugged my arms around her waist as she threw her arm over my shoulders.

"I'm glad you picked this one. This was my favorite," I said.

"I know, that's why I picked it," Theo said, and my heart fluttered like it always did around Theo. It never took much—she'd make breakfast for me or get me a card and flowers after practice or look extra sexy loading up the U-Haul for her move. Everything she did was the hottest, most incredible thing anyone had ever done. Iris was so relieved I'd gotten my shit together that she wasn't even making fun of me for my personality transplant. I had a feeling she'd eventually get sick of me gushing about Theo, not that she was any better when it came to Danny.

It was hard not to gush, though. Things had been storybook perfect with Theo. There were still hiccups—days when I was moody, times when she was so busy with meetings and training that there was little time for me—but it felt more than worth it to me. The good always outweighed the bad.

And things had been a lot easier since we knew we were both staying in Colorado. I'd accepted my offer at Cedar Creek University, the much smaller and much more city-centric school in the county. They offered a great benefits package and everything I wanted—including getting to stay close to my two favorite people in the world, since Iris was a shoo-in for a job at a hospital nearby.

My mom had even offered to fly out to see me a few times a year in Colorado; we'd been talking more regularly on the phone, and things seemed to be the best they'd ever been for us.

Iris and I were even going to stick together as roommates and agreed on finding a place with a guest room, which I was thrilled about. We knew friends from college were going to want a place to stay when they came into town to see Theo play.

Theo and I had discussed moving in together, but we agreed that we didn't want to rush anything. I had a feeling I'd be over here pretty much full-time—Iris and I were definitely going to make ourselves at home, even when Theo was away for games—and that was a good enough middle ground for me.

Moving in with Theo when our leases were up in about a year gave me something to look forward to—and I was more than looking forward to it.

I knew this was just the beginning. My girlfriend—a label we'd officially agreed to the night of that first Point Brook game—was moving an hour away from me. She was missing graduation because of her game schedule, and she wouldn't be there for those last few weeks of senior year when everyone wrote off classes and partied and cried about how much they were going to miss each other. It was going to be hard seeing her even less, knowing she was signing on to play basketball straight through until at least September, when the regular season ended in the pros.

I was sure even more changes and adjustments were to come. Nothing was going to be easy or predictable. But I was ready to take it one day at a time with her.

"I love you," I said, holding her close to me.

Theo kissed the top of my head. "I love you, too, pretty girl."

Acknowledgements

I fell in love with Maya and Theo from the first few words I wrote of this book and it never let up. I hope the time you spent with them gave you the same warm and fuzzy feeling I experienced every single time I read (and reread and reread and reread) *Tip In*.

But as a self-publishing author, writing is only half the battle and there are *so* many things that had to come together to get this book in your hands. I'm fortunate to have found amazing people who've helped me: My editor, Emily Ladner, for fixing the times when my brain worked faster than my fingers; Ruby and Rachel at Tales & Teacups for their incredible ARC distribution and release day support (two enormous things I'm eternally grateful I didn't have to navigate alone); my Canva dream team, Elena and Emily at Untold Stories; Sam and Deb at Ink & Velvet Designs who created unbelievable *Tip In* merchandise for the pre-order campaign (as well as the illustrations for the chapter headers which are *so* cute); Pooja at Epica Book PR for saving me from social media burnout; and my cover designer, Margauex, who brought my book to life and made this all actually feel real.

Outside of the business side of things, my friends and family are the most incredible and supportive people. I've talked about making the leap into self-publishing for *years* and I'm so grateful you've all stuck with me through it. Ivey and Daven, thank you for encouraging me to finally write and publish something gay. Kate and Simone, thank you for teaching me so much and being my industry big sisters (and please thank Darlene for her name). Anne, thank you for being the greatest and most levelheaded cheerleader anyone could ever ask for.

Now, onto book two!

Also by Josie Mae

Lakeside Green University:

Tip In

Paranormal America:

With Spirit

About Josie Mae

Josie Mae (she/her) is a lesbian who writes sapphic romance. She's a sports romance girl through and through despite being generally unathletic, and she says y'all far too much for being a city girl. She has worked a million odd jobs, lived a million different lives, and wants to live for a million more years. Josie writes all of her books with her small but mighty chiweenie, Baby Mae, by her side.

www.ingramcontent.com/pod-product-compliance
Lightning Source LLC
Chambersburg PA
CBHW060813120726
47909CB00006B/1901